Dear Readers,

Vengeance Is Mine wa̲ [illegible] ̲a̲.
Like you, we're sca̲r̲ [illegible] ̲e̲
U.S./Mexican border.

Thousands and thousands of illegals are pouring into the
U.S. each and every day. Yes, many of them are honest and hardworking, in search of the better life America has to offer. But
along with them are coming the scum of the earth—Middle
Eastern terrorists are infiltrating the porous borders with one
goal in mind: the destruction of the United States. *Time* magazine recently reported that al Qaeda, on direct orders from Osama
Bin Laden, has been trying to smuggle nuclear weapons across
the Mexican border—and in some cases they're working closely
with Latin American crime syndicates, according to some recent
reports. Just as dangerous are the ruthless drug cartels that are
flooding American cities and poisoning our children with their
heroin and cocaine. And the border jumpers are more brazen
than ever. Shootings, rapes, and carjackings of innocent, God-
fearing Americans are daily occurrences. Border towns are becoming war zones. Ranchers, many of whom have worked the
land for generations, are being slaughtered in their beds.

Make no mistake—we are at war. And this time the enemy is
bringing the battle to us. The Border Patrol is overwhelmed, outmanned, and outgunned. And our government is coping with the
situation by doing what they do best: not a damn thing.

We wrote this novel because, frankly, we were tired of poking
our fingers into the air and crying, "Why doesn't somebody do
something?" The horrifying events that befall John Howard Stark
are all based on true incidents that have been occurring along the
U.S./Mexican border. It's our hope that *Vengeance Is Mine* will
open America's eyes to the crisis on our border that grows more
perilous—to our friends and loved ones—with each passing day.

Respectfully Yours,
William W. Johnstone
Fred Austin
May 2005

BOOK YOUR PLACE ON OUR WEBSITE
AND MAKE THE
READING CONNECTION!

We've created a customized website just for our very special readers, where you can get the inside scoop on everything that's going on with Zebra, Pinnacle and Kensington books.

When you come online, you'll have the exciting opportunity to:

- View covers of upcoming books

- Read sample chapters

- Learn about our future publishing schedule (listed by publication month *and author*)

- Find out when your favorite authors will be visiting a city near you

- Search for and order backlist books from our online catalog

- Check out author bios and background information

- Send e-mail to your favorite authors

- Meet the Kensington staff online

- Join us in weekly chats with authors, readers and other guests

- Get writing guidelines

- AND MUCH MORE!

Visit our website at
http://www.kensingtonbooks.com

WILLIAM W. JOHNSTONE

WITH FRED AUSTIN

VENGEANCE IS MINE

PINNACLE BOOKS
Kensington Publishing Corp.
http://www.kensingtonbooks.com

PINNACLE BOOKS are published by

Kensington Publishing Corp.
850 Third Avenue
New York, NY 10022

All Kensington Titles, Imprints, and Distributed Lines are
available at special quantity discounts for bulk purchases for
sales promotions, premiums, fund-raising, and educational
or institutional use. Special book excerpts or customized
printings can also be created to fit specific needs. For details,
write or phone the office of the Kensington special sales
manager: Kensington Publishing Corp., 850 Third Avenue,
New York, NY 10022, attn: Special Sales Department, Phone:
1-800-221-2647.

Pinnacle and the P logo Reg. U.S. Pat. & TM Off.

First Printing: June 2005

10 9 8 7 6 5 4 3

Printed in the United States of America

BOOK ONE

Be sure you're right, then go ahead.

—Davy Crockett

Then . . .

The jungle smelled of death. Rotting vegetation, rotting animals—including man. But the odd thing was that it smelled of life, too, a rich, musky odor that proclaimed everything here was born anew, that the cycle of death and rebirth was ageless and unchanging.

John Howard Stark loved land. Loved to plunge his fingers into the earth and lift out great sticky clumps of dirt and rub his fingers together, smearing it into his skin so that when he brought his hand to his nose and inhaled, he could smell the life there.

John Howard Stark loved land—but not *this* land. Yes, the earth here in South Vietnam was fertile. It had supported its people for thousands of years and for that, he supposed, it should have been honored.

But now this earth had been watered by the blood of too many of his friends for him to ever honor it. The smell of death was too strong. It overpowered the scent of life.

Stark opened and closed his fingers on the stock of the carbine he held. They were out there in the darkness, waiting just like he was. He knew that. He supposed they were afraid, too, but he couldn't be certain of that. Though he had tried, he was unable to put himself in their heads. A naturally empathic man, Stark was still totally unable to make himself think like one of the enemy. They were just too damn alien.

The good thing was, you didn't have to be able to think like them in order to kill them. All you had to do was pull the trigger when they came at you, silent wraiths in black pajamas.

"What you think, John Howard?"

The whisper came from beside Stark. He glanced over at his buddy Rich Threadgill, who was standing guard with him on this side of the camp. Threadgill's face was blackened; he had even rubbed the stuff into the blond mustache that drooped over his mouth. But every so often there was a faint reflection off the glasses he wore. That worried Stark, but there was nothing he could do about it. Threadgill needed the glasses to see.

"I don't reckon it'll be much longer," Stark whispered in reply. He and Threadgill were both Texans, Stark from the Rio Grande Valley, Threadgill from Fort Worth, so it was natural they would be friends. Stark liked all the men in his marine unit, though. A few weeks in this isolated outpost north of Saigon had been enough to forge bonds between them that only death could break.

And to tell the truth, Stark sometimes wondered if even death could accomplish that.

Over on the other side of the camp were Jack Finnegan, a rich kid from Chicago whose banker daddy could easily have pulled some strings and kept his boy out of Southeast Asia, only Jack didn't want to be "protected" from something he considered his duty; and Will Sheffield from Knoxville, Tennessee, who claimed he was going to be a writer someday and to prove it carried around a notebook in which he scribbled ideas for stories and such. Both of them good men, already seasoned veterans of this dirty little war, and Stark felt confident with them watching his backside.

He was glad Threadgill was with him, though. Threadgill

was bug-fuck crazy sometimes, but he was probably the best natural warrior Stark had ever seen. All you had to do was point Threadgill at the enemy, say, "Rich, *kill*!" and stand back to watch the carnage.

A slithering rustle in the brush; Stark swung his carbine toward it. But it wasn't Charlie. "Del Rio," the newcomer hissed. Stark relaxed. Del Rio was the name of his hometown back in Texas. It was also the password used by the Vietnamese scout attached to their squad, Nat Van Linh.

Nat was only a kid, fifteen years old as opposed to Stark's twenty. But as with Stark, this war had made Nat grow up in a hurry, and he had lived with it a lot longer than Stark or his buddies had.

"They're coming," Nat said. "Any minute now."

Stark nodded. "Get the rest of the camp awake."

Nat slipped off, moving noiselessly in the jungle.

"Them little sumbitches gon' get a surprise," Threadgill said. "They figure to overrun us 'fore we know what's goin' on. But ol' Nat, he sees ever'thing that goes on out there. Don't nothin' get by him."

"That's enough," Stark said. "Quiet down now."

Threadgill hushed up. He had been in so many bar and barracks fights since he'd joined the marines, had been busted back from his hard-won promotions so many times, that all the brass thought of him as nothing but a troublemaker. They had never fought beside him, though. They didn't know that far from being the arrogant, insubordinate bastard they thought he was, Threadgill really didn't mind taking orders and being a team player, as long as he respected the man giving the orders.

He respected Sergeant John Howard Stark, all right. Stark had earned that respect.

The two men waited in silence. It must have been like this back home, Stark thought, a hundred years earlier when the Comanche moon rose over the vast Texas landscape and the settlers waited for the killing devils to come out of the darkness. When the hoot of an owl meant so much more, when savage death could strike with little or no warning. But if there was a Vietnamese moon floating overhead tonight, Stark couldn't see it. The overhanging jungle was too thick for that. Shadows ruled this world.

Shadows that suddenly lunged toward Stark and Threadgill, screaming and firing the automatic weapons that their good friends in the Soviet Union and China so thoughtfully provided for them.

Stark brought the carbine to his shoulder and started firing, squeezing the trigger smoothly as he targeted the muzzle flashes of the VC weapons. Threadgill opened up beside him, equally cool under fire. Stark heard shooting from the other side of the camp and knew the pajama boys were all around them.

They would hold their position or they would be overrun and die. Simple as that.

A mortar thumped, and a second later a blast went off in the jungle a couple of hundred yards out as the round exploded. The roaring bursts of fire marched in a line through the thick growth. That was Henry Macon's work, Stark knew. Macon was a black kid from Iowa, tall and gangling with the biggest hands Stark had ever seen. To look at those hands, you wouldn't think that Macon could do any sort of delicate work with them, but he was damned good with a mortar, one of the best ordnance men around. He wreaked havoc on the enemy's rear and contributed a great deal to breaking the back of the VC attack.

But there were still all the Cong up on the front lines to deal with. That job fell to Stark and Threadgill and the marines who came rushing out of the camp to reinforce them.

The chattering of automatic weapons, the sharp cracks of the carbines, and the screams of the enemy blended into an unnerving chaos. In the midst of such bedlam some men couldn't take it and simply shut down, crouching there in the darkness, not firing, not fighting, waiting to either live or die. Stark didn't hate or look down on men like that; he simply didn't understand them. The survival urge was strong in him, and it was more than that, really. It was the victor's urge, the need to win. He had known he had it when he was only a kid, the first time he had come up to the batter's box in the bottom of the ninth, with two outs and the winning run in scoring position. Even with two strikes on him, he didn't worry. He just waited for his pitch.

Someone had once called that mentality the triumph of the uncluttered mind. Stark didn't know that he'd go so far as to call his mind uncluttered, but it was certainly direct. He knew what he wanted and he knew how to get it. Tonight, deep in this damned jungle, he wanted to live and he wanted to kill the enemy.

He emptied the carbine, rammed another clip home. Charlie was all around.

Threadgill suddenly lunged over Stark's back. Stark heard him grappling with someone. A thin, bubbling cry that ended abruptly told Stark that Threadgill had just rammed his knife into a throat and ripped it wide open. Threadgill came to his knees and tossed a grenade out into the jungle. The place was so teeming with VC that the blast was bound to take out some of them.

But where there were so many, some were bound to escape, too. A couple of the black pajama boys came out of the shadows and crashed into Threadgill, knocking him backward so that he sprawled over Stark. Threadgill plunged his knife into the belly of one of them, but the other VC hit him with the stock of an AK-47 and stunned him.

Stark poked the barrel of his carbine against the black-clad enemy's back and fired, blowing Charlie's spine in two. The VC flopped to the side and thrashed around in his death throes as Threadgill groaned, only half-conscious.

Coming up on his knees, Stark twisted around to search for more of the enemy. He didn't see the one behind him who kicked him in the back of the head. Stark's helmet went flying as he pitched forward on his face. Fighting to hang on to consciousness, he forced himself to roll over so that he could try to defend himself.

It was too late. The VC who had knocked him down now loomed over him, and the flash from a mortar round showed Stark an image he would never forget: the snarling face of the man who was about to thrust a bayonet into his belly and rip his guts out. At that instant Stark knew he was staring death right in the eye.

And then, in the next heartbeat, before the poised bayonet could fall, the VC's head blew up, blood and brains raining down around Stark in a hot, grisly shower. Rich Threadgill shoved the corpse with its shattered skull aside, motioned with the .45 he had just used to blow Charlie's brains out, and said, "Come on, John Howard. Can't lie around all night."

Stark pushed himself up off the soggy, blood-soaked ground. Threadgill had regained his senses just in time to save Stark's life, but that didn't change the fact that he had been only seconds from death. He had been close enough to feel the Reaper's hand on his shoulder.

And the memory of that bony touch would always be there.

After so long a time—it seemed like hours but was probably only ten or fifteen minutes—the enemy withdrew and the shooting stopped. The marines remained alert for the rest of the night, unwilling to blindly accept that the fighting was over. Letting your guard down was the quickest way to get dead out here. Not until morning came did anyone relax.

They sat around a cook pot, Stark and Threadgill and Finnegan and Sheffield, all of them except Finnegan twenty years old and he was only a year older. Red-eyed, haggard, and unshaven, but still alive, by God. Nat Van Linh hunkered on his heels beside the pot and cut up some meat into the stew. The Americans didn't know what kind of meat it was and didn't ask. Stark hoped it wasn't long pig, but he was too tired and hungry to worry much about it.

He noticed Henry Macon standing not too far away. Macon seemed to want to join them, but he hung back. Whether his reluctance was because he was fairly new to the unit, or because his skin was black and three of the five men around the fire were southerners and he didn't know what to expect from them, Stark didn't know. Didn't care, either. He motioned Macon over and said, "Sit down. That was a hell of a job you did with that mortar, Macon."

Macon came over and sat down on a log. "Just doing what they trained me to do," he said in his soft voice.

"That mortar sure sang a sweet song," Finnegan said.

"Prettiest I've ever heard," Sheffield put in.

"You want some stew?" Nat asked.

Macon nodded, and he was grinning now, feeling more at ease, like he belonged with these other men. And he truly did. Combat had seen to that.

Once you go to war with a man, nothing is ever the same, and you never forget the lessons taught by the jungle and the night and the constant presence of death. You never forget.

Even though there are times when you might want to.

One

"Damn it!" John Howard Stark crumpled the newspaper and flung it away from him.

"What is it?" his wife, Elaine, asked from the stove where she was frying bacon. "The Cowboys do something you don't agree with again?"

"Worse'n that. They found another of those damn mad cows up in Washington."

"Oh." Elaine had been a rancher's wife for over thirty years. She knew how something thousands of miles away, like in the Pacific Northwest, could affect life here in the Rio Grande Valley of Texas. Every time there was another outbreak of mad cow disease anywhere in the country, it made beef prices go down, and that hurt ranchers everywhere.

Stark thought the smell of bacon cooking was just about the best smell in the world. He also thought his wife, still slim and straight with only a little gray in her blond hair despite her five-plus decades on earth, was the prettiest sight. But neither of them could cheer him up now. There had been too much bad news for too long. No real catastrophes, mind, just a seemingly endless stream of developments that made things worse and then worse and then worse again. Stark was fed up. Why, for two cents he'd—

He'd do exactly the same things he had done in his life, the rational part of his brain told him. Regrets were worth just about as much as a bucket of warm spit.

Sitting around and moaning wasn't a trait that ran in the Stark family. John Howard's great-great-grandfather had been a frontier judge, a man who had dispensed justice just as easily with a six-gun as with a gavel and a law book. His great-grandfather had worn the badge of county sheriff until settling down to establish this ranch up the Rio Grande from Del Rio. He had faced down some of Pancho Villa's men to keep it. The generations since had hung on to the Diamond S through good times and bad. John Howard himself had left the place for only one extended period of time in his life—to take a trip for Uncle Sam to a backwater country in Southeast Asia where little fellas in black pajamas shot at him for a couple of years. In the more than three decades since then, he had returned to his home, married his high school sweetheart, raised two boys with her, seen both his parents pass away, and taken over the running of the ranch. It was a hardscrabble spread and a hardscrabble time, here in the first decade of the twenty-first century. And Stark wasn't as young as he used to be. Fifty-four years old, by God. He had gone to Vietnam at the ripe old age of eighteen, little more than a boy. But he had returned as a man.

That was a long time ago now. For the first few years, Stark had sometimes woken up in the middle of the night shaking and drenched with sweat. He never could remember the dreams that provoked that reaction in him, but he knew they must have been bad ones. He had seen so many men that the war just wouldn't let go of, so they tried to escape it with drugs and booze and God knows what all. Ruined past, ruined present, ruined future. He'd been one of the lucky ones. He had Elaine and his folks and the ranch. Later he'd had the boys, David and Peter. They all got him through the nightmare landscape that had claimed so many other men, and these days Stark seldom ever thought about Vietnam. When he did he thought not about the dying but about the friends he had made there.

He'd been too busy lately to think about the past. Like all the other ranchers in Val Verde County, he was struggling to make ends meet. In the summer this part of Texas resembled the ass end of hell—hot, dry, and dusty plains dotted with mesquite trees, scrub oaks, and all-too-infrequent patches of grass. The old saying was that hereabouts it took a hundred acres of land just to graze one cow . . . and if the summer was bad enough, you could count the ribs on that cow. Now, to top it off, beef prices were in the crapper, and ever-spiraling taxes and overbearing government regulations didn't help matters, either. Most of the time he felt older than dirt.

But like the old saying went, gettin' old sure as hell beat the alternative. Most of the time Stark figured that was true.

Elaine put a plate full of bacon, biscuits, and scrambled eggs in front of him. The eggs had a lot of peppers and cheese in them, just the way he liked them. He poked at them with his fork and said, "This ain't some of that egg substitute stuff, is it?" He would have used a stronger word than "stuff" if not for the fact that Elaine didn't allow any cussing at the kitchen table.

"No, it's the real thing, John Howard," she said. "I've given up on trying to feed you healthy food. You kick up a fuss just like a little baby. Besides, you're going to be just like your daddy and your uncle and your granddaddy and all the other men in your family. You all pack away the red meat and the grease and you're still out reshingling the well house and roping steers when you're ninety-five."

"Yeah, but I don't drink much and only smoke one cigar a year, on my birthday."

She patted him on the shoulder. "I'm sure that's the secret."

She started to turn away, but Stark reached out, looped an arm around her slender waist, and pulled her onto his lap.

Despite her appearance, she wasn't a little bitty thing. She was tall and had some heft to her. But Stark was six feet four and weighed two hundred and thirty pounds—only up ten pounds from his fighting weight—and his active life kept him vital and strong in spite of the aches and pains that reminded him of his age. He put his other hand behind Elaine's head and kissed her. She responded with the eagerness that he still aroused in her. In fact, she was a little breathless by the time they broke the kiss.

"That right there, that's the secret," John Howard said.

"What, that all you Stark men are horny old bastards?"

"Damn right."

She laughed and pressed her lips to his again and when she slipped out of his arms he let her go this time. "Eat your breakfast," she said. "We've both got work to do."

Stark nodded as he dug the fork into the eggs and picked up a biscuit. "Yeah, I've got to go over to Tommy's in a little while. One of his cows got over on our range yesterday and bogged down in that sinkhole on the creek. I had to pull her out, and I've got her and her calf out in the barn. I need to find out what he wants to do about them."

"You be sure and tell him hello for me. And remind him that we're expecting him and Julie and the kids over here tomorrow evening."

Stark nodded. He couldn't answer. His mouth was full of bacon and eggs and biscuit by now, and somehow his bad mood of a few minutes earlier had evaporated.

Tomas Carranza—Tommy to his friends—owned the ten thousand acres next to John Howard Stark's Diamond S. It was a small spread for Texas, but Tommy had a small herd. The ranch had belonged to the Carranza family for generations, just as the neighboring land had belonged to the Starks. There had been Carranzas in Sam Houston's army at San Jacinto, fierce *Tejanos* who hated Santa Anna and the oppressive rule of the Mexican dictator every bit as much as the

Anglos did. Later the family had settled along the Rio Grande, founding the fine little rancho on the Texas side of the river.

John Howard Stark had always been something of a hero to Tommy Carranza. Tommy was considerably younger. When Tommy was a little boy, Stark was the star of the Del Rio High School baseball team, belting a record number of home runs. Tommy loved baseball, and it was special to have a godlike figure such as John Howard Stark befriend him back then.

But John Howard had graduated and gone off to fight in Vietnam, and Tommy had feared that he would never see his friend again. He had prayed to the Blessed Virgin every night to watch over John Howard, and when Stark came back safely from the war, Tommy felt a secret, never expressed pride that perhaps his prayers had had something to do with that.

Over the years since, the age difference between the two men, never all that important, had come to matter even less. They regarded each other as equals and good friends. John Howard and Elaine were godparents to the two children Tommy had with his wife, Julie. Hardly a month went by when the families didn't get together for a barbecue. In fact, one of the get-togethers was coming up the next day, the Fourth of July.

On this morning Tommy wasn't thinking about barbecue. He had driven the pickup into Del Rio to get some rolls of fence at the big building supply warehouse store on the edge of town. His land stretched for nearly five miles along the Rio Grande, and Tommy tried to keep every foot of it fenced. The fences kept getting cut, though, by the damned coyotes who trafficked in human cargo and the even more vile drug runners who smuggled their poison across the river.

Sometimes Tommy thought it would be easier just to give up and let the animals take over. But the spirits of his *Tejano* ancestors wouldn't let that happen. A Carranza never gave up the fight.

He wrestled the last roll of wire from the flatbed cart into the back of the pickup and then slammed the tailgate. He rolled the cart to one of the little corral places scattered around the big parking lot, and as he turned back toward his truck he was surprised to see a man standing beside it. The fact that the man stood there was less surprising than the way he looked.

The guy was wearing a suit, for God's sake!

Part of a suit, anyway. He had taken off the jacket and had it draped over one arm. He had also rolled up his sleeves and loosened his tie. The man was stocky, with thinning pale hair. His skin was turning pink in the sun. The suit and the shoes he wore were probably worth more than the battered old pickup beside which he stood.

Tommy thumbed back his straw Stetson with its tightly curled brim and nodded to the stranger. "Hello," he said. "Something I can do for you?"

"Are you Tomas Carranza?" the man asked bluntly.

"That's right. Oh hell, you're not a process server, are you? I told Gustafson I'd pay that feed bill as soon as I can!"

"Oh no, I'm not here to serve you with a lawsuit, Mr. Carranza. But I *am* a lawyer." The man took a business card out of his shirt pocket and extended it.

Out of curiosity, Tommy took the card and glanced at it. The name J. Donald Lester was embossed on it in fancy black letters. The address was in Dallas.

"What's a Dallas lawyer doing all the way down here in the valley?" Tommy asked with a frown.

"I represent a client in the area. Across the river in Cuidad Acuna, in fact."

Tommy grunted. "A Mexican with a Dallas lawyer. Must be a rich guy. What is he, a drug lord?"

"His name," J. Donald Lester said, "is Ernesto Diego Espinoza Ramirez."

Tommy went stiff and tight inside as he drew air sharply in through his nose. "*El Bruitre*," he said in a hollow voice.

"Yes, yes, the Vulture," Lester said impatiently. "It's a very colorful name, but my client doesn't care for it, so why don't we just refer to him as Senor Ramirez?"

Tommy dropped the lawyer's card onto the concrete of the parking lot. "Why don't we just call him a murdering, drug-running bastard and be done with it? And I think I'm done talking to you, too, Mr. Lester."

Tommy turned toward the front door of the pickup, but Lester stopped him with a hand on his arm. "Please, Mr. Carranza, I just want a few moments of your time."

Shaking off the lawyer's hand, Tommy said, "I don't talk to snakes, and if you work for Ramirez you're just as big a snake as he is, in my book."

"It's a matter of money," Lester said, raising his voice over the squeal of hinges as Tommy jerked the truck's door open. "A great deal of money."

A voice in the back of Tommy's head told him to get in the truck and drive away without paying any more attention to the gringo. But the mention of money piqued his interest. Not that he would ever take one red cent from Ramirez or his ilk. Any money they had would be indelibly stained with the blood and suffering of innocents.

Still, he was a naturally courteous man. And his youngest, Angelina, needed five thousand dollars' worth of orthodontic work to make her beautiful smile even more beautiful. That was what Julie said, anyway.

"I'll give you a minute," he said to Lester, "but I can tell you right now, I'm not gonna be interested in anything you have to say to me."

"Ten thousand dollars," Lester said.

Twice as much as what it would cost for Angelina's braces.

"What?" Tommy asked.

"Each month."

"You're offering to pay me ten grand a month?"

Lester nodded his sleekly barbered head. "That's correct."

"What for?"

"I think you know the answer to that, Mr. Carranza."

"Yeah," Tommy said. That brief moment of hope he'd had

came crashing down. No way would anybody pay that much money for something honest, especially not Ramirez. "You want me to look the other way while the Vulture's couriers bring that goddamn shit across my land."

"It would be a perfectly legitimate arrangement, an easement, if you will—"

"Easement this," Tommy said, and he brought up a hard fist and smashed it into Lester's mouth.

He struck out of anger, furious that this sleazy Dallas lawyer thought he could be bought off with drug money. And he struck out of shame as well, because he hadn't driven away without even listening to the bastard and because for a split second he had considered the offer. He didn't know whom he was angrier with, himself or Lester.

But it was the lawyer who got busted in the mouth. The blow sent Lester staggering back across an empty parking space. He slammed into another parked pickup. It had an alarm installed and activated, and the siren began to blare as Lester bounced off the driver's door and fell to the pavement. He looked up at Tommy, stunned, with blood on his mouth. His bruised lips began to swell.

"Lie down with dogs, get up with fleas, my daddy always said," Tommy told him, raising his voice so he could be heard over the yowling of the alarm. "Go back to Dallas, Mr. Lawyer." The words were filled with contempt.

Lester couldn't get up. All he could do was glare balefully as Tommy got in his pickup and drove away. Tommy didn't look back.

Two

Stark knew Tommy Carranza well enough to recognize that something was on the younger man's mind when Stark visited the Carranza ranch that day. Tommy didn't seem to want to talk about it, though, so Stark didn't push it. A man didn't go sticking his nose in another fella's business without being asked to.

Tommy had just gotten back from Del Rio with a load of fence wire. Stark offered to help him stretch it in the places where his fences needed repair, but Tommy shook his head. "You've got your own work to do, John Howard. Besides, I've got Martin to help me."

Martin Carranza was Tommy's boy, twelve years old and turning into a good hand. With school out for the summer, Martin was doing a lot of work around the ranch.

Stark nodded. "All right, but if you need any help, you know where I am. What about that cow of yours and her calf?"

"If you don't mind keepin' 'em another night, I'll bring the trailer with me when we come over tomorrow and get them then."

"Sounds like a plan to me," Stark agreed.

"I'm sorry they strayed onto your range, John Howard."

A grin creased Stark's weathered face. "Don't worry about that. Gettin' bogged down like it did, that old cow gave Uncle Newt an excuse to practice his roping."

Newton Stark was John Howard's uncle, brother to John Howard's daddy, Ethan. As a boy he had grown up in the saddle, riding before he could walk. By age twelve he had been a top hand, able to do a man's work and keep up with the cowboys who worked on the Diamond S. A few years later the Second World War had come along, and Newt had found himself trudging through the sands of North Africa behind some of ol' Blood-and-Guts Patton's tanks. Newt never talked much about the war except to say that parts of Tunisia looked a hell of a lot like west Texas.

After the war he had come home like hundreds of thousands of other former GIs and gone back to work. In Newt's case that meant cowboying. His like could have changed when his and Ethan's father passed away, but Newt wasn't having any of that.

He had sold his half of the Diamond S to Ethan back when they both inherited the place from their father. To hear Newt tell it, he was a cowboy, and cowboys didn't have no place in their lives for sittin' in an office and doin' book work. Any chore that couldn't be done from the back of a horse wasn't worth doing, to Newt's way of thinking. Now in his eighties, he still lived on the Diamond S and did a full day's work, blissfully ignorant of the business end of running a ranch.

"I thought you pulled that cow out of the sinkhole," Tommy commented.

"Well, Newt and me together got her loose," Stark said. "Anyway, her and the calf will be waiting for you tomorrow evening."

As Stark drove away in his pickup, he thought that he could just as easily have called Tommy and had this conversation by phone. Stark liked looking at a man when he talked to him, though. And he didn't mind overmuch the way Tommy's pretty wife, Julie, fussed over him and offered him lemonade when he visited. The lemonade had been cold and

mighty good. Even though it wasn't quite noon yet, the heat
of a Texas summer was in full force and the temperature was
already around ninety-five. It would likely top out at 105 or
106 later that afternoon.

When Stark got back to the ranch he found a note from
Elaine letting him know that she had gone into Del Rio to
finish buying everything she would need for the Independence
Day barbecue. She had left his lunch in the refrigerator since
she would likely be gone most of the rest of the day. Stark
got the bowl out and lifted the aluminum foil cover over it.
Salad. He sighed. Elaine might have said she'd given up trying to get him to eat healthy, but she really hadn't.

Dutifully, he ate the rabbit food. Then he followed it with
two thick peanut-butter-and-banana sandwiches he made
himself.

With it being the Fourth of July and all, John Howard and
Elaine had invited all their friends and neighbors. All the
local ranchers from along the river and quite a few folks
from town showed up at the sprawling, cottonwood-shaded
ranch house on a small knoll that gave a view of the Rio
Grande about a mile away. With help from Uncle Newt and
Chaco Hernandez, one of the ranch hands who was Newt's
best friend and companion, Stark had set up several picnic
tables in the yard. Those tables were packed with food, some
of it prepared by Elaine, some brought by the guests. Chaco,
who was pushing seventy, was in charge of the barbecue pit,
and wonderful smells filled the evening air.

It was hot, of course, because the sun was barely down
and the air wouldn't cool off much for a while yet. But there
was a good breeze and almost no humidity, so the weather
was bearable. Stark had once seen a T-shirt with a picture on
it of two sunbaked skeletons conversing. One of them was
saying to the other, "But it's a *dry* heat." That was meant to
be sarcastic, of course, but there was some truth to it. One

time Stark had visited Houston and felt like he was fixin' to drown every time he took a deep breath of the humid air there. He hadn't been able to get out of that place fast enough. It was the armpit of Texas as far as he was concerned.

The ranchers naturally gravitated together while the women talked and the kids ran around yelling and playing. Stark found himself standing in a group of five of his friends: Tommy Carranza, of course, plus Devery Small, W.R. Smathers, Hubie Cornheiser, and Everett Hatcher. The mood was glum despite the fact that this was supposed to be a celebration. All of the men had seen the newspaper and television reports about the latest outbreak of mad cow disease and knew what it would mean to their profits.

"It's not fair, damn it," Hubie said as they sipped from bottles of Lone Star beer. "Ain't never been a single mad cow found in Val Verde County. Every beef we raise is safe as it can be. But the buyers don't ever think about that."

W.R. nodded. "Prices are down across the board. That's what they always say, like it ain't their fault. And they claim they can't do a thing about it."

"They don't *want* to do anything about it," Stark said. "Naturally they want to pay as little as they can get by with."

"What they're gonna wind up doin' is starvin' us all out," Everett said. "Then they won't have to pay anything, so I reckon they'll be happy. But there won't be any beef no more, either."

Devery rubbed his jaw and said, "Yeah, beef prices are worrisome, all right, but to tell you the truth I'm more concerned about those damn drug smugglers."

Stark saw Tommy flick a startled glance toward Devery and ask, "What do you mean?"

Devery pointed toward the river with his beer bottle. "Hardly a night goes by when some o' that shit don't cross the range belonging to one or the other of us. You know, I really don't mind the illegals all that much, especially the ones who come across on their own. They're just tryin' to make a better life for themselves and their families, and I can almost respect that. But those drug runners ain't doin' anything except bringin' pure death across the river."

"I never have understood what would make a fella want to shoot that crap into his arm," W.R. said. "It just don't make no sense to me."

"The ones who do are too gutless to face up to life," Stark rumbled. "They'd rather run away, and they use the dope to do it."

"What's bad is that our daddies and our daddies' daddies and on back fought and died to tame this land," Devery went on. "They had to take on the Comanches and Mex bandidos—no offense, Tommy."

"None taken," Tommy said. "But there were Anglo bandits, too, you know."

Devery nodded. "Damn right, King Fisher and his like were every bit as bad, if not worse. Then you got your rattlesnakes and your scorpions, and the heat and the dust storms and everything else that those old boys had to put up with. But they beat all of it and made this valley a decent place to live. Now, though, it's bein' taken over by the same sort of bandidos who got run out of here a hundred years ago. They got cell phones and fancy guns and GPSs now, but they're still bandidos as far as I'm concerned."

There were mutters of agreement from the men. Hubie said, "Looks to me like somebody ought to do something about all this."

"Who?" Devery shot back. "The government?"

"Government?" a harsh voice repeated. The men looked around to see that old Newton Stark, John Howard's uncle, had come up to join them, all six feet, three inches of his cantankerous self. Newt continued, "All them fellas in Washington are a bunch o' black-suited, black-hearted bureaucratic robber barons, if you ask me. They ain't interested in helpin' anybody but their own selves."

"You don't think there are any good politicians?" W.R. asked.

Newt snorted. "I reckon there could be, but I ain't never seen 'em."

"It's not just the ones in Washington," Devery said. "There are plenty of 'em right here in Texas that I wouldn't trust as far as I could throw 'em. Like Norval Lee Hammond."

The sheriff of Val Verde County, Hammond was nearing the end of his second term in office. His first had been marked by controversy, but he had been reelected anyway, some said because of the campaign money that had poured into his coffers from unknown sources. Rumor had it those sources were heavily involved in the drug trade, but nothing had been proven. All anybody knew for sure was that arrests for drug trafficking weren't made very often, and when they were made, more of them were thrown out of court than seemed natural.

Stark and the others nodded in solemn agreement with Devery's comment about the sheriff. They might have gone on talking about the increased drug traffic across the border if Chaco hadn't called out at that moment, "Barbecue's ready!"

Certain things go with barbecue. Nobody sits down to a big plate of brisket and arugula. But you've got your beans, your potato salad, your coleslaw and sliced onions and corn bread, and for dessert peach cobbler or apple cobbler or both, topped with homemade ice cream from a freezer with a hand-turned crank, not one of those electric jobs. Wash it all down with a cold bottle of beer or a big glass of iced tea with sweat dripping off it. That's eatin', son.

John Howard Stark was pleasantly full as he sat on one of the benches with his back to the picnic table and his long legs stretched out in front of him. He thought about unfastening his belt buckle and the button of his jeans, but he knew if he did that Elaine would notice and likely swat him one on the back of the head. Country music played from the portable stereo he'd set up earlier, and a few couples were dancing as George Strait sang about getting to Amarillo by morning. Stark sipped his beer, content.

He watched Tommy Carranza dancing with Julie. Tommy was handsome enough in a rough-hewn way, but Julie was really a beauty, taut and tanned with hair as black as a raven's wing hanging straight down her back. Her high cheekbones and piercing dark eyes bespoke her Indian blood.

Elaine sat down beside Stark and said, "What are you doing?"

"Thinking about how pretty Julie Carranza is."

She punched him lightly on the arm. "What kind of a man says something like that to his wife?"

"The honest kind?"

"Well, if you want to put it that way . . . and she is awfully pretty."

"You know you don't have anything to be jealous about. I never said she was prettier than you. Nobody is."

"Thank you, John Howard. You never were a man with a smooth line of talk, but you say what you mean and mean what you say, and a woman appreciates that. This one does, anyway."

Stark put his arm around her shoulders and she rested her head against him. They sat there like that for several minutes, happy to be with each other and to be surrounded by their friends. At moments like this, all thoughts of trouble went away.

The problem was that moments like that never lasted long enough. In this case, the song ended, the dancing stopped, and Tommy and Julie came over to the bench where Stark sat with Elaine.

"John Howard, I need to talk to you for a minute," Tommy said.

"Uh-oh, I know that tone," Julie said. "Something's wrong, isn't it?"

Tommy shook his head. "Of course not. I just need to talk a little business with John Howard here."

"Man talk, he means," Elaine said as she stood up. "You'd

think they'd know by now that it's the twenty-first century and such chauvinistic attitudes are totally outdated."

"They're a couple of throwbacks," Julie said, but she was grinning as she said it.

Stark got to his feet, too, and jerked a thumb toward the barn. "Come on, Tommy, let's go get that cow and her calf and load 'em up. That'll give us a chance to talk in peace."

As they started toward the barn, Tommy asked quietly, "Elaine wasn't really upset, was she?"

"Naw, she was just hoo-rawin' us. She's feisty that way."

Tommy changed the subject by asking, "You hear anything from the boys lately?"

"Got e-mail from both of 'em a couple of days ago. They say they're doing fine, but they don't know when they'll be back from over there."

Both of John Howard and Elaine's sons were in the military. The older boy, David, was in the navy, a pilot flying off an aircraft carrier somewhere in the Middle East. Stark didn't know where, exactly. The younger one, Peter, was a lieutenant colonel in the marines, a leatherneck like his old man, and he'd been pulling a tour of duty in Iraq for the past year.

"You must worry about them being in harm's way," Tommy said.

Stark grunted. "This day and age, with all the evil loose in the world, every American is in harm's way no matter where he is or what he's doing. I reckon we're safer here than the boys are where they are, but at least they've got the weapons to fight back. Over here we're supposed to just roll over and take whatever's dished out to us, no matter how bad it is. Otherwise we ain't bein' sensitive enough to other folks' beliefs and cultures." He shook his head. "Just once I'd like to see other folks give a little respect to *our* beliefs and culture."

"Roger that," Tommy said.

Stark stopped, and the younger man did likewise. They were in a patch of shadow, and even though Stark couldn't see Tommy's face all that clearly, he looked at him head-on and said, "You didn't ask to talk just to hear me rant about such things. Something's bothering you, Tommy. What is it?"

"You can tell?"

"Hell, I've known you for over thirty years. Of course I can tell." Stark made a shrewd guess. "It's something about all the drug smuggling that's been goin' on. I saw the way you reacted when Devery brought it up."

Tommy shifted his feet uneasily. "When I was in Del Rio yesterday picking up those rolls of fence, a guy talked to me."

"What guy?"

"A lawyer from Dallas. He gave me his card. His name was J. Donald Lester."

"I never did really trust a man who uses his first initial and middle name like that. Seems like he's puttin' on airs. What did ol' J. Donald want?"

"I won't beat around the bush, John Howard. He works for the Vulture, and he wanted to pay me ten grand a month to look the other way while Ramirez's couriers bring drugs across my land."

Stark let out a low whistle. "The Vulture, eh? That ain't good. What did you do?"

"I'm ashamed to say I thought about it. I wouldn't admit that to anybody else, John Howard, not even to Julie."

"Thought about it for how long?" Stark asked grimly.

"About half a second."

"And then?"

"And then I busted him a good one in the mouth."

Stark couldn't hold back an explosive bark of laughter. "Good for you. I knew you wouldn't ever go for any sort of deal like that."

"Well, I'm glad you know that, because like I said, for a minute there I considered it. And it's been eatin' me up ever since."

Stark put a hand on his friend's shoulder. "No need for that. You did the right thing."

"Did I? I'm not so sure."

"You mean you think you should have taken the deal?"

"No, of course not. But doing what I did . . . it's bound to make an enemy out of Ramirez."

Stark rubbed his jaw, feeling the calluses on his fingertips scrape against the bristles of his beard. "Yeah, there is that. I didn't think about it at first."

"Neither did I. But now I wonder if I've put my family in danger."

One thing was sure, thought Stark. The Vulture was a bad man to cross. Just about the baddest man possible.

Three

The man in the white suit smiled. It was not a pretty expression.

"You know what to do, Alfonso," Ernesto Diego Espinoza Ramirez said.

The thick-bodied gunner nodded. "*Sí, jefe.*"

Ramirez—also known on both sides of the border as *El Bruitre*, the Vulture—picked up the drink from the round glass table beside him and sipped from it. "And take Ryan with you," he added.

Again Alfonso Ruiz nodded his assent. He glanced somewhat nervously over his shoulder at the man leaning indolently against the adobe wall around the courtyard. Electric lanterns shone in the trees around the pool, and in their yellow glow the man called Ryan looked half-asleep. But Ruiz knew that to be a false impression. Ryan was always alert, no matter how he looked, and he could kill in the blink of an eye. Ruiz knew that to be true, because he had seen it happen on numerous occasions.

Across the table from Ramirez, J. Donald Lester took a drink from his glass and winced at the pain from his swollen lips. The indignity of being assaulted like that, in the middle of a parking lot in broad daylight, still burned inside him.

But that damned greaser Carranza would get his comeuppance. Carranza had attacked J. Donald Lester while the lawyer was acting on behalf of Ramirez. That was just like attacking the Vulture. Ramirez would never let that pass. He was Colombian, and his pride would never allow him to be challenged like that without retaliation, fierce and swift. A Mexican might let the affront go out of sheer laziness, Lester thought, but not a Colombian.

"Let me know when it's done," Ramirez said.

"*Sí, jefe.*"

Ramirez waved a hand in dismissal. Ruiz faded back away from the table. Ryan straightened from the wall and joined him as they went inside the hacienda. That left Ramirez and Lester alone with the two girls stroking sleekly through the water of the pool.

They were watching Ramirez, and when he made a slight motion with his hand they swam over to the edge of the pool and pulled themselves out of the water. Both girls were nude, and neither was over the age of sixteen. Water streamed from their long black hair as it hung down their backs, and droplets gleamed on their bare, silky, olive-tinted skin.

"You have been through a great deal, my friend," Ramirez said to Lester. "You have suffered on my behalf. Therefore you deserve to be rewarded." He waved a hand toward the girls. "I give you your choice. Both are virgins, so you will not be disappointed."

Lester swallowed hard. "Well, I . . . I don't know." He couldn't take his eyes off the girls as they lifted their arms and ran their fingers through their dripping hair. That made their high, firm breasts rise even more. They smiled.

"I can't decide!" Lester burst out. "I want them both!"

Ramirez chuckled. "Then take them both," he decreed. "And enjoy them to your heart's content, amigo."

Lester stood up. The girls approached him. Each of them took one of his hands, and laughing they led him into the house. Lester stumbled a little in his excitement at what was about to happen.

When he was alone, Ramirez picked up his drink and finished it. He had planned to take one of the girls himself tonight, but he didn't really mind giving up that opportunity. There were other virgins in the world he could deflower, thousands of them, in fact. For a man with sufficient money, there was never a last chance for anything. The heart's desire could always be bought again. This lesson he had learned and learned well, in the years since he had crawled out of the gutters of Bogota a starving boy and set out to transform himself into a great man.

In many ways that transformation had been easier than he had believed it would be. The drug cartels that made up far and away the largest segment of the Colombian economy, larger even than the coffee industry, were like hungry machines, endlessly devouring the lower-level couriers. Ramirez had started small, working for the neighborhood dealer who supplied his whore mother with the drugs she needed to dull the pain of her existence. The job had gone well and Ramirez had been given more responsibility. Once one of the runners tried to steal from the dealer and had even gotten the drop on him with an automatic pistol. Ramirez, who was thirteen years old at the time, came up silently behind the man and cut his throat with a single swift stroke of a machete, killing him before he could even squeeze off a burst from the machine pistol. That was the first time Ramirez killed anyone.

It would not be the last.

Seeing how coldly and efficiently Ramirez could deal out death, his employer had given him more such jobs. Ramirez carried them all out to the best of his ability, and before he was eighteen years old he was known as *El Bruitre*, the Vulture, because wherever he went death was sure to follow.

Curiously, while he did not mind killing, he took no particular pleasure in it. Unlike some men whose eyes shone with a bright, sick excitement when they took a life, who were granted an almost sexual release by the sight of their victims' blood, Ramirez regarded the whole thing as a necessary part of the business he was in, nothing more. That detachment meant that he always weighed the odds and never took risks he didn't need to. His own urges never forced him into doing anything foolhardy.

And so he rose in the cartel, moving up more quickly than even he would have dreamed possible, because each killing removed an obstacle to attaining his ultimate goals. He wanted money and power, of course, and he wanted people to fear and respect him, not so much because he could kill them but because he could *crush* them if he chose to do so.

Now he was thirty-five years old and had come to Cuidad Acuna, to this magnificent hacienda, because right across the river was the United States of America, the source of nearly all the money that eventually made its way into his offshore bank accounts. Getting the drugs across the border was really the most crucial step in the entire process, and while he had not killed anyone personally for quite a few years, Ramirez still thought of himself as a hands-on manager. He was in charge of the smuggling and made all the decisions. Though simple at the heart of it—the drugs were taken from one side of the river to the other and then sent on their way into the distribution channels that would carry them all across the continent—the process was surrounded by a fairly complex maze of law enforcement and political corruption on both sides of the border. It took a skilled, intelligent man to keep up with everything, and Ramirez was that man.

Earlier today he had flown back into Acuna from a meeting with some of the other cartel leaders in Mexico City. While he was away from home, he had left his attorney with a simple matter to take care of. Lester was to arrange with the rancher Tomas Carranza for the unrestricted passage of Ramirez's couriers across Carranza's land.

Lester had failed miserably, and for a moment Ramirez had been tempted to have him killed as punishment for that failure. At the very least, he should have had his lead gunner, Alfonso Ruiz, cut off a couple of the lawyer's fingers. He might do that yet. Lester thought he was off the hook—what else could he think, when he had been rewarded with two teenage virgins?—but his ultimate fate was still to be decided.

In the meantime, Ramirez had turned his rage on Tomas Carranza. That fool had had the effrontery to strike the personal representative of Ernesto Diego Espinoza Ramirez. That was like slapping the face of Ramirez himself. There was no question about Carranza being punished. He would pay for his prideful, foolhardy gesture. Lester had a file on Carranza; the rancher had a wife and two children.

He drank the last of the liquor in the glass and stood up to stroll toward the house. By now Lester would have the two girls in bed in the guest quarters and would have them doing wanton things to him and to each other. Ramirez decided he would watch for a while on the monitor that was hooked up to the hidden camera in Lester's room. He was not a voyeur, really, but he did appreciate beautiful things, and watching those two girls would be no different from gazing at an exquisite painting or a splendid piece of sculpture.

There were five men in the crew, in an old Lincoln Town Car. Ruiz drove, and Ryan sat up front with him. The other three men—Guzman, Mendez, and Canales—rode in the backseat, jammed together rather uncomfortably. Ryan didn't feel sorry for them. Better them than him.

That was pretty much the story of his life, he mused. He had chosen the path of his own survival. No one could blame him for that.

He had been born in El Paso, the son of an Irish father and a Mexican mother. The father had left his native Ireland because he had been involved with the IRA and could no longer stand the political oppression of the bloody Englishmen. The fact that he was also fleeing several bank robbery charges and was suspected of being involved in a couple of murders had nothing to do with it, or so he claimed. He had slipped off a tramp freighter in Houston and made his way across Texas, picking up phony documents and a new identity along the way. Eventually he had settled in El Paso and gone to work as an enforcer for one of the local crime bosses.

Ryan's mother was in El Paso illegally, too, but nothing so elaborate as false identification papers was involved. She had simply waded across the Rio Grande one dark night with several of her friends and kept a low profile ever since, working as a domestic servant in several households, one of them belonging to the employer of the man who then called himself Allen Ryan.

The attraction between them had sprung up immediately. Juanita Gallego had surprised Allen Ryan by insisting that they be married before she would give herself to him. The idea had amused Ryan so much, and the desire he felt for her was so strong, that he had surprised himself by going along with it. Ryan had greased the wheels of the bureaucratic machine to get around the obstacle of Juanita's status as an illegal, and they were married in the church, all proper and fitting. A little more than nine months later, their son Simon was born.

It was a difficult birth, so difficult that Juanita would never be able to have more children. And Simon was a sickly child, given to crying for hours on end for no apparent reason. This infuriated Allen Ryan, who had of course become proficient in Spanish, working as he did for a man with criminal interests on both sides of the border. Angry and frustrated, Ryan often shouted, "*Silencio!*" at the infant, who didn't understand and kept crying. When Ryan raised his hand to the child, Juanita always moved in and took the beating herself, letting Ryan inflict his rage on her rather than on the baby.

One of his first words was "*Silencio.*" He heard it so much he thought it was his name. When he was old enough, he stopped crying, but it was too late by then. His father was already in the habit of beating his mother. Young Simon watched this going on as he grew older and outgrew the sick spells. By the time he was an adolescent he had begun running and lifting weights. He boxed in school, not playground fights but real boxing, as a sport, and was a Golden Gloves champion by sixteen.

By now Allen Ryan was quite an important man in El Paso's criminal underworld. The family had money and a comfortable life. There was no reason for him to feel rage. But he felt it anyway, and when it built up to a certain point, it sought release in the beating of Juanita, as it always had.

Until one night when Allen Ryan broke her arm in front of her son, and Simon beat his father to death.

There was nothing fancy about it. A punch to the solar plexus to knock the wind out of him and stun him, another to the jaw to knock him to the floor. Then Simon pinned him down with his knees and struck again and again, left, right, left, right, until the blood ran from his father's eyes and nose and mouth and his body was slack in death. It was not until then that Simon became aware of his mother screaming and trying to pull him off his father. Even with her arm broken and dangling loosely, surely causing her great pain, she had tried to stop him.

That made no sense at all to Simon. She should have been happy about what he had done.

He left El Paso that same night after a sobbing, half-hysterical Juanita told him that his father's business associates would kill him for what he had done. He had just turned eighteen, so he hitched a ride to San Antonio and enlisted in the army the next day.

It was 1966, and a year later he was in Vietnam, wearing a green beret on his close-cropped red hair. For the first time in his life he was happy.

No official charges were ever filed against him. Allen Ryan's associates in El Paso covered up his death. To tell the truth, despite what Juanita had said they were never that upset about the whole thing. Ryan had become too unstable to be depended upon. So they let Simon go and forgot the whole thing, although he never knew about that until years later.

His service record was exemplary, including several commendations and medals. He reupped in '69, stayed through the fall of Saigon, and was one of the last men off the roof of the American embassy. The way it all ended left a bad taste in his mouth. He'd had enough of the military, especially since it was no longer run by soldiers but by politicians instead. There were plenty of places in the world, though, where a man of his skills was still needed. He fought for money in little brushfire wars in a dozen tiny countries that nobody gave a damn about beyond their own borders. At first he tried to see to it that he fought on what he considered the "right" side, but as the years passed he grew to care less and less about that. Bit by bit he became more concerned with the money and the fighting. As long as there was plenty of both, that was all he cared about.

Eventually an urge came over him, an urge to go home. He returned to El Paso. His mother had believed she would never see him again. As soon as he laid eyes on her he knew something was wrong. She was eaten up by cancer and had only months to live, maybe less. She told him then that he wasn't in trouble because of what he had done to his father. He could stay without having to worry about vengeance coming down on him.

She needed money, and he knew how to do only one kind of work. He made contact with his father's old associates, or in many cases, the younger men who had taken over for those old ones. The jobs they gave him were easy for a man of his background and talents. Killing had never meant very much to him. No matter where his target might be, he could get in and out with military precision, with stealth and silence.

And so he took to calling himself Silencio. It was a good reminder, he thought, of where he had come from and why he had become what he had become.

His mother had no chance to defeat the illness that was slowly consuming her. One night she sat with him, small and fragile and in wracking pain, huddling against his rangy, powerful form as if he were the parent and she the child. He held her and talked to her in the soft Spanish of his childhood, and then he broke her neck, swiftly, sharply, unexpectedly, before she knew what was happening, ending her agony and letting her pass with at least a semblance of dignity and even happiness.

With her gone there was no reason for him to stay in El Paso. He drifted along the Rio Grande Valley until fate brought him to Ernesto Diego Espinoza Ramirez. The Vulture. A Colombian, a vicious, merciless man, but one who paid well. Silencio Ryan was no longer a boy, no longer a young, wild man. He still enjoyed the heady tang of danger and excitement, but he needed less of it now to satisfy him. He settled down in Cuidad Acuna, working for Ramirez. Alfonso Ruiz was nominally in charge of all the gunners, but Ramirez and Ruiz both knew that Ryan was pretty much his own boss, and they were all right with that. As long as the jobs got done, that was all that mattered.

Tonight Ryan, Ruiz, and the other three men were on their way to the ranch of a man who had defied the Vulture. In the trunk of the Town Car was electronic equipment that would jam the sensors the U.S. Border Patrol used to try to monitor the border for illegal crossings. The trunk also contained automatic weapons and night-vision goggles. Ryan had trained Ramirez's men in the use of such things. He would get Ruiz and the other men across the border, see to it that they reached their destination undetected, and then they would do the work of wiping out Tomas Carranza and his family. It was a shame that Carranza's wife and kids had to die, but that was the Colombian way of doing these things.

And as always, Ryan thought, better them than him.

Four

Stark and Tommy loaded the cow and calf into the trailer that was hitched to Tommy's pickup. As Tommy shut the tailgate, Stark said, "You ever think about going to the law?"

"To tell them about Ramirez, you mean? What good would that do, John Howard? Everybody says Sheriff Hammond is being paid off by him."

"You could try the Border Patrol," Stark suggested. "Go see Hodge Purdee."

Tommy gave a short laugh. "I'm surprised to hear you saying anybody should rely on the government for anything."

Stark shrugged and said, "Just because the government's too big and unwieldy to get much of anything done doesn't mean there aren't some honest men working for it. Purdee might be able to help."

"I'll think about it," Tommy promised. "In the meantime, I was wondering if you'd do me a favor."

"Name it."

"Let Julie and the kids stay here tonight. Maybe even for a few days."

The request caught Stark a little off balance, but he didn't hesitate in responding, "Sure, we'd be glad to have them. Plenty of room in the old place, what with both boys gone."

"You're sure Elaine won't mind?"

A grin creased Stark's face. "Hell, she'll be tickled to have some youngsters in the house again. She won't mind. I can promise you that. Besides, she thinks the world of Julie."

"Thanks, John Howard." Tommy squeezed Stark's arm for a second. "I . . . I just don't feel safe having them on the ranch right now."

"Because you're afraid Ramirez might try to get even with you?"

"They say he's Colombian. You've heard about those guys. They're crazy."

Stark nodded. "Maybe you'd better stay here, too."

"Oh no," Tommy said immediately. "That could put you and Elaine in danger."

"What you ought to do," Stark said with a frown, "is take your family and get the hell outta here for a while, until things cool off. You've got family in San Antonio and El Paso both. Head for one of those places and lie low."

"Run and hide, you mean. I'm surprised to hear talk like that from John Howard Stark."

"Don't get your back up," Stark said. "I'm talkin' about being reasonable and protecting your family, that's all."

Tommy sighed. "Yeah, maybe you're right. If I run away, though, Ramirez is likely to move in and take over my place. He'll see it as a sign that he's won."

"I'll talk to Hodge Purdee," Stark promised. "His boys can increase their patrols, sort of put the lid on things for a while. And me and Newt and Chaco can keep the place up while you're gone, tend to your stock and such. When it's been long enough for things to have blown over, you can come back."

"When will that be? I hear tell those Colombians hold a grudge for a long time."

"Maybe so, but Ramirez has a big operation. Sooner or later he'll move on to other things and forget all about you."

"Yeah . . . all right, John Howard, I'll do it. I'll get Julie and the kids tomorrow, and we'll go to my cousin's in San Antonio."

"Hell, let's put these cows back in the barn, and you stay the night, too."

Tommy shook his head. "No, I want 'em back on my range where they belong."

"But you're coming back here tonight, right?" Stark asked.

"Yeah, I'll just turn 'em out, unhitch the trailer, and drive right back over here. I don't much like it, but I guess it would be best all around."

Stark nodded. "Damn right. Wait just a few minutes, and I'll ride over to your place and back with you."

He left Tommy standing beside the pickup and went to the house. Most of the guests were still there, and the music still played. Stark looked around until he spotted Elaine. He caught her eye and she came over to him right away, sensing that there was trouble of some sort.

"What is it, John Howard?" she asked in a low voice.

"Come in the house with me," he said. "I need to get something."

Quietly, without wasting any words, he filled her in on what was going on with Tommy Carranza. Her first concern was for Julie and the children, which came as no surprise to Stark.

"We have to let them stay here where they'll be safe, John Howard."

He nodded. "That was Tommy's idea, too. I talked him into spending the night with us, and then tomorrow the whole family will head for San Antonio to stay with Tommy's cousin."

"Can't this man Ramirez track them down there?"

"Well, he could, I reckon," Stark said, "but he's less likely to try something in the middle of a big town like that than he would be out on an isolated ranch."

"I suppose you're right. Where's Tommy now?"

"Down by the barn waiting for me. He wants to take

those cows of his back over to his place tonight. I figured I'd better go with him."

They had reached the den by now. Stark went over to the gun cabinet on one wall, unlocked it, and took out a pump shotgun.

"John Howard," Elaine said, a faint note of alarm in her voice now. "What are you doing?"

"I don't think it'd be a good idea to go over to Tommy's place without havin' a gun along. Chances are, nobody's there, but just in case there is . . ."

Elaine began to shake her head. "I don't like it at all. I think you should call the sheriff's department."

"You know better than that."

"I know you think Norval Lee Hammond's not worth a rat's ass as sheriff, but surely he'd have to do *something* . . ."

Stark smiled. Elaine had never been one to pull her punches. She had told him that she admired the way he said what he meant and meant what he said. She admired that quality because she was the exact same way, whether she realized it or not.

"As soon as Tommy and Julie and the kids are safely gone, I'm going to talk to Hodge Purdee, who runs the Border Patrol office in Del Rio. I'm hoping he can convince his bosses in Washington to do something about the situation down here."

Elaine sniffed. "How likely do you think that is?"

"Maybe not likely, but worth a try, anyway." Stark opened a drawer in the desk and took out a box of shells for the shotgun. He loaded it and put a handful of extra shells in his pocket.

"I don't like this, John Howard. I don't like it at all."

"Neither do I. But it won't take long, and chances are, there won't be any trouble. Now, you go find Julie and the kids and keep an eye on them."

"All right. But you be careful."

"I intend to be," Stark promised.

He slipped out a side door of the house so that the folks

who were still enjoying the party wouldn't see him parading around with a shotgun. Stark headed for the barn.

When he got there, Tommy Carranza was gone.

Stark saw that the pickup and trailer were missing and knew right away what had happened. Tommy hadn't gotten tired of waiting; he had just taken it into his head that he ought to go back home by himself so that his longtime friend John Howard wouldn't be in any danger.

That dumb son of a bitch, Stark thought, torn between anger and concern. Chances were, nothing would happen to Tommy, but there was always the possibility trouble could be waiting for him when he got back to his ranch. For a moment Stark stood there debating his own course of action. He could get his own pickup and follow Tommy, or he could round up his friends and take a whole convoy over there. Most of them carried shotguns or rifles in their pickups, and Stark had plenty of extra weapons for those who weren't armed. That would mean ruining the party, and Elaine wouldn't be happy about that.

But hell, he decided, sometimes a party just had to be ruined.

Tommy knew he was being foolish. He should have waited for John Howard. But he would have felt even more foolish if he and John Howard had come over here armed to the teeth—he knew Stark had gone to the house to get a gun—and found that the place was deserted and as peaceful as could be. That was exactly the way it looked as he drove up to the barn. The house, about fifty yards away, was dark. Clearly, no one was around. Tommy began to relax.

He brought the pickup to a stop, killed the engine, opened the door, and got out. Going to the back of the trailer, he lifted the bolt that held the gate closed and shot it to the side. "Come on outta there, you two," he said to the cow and calf as he swung the gate open.

The animals didn't move.

Tommy walked around to the other side of the trailer. He reached in through the slatted side and poked the cow in the rump. "Move, you stupid cow," he said. "Go on, and take your baby with you." He leaned forward to poke through the slats again.

What felt like a bar of iron suddenly clamped itself across his throat and jerked him backward, cutting off his air. He didn't have time for even one squawk. Somebody kicked his feet out from under him, and then he was being dragged backward toward the barn. He wanted to fight, but all he could do was gasp for air that wouldn't come.

He had screwed up, he thought, screwed up beyond belief. And he was so scared he thought he was going to piss his pants. The man whose arm was around his neck was so strong that Tommy, a good-sized, work-toughened man in his own right, felt like no more than a child.

Maybe they wouldn't kill him. Maybe they just wanted to scare him real good. Maybe.

They were inside the barn now. Tommy slumped to the ground as his captor let go of him. He landed in cow shit. The stink rose around him, but he didn't care. He tried to get up, but a foot crashed down on his chest, pinning him to the ground.

"Here he is," a cold voice said in Spanish.

"The woman, the children?" asked another man.

"He was alone in the truck."

"He will not like that."

Tommy knew the one referred to in that comment wasn't him. It had to be Ramirez the man spoke of. *El Bruitre*. The Vulture.

"You can only do what you can do," the first man said, the one who had grabbed him. He didn't sound particularly worried or upset. He didn't sound like he felt much of anything.

"Yes," said the second man with a sigh. "All right. We might as well get started."

There were more than just two of them, of course. Several

men gathered around Tommy. He could see them looming over him. The interior of the barn was thick with shadows but not completely dark. Enough light filtered in from the moon and stars so that he could make out the shapes of his captors. The first man took his foot off Tommy's chest and moved back, as if his part was done and the rest was up to his companions. A couple of them leaned over to grab Tommy and hold him down. He tried to fight, but a fist slammed into his face, stunning him for long enough that they were able to get a good grip on him. He could still writhe around a little but no more as one of the other men leaned over the lower half of his body. He saw the flash of a knife, heard ripping sounds as his jeans were cut away, felt the cold kiss of the steel as it touched him.

"Go ahead," someone said.

And then Tommy began to scream as the terrible sawing pain hit him.

Silencio Ryan stood apart from Ruiz and the others as they slowly castrated Tomas Carranza, taking their time about it so the pain would last longer. Carranza fainted once from the agony of what they were doing to him, so Ruiz told Guzman, Mendez, and Canales to wait while he got a bucketful of water and dashed it into their victim's face. That brought Carranza back to a gasping, sputtering consciousness, and he started screaming again. None of them cared how loudly he screamed. No one was around to hear it but them, and to their ears it was just an affirmation that they were doing their job properly.

The Vulture would be happy when he heard how much Carranza had suffered.

So they cut his balls off, and when they were done with that they severed his penis as well and stuffed it into his mouth, muffling what had by now turned into wretched sobs. Blood had flooded from the hideous wounds between his legs, mixing with the cow shit and forming a black, muddy pool around him. The men had to step in it to continue their work, but they didn't care. One of them slit Carranza's belly open, and they pulled out his intestines and piled them on his chest so that he could see his own guts through bleary eyes in which the life was fading. By now Carranza had lost enough blood so that death was only moments away. His breathing was a ragged series of wheezing sighs. They had to move more quickly. They had brought an ax with them. Canales used it to chop off Carranza's hands and feet while Guzman sliced off his ears and nose and lips. Ruiz hunkered on his heels beside Carranza's head and scooped out his eyes with a knife.

Ryan leaned against the wall of one of the stalls with his arms folded across his chest. When he heard the distinctive rattle that he had heard so many times in his life, he said, "You can stop carving on him now. He's dead."

Ruiz glanced up. "Senor Ramirez wanted him to suffer."

"Well, he can't feel anything now." Ryan hoped Ruiz wouldn't make him say it again.

Ruiz took a deep breath, as if he had just realized something. Ryan didn't see how he could do that, leaning as he was over the stinking piece of butchered meat that had been Tomas Carranza. Ryan was off to the side, and he had to breathe shallowly because it smelled so bad in here.

"Yes, we are done here," Ruiz said. "I just wish we had found the woman and the children. Carranza should have had to watch what we would have done to them before we killed him."

Ryan started toward the open double doors of the barn. "Yeah, he's a lucky bastard, isn't he?"

He stopped short, just outside the barn. In the distance, probably still at least a mile away on the river road, were several pairs of headlights. It was entirely possible those vehicles weren't coming here . . . but Ryan knew they were. The instincts he had developed so keenly over the years told him that, and he trusted them.

"Let's go," he barked at Ruiz and the others. "Company's coming."

No one argued with him. Ruiz might give the orders most of the time, but when Ryan spoke in that tone, everyone did what he said. There was only a brief delay while Ruiz and Guzman emptied their clips into the trailer, the automatic weapons fire chopping up the cow and the calf as a last gesture.

Less than two minutes later, the Town Car pulled away from the spot where it was hidden behind the barn. A small dirt road led away from the house and the barn and looped back through the ranch, circling around until it connected with the river road a couple of miles away. Ryan had scoped it out earlier, just in case they had to leave the back way. He was behind the wheel now, driving without headlights, sending the Lincoln bouncing along the rutted trail. He wasn't worried about the car's suspension; it was specially reinforced, just like the door panels were. The glass was bulletproof. The Lincoln was almost as much a tank as it was a car.

They came to a locked gate where the trail met the river road. A burst of gunfire shattered the lock. Mendez swung the gate open and Ryan drove through. Once Mendez was back in the car, Ryan turned south. There was a place a few miles on the other side of Del Rio where the river could be forded. In the old days that would not have been possible, but now in many places the Rio Grande was only a pale shadow of the mighty stream it had once been. Dams and irrigation upriver, as well as the demands of industry in northern Mexico, had seen to that. The lowering of the river made it even more difficult for the Border Patrol to monitor all the possible crossings.

Ryan drove on into the night. He wondered briefly if those headlights he had seen meant that Carranza's friends were coming to check on him.

Then he forgot about it, putting what had happened out of his mind. He thought instead about a morning he had seen once in Africa, during a lull in one of the countless wars, when clouds and the rising sun had streaked the sky with orange above a snowcapped mountain. It had been a pretty sight. So pretty. He told himself he would have to go back there someday, and look at it again.

Five

Stark drove the first pickup. Uncle Newt sat beside him, cradling an old .30-30 carbine in his lap. Stark's shotgun was on the rack behind them. Following in three more pickups were half a dozen of his friends, all armed. They would be a match for any trouble they might find at Tommy's place, Stark thought.

Unless Ramirez had sent a small army up here to exact his vengeance.

That possibility worried Stark. He didn't really know what Ramirez was capable of. Like most folks along this stretch of the border, he had heard of the Vulture, but how much was true and how much was merely legend, he didn't know. It would pay Ramirez to foster the sort of gruesome stories that were told about him, because fear was his greatest weapon in his effort to control all the drug smuggling in the region. No one dared to cross him because of the terrible revenge he might wreak on them. It was possible, though, that he didn't really have that kind of power.

But if he did . . . if everything that was whispered about the Vulture in awed, terror-stricken whispers was true . . . then Tommy could be in very bad danger indeed.

The gate where the ranch road led off the river highway

was closed but not locked. Newt hopped out of the pickup, swung it back, and then climbed in again as Stark drove past. Devery Small, in the last pickup with Hubie Cornheiser, got out and closed the gate once all the vehicles were through. In this country, even in a possible emergency, a man didn't leave a gate open unless he absolutely had to.

Stark led the little convoy on to the ranch house. The place was dark. His headlights washed over Tommy's pickup and trailer, parked beyond the house near the barn. Stark swung his own pickup in that direction.

His foot hit the brake and he stopped the pickup short as his headlights shone more directly into the trailer. The cow and calf were still in there, both of them dead, cut up so badly it looked as though slaughterhouse workers had been at them with chain saws. The floor of the trailer was awash with blood, and the stuff had leaked out and formed a black lake on the ground around it.

"Son of a bitch," Newt breathed in horror at what his old eyes saw in the trailer.

Leaving the motor on and the headlights burning, Stark piled out of the pickup, snatching the shotgun off the rack as he did so. He reached under the seat and grabbed a powerful, heavy flashlight. He flicked it on and played the beam around as he shouted, "Tommy! Tommy, are you here?"

There was no answer, just as Stark had feared. The other men were out of their pickups now, clutching flashlights, rifles, and shotguns, and the beams danced around like lances of light. They called back and forth to each other, their voices touched with nervousness. They were scared, and Stark didn't blame them. These men were ranchers, family men, good citizens, tough as nails when it came to the everyday dangers of rural life . . . but they were not professional warriors.

Stark hurried toward the barn, thinking Tommy might be in there. His light touched something lying on the ground inside the cavernous building, but for a couple of seconds his brain didn't recognize the huddled shape as something that had once been human. Then beside Stark his uncle Newt said softly, "Sweet limpin' Jesus." Stark went forward, but only slowly, with dragging footsteps, as if he were being compelled to advance while at the same time feeling so horrified that all he wanted to do was back away from something so bad his mind could not comprehend it.

The thing on the ground, surrounded by blood and shit, was what was left of Tommy Carranza.

In Vietnam, Stark had seen men blown to pieces by grenades and land mines and artillery fire. He knew firsthand how much destruction could be wreaked on the human body. But he had never seen anything like this before. This carnage had not been inflicted at a distance. It had been carried out up close and personal. Men had sunk knives in Tommy's flesh and carved him up, and Stark knew from the look of agony and disbelief frozen on his friend's face that Tommy had been conscious and aware of what was being done to him.

Behind him, Stark heard somebody puking. He didn't know which of his friends it was. Could have been any of them. He felt like doing the same thing himself.

Uncle Newt's voice was dry, raspy, as he asked, "You reckon . . . you reckon he could still be . . . alive?"

"No." Stark moved closer, forcing himself to be detached as he played his flashlight beam over the thing that had been Tommy. "He bled out five, maybe ten minutes ago. And he would have passed out from loss of blood before that."

"Poor boy," Newt muttered.

Everett Hatcher came up beside Stark. He was wiping the back of a hand across his mouth. "Who'd do a thing like this?" he asked in an anguished voice.

"The Vulture," Devery Small put in from the other side of Stark. "Tommy crossed that lawyer fella who works for Ramirez. He has to have done this."

Stark said, "Not Ramirez his own self. He wouldn't dirty his hands. But he had it done, that's for damn sure. Tommy didn't have another enemy in the world."

"What do we do now?" Everett asked.

They were too late to help Tommy, Stark thought, but there were still Julie and the children. Ramirez's men probably didn't know where they were. Would they try to track them down? Would the trail lead to the Diamond S?

He swung toward his uncle and said, "Newt, take a couple of the boys and head back to the ranch as fast as you can. Don't tell Julie what happened, but make sure she and the kids are all right. Then keep 'em that way."

Newt nodded. "Don't worry, John Howard. Ain't nobody gonna get up to any shenanigans on the Diamond S."

Shenanigans, Stark thought as he glanced at Tommy's mutilated corpse. But he knew what his uncle meant.

"Get Elaine off by herself if you can," he went on. "Tell her, and let her tell Julie."

"That's a mighty hard burden to lay on the gal."

"I know," Stark said heavily. "And I pure-dee regret having to do it. But Elaine's the strongest woman I know. She can handle it."

Newt said, "If you say so, John Howard. Come on, Hubie, W.R. You're with me."

As the three men filed out of the barn, Stark patted his shirt pockets and then said, "Anybody got a cell phone? I left mine back at the house."

Devery handed over a phone he took from his breast pocket. Stark held it for a moment, then sighed and punched in 911.

Like it or not, it was time to bring the law into this.

Norval Lee Hammond had been an all-state defensive tackle for the Del Rio High Rams in 1970, was considered a blue-chip recruit, and his signature had been sought on a letter-of-intent by colleges and universities across the land. He had signed with Texas A&M and was all-conference his sophomore year, but then unexpectedly transferred to a smaller, less prestigious school for his junior and senior years. It was whispered that academic problems were behind the transfer, but there was nothing academic about the two coeds he had gotten pregnant or the other three he had beaten up. His time at the smaller school was unmarred by such incidents, and while his football career was much lower profile there than it would have been at A&M, the pro scouts had already seen enough to interest them. He was drafted in the third round by the New Orleans Saints, a fact that was appropriate in one way, since he never got above third team on the depth chart, and inappropriate in another, because he was far from being a saint in his behavior. He lasted two years before being released in training camp the third year. In those days NFL teams had what were called "taxi squads," the equivalent of what later became known as practice squads. Warm bodies, basically, who showed some promise. When he was released Norval Lee was confident that he would catch on with some other team as a free agent; if that didn't happen, surely the Saints would put him on their taxi squad.

Neither of those things came about.

With his pro football career at an end, Norval Lee had returned home to Del Rio. Most of the money from the two years he had spent with the Saints had already been spent. Contracts, while still lucrative by normal standards, were smaller back then, small enough that an athlete couldn't earn more money in a year or two than he could possibly spend over the course of the rest of his life.

Convinced that someday the phone would ring and it would be the Cowboys or the Bears or the Raiders on the other end, begging him to sign with them, to come back and help put them over the play-off hump so they could win the Super Bowl, Norval Lee lived with his parents and worked construction to make ends meet. He believed it was damned unfair that such a fate had befallen him. He had been young and stupid those first two years at A&M. He had cleaned up his act since then, hadn't knocked up any more girls, and hardly ever swatted one around and then only when she got so damned annoying that nobody could blame him for losing his temper. He didn't use dope, never drank more than a couple of beers when he went out. He was hardworking and clean-living, and it just wasn't fair that none of the NFL teams wanted him anymore.

Then Willa Sue McLaney, whom he had been going out with for a few months, called him one day and said she was going to have a baby and what did he intend to do about it? She had started bawling, but she didn't really need to do that to get what she wanted. Norval Lee liked her, he really did, and he was twenty-five years old by this point and felt he ought to start thinking about settling down. His dreams of continuing his pro football career weren't completely dead, but they were sure as hell on life support. Willa Sue getting pregnant was just what he needed to make him go ahead and pull the plug.

"Marry me," he had said to a stunned Willa Sue, and after sniffling a few times, she had agreed.

A man with a wife and a child on the way needed more than just a job, he needed a career. Norval Lee scraped up some money, borrowed a little from his folks, who weren't well-to-do by any stretch of the imagination, and rented a small house for himself and his new bride. Then he started taking law enforcement classes at the local junior college while still working part-time on construction jobs. Within a year he was a member of the Del Rio Police Department.

He'd been a good cop. He never had any doubts about that. He got along with the Anglos because he had once been a professional football player and so was considered a local celebrity. He got along with the Hispanics, too, because he spoke the language well and treated them fairly. There were a lot more brown faces than white ones in Del Rio, so Norval Lee considered it simply a prudent thing to keep them from hating him.

By the time he was thirty-five he was chief of police and had three kids. Willa Sue drank a little more than she used to, but by and large they got along all right, and if she knew about the two or three Mexican gals he had on the side, she never said anything about it. He was a big man, with big appetites. And by his standards, he was an honest man. He never took a bribe.

Until one of the local whorehouse owners offered him one that was just too blasted big to turn down.

He'd been cheated out of a fortune by bad luck, he told himself. He should have been a rich, famous pro football player. If he had been able to stay at A&M, he would have been taken in the first round, sure as hell. A first-round draft choice got a lot more money, and the Saints wouldn't have kicked him off the team after only two years, that was certain. He'd just never gotten a chance to really show what he could do.

So it was only right that his finances should take an upturn. He deserved it. Willa Sue and the kids deserved it.

The only problem was that a fella could never take just one bribe. The first bribe was never the last one.

He ran for sheriff before his reputation got too bad. He won, too, which didn't surprise anybody. By the time his first term was up, a lot of rumors had been whispered about him. He ignored them and went on about his business, enforcing the law to the best of his ability.

Well, 99 percent of the time, anyway, and that was a pretty damned good ratio, even if he did say so himself.

He had won reelection, and life was going along pretty smooth, pretty good. He didn't need any disruption. He sure as hell didn't need a gruesome, high-profile murder case.

But evidently that was what he had on his hands.

He got out of the Blazer with the official sheriff's department tags on it and slammed the door. The lights on top of the SUV kept flashing and turning. A couple of units, also with their lights flashing, were parked at angles between the house and the barn. The deputies assigned to them had been the first to respond to the dispatcher's alarmed bleating on the radio. Norval Lee had been at home, sitting in his den with his feet up, sipping a beer as he watched a baseball game on the satellite dish. It was late and Willa Sue and the kids had already turned in, tired out after going to the fairgrounds to watch the Fourth of July fireworks display, but the game was being played on the West Coast and still had a couple of innings to go. He'd had his radio on the table beside him, the volume turned low, but he had turned it up when the squawking started. He would have to have a talk with Alicia Gonzales about the proper on-air demeanor for a dispatcher.

Norval Lee hadn't bothered to wake Willa Sue before he left to see what was what. She would never know he was gone anyway, seeing as how they'd had separate bedrooms for the past several years.

He walked toward the barn, a big man in a polo shirt and jeans, a couple of inches over six feet and nudging 265. He would hate to have to go up against some of the offensive lineman they had in the league now, damn behemoths weighing well over three hundred pounds. Norval Lee didn't see how anybody that big could even move around enough to play football.

A couple of deputies stood in the open doors of the barn, keeping everybody out. Two more deputies were talking to several men who stood outside the barn, off to one side. Norval Lee spotted John Howard Stark among them. Norval Lee had been a few years behind Stark in school, but not so many that people weren't still talking about the thirty-nine home runs he'd belted in his senior year. Stark had been a good baseball player, all right, but he was still just a baseball player in a land where football was king. And he hadn't even been all-state, just all-district. Norval Lee had made folks forget about John Howard Stark pretty fast.

"What's the story here?" he asked as he came up to the deputies.

"Tommy Carranza's been murdered," Stark snapped. "Worse that that, he was tortured first."

Norval Lee put his hands in the pockets of his jeans. His

badge and gun were clipped to his belt. "I was asking my deputies," he said to Stark, keeping his voice level and civil.

"Mr. Stark's got the straight of it, Sheriff," said Deputy Willie Deeds. "The body's there not far inside the barn."

Norval Lee looked toward the open doors of the barn, craning his neck a little to see past the deputies who stood there. The overhead fluorescents in the barn had been switched on, so there was plenty of light for the sheriff to see the bloody, mangled corpse lying on its back.

"Least somebody could've done was put a blanket over him and cover him up," Stark said.

Norval Lee shook his head. "No, these boys done the right thing by not disturbin' the body. Medical examiner's on his way out. I called him before I left town."

"It's indecent, leavin' him layin' there like that," Devery Small said.

"You just let us handle this, Devery," Norval Lee said in his best sheriff's voice, stern so that nobody would give him any lip and soothing so they would just relax. Norval Lee didn't really expect these ranchers to relax, though. Not after what they'd seen inside the barn.

As for Norval Lee himself, he kept his eyes away from the corpse after that first look. He had seen plenty of ugly things in his years as a law enforcement officer—folks crushed and torn apart and sometimes decapitated in car wrecks, people with their bellies blown out by close-range shotgun blasts, cheating husbands whose wives had taken a butcher knife to them, wetbacks unlucky enough to have drowned in the Rio Grande, their bodies washed up and bloated in the hot Texas sun—but he wasn't sure he had ever seen anything quite as bad as what had been done to Tommy Carranza.

"Anybody got any idea who might've done this terrible thing?" Norval Lee asked Stark and the other ranchers.

Not surprisingly, it was Stark who answered. "We know who did it," he said flatly.

Norval Lee raised his eyebrows. "Oh? Well, that'll make my job a whole heap easier. Who done it?"

"Ramirez," Stark said. "The Vulture."

It took every bit of self-control Sheriff Norval Lee Hammond possessed to keep himself from crapping right in his pants.

Six

Stark saw the look of terror that appeared in Sheriff Hammond's eyes. It was only there for a split second before Hammond was able to bring it under control and banish it, but Stark had no doubts about what he had seen.

"Ramirez didn't kill Tommy himself, of course," Stark went on. "But he ordered it done."

Hammond lifted a hand to his forehead and wiped sweat away. It was a hot night, of course, being the Fourth of July. But he hadn't been sweating quite so hard a few moments earlier.

"Senor Ramirez lets you in on his plans now, does he, John Howard?" Hammond asked as if it were all a joke.

"Tommy had trouble yesterday with Ramirez, or with somebody who works for Ramirez, I should say."

"What sort of trouble?" Hammond asked sharply. He was more in control of himself now, Stark thought.

"A lawyer from Dallas who represents Ramirez approached Tommy and offered to pay him off if Tommy would look the other way while Ramirez's runners brought drugs across his land. Tommy punched the son of a bitch in the mouth."

"Where did this happen?"

"In the parking lot of that big lumberyard on the edge of

town. Tommy was there picking up some fencing," Stark explained.

Hammond rubbed his jaw and frowned in thought. "Seems like I saw a report cross my desk about a fistfight of some sort out there. But nobody called to report it officially, and since neither of the men came forward to press charges . . ." Hammond shrugged. "I just figured it didn't really amount to anything."

Stark slowly lifted a hand and pointed through the open barn doors. "That's what it amounted to," he said.

Stubbornly, Hammond shook his head. "You don't know that. Were there any witnesses to the attack on Carranza?"

"You know better than that, Sheriff. If there were any witnesses, their bodies would be in there, too."

"Carranza's got a wife and kids, don't he? Where are they?"

Stark hesitated. If rumors of the connections between the sheriff and Ramirez were true, then by telling Hammond where Julie and the kids were, he might just as well be telling Ramirez.

"They're in a safe place," he said.

It took a second for the implications of that answer to soak in on Hammond, but when they did the lawman's beefy face flushed even more than normal in the light from the barn. "Damn it, Stark," he said. "I asked you a question."

"And I gave you all the answer you need to know," Stark replied coolly. He knew he might be making a mistake, getting on Hammond's bad side this way, but at the moment he was too angry and too sick with grief over what had happened to Tommy to really care.

Everett Hatcher spoke up. "Senora Carranza and her kids are being took care of, Sheriff. Us ranchers along the river are sort of like a family, and we look after our own."

"That's all well and good," Hammond said, "but it doesn't excuse refusing to cooperate in an official investigation. I'll have to talk to her."

Stark said, "Morning's soon enough for that, isn't it?"

Hammond didn't answer for a moment. Stark could tell he was warring with himself over how he wanted to react to this challenge to his authority. Finally Hammond nodded and said, "Yeah, that'll be fine. Reckon somebody could bring her in to the courthouse?"

"I'll do that," Stark said.

"Fine. Guess I better take a closer look at the body."

Hammond turned toward the barn. The deputies standing guard at the doors, with their backs to the body, moved aside to let him by. Stark followed, not because he wanted to see yet again what had been done to Tommy, but because he wanted to observe Hammond's reaction to it. He thought the deputies might try to block his path, but they stayed out of the way and Hammond didn't order them to do otherwise.

Hammond's steps grew more ragged the closer he got to the mutilated corpse. He stopped about ten feet away as if he couldn't make himself go any closer. He stood there staring at what was left of Tommy. His chest rose and fell as he took several deep breaths. Then he murmured, "Good Lord."

"Ever seen anything like that, Sheriff?" Stark asked.

"You know I haven't. There's never been anything like this in Val Verde County."

"I've heard that Colombians are especially vicious when they take their revenge," Stark said. "Especially Colombian drug lords."

Hammond swung his eyes away from the gruesome remains. "If you've got something to say, Stark, why don't you just go ahead and say it?"

"Not feeling quite so friendly now, Sheriff?"

"Why should I be friendly to somebody who keeps ridin' me for no good reason?" The flush on Hammond's face deepened to a dark, furious red. He snapped a hand at the corpse. "You act like I had something to do with this! The first I knew about it was when the dispatcher's call came over the radio a while ago. Not that I owe you or anybody else an explanation!"

Stark kept his own temper reined in, though doing so cost

him in effort. "All I want to know, Sheriff, is what you intend to do about this."

"Get to the bottom of it, of course," Hammond answered without hesitation. "Find out who did this and arrest them. After that it's up to the district attorney and the grand jury and out of my hands."

"So you're going to carry out a full investigation?"

"Of course. Why wouldn't I?"

Stark shook his head, aware that he had pushed things about as far as he could tonight. "That's what I wanted to hear," he said. "Everybody along the river will want Tommy's killers found and brought to justice. You can start by looking at men who work for Ramirez."

"I'll start by examining the crime scene and following established procedure." Hammond glanced past Stark out the doors of the barn. "And since you've already given a statement to my deputies I'll have to ask you to leave now. The medical examiner's here."

Stark looked over his shoulder and saw more flashing lights as an ambulance pulled up. Its lights were on, but the driver wasn't using the siren. Somebody must have told him that there was no need.

Tommy wasn't going anywhere.

Stark gave Hammond a curt nod and walked out of the barn to rejoin the other men. "Let's get back to the ranch," he told them in a low voice.

They started toward their parked pickups, but one of the deputies called after them, "Hold on a minute, fellas. What if the sheriff wants to talk to y'all some more?"

"He knows where to find us," Stark said over his shoulder without slowing down.

To think that once he had actually voted for Norval Lee Hammond, Stark mused in disgust as he drove back toward the Diamond S. That had been when Hammond ran for sheriff the first time, before the rumors about his possible corruption had become so thick. All John Howard had really known about him at the time had been that he was some stud football player in high school, had played pro ball in the NFL for a few years, and had been a cop and then the chief of police in Del Rio for a while. Seemed a decent enough sort, other than being a little blustery when he talked to folks.

Then after the election the whispering about him had started in earnest. Stark didn't pay much attention to it at first; he wasn't the sort who went in for a lot of gossip. But he couldn't help but hear the talk about possible connections between the sheriff and the bosses of the drug gangs on the other side of the border, up to and including the notorious Vulture. Stark didn't want to believe it at first. His natural inclination was to give folks the benefit of the doubt. And although Hammond had a nice enough house and his personal car was relatively new, he didn't live the sort of flashy, expensive lifestyle that seemed to go with being a corrupt police official on the take. Of course, maybe Hammond was just too smart to flaunt it that way.

Stark was alone in his pickup, followed by Everett Hatcher, Devery Small, and a couple of other ranchers who had come over with them. His big hands were wrapped tight around the steering wheel. He couldn't seem to get that awful image of Tommy's body out of his mind. He saw it in the glow of the dashboard and in the long wash of headlights along the river highway. From the corner of his eye he even seemed to see Tommy sitting on the pickup seat beside him.

Settle the score for me, John Howard, that ghostly figure seemed to be saying. Pleading, actually. *Avenge my death. Find the men who did this to me and rain down fire and brimstone on their heads.*

That was crazy, of course, Stark told himself. No bloody wraith sat on the seat beside him. And he was just a rancher. He wasn't some sort of avenger. Raining down fire and brimstone was the Almighty's job, not his.

Something darted across the road in front of him, flashing

through the twin cones of light. Stark caught just a glimpse of it, barely enough to recognize it as a coyote. The real kind, not one of the lowlifes who smuggled illegals across the border for a high fee. The coyote was there and then gone, bent on some mysterious errand known only to its primitive brain.

The coyote was some sort of mythic figure in Indian legends, Stark recalled. A symbol of the trickster, the sly evildoer. If there was any truth to that, then surely tonight some coyote in the spirit world was laughing at the trick that had been played on Tommy Carranza. Less than thirty-six hours earlier, Tommy had been going along peacefully, enjoying his life, loving his wife, and raising his kids.

It was a travesty, an affront to the universe, that the scum who had done that to Tommy were still alive. Every breath they took was a waste of perfectly good air, Stark thought. Somebody ought to do something. . . .

It always came back to that. Somebody ought to do something. But who?

He had to put that question out of his head as he drove through the open gate of the Diamond S and piloted the pickup toward the house. He hadn't gone very far before he slammed on the brakes to avoid hitting the men who stepped into the road, rifles in their hands.

Stark cranked down the window and leaned out to call, "Damn it, Uncle Newt, I could've run over you!"

"We didn't know who y'all were at first!" Newt shouted back at him. "Hubie an' me figured we better stop you."

"By stepping in front of the pickup? If I'd been one of Ramirez's men, I would have floored it."

Newt gave a cackle of laughter as he stepped up to the vehicle. "Chaco's over yonder in the mesquites with a rifle, and ol' Ben Cobb's on t'other side o' the road with a twelve-gauge. They'd'a opened up on you if you hadn't stopped."

That made a little more sense, Stark thought. He asked, "Who's up at the house?"

"W.R. and the rest o' the hands, along with some o' the

folks who was here for the party and ain't gone home yet. W.R.'s in the house with Elaine and Senora Carranza and the kids. Ain't nobody gonna bother 'em."

"Did you tell Elaine what happened?"

Newt bobbed his head. "Sure did. And she told Senora Carranza, just like you said."

Stark felt a pang of sympathy for his wife. Breaking bad news was never easy. And this was just about the worst news of all.

"How did Julie take it?"

"How do you expect? There was a heap o' weepin' and wailin'. Elaine done the best she could to comfort her, but there weren't a whole lot she could do."

Stark shook his head slowly. "No, I imagine not."

"Any more news from over there?"

"The sheriff showed up."

Newt snorted in contempt. "What did ol' Norval Lee have to say about it?"

"Not much of anything. He said he would conduct a full investigation."

"That'll be the day."

"Maybe we should give him the benefit of the doubt," Stark said, but his words sounded hollow.

"What I doubt is that Hammond'll do anything to really find out who killed Tommy."

Stark couldn't argue with that.

"You and Hubie and the rest come on back to the house," he told his uncle. "All the neighbors can go home now. I reckon it's all over for the night."

"What if Ramirez's men come lookin' for Senora Carranza and her young 'uns?"

"There'll be plenty of men here to look after them, what with you and me and Chaco and the rest of the boys."

"Yeah, I reckon." Newt stepped back and waved the line of pickups on.

It looked like every light in the house was on as Stark drove up and stopped the pickup. As he got out, one of the ranch hands stepped out from under a cottonwood tree and said, "Senor Stark?" He held a shotgun.

"That's right, George." Stark moved past the man toward the house, resting a hand on his shoulder for a second as he did so.

He went inside, hanging his Stetson on a wall hook beside the door. Elaine must have heard him come in, because she hurried down the stairs toward him.

She came wordlessly into his embrace, wrapping her arms around his waist and hugging him tightly. She pressed her head against his broad chest as he folded his arms around her and returned the hug. He felt a little shudder go through her, then another and another as she began to cry.

Stark stood there holding her as she let the sobs well out of her. His own eyes were suspiciously damp. Tommy Carranza hadn't been so close that he was like a member of their family, but he had been a very good friend. And nobody—friend, foe, or anywhere in between—deserved what had happened to Tommy. Stark wouldn't even wish such a fate on the men who had tortured Tommy like that. A bullet in the head, now, he wouldn't have a problem with that.

Finally Elaine took a couple of deep, quavery breaths and seemed to calm down a little. She lifted her head and looked up at Stark. "Are you all right, John Howard?" she asked.

"As all right as I can be, under the circumstances," he answered. "What about Julie?"

"She's asleep. Doug Huddleston gave her something to help her."

Huddleston was a doctor in Del Rio, a friend of the Starks who had a place up near Lake Amistad. John Howard was glad Doug had been there to give Julie a sedative. Sleep was the best thing for her, although, when you got right down to it, that wasn't going to change a thing. She would still be a widow when she woke up.

"I put her in David's room," Elaine went on. "The children are in Pete's room and the guest room."

Stark nodded. "That's good. Do they know?"

"Not yet. I'm sure they're aware that something is going on, something bad, but they haven't been told about . . . about Tommy."

"If Julie's not up to it tomorrow, we'll have to do it."

"I know," she whispered. "In its own way, that's going to be even worse."

Stark nodded. He had lost his own dad, of course, but only after Ethan had lived a long, full life. Stark's mother had followed soon after her husband, as so often happened. It had been a hard, painful time, but at least there was some sense of life unfolding in its proper fashion, at its proper pace. A relatively young man's being ripped away from his family the way Tommy had been was made even more tragic by the very unnaturalness of it.

"How could anybody do such a thing?" Elaine asked.

"Something has to be missing inside them," Stark said. "I don't know what it is. The thing that makes them human just isn't there."

Elaine gave a ragged sigh and leaned against him. "You mind holding me some more, John Howard?" she whispered.

"Just try to get me to let go," Stark said as his arms tightened around her.

Seven

Norval Lee's mouth was drier than west Texas during a drought. That was a common reaction for him on the rare occasions when he paid a visit to this fancy, well-guarded compound outside Cuidad Acuna. Today was even worse because he had come down here on his own, instead of being summoned as he had been all the other times. As he sat nervously on the front edge of a thickly upholstered chair in a rustic den with a woven rug on the floor and guns and animal heads hanging on the walls, he thought about bolting. Just getting up and leaving. He knew he couldn't do that, though, because the elderly majordomo who had let him into the house had already gone to summon Senor Ramirez.

This morning Norval Lee was dressed in a western-cut suit, shiny boots, a white shirt, and a string tie. A white Stetson was balanced on his knee. He had unclipped his .38 from his belt and left it in the Blazer, knowing that he would not be allowed anywhere near Ramirez as long as he was armed. A bodyguard stood at one side of the room, near the fireplace that was cold at this time of year. The man had patted down Norval Lee to make sure he wasn't carrying any concealed weapons.

Ramirez strolled into the room wearing a short robe. His

thick dark hair was wet. He smiled as he said, "*Buenos dias*, Sheriff Hammond. Welcome to my home. I hope it is all right I finished my morning swim before seeing you."

Norval Lee was on his feet without any real memory of standing up. He felt bad for reacting with such deference to Ramirez. The man was unimpressive physically, slender and a little under medium height. Yet people just automatically snapped to attention around him, as if he were the commander of an army.

Which, of course, he was in a way. An army of drug smugglers and killers. Like the man Ryan who drifted into the room after Ramirez, moving smoothly and soundlessly, more like a ghost than a human being. Norval Lee had heard rumors about Ryan, and as he looked at the man's weathered, craggy face and cold eyes, he could believe every one of them.

"It's perfectly all right, Senor Ramirez," Norval Lee said. "I appreciate you seeing me without any notice like this."

Ramirez waved his visitor back into the chair. "Please, sit down. I rather expected that you would come here today, Sheriff."

Norval Lee hesitated as he sat, stopping halfway down. He forced himself to relax and sank the rest of the way into the chair. "You . . . expected me?" he said. He didn't like the sound of that, didn't like it at all. Even though logically he had known better, a part of him had desperately hoped that Ramirez really *didn't* have anything to do with the awful thing that had happened to Tommy Carranza. Ramirez's comment pretty much blew that hope out of the water.

Ramirez sat down in another chair and crossed his legs. "I'm told there was trouble on your side of the river last night," he said. "A man was killed?"

"That's right. A rancher named Tomas Carranza."

Ramirez nodded. "Yes, of course. I know of Senor Carranza. A very proud, stubborn man. It would seem that his pride and stubbornness caused a very evil fate to befall him."

Norval Lee felt himself sweating. He wanted to wipe the

drops from his forehead, but he didn't want to call attention to how nervous he was. Not that it really mattered. Ramirez never missed anything. He would already be well aware of how his visitor felt.

Norval Lee hesitated, unsure of how to go on. He couldn't just come out and ask, *Did you have Carranza killed? Did you tell your men to slaughter him like an animal?* He had to take his time about this, had to be discreet and cautious.

"I, ah, I was wondering, Senor Ramirez, since you're always so well informed about what goes on in the area, on both sides of the border, if you might have . . . well, if you knew anything about . . . could tell me anything about what happened."

Fool! he yelled at himself. *Stammering fool! Buck up, man. Grow a damned spine.*

But it was too late for that.

The majordomo came into the room carrying a heavy silver tray on which sat two cups. Norval Lee smelled coffee, strong and sweetened with chocolate. The servant gave one cup to Ramirez and brought the other over to Norval Lee. Ryan and the bodyguard declined.

"Please," Ramirez said. "Let us sit and enjoy our coffee before we talk of less pleasant things."

The last thing Norval Lee wanted to do was drag out this visit, but he had no choice. He sipped the coffee, but even though it was excellent he barely noticed. It did keep his mouth from being so dry, though.

After so long a time, Ramirez set his cup aside on a little table and said, "I would imagine there is considerable pressure on you to solve this horrible crime, Sheriff. To establish the identity of the killer and arrest him."

"Well . . . yeah. Carranza was well liked."

"And naturally the citizens of Val Verde County would like to see justice done."

"That's right."

"Unfortunately, this will be impossible."

"Why . . ." Norval Lee had to stop and swallow hard before he could go on. "Why is it impossible?"

"Because no doubt Carranza was killed by a drifter who has already moved on and is long gone from the Del Rio area. A serial murderer who deals out death and then vanishes into the night, never to be seen again."

Norval Lee couldn't help but stare. When he got his voice back he said, "What?"

Ramirez smiled thinly as he repeated, "A serial killer. America is famous for them, you know."

Was he joking? Both of them knew good and well what had happened to Carranza.

"I am trying to help you, Sheriff," Ramirez went on. "Go back across the river and tell the newspaper and television reporters that Tomas Carranza was murdered by a serial killer. Say that you have some leads and expect to make an arrest shortly if you like. But of course, you will make no arrests."

Suddenly, something welled up inside Norval Lee. Some pride and stubbornness of his own, maybe. To his own surprise he heard himself saying, "I'll make an arrest if I find the man responsible for this. And I'm not so sure it was a serial killer. It doesn't fit any pattern I ever heard of."

Ramirez's outwardly placid expression didn't change, but his dark eyes flashed and then hardened at this display of defiance, mild though it was. "Be careful, Sheriff," he said.

"I'm not the one who needs to be careful. Whoever killed Carranza—" He still maintained that facade of ignorance, no matter how angry he was. "He's the one who needs to be careful. Whoever did it really crossed the line this time." More words rushed out, while he had the momentum from that surge of unexpected courage. "People on the other side of the river are talking too much. There's gonna be another election over there before too much longer, and I want to win. You need for me to win it, Senor Ramirez."

"I saw to it that you won the last one, did I not, Sheriff?" Ramirez asked tautly.

"I appreciate your support," Norval Lee said. "Our arrangement, it's good for both of us, good for everybody concerned. If you want it to continue, I can't have a bunch of wild-ass stuff going on in my jurisdiction. Ranchers being slaughtered, I just can't have it, senor."

He glanced nervously at Ryan. The man wasn't watching him. Ryan's eyes were on Ramirez, Norval Lee realized. Ryan was just waiting for a command, waiting to be told to kill this impudent visitor.

Norval Lee had a couple of inches and at least thirty pounds on Ryan. He had a bad feeling, though, that it wouldn't make a bit of difference. All Ramirez had to do was snap his fingers. Hell, even lifting one finger might be enough to set Ryan on him. After a long moment, Ramirez said quietly, "I see that I must speak plainly, Sheriff. You take my money, so you must do as I say, not the other way around. You give no orders here. Go back across the river and tell the press that Tomas Carranza was murdered by a serial killer. Put on as much of a show as you need to put on, and then let the matter drop. If you do not . . . life will become unpleasant."

It couldn't get plainer than that, no, sir, Norval Lee thought as he struggled with the fear and anger coursing through him. Fear won out. Ramirez was right, of course. Ramirez was always right. Norval Lee swallowed hard again and said, "A serial killer."

Ramirez nodded.

"Yeah. I think it . . . it was a serial killer. Had to be, to do something that crazy." Then he realized how that might sound and added hurriedly, "I mean—"

"I know what you mean, Sheriff." Ramirez uncoiled from the chair, smiling again now. "Please, finish your coffee, and then Hector will escort you out. You will excuse me if I return to the pool. This is a dry country. I find myself drawn to water."

"Sure. And thank you, senor."

"No thanks are necessary. Just remember everything we have spoken of here today." Ramirez started to turn away, but then he stopped and added, "And please convey my best wishes to your lovely wife and your children."

Norval Lee went cold inside. He didn't want Ramirez mentioning Willa Sue and the kids. He wished Ramirez didn't even know they existed. That was impossible, of course, as Ramirez knew everything about the people who worked for him. From this he got his power.

Norval Lee managed to smile weakly and nod. Ramirez left, trailed by Ryan, who didn't even look at Norval Lee as he went out of the room. The old servant came up beside him and said, "You wish to finish your coffee, senor?"

"No. No, thanks. I . . . I've got to get back."

"Very well. This way, please."

Norval Lee followed the majordomo out into the sunshine. It was bright, so bright it almost blinded him at first, and it already packed a potent, energy-sapping heat despite the early hour.

The heat didn't reach inside Norval Lee Hammond. His guts stayed ice-cold all the way back across the river to Del Rio.

John Howard Stark had heard the old saying about how sleep knitted up the raveled sleeve of care. Sleep on it, people always said. Things will look better in the morning. When somebody was deep in grief and shock, sleep was what they needed more than anything else, according to some folks.

And maybe there was some truth to that. The idea that the earth was still turning, that the sun goes down at night but also rises the next morning, well, there was some comfort in that.

But in its own way, sleep was a trickster, too, because it fooled a fella into thinking that everything was all right. For just a moment, maybe only a few seconds, when the mind emerged from sleep it didn't quite remember everything that had happened, didn't quite grasp the depth of the tragedy, the loss that had occurred.

For just a heartbeat, as Stark woke up, it seemed as if his friend Tommy Carranza were still alive.

But then, crashing down on him like a blow, came the memory of what he had seen in that blood-soaked barn the night before. He sat up in bed, heaved a heavy sigh, and muttered a heartfelt "Damn!"

Elaine was already up, of course. She had always been an earlier riser than him, even though the ranch work usually dictated that he be up and about before dawn. Today it was later than that; sunlight already slanted in through the windows of the master bedroom. Stark swung his legs out of bed and stood up, trying to recall just when such a simple thing had started causing him to groan. Must've been about the same time he got old, he decided.

When he came downstairs twenty minutes later, freshly showered and shaved, he felt some better. Though the horrible images of Tommy's death still lurked in his mind, he had shoved them all the way to the back of his brain. He wouldn't forget, but he couldn't let himself become mired in anger and grief. He had to move on. He had things to do.

The twin smells of coffee and bacon perked him up. He went into the kitchen and found breakfast waiting for him on the table. Elaine was at the stove, cooking more bacon. Stark came up behind her, rested his left hand on her shoulder, and used his right to caress her butt, which was still very nicely rounded in a pair of blue jeans.

"Good morning, John Howard," she said as he leaned over and kissed her neck. "If you want a second helping of bacon, you'd better let me get on with cooking it and not distract me."

Elaine lifted the bacon from the pan onto a plate with a paper towel on it, to soak up the grease. "Go ahead and eat," she told Stark. "I imagine you've got plenty to do."

He nodded. "Newt and the boys can keep things running just fine here on the ranch. I'll go into Del Rio and talk to Father Sandoval, see about making arrangements for the funeral." The Starks were Baptists—backslid for the most part,

but still Baptists—but of course Tommy had been Catholic.
"Then I plan to go see Hodge Purdee."

"Why do you want to talk to him?"

"To see if something can be done about all this drug
smuggling. It's bad enough that that damn poison comes
through here and gets spread all over the country. Now it's
been responsible for what happened to Tommy."

"A lot of other people have probably died from it, too. It's
just that we never saw them. They weren't our friends."

Stark knew she was right. "I know we probably should
have gotten more worked up about it before now. It's too
easy to just let things go until they finally get bad enough to
hit close to home. When there's evil loose in the world, we
need to take steps to stop it before it winds up right in our
own backyard."

"You sound like you're talking about terrorists now."

Stark looked at her and said, "What else would you call
somebody like Ramirez? He rules by fear and thinks he's a
law unto himself. He's just as much a terrorist as any of
those assholes David and Pete are dealing with in the Middle
East. What Ramirez needs is for a company of marines to go
in there and blow his sorry butt off the face of the earth."

Elaine moved closer to the table. "Take it easy, John Howard.
It's not going to help anything for you to get all riled up."

"Somebody needs to get riled up enough to *do* something." He couldn't shake the memory of that ghostly visita-
tion he'd had the night before, when he was alone in the
pickup. When Tommy Carranza had pleaded for someone to
avenge his death.

"Whose sorry butt are you talking about, Mr. Stark?"

The childish voice made both Stark and Elaine jump.
They looked around to see Tommy and Julie's daughter,
Angelina, standing just inside the kitchen, rubbing her eyes
sleepily. She still wore the same clothes she had worn to the
party the night before.

"Nobody, sweetheart," Stark said quickly in reply to her
question.

"But I heard you say—"

"Would you like some pancakes, darling?" Elaine asked. "And some bacon?"

"Yes, please," Angelina said. She looked around the kitchen. "How come we didn't go home last night? Where's my mama and daddy?"

Stark hadn't had that second helping of bacon, but he drained the last of his coffee and shoved his chair back anyway. "I've got to get going," he said.

"John Howard . . . " Elaine said, a faint note of desperation in her voice.

He stepped over and kissed her quickly on the forehead. "Honey, I once stood up to a whole howlin' horde of kill-crazy Vietcong, but there's some things I just can't do."

And with that, although he felt like shit for doing it, he hurried out of the kitchen and left his wife there with the little girl who wore a quizzical expression on her face.

A little girl who had to be told that she would never see her precious daddy again, would never hear his laugh or feel the loving touch of his hand.

I can't make it right, Tommy, Stark thought as he went outside. *But I can see to it that they pay for what they did.*

Somehow, I'll see to it.

Eight

Hodgson "Hodge" Purdee was a barrel-chested man in his forties with a pugnacious jaw and a close-cut brush of iron-gray hair. Even in a suit, he looked like a boxer, which in fact he once had been. Champion of the entire crew of the aircraft carrier on which he had served as a young man. Later he had refined his technique as a Shore Patrolman stationed in San Diego. Knowing how to knock out a man with one punch came in mighty handy when dealing with a bunch of drunken sailors. After leaving the navy he had become an agent of the United States Border Patrol, and his years of service there had seen him rise to become the head of the office located in Del Rio, one of the Patrol's busiest areas. Stark knew Hodge Purdee to be an honest man.

But that toughness and honesty didn't mean that Purdee could work miracles.

"I'm sorry, John Howard," Purdee said as he looked across his desk at Stark. "I just don't know what to tell you."

Stark had his cream-colored Stetson balanced on his knee. His hand clenched on the brim, bending it a little. "Tell me you'll find the bastards who killed Tommy Carranza and put them in jail," he said. "Better yet, tell me you'll blow holes in their sorry asses."

"Nothing I'd like better," Purdee said. "Carranza was a good man. I didn't know him as well as you did, of course, but he was always cooperative and helpful with us. I'd like to see his killers brought to justice. But you and I both know that's not the way these things work."

"It's not? I thought that was the job of our legal system, to see that justice is done."

Purdee laughed, but there was no humor in the sound. "If that was the real goal, John Howard, then cold-blooded murderers wouldn't go free because they have enough money to hire better lawyers than the state has. Federal judges wouldn't step in and try to micromanage everything from the military down to the local elementary school according to some half-assed theories of political correctness. Liberal politicians wouldn't whine every time the law tries to get the least little bit tougher on killers and rapists and terrorists. Remember the old joke about a hockey game breaking out in the middle of a fistfight? That fistfight is what our legal system has become, John Howard. Every so often some real justice breaks out in the middle of it, but it's rare. Chances are, this whole thing will be swept right under the rug."

Purdee spoke with the voice of bitter experience. Stark let the emotional outburst run its course, and then he said, "So what you're tellin' me is that nothing can be done? Ramirez's thugs will go scot-free?"

"There's no proof Ramirez had anything to do with Tommy's murder. The killers brought the weapons they used with them and took them away when they were finished. They didn't leave any forensic evidence, at least according to Sheriff Hammond's crime scene investigation team."

Stark made a sound of disgust and contempt. "Hammond doesn't want any evidence to be found. He's in bed with Ramirez, and you know it."

"I don't have any proof of that, either."

Stark stood and began to pace back and forth as best he could in the narrow confines of the small office. He just couldn't sit still anymore.

"So what *can* you do?"

The question lashed out from him, and he saw anger and resentment in Purdee's eyes. Stark felt bad about upsetting his friend. Purdee might not be a Texan—he was originally from Michigan or Wisconsin or one of those states up around the Great Lakes—but he was still a good man and had been a friend to Stark for the past five or six years, ever since he had been assigned to Del Rio.

Purdee stood up, too, resting the knobby knuckles of both hands on the desk. "I'll tell you what I can do," he said. "I can step up the patrols along the river. I don't have the manpower for it, but I'll find a way. I can put out the word to my sources on the other side of the border to let me know if they hear anything pointing to Ramirez as being responsible for Tommy's murder."

"You know he was—" Stark broke in.

Purdee held up a hand to stop him. "I can ask Washington to send me more agents and to authorize more man-hours. I'll do those things, but that's all I can do, John Howard. My hands are tied. The official investigation belongs to Sheriff Hammond."

Stark snorted in disgust at the mention of Hammond's name. He knew just how much good an investigation by the sheriff would do: none at all.

"Sit down," Purdee went on. "I know you want to barge in and fix things, John Howard. That's just your way. But this is one time when it won't work."

"Why the hell not?" Stark demanded.

Purdee said, "Because there is no quick fix in this situation. Think about it . . . the border between the U.S. and Mexico is over a thousand miles long, stretching from the mouth of the Rio Grande to the Pacific Ocean. Patrolling the border is a little higher priority now than it used to be, because we know that Islamic terrorists sometimes slip across pretending to be Mexicans. But we're still so outmanned it's scary. Every night there are hundreds, if not thousands, of illegal crossings. There's a floodtide of illegals that we can't even begin to stem. Many of them are relatively honest, hardworking folks who just want to make a better life for themselves and their families, but a lot of them are drug smugglers, like the couriers who work for Ramirez. And he's not alone. The drug cartels have operations going on at every conceivable point along the border where they think they can get their shit across without getting caught. Ramirez is a big fish, no doubt about it, but he's just one fish in a mighty big ocean."

"I get it," Stark said tightly. "The Border Patrol is over-worked, so you just give up and let the bastards do whatever they want."

Purdee's jaw thrust out even more than usual as he said, "John Howard, I'm gonna cut you some slack because I know how upset you are about Carranza. But don't ever accuse me of giving up just because I can see the reality of the situation."

For a moment the strained silence between the men continued as they glared at each other. Then Stark gave a little shake of his head and said, "Sorry, Hodge. I know better."

Purdee leaned back in his chair. "I know you do. That's why I didn't tell you to get the hell out of my office."

"You said you'd ask Washington for more men . . . you reckon they'll give 'em to you?"

"I'm not gonna hold my breath waiting. They'll issue statements to the press saying how much they want to increase our budget so we can put more men out on patrol, but until those bright boys in Congress realize that protecting the country is more important than social experimentation and increasing everybody's self-esteem, nothing's really going to change. And to tell you the truth, I don't see that happening in my lifetime."

Stark hated to admit it, but he didn't, either. Despite all the hot air coming out of Washington, politics changed about as fast as a glacier.

"All right," he said as he leaned forward. "Let's forget about proof and jurisdiction for a minute."

"I told you, I can't—"

This time it was Stark who held up his hand to forestall Purdee's protest. "Just for a minute," Stark said, "let's talk plain, man to man, without it leaving this office."

Purdee glared for a few seconds, but then he gave Stark a curt nod. "Man to man," he said.

"We both know Ramirez ordered that Tommy be killed for defying him and hitting that lawyer," Stark said.

"Yeah. That's the way I see it, too."

"Ramirez is a Colombian. They don't just strike back at their enemies. They go after the family, too."

Purdee nodded. "Usually."

"So, can you protect Julie Carranza and her kids?"

"That's not in the purview of this agency . . . I hate that legalistic mumbo jumbo, but when you work for the government it's hard not to start spouting it. The simple answer to your question, John Howard, is that no, I can't. I can't guarantee a thing where they're concerned."

"Then I'm going to see to it they're protected until after Tommy's funeral, and then I'm going to get them as far away from here as I can, as fast as I can."

"I think that's a good idea," Purdee agreed. "At least for a while."

There was nothing left to say. With the bitter taste of disappointment in his mouth, Stark stood up and put his hat on. Purdee walked out with him. The two men paused in the doorway of the office building. Purdee put out his hand. Stark took it without hesitation. Purdee was still his friend.

"It's a helluva shitty situation, John Howard," the Border Patrol agent said, "but we just have to live with it."

"No," Stark said. "We don't."

Then he was back in his pickup and driving away before Purdee could ask him what in blazes he meant by that.

He was still as mad when he reached the ranch. All the way back he had been thinking about that last comment he'd made to Hodge Purdee. Purdee had said they had to live with their country being under attack by vicious killers, and Stark had declared that they didn't.

But what could be done to stop it? What could one man do, where the full force of the federal government had failed?

Well, for one thing, Stark thought, the full force of the government *hadn't* failed, because it had never been brought to bear on the problem. Build a high enough fence and station enough heavily armed soldiers along that fence, and the southern door to the United States would be slammed shut. That floodtide of drug smuggling and illegal immigration would quickly diminish to a trickle.

That would never happen, though. Too many politicians would squawk about how unfair it was and how expensive it was, and behind the scenes too many businessmen who depended on the cheap illegal labor would be doing plenty of squawking of their own. Too many officials with bribes in their pockets would continue to turn a blind eye to the illicit trade in human misery.

What could one man do?

Devery Small and W.R. Smathers were sitting in chairs on the front porch, evidently waiting for him. Both men had rifles across their knees. Stark thumbed back his hat and nodded to them. "Boys."

"John Howard," Devery said. "Hope you don't mind. Me an' W.R. thought we'd come over and set a spell, just to make sure everything stays peaceful around here."

"Everett and Hubie said they'd be along later to spell us," W.R. added.

Stark frowned. "You fellas have places of your own to look after."

Devery waved a hand and said, "Our spreads can get along just fine without us for a few days, until things quiet down." He lowered his voice. "We don't want anything to happen to Julie and those kids."

Stark had figured out that much as soon as he saw his friends on the porch. He said, "I appreciate it. It shouldn't be too long. I'm going to talk to Julie and see if she and the kids will go somewhere safer after the funeral tomorrow."

"Funeral's that soon, huh?" W.R. said.

"No reason to wait. The sooner the better, I expect."

"You think Julie will go?" Devery asked.

"She's got some stubbornness in her," Stark said. "She has to, the way she put up with Tommy. But she loves her kids and will want to make sure they're safe. She'll go."

"Yeah, I expect you're right." Devery patted the stock of his Winchester. "But until then, there'll always be some of us close by."

Stark took off his hat and sleeved sweat from his forehead. "I guess I've got to go talk to her now. You know if anybody's told the kids yet?"

"Yeah, Julie told 'em," W.R. said. "Elaine helped a little. But it was pretty bad, I reckon."

Again Stark felt a twinge of guilt for leaving that in his wife's lap. But Elaine was better with people than he was, and that was no self-serving rationalization. It was the truth. As bad as it must have been, it would have been even worse if he had delivered the news.

He went inside the house, taking a deep breath of the cool, air-conditioned air. Elaine must have heard his steps, because she called from the den, "We're in here, John Howard."

Stark saw that the curtains had been drawn in the room, and no lights were on. There was something horrible about a darkened room in the middle of the day, something that spoke of sickness or death. A part of him wanted to turn around and plunge back into the clean sunlight. Instead, he steeled himself and went on into the den.

Elaine and Julie sat on the sofa, close enough so that Julie could reach out and touch the other woman if she needed to. Stark saw that Julie's eyes were swollen from crying, but she seemed to be under control. She said softly, "Hello, John Howard."

He went over and perched on the arm of the sofa next to her. "Julie," he said. "How are you?"

She took a deep breath. "I'm . . . all right. Elaine said you went to see—" Her voice broke for a second, but she got it back. "To see Father Sandoval," she finished in a stronger voice.

"That's right. I saw Manny Ortega at the funeral home, too. Both of them said they'd be out to visit with you this afternoon, to work out all the . . . arrangements. Father Sandoval thought it would be best, though, to go ahead and have the service tomorrow."

Julie managed a weak nod. "I agree."

Stark looked over at Elaine. "Where are the kids?"

"Newt and Chaco took them out on the range," she replied. "A couple of the hands are with them."

Stark nodded, knowing that Angelina and her brother, Marty, would be safe with the men. "How are they doing?"

"They were devastated, of course," Elaine said. "But children are resilient. That's one more thing us older folks can envy them for."

Julie said, "They're very strong children. *They* tried to comfort *me*. But I know they'll never really get over this . . . this terrible thing. . ."

Tears began to roll down her cheeks.

He hadn't talked to Julie about her taking the kids and leaving, going to San Antonio or some place even farther away, where they would be safe. How far away would that have to be, though? Ramirez had a long reach. They might have to leave Texas. Even that might not be far enough.

Of course, it was possible Ramirez wouldn't come after them. The Vulture might be satisfied with what he had already done. Stark hoped that would be the case.

Anyway, Ramirez might soon have a bigger problem. Hammond wouldn't do anything, and Purdee couldn't do anything, but Stark's hands weren't tied. Somebody should do something, he had thought, and the answer had come back, *Why not you?* What could one man do? he had asked, and the answer was, *You never know until you try.* As he stood up, twisting his hat in his hands as he watched Julie Carranza sob out her grief, he realized he had known from the first that it was going to be up to him to set things right. As soon as he had walked into that barn and seen the bloody ruin of his friend, something deep inside him had hardened and crystallized into a pure, righteous anger that would not be denied.

What could one man do? He was about to find out.

And so was that bastard Ramirez.

Nine

The next morning thunderheads loomed over the range of low mountains known as the Serrianas del Burro to the southwest of Del Rio, across the border in Mexico. Stark stood on his front porch looking at the clouds and saw the faint flicker of lightning among them. He hoped the storms wouldn't disrupt Tommy's funeral, which was scheduled for two o'clock that afternoon.

Of course, a bleak, pouring rain would be appropriate for the occasion, as if the heavens themselves were crying out their grief over a good man's tragic death.

The thunderstorms drifted from southwest to northeast, toward Del Rio, and out in front of them blew a cool breeze that carried the ozone tang of rain. But when the storms left the mountains and hit the desert, they broke apart for lack of moisture, as they usually did. Later in the summer, in the last half of August and on into September, the chances for rain would be better. Until then, the dryness would likely continue.

The Starks had an SUV in addition to several work pickups around the ranch, and Stark drove it into Del Rio that afternoon with Julie Carranza sitting stiffly in the front with him while Elaine rode in the back with the Carranza children. That morning the wives of Hubie, Devery, and Everett had gone over to the Carranza ranch and picked out appropriate clothes for Julie, Angelina, and Martin, then brought them to the Diamond S. The ladies had been accompanied and well guarded by some of their husbands' ranch hands.

As Stark drove he wished he could pull off the tie that was cinched tightly around his neck. He had always hated the damned things and never wore them unless he absolutely had to. This was one of those occasions.

He kept his eyes on the road and didn't look over at Julie. She was keeping a tight rein on her emotions, but he knew how shaky her grip was. The funeral and the burial service would be hard enough on her. No need to make things worse with a lot of unnecessary talking now.

As he left the ranch, Stark thought he saw a momentary reflection from the top of a small knoll about half a mile to the north. But it was there and gone so fast he couldn't be sure that he hadn't imagined it. Still, imagination or not, his hands tightened on the steering wheel and what felt like an icy fingertip played along his spine. He took a deep breath and told himself not to start thinking crazy thoughts. He already had plenty of those running around inside his head.

But the feeling didn't go away until he had covered a mile or more of the river road and the knoll was out of sight behind them.

Silencio Ryan rolled onto his back and let the sun beat down on him. Like a snake, he enjoyed its warmth. With his red hair and green eyes, he looked like he ought to be fair-skinned as well, the sort of complexion that burns easily in the fierce glare of the Texas border country. Instead he had inherited from his Mexican mother skin the same color as old saddle leather, and he could stay out in the sun all day without burning.

After a while he sat up, took out a cigarette, and lit it. Beside him lay the high-powered rifle with the equally high-powered telescopic sight mounted on it. For an instant John Howard Stark's head had filled that sight, and the crosshairs had been centered on Stark's temple, right where the silver was thickest in his graying dark hair. A slight squeeze of the trigger at that moment, just a few pounds' worth of pull, and Stark's head would have exploded under the impact of a bullet. That would have stopped the SUV, and in the next ten heartbeats Ryan could have put ten more rounds into the vehicle, killing everyone in it. Several pickups full of men had been following the SUV, and no doubt some of them were armed. They hadn't worried Ryan, and they weren't the reason he had held off.

"*If there is a chance,*" Ramirez had said, "*I want them all dead, Carranza's slut and both of their whelps. Fate spared them once, but it shall not do so again.*"

That was where the Vulture was wrong, Ryan thought as he dropped the butt of his cigarette in the gravelly dirt beside him. Fate had once more spared Julie Carranza and her children. Fate was named, in this case, Silencio Ryan. He could not have said *why* he had decided not to shoot. It was enough for him to know that he had the option to do so. Of all the men who worked for Ramirez, Ryan was the only one who had any sort of discretionary power. With everyone else, Ramirez expected total, instantaneous obedience. When Ryan returned to the compound and delivered the news that Julie Carranza and her children were still alive, Ramirez would be disappointed, but he would shrug off that disappointment. If Silencio Ryan thought it best not to pull the trigger, then so it must be.

Ryan's weathered face creased in a smile. He took a pair of sunglasses from the breast pocket of his khaki shirt, slipped them on, and stood up. He picked up the rifle and carried it toward the jeep that had brought him here.

On another day it might all be different, he thought. But only he would know when the time was right.

* * *

Baptist funerals were sad, of course. How could any funeral not have an element of grieving to it? But at the same time, Baptist funerals were sometimes like Irish wakes. There wasn't any drinking, of course, unless you wanted to count iced tea. But relatives and friends usually got together before a Baptist funeral, and folks brought food—casseroles and bowls of mashed potatoes and sweet potatoes and English pea salad and macaroni and cheese and plates full of home-made rolls and pies and cakes—and people who hadn't seen each other since the last funeral shook hands and slapped each other on the back and asked how everybody was doing. There were smiles of greeting and even a little laughter as people caught up on each other's lives. It was all muted by the solemnity of the occasion, but it was there nonetheless.

Tomas Carranza's funeral mass, on the other hand, was filled with ritual and weeping, and Stark hated every minute of it. Tommy had been such a vital man, full of life and passion, quick to anger but even quicker to give out with a booming laugh, that it seemed impossible to believe he was really up there in front of the altar in that closed, flower-draped coffin.

Elaine took Stark's hand as they sat side by side on the hard, uncomfortable pew. He squeezed it and wished this was all over.

Eventually, it was. Tommy was laid to rest in the cemetery beside the church. Stark approached the crowd of people around Julie. He recognized one of them as her brother Rigoberto from Austin. Stark drew him aside, shook his hand, and said quietly, " 'Berto, I think it'd be a good idea for Julie and the kids to get away from here for a while."

"So they won't be reminded of what happened to Tomas, you mean?"

"So it won't happen to them, too," Stark said bluntly.

Rigoberto caught his breath and stared at Stark. "This man Ramirez," he said after a moment. "You really think he would . . . would come after them, too?" He sounded outraged and afraid at the same time.

"I think there's every chance in the world that he will. He's a Colombian. They don't stop with just killing their enemies."

"No. I've never dealt with them directly, but I've heard stories. Plenty of stories." 'Berto was an assistant district attorney in Travis County. He fingered his chin as he thought. "We have relatives all over south Texas, but that's too close," he finally said.

Stark nodded. "I was thinking the same thing."

"But I have a good friend in Cheyenne, Wyoming, a fellow I went to law school with. He owes me plenty of little favors. If I combine all of them into one, he might be willing to look after Julie and the kids. He and his wife have plenty of room in their house. They have a place up in the mountains that might be even better."

"Not too isolated," Stark warned. "Sometimes that works against you when you're trying to protect somebody. Gives the bad guys too much room to operate."

'Berto nodded. "I'll go up there with them and check it all out myself."

"Good idea. How soon can you leave?"

"Well, I've got to get back to Austin for a trial day after tomorrow . . ."

"Let somebody else handle it. Leave from here and head north. Don't go back out to the ranch or anywhere else."

'Berto stared at him, not quite comprehending for a few seconds just what Stark proposed. Then he said, "But none of us are prepared for a long trip like that."

"I'd be willing to bet that if Ramirez has somebody watching Julie, he's not ready to take off on a long trip, either. Go to San Angelo and catch a plane there, doesn't matter where it's headed as long as you can get a connecting flight to Denver. You can rent a car and drive to Cheyenne from there. If you move fast enough, Ramirez won't be able to track you. Buy whatever Julie and the kids need when you get to Wyoming. If it's a matter of money, I can—"

"That's not necessary, Mr. Stark. I know from talking to Tommy what a hard time all you ranchers down here in the valley are having. I can take care of my sister." 'Berto flashed a grin. "Hey, that's what plastic's for, no?"

"Thanks, 'Berto."

"I just wish there was something I could do to even the score for Tommy."

"Don't worry about that," Stark said. "I'm already working on it."

But to tell the truth, he didn't know what he was going to do. He didn't like to think that he might be just full of hot air, that he really wouldn't get around to doing anything about Tommy's murder. He had always despised people who were big talkers but who never actually got anything done, or even tried to.

After the funeral, after Rigoberto had hustled a confused Julie and Angelina and Martin into his car and driven off, Stark and his friends gathered at the Diamond S. It was late in the afternoon when they all sat in the rocking chairs on the front porch of the ranch house. Neckties had long since come off, along with suit coats. Collars were unbuttoned and sleeves were rolled up. Elaine had brought out bottles of beer for the men and some of the women. W.R. was the only old bachelor in the bunch. The rest of the men had brought along their wives. It was reminiscent of the barbecue two nights earlier, but this was a much smaller, much more somber gathering.

Devery lifted his bottle and said, "To Tommy." The others echoed the toast and drank.

When Everett lowered his bottle, he asked, "What are we gonna do about this?"

"What do you mean?" his wife, Mary, asked. "You boys have already done everything you could."

"We ain't done squat!" Everett said heatedly. "Tommy's in the ground, and we ain't done a thing to settle the score."

"That's crazy talk," Kate Small said. "Tommy's murder is a matter for the police to handle."

"Hammond ain't gonna do anything about it," Devery said. The other men nodded and muttered agreement.

W.R. belched and said, "We could get our guns and go down and roust ol' Ramirez outta his hidey-hole."

"And get yourselves killed doing it," Elaine said. "John Howard, you'd better talk some sense into these friends of yours."

"Nobody could talk sense to an old pelican like W.R.," Stark said with a smile.

W.R. snorted. "Old pelican, is it?"

"Anyway, I'm not sure but what he's right," Stark went on, "at least in theory."

Hubie asked, "What do you mean by that in-theory business?"

"We *could* go after Ramirez, like W.R. suggested," Stark said, "but Elaine's probably right, too. We'd just get ourselves killed. Ramirez has got himself a damn fort down there on the other side of the river. Y'all read the story about it in the paper last year."

Sober nods went around the group. A newspaper reporter named Acosta had somehow gotten some inside information about the Vulture's drug-smuggling operation and his opulent home, including photographs, and he had written an exposé about the whole thing. A few days later, Acosta had disappeared . . . and it had taken a week to find all the parts of his body scattered up and down the Rio Grande.

"It would take an army to pry Ramirez out of that stronghold of his," Stark went on. "I'm afraid five broken-down old ranchers are a far cry from an army."

"So we just let it go?" Everett asked indignantly.

"I didn't say that. But we're gonna have to do some figuring."

"You can figure a thing to death."

That was exactly what Stark was afraid of, but he didn't

say that. He just said, "It won't bring Tommy back for the rest of us to get killed."

Kate Small, Mary Hatcher, and Doris Cornheiser all nodded emphatically in agreement. Doris said, "You boys listen to John Howard. He makes good sense."

There was more muttering, but talk of attacking Ramirez was dropped. Eventually the conversation turned, as it always did, to the price of beef and the way the government made things harder than they had to be for ranchers.

When the sun began to dip below the horizon and the visitors got up to leave, Stark said, "Better pass the word among your hands to be extra careful for a while. Ramirez is liable to get more aggressive than ever now that he probably thinks he's got us scared."

"He's right about that," Kate Small said. "I *am* scared, and anybody else with any sense would be, too."

Devery sighed. "Yeah, this valley sure ain't the kind of place it once was. Never thought I'd live to see the day when it got so dangerous and all-fired *mean* around here."

The visitors left, Stark and Elaine standing on the porch to wave good-bye to them as they drove off. Then, as Stark turned and started to go into the house, Elaine said, "Hold on a minute, John Howard. You don't think you fooled me, do you?"

"Fooled you about what?" Stark asked, although he had a sneaking suspicion that he already knew the answer.

"All that talk about being cautious and figuring and not trying to even the score for Tommy. I've known you for too long. You're up to something, but you don't want your friends to get drawn into it and get hurt."

"I don't know what you're talkin' about."

"Don't lie to my face," she said. "I deserve better than that."

Stark just looked at her for a moment, and then he drew in a deep breath and blew it out in a sigh. "You always did know me too well, woman," he muttered. "You're right. I do want to do something to avenge Tommy's murder. I know Ramirez was behind it, and I know the law can't or won't do a damned thing. But the hell of it is, I really don't know what to do. One man can't get to Ramirez."

"The others offered to help."

Stark shook his head. "They're tough old birds, but they're no match for Ramirez's men."

"Not like you, an old marine who chews nails for breakfast."

Stark smiled ruefully. "I'm afraid my nail-chewin' days are over. No, I've got enough sense to know that I can't launch some one-man crusade. But we can sure keep a closer eye on the border and try to keep the Vulture's men off our land. That's something, anyway."

Elaine's eyes narrowed in the dusk as she studied him. "I'm still not sure I believe you. It's been a long time since you did anything crazy, John Howard, but you cut some pretty good capers when you were a youngster. If you get too worked up, just remember that you're fifty-four years old."

"I ain't likely to forget it," Stark said.

Elaine gave him a kiss on the cheek and went on inside. Stark lingered on the porch, watching the orange glow of the sunset fade from the western sky.

"That girl just thinks she knows how crazy you can be."

Stark looked toward the shadows at the end of the porch. "How long you been skulkin' there, old man?"

"Long enough," Uncle Newt said as he shuffled forward. "Long enough to see the look in your eyes when you talk about that fella Ramirez. You can sound mighty calm and reasonable-like when you want to, John Howard, but I know better. I ever tell you I knew Wyatt Earp?"

"Only about a thousand times. And you didn't really know Wyatt Earp. You were too young to even remember that time Grandpa saw him out there in California."

"No, I weren't!" Newt protested. "I was three years old, and I remember it clear as a bell! Nineteen and twenty-eight it was. We was walkin' down the street and Daddy was holdin' my hand and this old man come a-walkin' down the sidewalk the other way. He was a mite bent from bein' so old, but he straightened up and give Daddy a nod as he went past, and when he'd gone on Daddy leaned over to me and said, 'Son, you remember this day, because that there was Wyatt Earp, the last o' the old-time gunfighters to still be alive. He's outlived 'em all, Smoke Jensen, Doc Holliday, Frank Morgan, Ben Thompson, Falcon McAllister, an' all the rest. He's the last o' his kind.' That's what he said to me, an' I remember it, by golly!"

"Maybe so, but what's that got to do with anything?"

"When Wyatt Earp walked past us, I looked in that old man's eyes. What I seen there, I never saw in any other man's eyes . . . until now."

Stark felt that coldness along his spine again, but this time he didn't feel like he was being watched. Not by human eyes, anyway.

Newt turned and started to limp away. Stark said, "Where are you going?"

"Back to the bunkhouse," the old man said over his shoulder. "*Wheel o' Fortune*'s on the satellite, an' that gal who turns the letters, whoo-ee, she's a looker!"

Ten

Stark went inside a few minutes later. Elaine was putting together a quick supper. They ate together in the kitchen, but neither of them had much of an appetite. Afterward, when Stark asked her if she wanted to watch some TV, Elaine shook her head and said, "I'm worn out, John Howard. I think I'll just go on up and read for a while."

"Suit yourself." Stark was too restless to even consider turning in this early. He went into the den/office and fired up the computer that sat on the desk. He would never be the type to spend hours on end surfing the Web or the Net or whatever they called it, but he enjoyed the convenience of e-mail and there were a few ranching-related Web sites that he visited fairly regularly. As he waited for the computer to boot up, he hoped there would be e-mail from David or Pete or both. These days that was the easiest way for the boys over-seas to communicate with the folks back home.

He connected and started to retrieve his e-mail. He'd heard a lot about that so-called spam, the e-mail ads for everything under the sun from porno to mortgages to printer ink, but he didn't get that many of them, probably because he didn't use the Internet all that much. Only a handful of messages came in, and none of them amounted to anything.

Until the last one popped up and he saw that the subject line was blank. That wasn't all that unusual, and when it happened it was usually just another piece of junk e-mail. On this one, though, the sender's name caught his eye and made him sit up straight in shock.

The name was "Carranza."

"Damn it, Tommy," Stark said under his breath, "are you sendin' me e-mail from beyond the grave now?"

That was impossible, of course. Stark was too hard-headed to believe in ghosts, and he wasn't going to start now. This was some sort of fluky coincidence. Either that, or somebody was playing one hell of a cruel practical joke. The message had no attachment, and when Stark checked its properties he found that it was small, less than one kilobyte. So it seemed safe enough to open it. He double-clicked on it.

The message screen that came up had only a few words on it:

GUZMAN MENDEZ CANALES
THE BLUE BURRO
TOMORROW NIGHT

What the hell? Stark thought. Those first three were names, of course, but they meant nothing to him. "The Blue Burro"? That could be anything, but for some reason it sounded to Stark like the name of a cantina or a nightclub. "Tomorrow night" was clear enough on the face of it, but what did it mean? That Guzman, Mendez, and Canales would be at some place called the Blue Burro tomorrow night? That made sense, Stark decided, but he didn't know who the men were or why their whereabouts tomorrow night should have any meaning to him.

And then one possible answer hit him like a punch between the eyes.

Hodge Purdee had said that he would put the word out to his informants south of the border that he was looking for information about Tommy Carranza's murder. Maybe Purdee had come up with something, like the names of three of the men involved in the killing, and was passing them along to Stark with a tip as to where those men would be on the coming night. That was possible, wasn't it? Purdee knew he couldn't act officially, but he could send an anonymous tip. . . .

Somebody who knew more about computers than Stark did might be able to figure out exactly where that message had come from. On the other hand, if he was right in his guess about what it meant, whoever had sent it would have been very careful to conceal his identity, especially if he worked for a bloated, unresponsive, but sometimes petty and vengeful government. The more Stark thought about it, the more convinced he was that he was right.

The question now was, what was he supposed to *do* with that information? The Border Patrol was powerless, Hammond wasn't interested, and the Mexican authorities just weren't about to interfere with one of the primary sources of the graft on which they thrived.

First, thought Stark, he needed to find out just what, and where, the Blue Burro was.

He had a Ciudad Acuna phone book in the desk along with the Del Rio book. He hauled it out and flipped through the pages until he found a listing for El Burro Azul, which translated to the Blue Burro. The address was on Boulevard Guerrero. Stark had made many trips across the river as a young man and knew the town fairly well. He thought this Blue Burro must be somewhere on the southeastern edge of town, not far from the Plaza de Toros, or bullfight ring. Stark stared at the phone book for a long moment, then pulled the telephone over to him and punched in the number.

A loud, male voice answered in Spanish. The voice had to be loud because so was the music that was playing in the Blue Burro. It sounded like a Tejano version of hard rock and confirmed Stark's suspicion that the Blue Burro was some sort of bar or strip joint, something like that. He hung up without saying anything.

Though he still couldn't be certain of who Guzman,

Mendez, and Canales were, it was obvious whoever sent him that e-mail wanted him to go to the Blue Burro tomorrow night.

It was equally obvious that the whole thing might be a trap.

Stark had left the computer alone long enough so that the screensaver had come on. It was a constantly shifting, panoramic landscape of west Texas scenery that Pete had programmed into the machine. Stark sat there for a long time, staring at the beauties of the land he had grown up in and thinking.

With the funeral over and the rest of the Carranza family safely ensconced in Cheyenne—Stark had gotten a call from 'Berto the night before, confirming that they had reached their destination without actually revealing what it was, just in case anybody was listening in—things ought to get back to normal around the Diamond S, Stark thought the next morning. He spent the afternoon doing chores around the ranch headquarters, and then, after lunch, drove out to work on one of the ranch fences. He had to replace a cedar post that Newt had accidentally backed into with the pickup, breaking it off at the ground. He had a new post in the back of the pickup, along with a roll of barbed wire in case some of the old wire had to be replaced.

With the post being broken off, that meant he had to dig the lower part out of the ground. He dug around it with a sharpshooter shovel, then reached down with gloved hands and worked the piece of post back and forth until he could pull it up. The new post would go back in the same hole, so that was no problem. Then he had to take the upper part of the broken post loose from the field fence and barbed wire to which it was attached, set the new post in the hole, and re-attach the fencing.

He worked hard, enjoying the heat of the sun and the sweat that flowed freely and the way his muscles loosened up until he felt twenty years old again. A little hard work always made him feel his age; a lot of it seemed to make the years fall away so that for a time he almost recaptured his youth. Of course, he would pay for it with some soreness the next day.

The only other break he took was to talk briefly with Newt and Chaco, who rode by on horseback, making their usual rounds of the place. Newt was on his old Biscuit horse, his favorite mount.

In late afternoon, Stark loaded up everything. He had tossed the broken pieces of cedar post into the back of the truck earlier, next to the roll of barbed wire, the shovel, and a posthole digger he hadn't needed. Stark wasn't sure what he would do with the pieces of post. He never threw away anything that was still potentially usable, though. One of his father's favorite expressions, which could refer to almost anything, had been, "You never know when you might need something like that," and Stark still lived by that doctrine.

As he drove back toward the ranch house, he wondered if in the back of his mind had been the idea that if he worked hard all day, he would be too tired to go down to Cuidad Acuna tonight and pay a visit to the Blue Burro. If that was what he had been thinking, it hadn't worked out too well. He felt as vital and alive as he had in a long time. He was rarin' to go, in fact.

Elaine had supper ready by the time he had cleaned up and changed clothes. As they ate, she commented on how cheerful he seemed. "You're definitely more chipper today, John Howard," she said.

"Yeah, I feel pretty good," Stark agreed.

He couldn't tell her that he felt good because he had finally reached a decision. He couldn't forget or ignore what had happened to Tommy. There had to be some sort of reckoning, and it was up to him to do it. He couldn't get to Ramirez; Stark knew that and accepted it, although it was a pretty bitter pill to swallow. But if those men who were going to be at the Blue Burro tonight worked for Ramirez and had had something to do with Tommy's murder . . .

Well, he could get at them, sure enough.

When he was finished eating, he shoved back his chair and said, "I've got to go into town for a while."

"What for?"

"Just to pick up a few things."

"If you're going to Wal-Mart, I'll go with you—"

Stark shook his head. "I'm not going to Wal-Mart."

Elaine looked a little surprised at the curtness of his voice. "Oh. Well then, how long are you going to be gone?"

"I don't know, but it shouldn't be long. An hour or two, maybe." In truth, he had no idea how long this trip would take.

"All right. I'll wait up for you."

He didn't tell her not to. That would just worry her more than she was worried already.

As he got his hat, she said, "John Howard . . . you're not about to do something foolish, are you?"

"Me?" He managed to smile. "When did I ever do anything foolish?"

"Oh my God," she said, but by the time the words were out of her mouth, he was already out the door. He got in the pickup and drove off. He almost stopped when he glanced in the rearview mirror and saw her standing on the porch, one hand lifted to her throat in alarm. But his foot came down harder on the gas. He knew that if he stopped now, he might never go on, and that would be the end of it, the end of any justice for Tommy Carranza.

Night was settling down over the Rio Grande valley by the time he reached Del Rio. He drove on through town toward the International Bridge. Stark had Mexican insurance on all his vehicles, since he sometimes had to cross the border to do business, so taking the pickup into Cuidad Acuna was no problem. Nor was the traffic too bad. This border crossing wasn't as heavily traveled as the ones at El Paso and

Eagle Pass and Brownsville, so the approaches to the bridge didn't get clogged with cars and trucks. Stark was able to make it across in short order, telling the guards at the Mexican end of the bridge that he would be staying less than seventy-two hours. They waved him through, figuring he was just another gringo in search of cerveza and pussy.

He drove along brightly lit Hidalgo Street, the main tourist drag, for several blocks until he came to Boulevard Guerrero. Waiting for traffic to clear, he hung a left and drove past the bullring. Cuidad Acuna had a larger population than its sister city across the border did, but its citizens were packed into a much smaller area. Town ran out in a hurry, giving way to scrubby grassland. Not all the vestiges of civilization disappeared, however. Up ahead, blue neon blazed in the night.

As Stark came closer, he saw that the neon tubes were curved into the shape of a cartoonish donkey, with blue letters underneath that spelled out EL BURRO AZUL. The sign went with a sprawling, one-story adobe building with a large gravel parking lot in front of it. As Stark pulled in, he saw that the lot was only about half-full. The vehicles ranged from battered pickups, some of them so old they had running boards, to newer SUVs and sedans. Stark found a place to park without any trouble.

When he had killed the lights and the engine, he sat there for a long moment, hands tight on the steering wheel. He could still leave, could turn around, and head home without ever going into this sleazy club where God-knows-what awaited him.

But if he did that, he would never know why someone had wanted him to come here tonight. He took a deep breath, opened the pickup door, and got out.

He heard the music pounding out of the place even though all the doors and windows were closed. Stark walked determinedly toward the entrance. A burly young man with a ponytail and a dark Indio face, wearing a black T-shirt, was stationed there. "Hey, man," he greeted Stark. "You looking for pretty girls?"

"Sure," Stark replied, even though strippers were about the last thing he had on his mind right now.

"We got plenty. You not gonna cause any trouble, right?"

"Right," Stark lied.

"Go on in." The arrogant smugness in the kid's voice said that he had seen plenty of middle-aged gringos down here before and would again. The Blue Burro probably made a lot of its money off visitors from the other side of the border, slumming tourists and locals who had left their wives behind for a night of excitement.

In a way, Stark thought, he supposed he fit into that last category.

The air was thick with tobacco and marijuana smoke, along with the sharp tangs of whiskey, beer, and cheap perfume. Stark's jaw tightened as the stink assaulted his senses. The lighting was dim, with shadows interspersed with garish bursts of illumination from colored spotlights that played over the nude, writhing flesh of dancers atop elevated stages on both sides of the room. In front of him was a big U-shaped bar that enclosed another stage where two girls danced together. As Stark approached the bar the dancers rubbed their breasts against each other and kissed openmouthed, with plenty of tongue action visible. The patrons at the bar shouted their appreciation.

What the hell was he supposed to do *now*? Stark thought.

Getting a drink seemed to be the logical place to start. He had already looked around the room as best he could in the dim, smoky light and hadn't seen anyone he recognized. He found an empty place at the bar and ordered a beer. The bartender was a Mexican woman, older and heavier than the young, slender dancers but still attractive with a wild mane of midnight-black curls and big breasts with dark brown nipples that were clearly visible through the almost sheer blouse she wore. Stark tried not to look at them, but it was damned difficult with them poking out that way.

"Howdy," a voice with a Texas twang said from beside him. "Quite a place, ain't it?"

Stark glanced over and saw a middle-aged man in jeans, a cowboy shirt with silver snaps, and a black Stetson. The man grinned and went on, "Your first time here?"

"Yeah," Stark replied. He lifted the bottle of beer that the woman placed in front of him. It wasn't too bad, and was surprisingly cold.

Stark's newfound drinking buddy grinned and inclined his head toward the dancers who were now licking each other all over as much as they were dancing. "Pretty hot stuff, huh?"

"If you like that kind of thing."

"If you don't like it, why are you here?"

Stark shrugged. "Just getting a drink."

"Well, it's good to see another American face in here."

"Looks like quite a few Americans around to me."

That was true. Probably 25 percent of the customers were Anglo, ranging from cowboys like the man talking to Stark to businessmen in suits and loosened ties.

"Well, some folks in here don't much like us. In fact, I just heard . . . Nah, it ain't none o' my business."

"You just heard what?" Stark asked, turning to look at the man.

After a moment's hesitation, the man said, "There are some guys back there at that table in the corner who are . . . well, they're braggin' about killin' some guy on the other side of the river a few nights ago. I heard 'em talkin' about it, and I don't mind tellin' you, it scared me. I'm thinkin' I might ought to get out of here while the gettin's good."

"Maybe so," Stark said. "They mention the name of this guy they killed?"

"I think they called him Tommy."

That came as no surprise to Stark. He had already figured out this stranger in the black hat must be the one responsible for that e-mail he had gotten. It would be just too wild a co-incidence otherwise for him to have waltzed in here and

.ound the men he was looking for so quickly. Stark took another drink of his beer and asked, "Which ones exactly are you talking about?"

"The ones right under that Dos Equis sign," the man said.

"Thanks," Stark said. He drained the last of the beer, set the empty on the bar, and turned to walk out of the noisy strip joint.

Hodge Purdee had set this up. Stark was sure of it now. Frustrated, Purdee couldn't do anything directly about Tommy's murder, but he had located some of the men responsible for it and now through this intermediary, probably one of his informants, he was pointing Stark right at them, as if Stark were some sort of human weapon.

Well, maybe he was, he thought as he reached his pickup. He put his hat on the front seat, then relocked the door, went to the back, and lowered the tailgate. He reached into the bed and picked up the pair of work gloves he had left there earlier. He had put the shovel and the posthole digger back in the toolshed at the ranch, but the broken pieces of cedar post were still in the back of the pickup, as was the roll of barbed wire. He drew the gloves on and then picked up the longer length of cedar post that was still rattling around back there. It was solid, about four feet long. Stark hefted it and nodded in satisfaction.

He started to turn away, but then he stopped and reached back into the bed of the pickup, getting the roll of barbed wire. He took hold of the end and pulled out a couple of feet of wire, using a pair of pliers that were also in the back of the truck to cut it off. He started twisting the wire around the length of post in his other hand, bending it around itself to fasten it in place. When he was finished, he had about eight inches of the post covered in barbed wire.

There, he thought. *That ought to do it.*

Still wearing his gloves, carrying the barbed-wire-studded piece of fence post, Stark walked toward the door of the Blue Burro.

Eleven

The guy in the black T-shirt at the door saw Stark coming with the piece of post and took a quick step toward him, holding up a hand and saying, "Hey, man, you can't—"

Stark moved fast, muscle memory kicking in as all the hand-to-hand combat techniques the marines had taught him came back to him. He rammed the end of the post into the guard's stomach with a quick, hard jab that knocked all the wind out of the guy and made him double over in pain as he gasped for breath. Stark used his hand to chop a short, hard blow down on the back of the man's neck. The guy collapsed, his face hitting the gravel hard. He let out a groan but didn't move. He was out of the fight for a while.

Stark reached for the door handle. Leaving an enemy alive behind him went against the grain, but even though the guard was a thug and probably had committed crimes of his own in the past, Stark was here for Tommy's murderers. That was all. He would take care of anybody else who got in his way, but he wouldn't deliberately try to kill them.

Stark pulled the door open and stepped inside. The noise and the stink assaulted his senses again as he let the door swing closed behind him. Holding the length of fence post down beside his leg so that it wouldn't be so noticeable, he stalked across the room toward the men who had been pointed out to him. They still sat at the table under the Dos Equis sign, drinking and talking and laughing, having a fine old time. A couple of the strippers who weren't up onstage at the moment had come over and joined them, sitting at the table in skimpy, tasseled costumes, rubbing the thighs of the men under the table, and sipping twenty-dollar "drinks" that were really just weak iced tea.

A glance at the bar told Stark that the cowboy who had pointed out Tommy's killers was nowhere to be seen now. He had done his job and had probably taken off so that he wouldn't get caught up in the trouble. Stark didn't blame him. He wouldn't be here himself, if not for the fact that if he didn't do this, nobody else would.

Nobody seemed to be paying any attention to him. Most of the eyes in the place were fixed on the erotic gyrations of the strippers. Stark had known girls like them before, back when he was single, and he knew that they were more likely to be thinking about such things as late car payments and kids with the sniffles and what they needed to buy at the grocery store on their way home after work, than they were about the lust-charged fantasies of the men watching them. That knowledge sort of took the appeal out of it for Stark. Not that it really mattered right now. All his attention was focused on the three men sitting under the neon beer sign. The sign had a small electrical short in it, so that one section flickered from time to time.

Stark turned his body slightly as he came up to the table, keeping the post out of easy sight against his leg. The Mexicans looked up with sullen, resentful expressions at the tall, muscular gringo standing there, and one of them said in a surly voice, "What you want, man?"

"I think you boys know an amigo of mine," Stark said. Somewhere inside himself he found the self-control to keep his voice steady. He had to be sure he was doing the right thing, had to be certain these were the men who had tortured and killed Tommy before he started flailing away at them with the barbed-wire-wrapped fence post.

"We don' know anybody you know, *cholo*," one of the other men said disdainfully.

"I think you do," Stark said. He noticed that the strippers were starting to edge their chairs back away from the table. They had a keener instinct for trouble than these half-drunk thugs did. "His name was Tomas Carranza."

The shocked, wide-eyed stares the men gave him, the startled curses that ripped from their mouths, the way they started up out of their chairs and reached hurriedly for the weapons in their pockets all told Stark that his information was correct. He brought the piece of fence post up in his right hand, and as he did his left reached across his body and wrapped around the post as well, and he pivoted at the hips and brought his hands back and it was just as if he were back on the baseball field, stepping to the plate in the bottom of the ninth, two outs, bases loaded, the home team three runs behind, the only hope a grand slam.

Batter up.

Stark swung as a couple of switchblades came out and flicked open, the glare from the beer sign reflecting from the cold steel. The third man had a small, flat automatic, probably a .25. Stark wished he could have gone for the gunman first, but the other two were in the way.

The strippers screamed and flung themselves out of their chairs, stumbling into the crowd. The music pounded and the women still onstage twisted and posed in time to the beat.

The fence post slammed into the face of the nearest man. The barbed wire ripped his skin and gouged into his flesh, tearing off little chunks of meat as it pulled free. The force of the blow shattered his cheekbone and pulped his nose as well. He gave a strangled cry and slumped backward as blood spurted from his mangled face. The switchblade slipped from his fingers and fell unnoticed onto the table.

That first impact stole some of the speed and force from Stark's swing, so that the second man was able to twist aside and avoid taking the post across the face like his companion. Instead it thudded against his left shoulder. The barbs dug in again, drawing a howl of pain. Stark knew he had probably broken the man's shoulder. At the very least, that whole arm would be numb and useless.

Unfortunately the man held his knife in his right hand. Fighting through the pain, he lunged forward and jabbed the blade at Stark. The only good thing about that from Stark's point of view was that the knife wielder's move put him between Stark and the man with the gun. The guy was trying to line up a shot but had to hold off for fear of hitting his friend.

Stark felt the bite of the blade on his right forearm as he jerked the post back for another swing. He didn't think the wound was a bad one, only a scratch, but in the middle of the fight, with his blood pumping so hard and his adrenaline up, he couldn't be sure about anything. He swung the post again, a shorter swing this time, not the roundhouse going for the fences but more like just trying to punch the ball into the hole between third and short. He hit the second man on the left ear and tore it off. Blood poured down the side of the man's neck. He clapped his right hand to the wound and shrieked. Worse luck for him, he was still holding the switchblade in that hand and accidentally sliced a deep gash in his head above where the ear had been. He slumped forward onto the table.

The third man's little automatic cracked wickedly. Up until now the fight, while it hadn't gone unnoticed, hadn't attracted a great deal of attention. The thuds and screams had been partially drowned out by the loud music. Gunfire was a different story, though. People heard that, even through the heavy beat. With shouts of alarm and confusion and a lot of bellowed curses, many of the club's patrons took off for the tall and uncut, heading for the exits as fast as they could without even waiting to see what was going on. There was a back door, down a little hall past the filthy bathrooms, but both it and the front door soon jammed up as the frightened mob tried to pour through them. The strippers had leaped down from the stages—the smart ones kicking off their spike heels first so they wouldn't break their ankles when they landed—and joined the exodus.

Stark didn't know where the first shot had gone, but he was pretty sure he hadn't been hit. Recovering from the momentum of his second swing, he brought the makeshift club around in a backhand that swatted the automatic from the guy's fingers just as it went off again. That bullet creased the right butt cheek of one of the fleeing strippers and made her yelp. Stark thrust the post out like a sword, jamming it into the third man's belly. As the man bent over, Stark brought the post up so that the end wrapped in barbed wire caught him under the chin. Crimson drops of blood flew through the air like rain.

A heavy weight landed on Stark's back, knocking him forward. He hadn't expected that everyone else in the place would stay out of the fight. Whether the three killers had friends here or not, the club would have bouncers who would jump on anybody who started a fight; not to mention that some of the men in here would probably be glad to pound on him awhile just because he was an Anglo. The man on his back forced him down onto the table, on top of the man whose ear had been torn off. That one began to squirm and scream.

The coppery smell of blood filled Stark's nostrils. He brought his right elbow up and back, driving it into the midsection of the guy who had tackled him from behind. He had to do that three times before the man's grip came loose. Stark meant to put his hand down on the table so he could shove off of it, but he grabbed the back of the other guy's head instead and rammed his face against the table. The man went limp. Stark shoved off anyway, rolling over onto his back, half on and half off the table.

He saw a chair coming at him and barely got the post up in time to block it. The impact was still enough to half stun him, but at least he was able to turn the chair aside so that it shattered against the table. Stark brought his right leg up and snapped a kick into the groin of the man who had swung the chair. The heel of his boot landed solidly, crushing the man's genitals. He shrieked and fell back, clutching at himself.

Stark kept rolling, came completely off the table, and surged up onto his feet, stumbling a little as he caught his balance. Catching a glimpse of several men coming toward him, he whipped the post back and forth, driving them back. Part of the barbed wire had come loose, and when Stark swung the post the wire sang through the air like one strand of a cat-o'-nine tails.

The old combat instincts that never went away completely warned Stark. He whirled around to see two men coming at him. One of them was the guy who'd had the gun. He had snatched up the switchblade his friend had dropped. The other one was the first man Stark had clobbered. His face was covered with blood and grotesquely swollen from the broken cheekbone. He blubbered incomprehensible curses as he lurched toward Stark, arms outstretched, hands twisted into claws.

The one with the knife was more dangerous, but armed with the fence post, Stark could keep him at bay. He swung a couple of times, making the man dart back. That gave the other guy a chance to reach Stark, though. He crashed into Stark and fumbled at his throat, trying to get a death grip on it.

The end of the post Stark had been using as a handle was jagged where it had broken off. He reversed it and brought it up between them, driving the post into the man's throat. The jagged wood tore through flesh and severed arteries. The man gave a hideous, bubbling scream right in Stark's face as blood fountained from his ravaged neck. He fell away and landed in a heap, pawing at his torn-open throat for a couple of seconds before he jerked and quivered and gradually settled into the stillness of death.

Something bit into Stark's side. The man with the knife

was close again, too damned close. He had just sliced a gash under Stark's ribs. Stark let go of the post with his left hand and jabbed that fist into the guy's face. The blow knocked him back a step, and that gave Stark the room he needed to swing the post one-handed. The gnarled wood crashed into the side of the man's head and shattered his skull. The bone collapsed under the force of the blow, and his left eye popped out of its socket and hung dangling on his cheek. He went down like a puppet with its strings cut, dead before he hit the floor.

Breathing heavily, Stark kept an eye on the other men and stepped over to the table where the final member of the trio that had killed Tommy Carranza lay facedown. The music had stopped sometime during the fight, so now an eerie silence hung over the place, broken only by Stark's rasping breaths. He grabbed the man by the hair and lifted his head, only to see the glassy stare of death in the man's eyes. Having his face smashed into the table like that must have driven bone fragments from his nasal cavity back and up into his brain. Stark released him and let his head thump down on the table again. Stark left the body there, splayed across the table.

Even though he was heavily outnumbered by the men still in the club, evidently none of them wanted anything to do with him. They watched him warily as he stepped away from the table, leaving the three dead men behind him. His side and arm throbbed where he had been cut, and he felt revulsion roiling in his stomach as he realized that he was covered in the blood of those bastards. He hoped like hell that none of them had some filthy disease he could catch.

That was assuming, of course, that he got out of here alive. That outcome was still very much in doubt.

Stark limped over to the bar, a pulled muscle in his leg catching a little. He had no idea when he had suffered that injury. He hadn't noticed it when it happened.

Men pulled back, keeping a good distance between him and them. He held the post down by his leg again and leaned his other hand on the bar. The lady bartender with the big nipples was still behind the hardwood, pressed back as far as she could get against the now deserted horseshoe stage.

Stark managed to hold up a finger and say, "*Una mas cerveza, por favor, senorita.*"

With shaking hands, the woman uncapped a beer and leaned forward to set it gingerly on the bar in front of the blood-covered, wild-eyed, gringo lunatic. Then she backed away again hurriedly.

Stark picked up the bottle and tilted it to his mouth. He had never tasted anything as good as the cold beer that flowed down his throat. He drank half the beer before he lowered the bottle. He set it on the bar.

Then he turned to face the silent, wary crowd. Lifting the fence post, he pointed at the dead men and said in fluent border Spanish, "Those three tortured and killed a good friend of mine and would have done the same to his wife and children if they had caught them. I have repaid them for their evil and avenged my friend's death. My fight is with none of you."

"Hombre, jus' get outta here," the woman behind the bar said in English. "We don' wan' no part of your troubles." She added, "Those three, they work for . . ."

She couldn't bring herself to say the name, but everyone in the place knew it, Stark sensed.

"They work for the devil now," he said. *Or maybe they always did.*

He started slowly toward the door. It opened before he got there, and the man in the black T-shirt stumbled through it, groaning. His bleary eyes fastened on Stark, and he stopped and clenched his hands into fists as he growled a curse.

"No! Let him go!"

The sharp command came from the woman behind the bar. The man ignored her at first until she unleashed a rapid torrent of invective in their native tongue. Then, grudgingly, he stepped aside out of Stark's way.

Stark trudged out of the place, halfway expecting some of

them to come after him as soon as he was outside. That didn't happen, though. Maybe what he had said about avenging a friend's death had struck a chord in them. They were a people with a deep sense of honor. Scum like Ramirez were an aberration, and he reminded himself that Ramirez was Colombian, not Mexican.

He made it to his pickup, awkwardly fished out his keys—his left hand was swelling some from the punch it had delivered—and unlocked the door. After tossing the bloody fence post in the floorboard on the passenger side, he pulled himself up behind the steering wheel. It took him longer than usual to get the keys in the ignition and start the engine, but after a minute he was ready to pull away.

He paused to look at the flickering blue neon of the club's sign. He was just as big a jackass as that blue burro, he told himself. He had taken a huge chance by coming here tonight, and he knew he was damned lucky to still be alive.

But he had made a start on settling the score, and it felt good. When he thought about that he forgot his aches and pains for a moment. People said that revenge was hollow, that all the retaliation in the world wouldn't bring someone back after they were dead. And Stark couldn't deny that Tommy was gone. No matter what he did, he couldn't change that.

But there was a question of justice, too, and when Stark thought about the way the impact had shivered up his arm as that son of a bitch's skull broke apart when the fence post hit it, he knew that justice had been served. A rough justice, an extreme justice, to be sure, but justified nonetheless.

They'd had it coming. Pure and simple, boiled down to its essence, that was all there was to it. They were bad men, and they'd had it coming.

Stark put the truck in gear and drove off into the night.

He wondered what the American guards at the other end of the International Bridge would say when he tried to reenter the country covered in blood.

* * *

The music hadn't started up again in the Blue Burro. All the strippers were so shaken by what had happened, and upset because one of the girls had actually gotten shot in the ass, that there might not be any more shows tonight.

On the other hand, once the bodies were hauled out and the blood was cleaned up, enough of the night would be left so that more money could change hands, and that was the way of the universe, was it not?

Silencio Ryan emerged from the men's room. He had watched the whole thing from there, through the door held open a few inches. After talking to Stark at the bar, he had stepped into the hallway beside the restrooms when the big gringo went outside, then retreated into the bathroom itself when the mob tried to get out the rear door. Ryan had known Stark would be back, and then all hell would break loose. Otherwise Ryan never would have sent Stark that e-mail and lured him here tonight.

That was exactly the way it had happened. Stark had waded in, swinging that fence post like a baseball bat, and when it was all over, Guzman, Mendez, and Canales were all dead. As far as Ryan was concerned, their lives were a small price to pay to find out just how much of a badass Stark really was. Ryan knew now why he had held off on pressing the trigger when he could have killed Stark the day before. It was curiosity. Ramirez might not like it, but a worthy enemy deserved more than a bullet in the head from four hundred yards away. A worthy enemy deserved to meet his fate at close range, and now Ryan knew.

John Howard Stark was worthy.

BOOK TWO

No man in the wrong can stand up against a man in the right who keeps on a-comin'.

—William "Wild Bill" MacDonald, captain,
Texas Rangers

Twelve

Stark stopped before he got back to the bridge and dug around under the front seat for an old work shirt he'd remembered was there. It had oil stains on it and stank of sweat, but at least it wasn't soaked with blood. He took off the shirt he had on and used the tail of it, which was fairly clean, to scrub as much of the blood off his face as he could. He checked the wounds on his arm and side while he was at it. Both of them hurt, but they didn't look too deep and had already stopped oozing crimson. The wounds would need to be cleaned as soon as possible, but he thought that could wait until he was back at the ranch.

He checked himself in the rearview mirror and saw that he looked as presentable as possible under the circumstances. It was when he reached for the key to start the truck again that the reaction hit him. His shoulders hunched up and he had to grab the steering wheel to keep from shaking. He had killed three men tonight and possibly injured several others severely. The three dead men had deserved their fate, no doubt about that. Arguably they had deserved death more than the hundreds of men Stark had killed in Vietnam. Stark had never felt the sort of personal hatred for the enemy during the war that he had felt tonight for the men who had murdered Tommy. Morally he had absolutely no doubt that he had done the right thing.

But still, for the past thirty years he had been just a common man, a husband, a father, a rancher. He had worked at his living, raised his kids, and loved his wife. He had watched TV and gone to the movies and read books and pushed a cart up and down the aisles of the grocery store and written out checks each month for the electric bill, the insurance bill, the feed bill, the telephone bill. He had eaten Sunday dinner and midnight snacks, laughed at David Letterman, cheered at high school football games, and gotten a lump in his throat when the band played the National Anthem before those games. At times in his life he had known moments of heart-stopping danger, of desperate heroism and gallant bravery, but they were long in the past, the sort of things that a fella could go for months or even years without thinking about too much. In short, there was nothing really special about him.

And yet, when push came to shove, when injustice had forced him into a corner, he had waded in and killed three men who were undoubtedly younger, quicker, stronger, and more ruthless than he was. How? *How?*

Stark lifted his hands from the steering wheel and held them in front of his face, staring at them in the light from the businesses that lined Hidalgo Street, turning them back and forth and studying them as if he would find the answers to all his questions engraved upon them in letters of fire.

But there was nothing there except dried bloodstains. Stark slowly closed his hands into fists and took a deep breath. He was all right now. For a second he had feared that he was going mad, but now he knew he was all right.

It was over. He had done what he could. Earlier he had thought that tonight's work was a good start, but he knew now that was it, the beginning and the end, the alpha and the omega. He prayed that Tommy was resting easier now. It was time for Stark to go home.

As it turned out, the customs agents on duty at the U.S. end of the bridge gave him no trouble at all about reentering the country. They just looked at his driver's license, glanced in the back of the pickup to make sure he wasn't hauling any obvious contraband, and waved him on through the checkpoint with a cheerful "Have a good night."

Too late for that, Stark thought as he drove away. A productive night, yes, but he didn't know that he'd call it good.

It took him half an hour to reach the ranch. During that time he pondered a question that he hadn't really considered before: what was he going to tell Elaine? He had been so caught up in figuring out what, if anything, he ought to do about Tommy's murder that he hadn't even thought about what he was going to tell his wife.

And he would have to tell her *something*. He couldn't come in wearing a different shirt, bruised and battered and with knife wounds on his arm and side, and expect Elaine just to ignore it. He knew her way too well for that.

The house was dark when he got there. That was unusual. Hard to believe with everything that had happened, but it really wasn't all that late. Stark felt a shiver of worry go through him when he saw that all the lights were out.

He brought the pickup to a halt in front of the house and was out the door almost before the engine stopped turning over. When he reached the steps, Elaine's voice came from the shadows along the porch. "No need to hurry, John Howard. I'm right here."

"Elaine," he said. "Are you all right?"

"Why wouldn't I be? I'm not the one who went off to do something stupid."

He saw that she was sitting in one of the rocking chairs. As he went toward her, he lifted a hand and said, "All the way home, I've been trying to figure out what I was going to say to you."

"Don't say anything," she told him. "Just stand there and let me look at you for a minute." Her voice trembled slightly as she added, "I was afraid I'd never see you again. Not alive, anyway."

If she had been sitting out here in the dark for a while, as Stark guessed she had, then her eyes were more adjusted than his were and she could see better. He couldn't make out the details of her face. All he knew was that she was sitting there hugging herself, staring up at him.

Finally she sighed and said, "All right. I've convinced myself that you're real and not just wishful thinking or a figment of my imagination. *Now* you can try to explain what the hell you were thinking when you went off like some sort of avenging angel. I warn you, though, I don't think you're going to be successful."

"Somebody had to," Stark said. "Hodge Purdee's hands are tied, and Hammond's worse than useless. He's actually on the other side. So it was up to me."

"You were the voice of reason last night, telling Devery and the others that they couldn't go after Ramirez no matter how much they wanted to. You told them they'd just get themselves killed. What happened, John Howard? What changed your mind? Or was it just an act all along? Did you intend to pull this Lone Ranger stunt right from the first?"

"I got an e-mail," Stark said.

"An e-mail?" Elaine's voice cracked a little. "My God, what sort of e-mail inspires you to go off and try to get yourself killed?"

"I wasn't trying to get myself killed," Stark said. "In fact, I did my damnedest not to. But that e-mail told me where I could find the three men who actually killed Tommy. Not Ramirez, who ordered it, but the men who carried out the order." He shrugged. "It was better than nothing."

She stood up and took a step toward him. "So you went after them." The words weren't a question.

"I had to. The e-mail was anonymous, but I figure Hodge Purdee sent it to me. He found out somehow who the men were, but he couldn't do anything about it. I could."

"Where did you go?"

"A club over in Acuna called the Blue Burro. A strip joint." Stark chuckled humorlessly. "But don't worry. I didn't look at the girls . . . much."

She stepped closer. "You . . . you idiot!" She punched him in the chest. Stark barely felt it. "You think I care whether or not you look at a bunch of strippers? You went there after some killers!"

"Found 'em, too," Stark said quietly.

"What happened?"

"I confronted them, their reaction told me that they really were mixed up in Tommy's killing, and there was a fight."

"You're lucky to be alive."

"I know that," Stark agreed. "They weren't that lucky."

Elaine stared at him for a long moment without speaking. Then she whispered, "Dead?"

"All three of them," Stark said.

She lowered her head. "My God," she breathed. "My God."

"It had to be done."

Elaine looked at him again. "Did people see you? Will the Mexican authorities be coming after you?"

"Plenty of people saw me, but I don't think I have anything to worry about from the police over there. As far as they're concerned, it was just a bar fight. People get killed in bar fights all the time. They're not going to press the investigation."

Of course, Stark thought, he had stood there in the Blue Burro and made it perfectly clear to everyone in earshot that it was much more than a bar fight. All those witnesses knew it was a personal vendetta. They knew as well that the three dead men worked for the Vulture. It was possible that the deaths wouldn't even be reported to the police.

But Ramirez would know. The word had probably gotten back to him already.

"Oh, John Howard," Elaine said. She came closer, and although he hated to hug her while he was wearing that filthy shirt, he put his arms around her and pulled her even closer.

"It's all right," he said. "It's all over now. Nothing more to worry about."

But there was plenty to worry about, he thought. What would Ramirez do when he heard about what had happened?

What had he done? Stark asked himself. What had he *done*?

Elaine put her arms around him and hugged him, and he flinched as she pressed against the wound in his side. Immediately she drew back in concern and said, "John Howard, you're hurt!"

"Not too bad," he assured her. "Just a little scratch in my side. There's one on my arm, too. You reckon you'd be up to doctoring them?"

"You come on in the house right now," she said briskly as she took hold of his hand. She led him to the front door but paused there to say, "Earlier tonight, when I figured out you were up to something dangerous, I asked Uncle Newt if he knew where you had gone. He just laughed and said something about the O.K. Corral. What did he mean by that?"

Stark laughed softly. "He's just a crazy old man, honey. Don't put too much stock in what he says."

They went on inside, to the bathroom upstairs where Stark took a shower, and then Elaine cleaned and disinfected and bandaged the cuts and said that they probably wouldn't need stitches but that he ought to have the doctor take a look at them just to be sure. Stark agreed that he would do that.

But all the time, Newt's comment about the O.K. Corral lingered in the back of his mind. Stark had read enough western history books to know that the famous shoot-out in which Wyatt Earp had been involved had taken place near the O.K. Corral but not actually in it. He also knew that the gun battle, epic though it had been, had not ended the violent clash between the two factions vying for control of Tombstone.

That day had been, in fact, not the end of the killing . . . but the beginning.

* * *

Normal people might have expected to find Ernesto Diego Espinoza Ramirez snorting cocaine or having sex with an underage girl—or two—or some other disgusting and depraved activity in which Colombian drug lords might indulge. But no one had ever accused Silencio Ryan of being normal, and besides, he had worked for Ramirez long enough to know his boss's habits. So he wasn't surprised to find Ramirez in the office, in front of the computer, going over a spreadsheet that detailed all the cartel's activities for the past year. A federal prosecutor would probably sell his mother into slavery for that file, but even if he got his hands on it, it wouldn't do him any good. There were so many levels of encryption that no one except Ramirez or one of his trusted—i.e., drug-addicted—technogeeks could ever retrieve any incriminating data.

It wasn't that Ramirez was immune to the charms of tender young female flesh; he wasn't. There were always girls around the place, and Ramirez indulged himself with them often. He never touched drugs himself, having seen with his own eyes the dangers of a dealer becoming his own best customer. And he liked working with the computer. Guns, knives, bombs, torture . . . these time-honored traditions of the drug-running business all had their places, of course, but this *was* the twenty-first century, after all.

Ramirez switched off the monitor as Ryan came into the office. Trusting Ryan with his life was one thing. Trusting him with confidential information was something else entirely. "Any leads on Carranza's wife and kids?" Ramirez asked casually.

"Not yet." The woman and the children had given the slip to the men who were watching Tomas Carranza's funeral, and so far they hadn't been located. That wouldn't have happened if Ryan had been handling the chore personally, but he had already handed it off to one of the Vulture's other men. To tell the truth, Ryan hadn't been working all that hard at finding Julie Carranza and her kids. He would have put bullets through their heads without hesitation if they were right there in front of him and Ramirez ordered him to do so, but he wasn't really all that interested in the job. If they escaped Ramirez's vengeance, it was all right with Ryan.

He had found something a lot more intriguing tonight.

"What have you been doing, then?" Ramirez asked, the question little more than an idle one.

"I went to the Blue Burro with Guzman, Mendez, and Canales."

Ramirez arched an eyebrow in surprise. "You went to a strip joint with some gunners? I didn't think you liked to associate with that type unless you were working, Silencio."

Ramirez didn't know Ryan's real first name, Simon. That was just fine with Ryan, and he intended to keep it that way. He shrugged and said, "They asked me to go out with them. I thought it might be good for morale."

That was a lie. Ryan had invited the three men to the Blue Burro. He knew they were good men, experienced gunners, and he would not have been surprised at all if they had killed John Howard Stark with ease. The fact that Stark had killed them and injured several other men spoke volumes about the big Texan and indicated that he was not a typical middle-aged rancher at all, which was exactly what Ryan had been trying to learn.

With Guzman, Mendes, and Canales dead, Ramirez would never know that Ryan was lying. Ryan felt no particular disloyalty in doing so. He had always followed his own path, done things his own way.

"So how was the Blue Burro?" asked Ramirez. "Any new girls that were particularly interesting?"

"Not really. But something happened while we were there."

"What's that?" Ramirez asked when Ryan paused.

"That fellow Stark showed up, picked a fight with Guzman and the others, and killed them all."

Ramirez started to nod, and Ryan realized that he hadn't really been paying attention. But then the shocking truth of what Ryan had said soaked in on Ramirez, and he started up out of his chair, eyes widening.

"What?" he shouted. "Stark . . . you say . . . killed them all!"

Ryan nodded. "That's right."

"He came in with a . . . a machine gun or something . . . ?"

"He had what looked like a piece of an old fence post with some barbed wire wrapped around one end of it," Ryan said, relishing the telling of it. "He laid into them, swinging that post like a baseball bat."

"*Dios mio*," Ramirez muttered as he sank back into his chair. "*Dios mio*. Alfonso will be upset. They were some of his best men. Stark killed them with nothing but a . . . a club?"

"I saw the whole thing."

Anger flashed in Ramirez's eyes. "And you did not step in to help them?"

Ryan allowed his voice to harden a bit as he replied, "You know our agreement, Senor Ramirez: I kill in defense of your life, my life, or on direct orders from you. Otherwise my conduct is left to my own discretion."

Ramirez was still mad, but he was in strict control of his emotions, at least where Ryan was concerned. Where Stark was concerned, it was different. Ramirez nodded and said, "Of course I trust your judgment, Silencio. I have ever since you came to work for me. But this man Stark, why would he do such an insane thing?"

"To avenge his friend's death, I assume."

"But he had to know that he would probably be killed!"

"Some men don't care about that," Ryan said. "They do what they think they have to do."

Ramirez slapped a hand on the desk beside the computer and came to his feet as his anger bubbled up. "That bastard! That no-good son of a whore! That gringo motherfucker!" The curses spewed out of him and became more obscene and blasphemous the longer he ranted. Caught up in rage, Ramirez grabbed some of the papers scattered on the desk and flung them across the room. "I want him dead, Silencio! You understand? I want him dead, and his wife, too, and his children and all his friends and anyone who has ever spoken a friendly word to him or had a good thought of him!"

That fierce, widespread hatred was part and parcel of Ramirez's Colombian heritage, Ryan thought. That was the way Ramirez and his countrymen in the drug business operated. That was why they were so feared.

Ryan just stood there and let Ramirez erupt for several minutes, and when the Vulture finally ran out of steam, he stared at Ryan and said, "You will take care of it, Silencio?"

"Of course," Ryan replied with a nod. "But I saw what Stark did tonight. It won't be easy to take him out."

Ramirez frowned. "The great Silencio Ryan says this? I thought there was no man you could not kill!"

"I can kill Stark," Ryan said with easy confidence. "I can kill his friends and family. His sons may take a while—they're both in the American military, serving overseas. But I'm sure they'll get compassionate leave to come home for their parents' funeral, and I can take care of them then."

Ramirez nodded. "Good, good."

"After tonight, though, Stark will be on his guard. He'll know that you'll send someone after him. So the best thing to do might be to try to draw him out in the open, where I can get at him easier. In order to do that, we should strike at his loved ones first. He won't stay hidden then."

"I trust you, Silencio. Handle this matter as you see fit. I make only one request, other than that Stark and those around him die."

"What's that?" Ryan asked, relatively sure that he already knew the answer.

Ramirez leaned forward and rested his hands on the desk. All his computer expertise and businessman's facade had vanished. At this moment he was nothing but an outlaw and a savage. His lips pulled back from his teeth in a snarl, and he said, "Make sure this man Stark truly suffers before he dies. Not like with Carranza. Simple torture was enough for the likes of him. Stark is different. I want him to suffer the torments of the damned."

Thirteen

Stark hurt like blazes when he woke up the next morning. Getting out of bed usually required a few grunts of effort since fifty-four-year-old muscles tended to stiffen up a little during the night, but this was different. He hadn't realized that he'd been banged up so much during the fight at the Blue Burro, over and above the knife wounds. After some groaning and cussing under his breath, he made it out of bed and into the bathroom. When he looked at his naked body in the mirror before climbing into the shower, he saw that it was mottled with livid bruises. Stark turned the water in the shower as hot as he could stand it and stood under the spray for a long time, letting the heat massage away some of the aches and ease others. At the same time he checked the gash on his arm and looked at the one on his side as best he could. While both wounds were painful, the flesh around them looked normal. There was no redness and swelling such as would have been present in the case of infection. Elaine had done a good job cleaning them.

He was thinking about that as the shower curtain rustled and moved back slightly. Stark took a sharply indrawn breath and turned more quickly than he would have thought possible, considering how stiff and sore he was.

But this was no threat. Instead, a nude Elaine stepped into the shower with him and closed the curtain again. She smiled up at him and said, "I thought you might want a little help, John Howard. Since you're stiff and all."

Stark felt the surge of blood into his penis as he looked at his naked wife, who was standing so close to him that the erect nipples of her breasts brushed against his lower chest. Elaine's body, though no longer that of a teenager, was still slender and fairly firm. He thought she was beautiful, and his erection agreed with him.

She reached down and clasped her hand loosely around his penis. "Just like I said," she murmured. "Stiff." She gave him a squeeze and then said, "Turn around."

"What?"

"Just turn around."

Stark did as she told him, and her hands touched his shoulders. She began massaging him with a firm, expert touch, kneading and stroking and rubbing muscles that were still tense even after a night's sleep. Stark felt relaxation spreading through him like a warm tide. The combination of hot water and his wife's loving touch was magnificent. Elaine worked her way down his back, lingering anywhere that her prodding produced a groan from Stark. She didn't move on until all the tension in those muscles had eased. She knelt to massage his buttocks and the backs of his thighs and slipped a hand between his legs to cup his scrotum for a moment. Stark's erection hardened even more. How could any man be so relaxed and so excited at the same time? he wondered.

Elaine stood up, kissed the back of his neck, and whispered in his ear, "I need you to make love to me, John Howard."

Stark turned toward her. She faced away from him, bent over slightly, and Stark took her from behind, clutching her trim hips. Elaine cried out softly as he penetrated her.

Time had not changed the way he felt about her. His passion for her was as strong as ever, and hers for him, too. The years fell away, like leaves plucked from a tree by an autumn wind.

"Rock Around the Clock" played on the radio, already an oldie; otherwise it wouldn't have been playing on XERF, the Mexican station across the river in Cuidad Acuna that blasted out a hundred thousand watts of clear channel power all across Texas and up through the Great Plains and the Midwest. On a good night, when the weather was just right, XERF boomed in for listeners in Chicago and Detroit and could be heard more faintly in Los Angeles and New York. John Howard Stark sometimes wondered if Wolfman Jack, the howling, fast-talking nighttime disc jockey on XERF, could be heard on the moon if there had been anybody there to listen to him. President Kennedy had said that the United States would put a man on the moon and return him safely by the end of the decade. There were still a few years to go on that deadline. Stark, lying in the back of a '48 Ford pickup, looked up at the moon and wondered what it would be like to walk on its surface. He wondered what the astronauts would find when they finally got there; a moon maid, maybe, like in that Edgar Rice Burroughs paperback he'd read not long before. The science textbooks said that gravity was a lot less on the moon than on Earth. Six times less, Stark thought. Did that mean that one of the three-hundred-fifty-foot home runs he had hit would travel over two thousand feet on the moon? That seemed logical enough to him, even though math and science had never been his strongest, or his favorite, subjects in school. He still did well enough in them to trust his calculations. Not that it really mattered, he thought, because it was highly unlikely that he would ever go to the moon, let alone hit a baseball on it. But if he ever did, boy, that sucker would be outta the park.

Stark thought a lot of things on that warm night. He had to keep his mind occupied so that he wouldn't think too much about the fact that his hands were filled with Elaine Parker's bare tits and that his dick was way up her pussy and she was riding him as if she were galloping toward the finish line in the Kentucky Derby and he was fucking the girl he loved, who just happened to be the head cheerleader, and he was fucking her like there was no tomorrow, which in fact there might not be, but Stark didn't want to think about that, either, so he looked at the moon and thought about how far you could hit a baseball on it, and then she cried out and he was coming, too, wrapping his arms around her and holding her so tightly, so close, moving so deeply inside her it seemed they were no longer two organisms but one instead.

It was the best feeling John Howard Stark had experienced in a little more than eighteen years of life.

Elaine gave a last little shudder as her orgasm faded. Still holding her tightly to him, Stark lay back on the thick pile of blankets in the back of the pickup and cuddled her on his chest. The clean scent of her thick blond hair filled his nostrils. He reached up with one hand and stroked it softly.

Both of them were breathless. Elaine's bare breasts were flattened against his chest now. He felt the rapid flutter of her heart.

She had unbuttoned her blouse and somehow gotten her bra off without removing the blouse. That seemed a little like magic to Stark. He'd wanted to say "Shazam!" when he saw her do it the first time, but she would have thought he was crazy. Anyway, he was too impressed by those firm globes of flesh with their large brown nipples to be thinking about comic book wizards or Gomer Pyle, either one.

They had been dating for eight months, since not long after senior year started, and Stark had seen her breasts plenty of times before. She had let him fondle them through her clothes on their fifth date and he'd been under her bra after a few more dates. She'd started that trick with taking the bra off after yet a few more dates. It was a natural progression. As the months passed they did a little more and a little more, and he felt the smooth cotton of her panties and then a few weeks later he slipped a finger under the edge of them and for the first time touched the mysterious wet heat that constantly occupied the thoughts of John Howard Stark and most other teenage boys on the planet.

Elaine was a more than willing participant. It wasn't long

before she was grabbing his hand and pulling it between her legs so that he could slip a finger or two inside her as they sat in his pickup under the stars after their dates. Nor was Stark the only one doing the caressing. After a little initial hesitation, Elaine grew quite bold about freeing his penis from the confining blue jeans he wore and stroking it until he groaned and spent in her soft palm. She even leaned over and took it in her mouth a few times, to Stark's amazement. He didn't think nice girls were supposed to do that, or even know that such a thing was possible, and he had a few bad moments when he wondered if she was really a whore, even though he had known her for years and years and had never heard anything remotely like that said about her. She was awkward enough at it, though, that he realized she was just as new to all this as he was, and when he finally, delicately, broached the subject, she had just smiled that shy, pretty smile of hers and said, "I thought you might like it, John Howard." Her voice dropped to a whisper. "I've heard that boys like it a lot."

Stark could have laughed and hugged her and said that oh yeah, did they! but instead he kissed her, softly and tenderly, and he knew that he was in love with this girl.

It hadn't all been about sex, of course. They had done a lot of other things. It took a while for new movies to reach Del Rio, but eventually they saw *The Graduate* and *Bonnie and Clyde* like everybody else. They went out to dinner and they crossed to Acuna and wandered around the big public market there, where Stark bought turquoise and hammered silver jewelry for Elaine and she bought him a big, goofy-looking sombrero that he wore anyway, and wore proudly because she got it for him. They saw each other at football, basketball, and baseball games, since Stark was a three-letter man and Elaine was, after all, the head cheerleader. They spent quite a few evenings at her house, helping each other with their homework or just watching TV. Elaine was a Methodist and Stark a Baptist, but somehow they managed to span the vast denominational differences between Sprinklers and Dunkers and often went to church together. Stark held her hand as they sat side by side on one of the hard pews, and he felt like the worst kind of hypocrite because there they were in church on Sunday morning when on Saturday night they'd been in his pickup masturbating each other for all they were worth. But they couldn't help it, and Stark could only hope that the Almighty was understanding about the fierce passions that burned within them. There was an old joke about how God must love poor people because he made so many of 'em. Stark fervently hoped the same thing was true when it came to horny teenagers.

But there was never any doubt in Stark's mind that he loved Elaine and she loved him. Earlier tonight, when she had whispered, "I want to do it. I want to go all the way with you, John Howard," he had nodded and asked her only if she was sure. She was.

So here they were, and although people said that the first time was sometimes awkward and even unsatisfying, with them it had been wonderful, glorious, better even than Stark had dreamed it would be . . . and he had dreamed about it plenty of times!

The only problem was, the timing wasn't all that good since he was leaving soon and didn't even know if he would ever see her again once he was gone.

Elaine lifted her head from his chest and reached up to kiss him. Her lips tasted as sweet as ever. She smiled down at him, and he wondered, as he often did, how she could look so wholesome and clean and innocent and yet be so damned sexy at the same time. She was close to the perfect woman. No, not close to it, he corrected himself. She *was* the perfect woman. Perfect for him, anyway.

So why was he even thinking about leaving her?

Honor. Duty. Love of country.

But those were just words, a part of him insisted. Words that didn't mean anything, especially when they were contrasted with the soft, warm, sleek reality of the young woman he held in his hands. What they had between them was the only thing that really mattered.

If he truly believed that, it would sure make things simpler, Stark thought. But he knew that the words *did* mean something. They were part of him, road signs on the map of his heart and soul, his conscience. He couldn't turn his back on them, no matter how much it was going to hurt when he left her.

"Elaine," he said as she looked down at him, "I'm joining the marines."

At first she didn't comprehend what he was telling her. He could tell that by the way she continued to smile. But then the smile began to go away, and a line appeared between her perfectly arched eyebrows, a line that turned into a frown.

"What?" she said as if she hadn't quite heard him.

"I'm joining the marines," he repeated. "I'm going next week to sign the enlistment papers."

"The . . . marines? But . . . you can't. You're not—"

She stopped short, and he knew she had been about to say that he wasn't old enough. He was, though. His eighteenth birthday had been two weeks earlier. In the past they had discussed what they would do if he was drafted, but no mention had been made of him enlisting voluntarily.

"I know this is a lousy time to bring it up—" he began.

"Yes," she broke in. "Yes, it is! My God, John Howard, we just . . . we just made love!" Tears welled from her eyes and began to roll down her cheeks. A couple of them fell on his face.

Stark tried again. "That isn't fair—"

"No, what isn't fair is that I love you, and you're talking about going away!" She pushed herself up into a sitting position beside him and turned her head away from him.

Stark sat up, too, and tried to touch her shoulder, but she flinched away. Without putting her bra on, she started buttoning her shirt.

"Well," Stark said, "that's not really what I expected of you."

She turned sharply toward him. "What *you* expected of *me*? Don't you dare act like I'm the one being unreasonable here, John Howard Stark! We talked about the war. We said if you were drafted, you'd have to go, no matter how much we'd hate being apart. You're no . . . no draft dodger, and I wouldn't love you if you were a coward! But to enlist . . . to put yourself in harm's way like that on purpose . . . i just don't understand it."

In harm's way . . . They had seen the movie of that title not long before. Stark never missed a John Wayne movie. That picture had been about a different war than the one now being fought in Southeast Asia, but still it had vividly demonstrated the bloody human toll that was paid whenever men took up arms against each other.

Stark said, "I've been thinking about it a lot—"

"Not enough!"

He pushed on doggedly. "I've been thinking about it a lot, and the reasons I could never dodge the draft are the same reasons I have to enlist. I love my country. We're trying to stop the spread of communism. That's important, Elaine."

"You're not convinced we're doing the right thing in Vietnam. You've said so yourself, John Howard."

"I'm not convinced we're fighting the war the right way. The politicians are too mixed up in it, and it seems like they don't even care whether we win or not. And those protesters!" A bitter anger came into his voice. "It's like they *want* us to lose! Their own country! Good Lord, what can they be thinking? Don't they know that the leaders in Hanoi and Peking and Moscow just love it when they see news footage of all the marching in the streets and waving signs? Why would they want to reach any kind of settlement with us when they know we've got this cancer growing inside us? They know that eventually the protesters and the politicians will win the war for them!"

Elaine looked at him coolly and asked, "So why are you

so determined to throw your life away in what you think is a lost cause?"

He stared at her for a long moment, blinked a couple of times, and said, "Sometimes lost causes are the only ones worth fighting for."

She hauled off and hit him, punched him hard in the chest. "Damn you!" she cried. "Don't you go quoting Jimmy Stewart to me! This isn't *Mr. Smith Goes to Washington*! It's Mr. Stark Goes to Saigon!"

Then she gave a little hiccupping sound that was half sob and half laugh, and she slumped forward into Stark's embrace and continued crying and laughing at the same time, and he held her and patted her back and knew exactly how she felt because he recognized the ludicrous tragedy of the situation, too. But that didn't change anything. He loved this young woman and wanted to spend the rest of his life with her. He loved his country and had to do right by it. Those two emotions were at odds, and there was no way to reconcile them.

"Look, there's no guarantee I'll be sent to Vietnam," he said. "I may wind up staying stateside for my whole hitch. Remember when we saw George Gobel on *The Tonight Show* and he was telling Johnny Carson about how he spent World War Two stationed in Oklahoma?"

"Yeah. He said . . ." Elaine straightened and wiped away some tears. "He said not one Japanese airplane ever made it past Tulsa."

"Maybe it'll be the same way with me."

"You don't really think that."

"Why not? There's no way of knowing."

She reached up and touched his face lightly with her fingertips. "You're determined to do this?"

"Yes. I am."

"Then you have to promise me something."

"Anything," Stark said.

"Promise me that you'll come back alive and whole and

that you'll marry me and we'll have a house full of children and live a long and happy life together."

"You're proposing to me?"

"No," she said as if she were trying to explain something simple to a particularly backward child. "You'll do that when you get back. Now, are you going to promise me or not?"

"I promise," Stark whispered.

"There's one more thing. . . ."

"Name it."

"You said you go to sign the papers next week?"

"That's right, and it'll be another week or so after that before I report for duty."

"Then we have about two weeks. Can you make love to me a hundred times between now and then?"

Stark felt a smile on his face. "I can try."

He had tried, too. Done his damnedest, in fact. But there just wasn't time. They managed to do it only sixty-two more times before he went off to that crazy little war.

He had wondered briefly at the time if she was trying to get pregnant, so that if he did wind up in Vietnam and was killed over there, she would have at least a part of him still with her in the form of a child. He never asked her if that had been her goal or not. But she wasn't pregnant when he left Del Rio. That part of it had to wait until he came back, alive and whole as promised, and began to fulfill the rest of his pledge to her. They were married, and while two sons didn't exactly constitute a house full of children, they were so loud and rambunctious and overflowing with life that sometimes they seemed like a houseful all by themselves. They were the only children John Howard and Elaine were blessed with, and it was fine. The long happy life together that she had demanded and that he had promised her had come about, the years flowing by, not by any means without bumps in the road, the small trials and tragedies that came to any family, luckily more than offset by the successes and the proud moments and most of all the love that was still there between them, strong and steady. Stark still loved Elaine as much as he ever had, the abiding love that was composed of friendship, trust, years of companionship and laughter and tears; and passion, oh yes, the passion was still there, and it flowed from Stark into her and from her back to him as they made love in the shower with the hot water pounding down on them and streaming over their bodies.

Funny thing. He didn't hurt at all anymore.

Fourteen

Newton Stark was up early, well before the sun, as usual. He had his own apartment in the bunkhouse with a little kitchen. While he was waiting for his coffee to brew he sat at the table and smoked the first cigarette of what would be two packs of filterless Camels before the day was over. He'd been smoking them for over sixty-five years and figured it was too late to quit now. Since he was well on the shady side of eighty, it appeared that they hadn't harmed him too much. Nor had the quart of bourbon he drank every day, starting with a healthy slug in his coffee. Folks on the television liked to pontificate about all the things that were bad for you. Don't smoke, don't drink, and you'll live longer. Stay out of the sun or you'll get skin cancer. Avoid red meat and fatty food and save your heart. Newt had been smoking and drinking and working outdoors for damn near seven decades, and he loved a thick steak burned black on the outside and still bleeding in the center, and he was still as spry as ever. Well, almost.

He was damned if he was gonna be put out to pasture. Give him a good mount, especially that ol' Biscuit horse of his, and he could still chouse cows out of the brush as well as anybody. Better'n most of the kids who passed for ranch hands these days, in fact. He was sure glad that John Howard was running things here on the ranch. The thought of doing a bunch of book work and dealing with cattle buyers and feed dealers and county agents and such-like just made shivers go through Newt's body. He wasn't made for that. He was made for riding the range, taking care of the stock in blistering heat and bone-numbing cold, working from can to can't, being the last to quit a chore and the first to buy the beer, as that LeDoux boy sang about in one of his songs. Fella was one of the few decent country-and-western singers left. The rest were a bunch o' sissified Nashville hat acts who'd probably never stepped in a pile o' cow shit in their whole damned lives. Newt took a deep drag on the Camel between his lips and got up to check the coffee.

Sometimes, when he was out riding a few miles north of the ranch house near a narrow draw that fed into the Devil's River, he would nudge ol' Biscuit into a gallop and race across the mostly flat landscape toward that draw. The first time he'd done that when Chaco was with him, the Mexican had thought he'd lost his mind and had galloped after him, yelling for him to stop. Newt never drew rein, though. He just reached up and jammed his high-crowned hat down tighter on his head so that it wouldn't blow off and let out a high-pitched cackle of laughter as he and Biscuit swept toward the draw, never slackening their pace.

Then at the last moment Biscuit would bunch his muscles and gather himself and launch out into the open air above that draw, sailing clear over it to land on the other side, his hooves throwing up a cloud of dust and grit. Newt was an old bachelor, but he had known women in his life, and that instant when he and Biscuit were suspended there, seemingly almost weightless, well, that was almost as good as Newt remembered sex being. As close as he was ever gonna come to it again, that was for damned sure.

That first time Chaco had witnessed the stunt, he had sat on the other side of the draw and hollered about how Newt was a crazy old man and could've killed himself. If Biscuit hadn't been able to make the jump, Newt would have broken every bone in his body when he and the horse crashed down into the draw, Chaco claimed.

Newt just set fire to a gasper, nodded toward the draw, which was eight feet wide and six feet deep, and said, "It ain't like we're jumpin' over the goddamned Grand Canyon, now, is it?"

That shut Chaco up. Now whenever he was around when Newt let out a whoop and took off for the draw, he just rolled his eyes and crossed himself, saying a prayer for his crazy gringo friend.

The coffee was almost ready. Newt turned on the little radio on a shelf over the counter. It was tuned to a station that played country oldies: George Jones, Loretta Lynn, Hank Snow, Porter Waggoner, Buck Jones, Hank Williams Jr., Roy Acuff . . . the real stuff. He fixed himself a bowl of Post Toasties with a banana sliced up on it and a piece of toast, the same breakfast he had eaten for more than sixty years. He was what they called a creature of habit and didn't give a damn if he was. He knew what he liked. Black coffee with that dollop of bourbon in it, cereal and toast, a few cigarettes, good music on the radio . . . that was the way a fella ought to start the day.

And so he did.

The sun still wasn't up when Newt walked out to the corral carrying his rope. He didn't really need it, since Biscuit would come right up to him if he just held out his hand and made a little clucking noise. But Newt liked the feel of shaking out a loop and twirling it over his head, and he liked to test his hand and his eye, too, by casting out that loop so that it sailed straight over Biscuit's head and settled down around the buckskin's neck. Maybe it was just a game, but he enjoyed it and Biscuit seemed to as well.

The sky blazed orange over a shallow butte to the east. A cool breeze blew as Newt got his old saddle on Biscuit. The summer heat would hammer down on Texas before the day was over, as usual, but right now the temperature wasn't bad. This was just about the most pleasant time of day, in fact, and so Newt always made sure that he was out and about by now, so that he could enjoy it.

Chaco came out of the bunkhouse and greeted Newt with a soft-voiced "*Hola, amigo. Buenas dias.*"

"Mornin' to you, too," Newt said. "Ready to ride? I thought we'd take a paseo up north today."

"Of course," Chaco said with a smile. He knew what Newt had in mind. It would be a good day for jumping over that draw and feeling fully alive again.

Chaco saddled a roan gelding from his string and swung up onto the animal's back. He was a spare little man with a narrow mustache and iron-gray hair cut short under his straw Stetson. He was probably the neatest sumbitch Newt had ever known, with his shirts and jeans always freshly laundered and pressed and a shine on his boots. Cowboyin' was dirty work, no doubt about it, and Chaco didn't hesitate to get right down in the mud and shit when that was needed, but all the rest of the time he was downright spiffy.

The two old men rode out just as the sun was peeking over the horizon. They headed northeast, working around in a wide circle that brought them to the boundary of the Diamond S. Then they cut west, checking the fences and making mental notes of the number of cattle and the condition of the animals they passed. They worked mostly in silence. They didn't need a lot of words. Men who rode together as long as Newt and Chaco had got to know each other almost as well as if they could read each other's mind.

In the middle of the morning, as was their habit, they stopped and ate some tortillas that Chaco had brought along in his saddlebags, rolled in tinfoil so that they had stayed warm. Newt had a thermos of coffee laced with bourbon. It was a good snack and would tide them over just fine until they got back to the house for lunch. They ate in the shade of a scrubby mesquite tree, hunkered on their heels. Their horses cropped peacefully at some grass that grew nearby.

When the break was over they rode west again, and Newt felt a familiar excitement stirring in him as they approached the draw. It had been more than a week since he'd been out here. So much had been going on, what with the Fourth of July celebration and then Tommy Carranza's terrible murder, that Newt hadn't been able to follow all of his usual routines. Now it was time.

Then Chaco had to go and ruin it by saying, "Some smoke over there, amigo."

Newt reined Biscuit to a halt, hipped around in the saddle, and looked where Chaco was pointing. Off to the southwest, a quarter of a mile or more distant, a narrow plume of smoke rose against the blue Texas sky. Newt frowned. As far as he knew, none of the other ranch hands were working in that area today. Even if they were, there was no reason for them to have built a fire. They weren't doing any branding at this time of year.

"We'd best go check it out," Newt said as he lifted the reins. "Whoever set that fire didn't have no right to do it. They're trespassin' on Diamond S range."

There had been no storms; the sky was clear and had been all night. So lightning strikes couldn't be blamed for the fire. Humans had to be responsible for it. Newt had a bad feeling about this, a mighty bad feeling. He heeled Biscuit into a trot.

Chaco rode beside him as they headed for the smoke. Newt hoped it wouldn't take too long to run off the varmints, whoever they were. Then he could get back to jumping his horse over that draw, like he had intended.

They came to a little creek, its banks dotted with mesquite and cottonwood, and followed it for a few hundred yards. The trail led around a bend, and there on the other side Newt and Chaco came in sight of the fire. A big red SUV was parked nearby, its tailgate open with a boom box sitting on it blasting out Tejano music. Four men stood by the fire, roasting large chunks of beef that still dripped blood. The blood sizzled as it dropped into the flames.

As if all that weren't surprising enough, Newt reined in sharply as he spotted the source of the beef. It was a freshly slaughtered cow, a Diamond S cow, that lay on its side by the creek, its throat cut. The steaks had been crudely hacked from its carcass. The gruesome wounds were covered with a black, roiling carpet of flies, as was the cow's slashed throat. Clearly, the trespassers meant to make a meal off the cow and then leave the rest of the carcass to rot.

"*Madre de Dios*," Chaco muttered as he brought his horse to a stop alongside Newt. "What have they done? Who are they?"

"Goddamn rustlers, that's who they are!" Outrage filled Newt. The idea that anybody would dare to come onto Diamond S range, slaughter a Diamond S cow, and then stand there calmly roasting hunks of it was almost too much for him to comprehend.

The strangers were Hispanic, all of them wearing Stetsons and jeans and khaki work shirts with the sleeves rolled up. They didn't seem surprised to see Newt and Chaco. One of them turned and grinned at the two old range riders. "*Hola, amigos!*" he called. "I would invite you to join us for lunch, but as you can see . . ." He waved a hand toward the slaughtered cow. "There is only enough for us."

"That ain't your cow, you son of a bitch," Newt barked. He was vaguely aware that beside him Chaco was making worried noises and trying to motion him away, but Newt ignored him. "You had no right to kill it!"

The spokesman, a short, stocky man with bulging muscles under the sleeves of his shirt, shrugged and said, "Go to hell, *viejo*. We do what we want and take what we want."

Newt's pulse pounded heavily inside his head. He couldn't remember the last time he'd been this mad. He wished he had his Colt double-action Peacemaker. The revolver was over a hundred years old but worked just as well as the day it had been manufactured. It had belonged to Newt's grandfather, and Newt had kept it in perfect condition. If he had it now, he'd do some damage, by God! But the Colt was back at the house. Newt never carried it anymore. It had seemed to him that the time for such things was past.

He had a .30-30 carbine in a saddle sheath, though, and so did Chaco. Any man with sense carried a varmint gun when he rode out on the range. Newt didn't think he'd ever seen any bigger varmints than the ones standing around that fire, laughing at him with shit-eatin' grins on their faces.

Before Newt could reach for the carbine, Chaco took hold of his arm and said urgently, "Come, Newt. We must get out of here."

Newt jerked his arm free from his friend's grip and said, "Damn it, I ain't goin' anywhere until I settle things with these sorry-ass rustlers!"

"Hey, I am insulted!" the spokesman said. "You keep calling us rustlers, old man, but we didn't steal no cows. It's no crime when you got to butcher a cow to eat."

"You don't look like you've missed many meals, fattie," Newt snarled.

The man glared. "You call me names now. I am getting tired of this, old man. You want to know who we are?" He thumped a fist lightly against his chest. "We work for *El Bruitre*. You know him?"

"I know who he is," Newt replied. "He's a piece of shit, and so are you. Now get off this range, and make it pronto!"

"We are not going anywhere until we finish our lunch," the man said coolly. "But you are."

"Newt . . ." Chaco said warningly.

Suddenly, Newt saw what was happening. While he'd been talking with the stocky drug runner, one of the other men had drifted over closer to the SUV. Now the man reached inside the back of the vehicle and took out a rifle, some sort of military weapon. He swung it toward Newt as the old cowboy made a lunging grab at the stock of the carbine.

The rifle cracked while Newt was still trying to pull the carbine from its sheath. He felt a heavy blow against his chest that knocked him backward. Before he knew what was happening, he had tumbled out of the saddle and thudded to the ground. His left foot was still in the stirrup, but Biscuit didn't bolt. The horse was too well trained for that.

"Newt! Amigo!" Chaco cried.

The Mexican ranch hand didn't try to pull his carbine. He leaped down from the saddle instead and ran around Biscuit to reach Newt's side. He jerked Newt's foot from the stirrup and dropped to one knee beside him.

Newt was aware that he had been shot, but he didn't feel much pain. Instead he was just sort of numb and shocked, with only a few little jabs of pain beginning to creep in around the edges of his consciousness. His hat had come off when he fell, and he missed its broad brim shading his face. The sun was bright and shone in his eyes, annoying him. It was a relief when Chaco leaned over him, blocking out the glare.

"Lie still, Newt," Chaco said. "I will get help."

"You will get nothing, *viejo*," said the stocky drug runner, "except perhaps a grave next to this worthless old fool."

Chaco came up out of his crouch, turning as he did so. But as soon as he came around, a shotgun roared and a double charge of buckshot tore into his chest. The impact of the terrible blast threw him backward. He landed next to Newt, his chest shredded and blown open. His back arched once as a gurgling, incoherent cry came from his throat, and then he sagged loosely into death's embrace.

The four men gathered around Newt and Chaco. "You ruined our lunch, old man," the spokesman said. "You got what you deserve. You'll be dead soon, and as you die, remember who killed you."

Newt's tongue came out and rasped over dry lips. "You . . . polecats," he husked. "Go to . . . hell . . ."

He tried to get up but couldn't do it. A vast weakness had stolen over him. He knew he had only minutes, perhaps just seconds, to live.

Dying wasn't so bad. He'd made his peace with that prospect a long time ago. But it bothered the hell out of him that he'd let himself be killed by low-class trash like these drug runners. He had always figured he'd be crushed by a maddened bull or bit by a rattlesnake or trampled in a stampede or hit by lightning on some lonely range. To be shot by a common criminal . . . well, it just wasn't fittin'.

And even worse, they had killed Chaco, too. His oldest and best friend in the world. Newt had heard Chaco's last breath and recognized it for what it was.

Well, he thought, the world wasn't worth livin' in anyway with Chaco gone. What really worried Newt now was what was going to happen to John Howard and Elaine. Ramirez must have sent his boys up here to strike at the family on account of what John Howard had done down in Acuna the night before. He had been listening from the shadows and had heard enough of what the boy had told Elaine when he got back. That had taken *cojones*, goin' after those three killers like that. But at the same time, maybe it hadn't been the smartest thing in the world to do. It had made the Stark family a bad enemy. *Muy malo*. Killing him and Chaco was probably just the start of Ramirez's vengeance.

But Ramirez might have broke off a bigger chunk of hell than he realized. Being a criminal and a thug, Ramirez had no respect for a common, ordinary, law-abiding man. He didn't know just how dangerous such an hombre could be when he was riled up enough.

Newt heard coarse laughter, followed by the sound of the SUV's engine starting up. It drove away with a spurt of gravel and dirt from the wheels. Where had the sun gone? Newt couldn't see it anymore. And the midday heat had vanished as well, to be replaced by a creeping coldness.

He laughed. "This is what it feels like to die, you dumb old coot," he said aloud. Or maybe he just thought it. He really didn't know.

Something nudged his arm. With an effort, he turned his

head and looked up to see Biscuit standing beside him, head lowered. The horse nudged him again with its muzzle.

"Sorry, fella," Newt rasped. "We ain't gonna . . . jump the draw today. . . . I got a heap bigger . . . jump to make . . . all the way outta this world. . . ."

Fifteen

Stark was on his way out to the barn when he heard the distant crack of a rifle shot. It wasn't that unusual to hear such a shot; one of the hands could have killed a rattlesnake or chased off a coyote—the four-legged kind. But something about the shot didn't sound quite right to Stark. He knew from talking to some of the hands that Newt and Chaco had set off in that direction early that morning, and both of the old-timers carried .30-30s. The shot Stark had just heard sounded more like it came from a higher-powered weapon.

When it was followed after about a minute, while Stark was still staring off to the north with a frown, by the dull boom of a shotgun blast, he knew something was wrong. Nobody who had any business being up there would have fired off a shotgun. As far as Stark knew, Newt and Chaco were the only ones on that part of the ranch this morning.

Fear stabbed him in the chest like a physical pain. Something was wrong, bad wrong.

He turned and ran for the house, yelling, "Elaine! Elaine!"

She slammed out the front door before he got there, wearing jeans and a sleeveless blouse. Her eyes were wide with surprise and worry. "John Howard!" she said. "What's wrong?"

Stark was thinking rapidly. Elaine was just as good a driver as he was, if not better. "Get the truck!" he said as he bolted past her. "Somebody's shooting up in the north pasture!"

Calling the northern reaches of the ranch a pasture was putting it mildly. The Diamond S covered a lot of square miles. But Stark knew every foot of it, and he thought he could drive to within a few hundred yards of the place those shots had come from. He could navigate, rather, since he wanted Elaine to drive.

He figured he might be too busy to handle the wheel . . . too busy with the guns he grabbed from the rack in the den.

He took down the pistol his father had carried as an officer in World War II, the standard-issue Colt Model 1911A, which was still one of the best handguns ever made. Stark kept it in excellent working condition and had practiced with it ever since he was a young man. He took a loaded clip from a desk drawer and rammed it home but didn't work the slide, leaving the chamber empty. He stuck two more clips in his pocket. Then he grabbed a couple of shotguns and a box of shells and ran outside with them just as Elaine pulled up in the truck, stopping short in front of the house so that dust billowed up from the wheels.

Stark ran through the dust, yanked the passenger door open, and piled in. "You know where that draw is that Uncle Newt likes to jump Biscuit over?" he asked.

Elaine nodded.

"Head for it as fast as you can!"

Chaco had told them about Newt's antics, probably hoping that Stark would somehow put a stop to them. But Stark knew his uncle too well to think that anything he could say would stop the old man from doing what he wanted to do. That just wasn't the way Newt operated. He was too stubborn to be bossed around, and that was how he regarded even a suggestion that he might change his behavior. He was as stiff-necked as any mule Stark had ever seen.

But that didn't mean he was crazy, despite the fact that he sometimes acted like it and even seemed to revel in that perception. Newt was hardheaded and practical at heart, and he wouldn't attempt anything he knew he couldn't do.

Stark loved the old man and hoped he was all right. But those shots were mighty worrisome. They hadn't come *from* Newt and Chaco, so the most logical explanation for them was that somebody was shooting *at* the old-timers.

Elaine knew the ranch trails as well as Stark did. She had ridden all of them herself, almost as much at home in a saddle as her husband and his uncle. Some of them were more difficult to negotiate in the pickup than they were on horseback, but she managed. They came to the creek that meandered through that part of the ranch, and Stark said, "Turn right. Follow the creek."

Elaine jabbed the brake, spun the wheel, stomped on the gas. "What's going on, John Howard?" she asked. "Why are we doing this?"

"I think somebody was shooting at Newt and Chaco a while ago."

"Shooting—My God!" Her eyes widened even more, but she didn't take them off the trail in front of the pickup. "Ramirez?"

"I don't know," Stark said grimly. He was afraid they were going to find out.

He saw smoke up ahead, on the other side of a bend in the creek. That was a sign of trouble, too. There shouldn't be a fire up here. Elaine sent the pickup rocking around the bend.

"Stop!" Stark yelled.

On the way out here he had loaded both shotguns. He thrust one of them into Elaine's hands now and said, "Anybody comes at you that you don't know, don't hesitate. Just shoot!"

With that he piled out the other side of the truck and started running toward the sprawled shapes beside the creek. Two of them were human, the third a butchered cow. As soon as Stark had seen the two men lying on the ground, not far from the small fire, he had known what he was going to find, even though a part of him rebelled at the very idea. The two horses, standing nervously nearby, were all the proof he needed, though. One of them was Biscuit, the other an animal that Chaco often rode.

His hands tightened on the shotgun as he saw the bloody ruin of Chaco's chest. The old Mexican was dead, no doubt about that. Newt had been shot in the chest, too, but there wasn't as much blood. That told Stark that Newt had been shot first—with the rifle Stark had heard—and then Chaco had been cut down by the shotgun blast when he ran to help his longtime friend.

Stark held out a bare hope that Newt might still be alive. He dropped to both knees beside his uncle and set the shotgun aside so that he could check for a pulse in Newt's neck. The .45 was handy behind his belt if he needed a weapon in a hurry.

Stark's fingers probed at the old man's stringy neck. Newt's eyes were closed, and he certainly looked dead. To Stark's surprise, he found a tiny thread of a heartbeat pulsing feebly and raggedly through Newt's arteries.

"Newt!" Stark said. "Newt, can you hear me?"

"John Howard," Elaine said from behind him as she left the pickup and approached the bodies, "I think he must be dead—"

"No, he's not! He's got a pulse!"

Stark ripped Newt's shirt open, exposing the red-rimmed bullet hole in his chest. The wound hadn't bled much, but a wound in that area didn't have to in order to be fatal, Stark recalled from Vietnam. Sometimes a man who had looked like he was barely injured had died from such a wound in a matter of minutes, while another man who appeared to have been shot to pieces survived. You just couldn't tell.

"Get back to the house and call for help, Elaine."

"I'll do no such thing! The men who did this might come back."

"All the more reason for you to go."

"Forget it, John Howard. I'm here, and here I'll stay as long as you do."

"Damn it, at least go back to the truck and call nine-one-one!"

"Oh," she said, remembering that there was a cell phone in the pickup. "Yes, I can do that." She turned and ran to the truck.

"Are you two . . . gonna fuss all day?"

The raspy whisper took Stark by surprise. When he looked at Newt's face, he saw that the old man's rheumy eyes were open now. Open, and filled with pain.

"Hang on, Newt," Stark said as he leaned over him. "We'll get you some help, get you to the hospital."

"Don't be . . . a damn fool, boy . . . I'm too far gone. . . . Ain't nobody who can . . . help me now."

"You don't know that," Stark insisted.

Newt coughed, and his eyes closed for a moment. When they opened again, Stark saw even more pain there.

"I damn sure . . . do know it," Newt said. "Listen . . . to me, boy."

Stark leaned closer. "Who did this?"

"That's what I'm . . . tryin' to tell you. . . . *El Bruitre* . . . the Vulture . . . some o' his men . . ."

"They told you who they were?"

"They was . . . proud of it. . . . Damn skunks . . . Wish I could'a . . . ventilated one or two of 'em. . . ."

"Take it easy now," Stark said. "We'll take care of you, Newt."

"Chaco . . . see to Chaco!" The old man lifted his head as he spoke vehemently.

Stark took hold of his gnarled hand. "Of course. Don't you worry about that, Newt. We'll see to it."

Newt lay back and closed his eyes again. A long sigh came from him, and for a second Stark thought that his soul had departed with that sigh. But Newt had one more thing to say, and his hand tightened on Stark's hand as he did so.

"John Howard . . . avenge me."

"I will, Newt," Stark pledged. "You got my word on it."

But now it really was too late. Newton Stark was gone. The withered chest fell, never to rise again.

"Oh, John Howard," Elaine said, having returned from the truck. "I'm so sorry."

Stark laid his uncle's hand on his breast, then brought the other hand over to join it. "So am I," he said with his head down in a prayerful attitude. Then, slowly, his head came up, and he said, "But not as sorry as the bastards who did this are going to be."

He got to his feet. Elaine took a step toward him, her hand outstretched. "I've called nine-one-one," she said. "Let the authorities handle this."

Stark was looking around. He spotted tire tracks nearby and walked over to look at them. The tracks indicated good-sized tires. A pickup or an SUV, he thought. The men who had butchered the cow and then slaughtered Newt and Chaco must have driven off in it.

"The sheriff's office will get the call," he said. "You know what that means. Hammond will come out, and he'll make the proper noises but nothing will really get done. He won't even try to find the men who did this."

"You don't know that."

Stark nodded. "Yes, I do, and you do, too. Wishing it was different won't change anything." He turned and started toward the pickup.

She caught hold of his arm as he went by, stopping him. "What are you going to do?" she asked tensely.

"Go after them."

"They've been gone from here for at least fifteen or twenty minutes. You can't catch up to them now."

"I can try," Stark said. "Stay here and wait for the sheriff." Stark's tone made it clear what he thought of Norval Lee Hammond.

"The hell with that," Elaine said, looking up into his eyes. "I'm going with you."

Stark opened his mouth to argue with her, but then he realized that she was probably right about not being able to catch up to the killers. In that case, she wouldn't be putting herself in danger by going along. Even though he held out little hope of catching the men, Stark wanted to trail them and see where they had gone. It might help in identifying them later.

"All right," he said with a nod. He glanced at the bodies of Newt and Chaco. He hated to leave them here unattended, but there seemed to be no choice. "Come on."

They got into the pickup. Elaine had left the engine idling, so all she had to do was shift into gear and press the gas. The rugged old work truck took off, following the tire tracks alongside the creek.

The killers had gotten in here, so they shouldn't have had any trouble finding their way back out. Stark peered through the windshield at the tracks and picked out two sets of them, one coming and one going. The killers had followed the creek for a while, then veered off to the southeast. Stark wondered if they had cut some fence or shot the lock off a gate in order to get onto the Diamond S. It didn't really matter, of course, how they had gotten onto his range. What was important was what they had done once they were here.

They were going to pay for it, Stark vowed, just like the murderers of Tommy Carranza had paid for their crime.

As he looked out across the rolling, brush-covered hills that formed this part of his ranch, Stark's eyes suddenly caught a flash of red where nothing that color should have been. He leaned forward excitedly. "I think I saw them," he said.

"Where?" Elaine asked.

"Over there not far from Espantosa Arroyo. Something must have happened to delay them."

Elaine glanced over at him. "I can take a shortcut that'll get us there quicker if you're sure it's them, John Howard. But it'll mean abandoning these tracks."

Stark considered rapidly. "The way the trail's liable to wind around, they'd be gone by the time we got there if we keep following the tracks. Take the shortcut."

"Damn straight," Elaine said as she punched the gas. The truck lunged forward, picking up speed.

Stark's fingers opened and closed on the stock of the shotgun in his lap. He hoped he had guessed right.

With Elaine at the wheel, the pickup roared along dry washes and climbed rocky ridges. A couple of times as it topped a rise, it came down hard, putting a strain on the shocks. Everything held together, though, and faster than most people would have thought possible, they were closing in on the spot where Stark had seen something. He leaned forward again and peered through the glass.

"There!" he suddenly exclaimed, pointing. Three hundred yards away, across a shallow valley, a red SUV sat with its tailgate open and several men scurrying around it. "They had a flat! They're just putting the bad tire in the back and getting ready to go!"

Sure enough, seconds later the men hurriedly got back into the SUV, and it took off with its tires skidding on the gravel and its rear end fishtailing. They had seen the pickup coming after them.

Elaine almost floored the accelerator as she started across the valley. "How can you be sure it's them, John Howard?" she asked.

"Who else would be out here on our range, running away from us?" Stark replied. "There's no doubt in my mind."

But far in the back of it, there was. The overwhelming likelihood was that the SUV belonged to the men who had killed Newt and Chaco. But that could be joyriding kids up there, or somebody else who didn't belong on the Diamond S but wasn't a killer. He couldn't just start blazing away when he and Elaine caught up to the SUV, he told himself. He would have to make sure its occupants were really the men they were after.

But they *would* catch up, he told himself. Providence had given them this chance, and they weren't going to blow it.

The SUV disappeared over the rim of the valley. The driver was forced to take it easy now. If another tire blew, they would be stuck. Elaine could afford to take a few more chances, even though if anything happened to the pickup, she and Stark would lose their chance to overtake the other vehicle.

Stark had confidence in his wife's driving and in the sturdy old work truck. He took shotgun shells from the box of ammunition and stuffed them in his pockets.

They were nearing the boundaries of his ranch. Stark knew that and wanted to catch up to the SUV while they were still on Diamond S range. It was beginning to look like that would be impossible, though. The fence was less than half a mile away now. Elaine had cut the gap between the two vehicles down to about a hundred and fifty yards, but Stark didn't think she would be able to catch the SUV before it reached the fence.

Suddenly he saw a flash from the back of the SUV, followed by a couple more. Something hit the roof of the pickup right over his head and ricocheted off. "Oh my God!" Elaine yelped. "They're shooting at us!"

She didn't let off on the gas, though. She kept the pickup rocketing after the SUV.

Stark bit back a curse. Now any doubts in his mind had been erased. Those men had high-powered rifles, just like the one he'd heard, the one that had taken his uncle's life. Those were some of Ramirez's drug runners and hired killers. Righteous anger filled Stark to overflowing.

He wasn't so angry, though, that he forgot about his wife's safety. "Slow down," he said to Elaine. "We can describe their vehicle now. I was even able to make out some of the letters on the license plate. We'll turn the information over to the law."

"The hell with that!" she said. "Newt told you to get 'em, John Howard, and that's just what we're gonna do!"

He had never seen her this way before, as caught up in the rage and excitement of the moment as he was. He knew what happened to men in combat, the way chemicals flooded their bloodstream and made them forget all about fear, so that all they knew was forging straight ahead and taking the fight to the enemy. Obviously, women weren't immune to that, either.

He thought about reaching over and stomping his own foot on the brake as he grabbed the wheel from her. But if he did, he knew she would never forgive him for letting the killers go just because he was worried about her safety. Stark couldn't bring himself to do it.

"Keep your head down as much as you can," he said. "And get me close enough for a good shot at those sons of bitches."

He saw the fence up ahead. Sure enough, there was a gap in it where the wire had been cut. The SUV careened through the opening and onto the two-lane blacktop of the river road. The pickup shot through the gap fifty yards behind the SUV.

Elaine spun the wheel and sent the truck sliding onto the highway..The SUV had a powerful engine and was pulling away, but as she pressed the gas pedal all the way to the floor, the pickup began to cut the gap again. Pete Stark was as good a mechanic as could be found in Texas, and during his last leave he had tuned up all the vehicles on the ranch and gotten them in peak working condition, despite their battered exteriors. He had even rebuilt some of the engines.

The men in the SUV had opened the tailgate window and fired out of it again now. Stark saw sparks fly as a bullet spanged off the truck's right front fender. So far the accuracy of the gunmen wasn't very good. They outnumbered their pursuers, though. Stark and Elaine were close enough now so that Stark could count four men in the vehicle.

"Swerve into the other lane!" he called to Elaine over the roar of the engine. She twisted the wheel without hesitation, sending the truck over into the oncoming lane, which luckily was empty of traffic at the moment. Stark hadn't seen another car on the road, which was a good thing considering what was about to happen.

He leaned out the passenger-side window and brought the shotgun to his shoulder. The SUV was about ten yards in front of the pickup. Stark fired one barrel and had the satisfaction of seeing the SUV's left rear tire shred as the charge of buckshot tore into it. More sparks flew as the wheel rim hit the road. More muzzle flashes came from inside the SUV, but Stark didn't think any of the bullets came close to the pickup. The SUV was jolting and weaving around too much for any sort of accurate aiming.

"Back over!" he shouted at Elaine, and as she instantly responded, the pickup moved toward the shoulder again. Stark fired the second barrel and took out the right rear tire. The rim hit the road with a scraping screech that was enough to put a man's teeth on edge. The wildly fishtailing rear end drifted off the pavement, and the rim dug deep into the gravel shoulder. The rear end slid farther in that direction.

Stark knew what was going to happen if that kept up, and suddenly it did. The SUV was airborne, turning in the air as its high center of gravity caused it to flip. It slammed down on its roof, partially crumpling it, and bounced even higher in the air. Once, twice, three times the SUV rolled, doing more damage each time it landed for a split second between flips. With a shriek of brakes, Elaine brought the pickup to a stop so that she and Stark could watch the crash.

The SUV, bent and crumpled until it hardly resembled itself, came to rest upright on its wheels. Only a couple of seconds ticked by before flames burst out underneath it. Two of the doors opened, one of them kicked open desperately by the man who tumbled out through it. He and his companion stumbled away from the wreck, moving just fast enough to put a little distance between themselves and the SUV before the vehicle went up in a fiery explosion that threw the men facedown on the road.

Stark opened the passenger door and stepped out of the truck.

He heard Elaine calling his name as he strode toward the two men, but he didn't pause or look back. He had picked up the second shotgun and held it at his hip, ready to fire. The SUV was an inferno now, fierce flames shooting out of its windows. If the other two men had survived the rollover, they certainly hadn't survived the gas tank blowing up. They would be well roasted by now.

The two on the road were burned and bloody and wracked by coughing, but they managed to struggle to their feet. One of them still held a pistol in his hand. The other man had been carrying a rifle. It had fallen beside him when the force of the blast knocked him down.

The man with the pistol looked up, saw Stark approaching, and brought the weapon up. Stark didn't give him a chance to fire. He touched off the right barrel of the shotgun first. The buckshot smashed into the man, lifting him off his feet and tossing him backward . . . much like Chaco must have been killed, Stark thought.

The other man made a dive for the rifle. Stark fired the shotgun's second barrel. The charge practically tore off the man's right arm and sent him rolling across the ground, away from the rifle. Stark walked closer. As badly wounded as the second man was, he might live long enough to be questioned. Stark would insist on it, in fact. He wanted it on record that Ramirez was behind what had happened this morning. Maybe Hammond wouldn't be able to ignore *that*.

The wounded man was still alive, all right, alive enough to use his left hand to grab the pistol his companion had dropped. The man came up on his knees and screamed curses in Spanish at Stark as he tried to bring the gun to bear.

Stark dropped the shotgun, which he hadn't reloaded right away, an oversight that might cost him his life. He snatched the Colt Model 1911A from behind his belt, remembering that he hadn't worked the slide, and racked a cartridge into the chamber. His right hand squeezed the checkered grip as his left grasped the slide and shoved it back. The surviving killer fired, the bullet kicking off the blacktop at Stark's feet. Stark extended his arm, lined up the blade sight on the front of the barrel, and fired. The bullet caught the man just above the left eye. It shattered the skull and bored on through his brain before exploding out the back of his head. The man flopped backward, already dead even though the twitching nerves in his arms and legs didn't know it yet.

"John Howard!" Elaine cried as she came running up behind him. "John Howard, are you all right?"

Stark lowered the Colt, turned to his wife, and slid his left arm around her shoulders. "I'm fine," he said as he hugged her to him. "How about you?"

"Not a scratch," she told him, to his great relief. "What about . . . them?"

"They're all dead," Stark said.

The SUV continued to burn, the flames crackling almost merrily now. Somewhere in the distance, sirens wailed.

Sixteen

The burning SUV sent up a dense column of black smoke, more than enough to draw the attention of the sheriff's deputies who were already on their way out in response to Elaine's 911 call. Only a few minutes later, a cruiser pulled up on the edge of the road a hundred yards away, and two deputies leaped out, running toward Stark and Elaine with their pistols drawn. Stark stepped away from his wife and held his arms out to his sides, making sure that the deputies saw his hands were empty. He had already placed the .45 on the ground at his feet.

"What happened?" one of the deputies yelled. He was young and nervous, a dangerous combination.

"I'm John Howard Stark, the owner of the Diamond S," Stark said, speaking as calmly as possible, hoping the attitude was contagious. "This is my wife, Elaine. She called in about the murders of my uncle and one of our ranch hands."

"Yeah, there are units on their way out there now," the other deputy said. He was a little older, a little less shook-up by the sight of the blazing SUV and the sprawled bodies. "We were running backup for them when we saw this smoke and figured we'd better take a look."

Stark inclined his head toward the burning wreck. "Those

are the men who killed Newt and Chaco. We followed them, caught up to them, and then they tried to kill us."

"Looks like it backfired on them," the older deputy said dryly.

"We defended ourselves," Stark declared.

"Maybe so, mister, but why don't you and the lady go over there and sit down until the sheriff gets here? He'll sort out all of this."

Hammond couldn't sort shit from Shinola, Stark thought, but he kept that to himself. He and Elaine sat down on the running board of the old truck, grateful for the shade that the pickup's body provided.

The older deputy went back to the car to call for help on the radio, while the younger one stood there staring at the bodies and the burning SUV. He didn't bother getting the fire extinguisher from the cruiser. The SUV was too far gone and would just have to burn itself out. With its lying on the pavement like it was, it was unlikely the flames would spread to the grass beyond the bar ditches.

"What'll happen now, John Howard?" Elaine asked quietly.

Stark shook his head. "I don't know."

"Will we be in trouble with the law for this?"

"I don't see how. We acted in self-defense. Just to be sure, though, I'm not saying anything else until I've had a chance to talk to Sam Gonzales."

Gonzales was the Stark family lawyer, the sort of attorney who handled wills and trusts and the occasional minor lawsuit. He wasn't a criminal defense attorney. But Stark trusted his judgment and knew that Sam would look out for their interests. If he couldn't, he would find someone who could.

Twenty minutes later, after the deputies had turned away traffic from both directions, Stark spotted a black Blazer with Mars lights on its roof coming toward them from the direction of Del Rio. That would be Sheriff Hammond, he thought, and a few moments later he saw that he was right.

The Blazer came to a stop and Hammond climbed out, moving heavily and stiffly. He came toward the pickup with an unreadable expression on his face.

Stark stood up to meet him but motioned for Elaine to stay seated. "Sheriff," Stark said with a curt nod.

Hammond ignored Stark and looked at Elaine. He lifted a finger to the brim of his Stetson and said politely, "Ma'am."

"Hello, Sheriff," she said.

Hammond shifted his gaze back to Stark. "Looks like a battlefield out here," he said.

"That's about what it amounts to," Stark agreed. "You heard what happened to my uncle and Chaco Hernandez?"

"I heard. That's where I was headed when the call came over the radio about this. What did you do, Stark? Take the law into your own hands?"

Stark had vowed to himself that he would stay calm and not let Hammond get under his skin, but that was mighty hard to do in the face of the lawman's arrogance. Bristling a little, Stark said, "I did what anybody would do under the same circumstances: I went after the men who killed my uncle and my friend."

"That's not your job," Hammond snapped. "It's up to the proper authorities to deal with criminals."

"You can still deal with them," Stark said. "You can put them in body bags and haul them off."

Hammond grunted angrily. "You killed them all?"

"I don't think I'll be making an official statement just yet, Sheriff. Not until I've talked to my lawyer."

"Got something to hide, do you?"

Stark just smiled, not rising to the bait. "No comment."

Hammond stepped closer, his face red, as he obviously battled with his own temper. "Damn it, Stark, every time I see you lately, somebody's dead. I'm gettin' mighty tired of it."

Stark returned the sheriff's angry stare. "Not as tired as I am."

The two men faced off for a long moment, and then

Hammond said, "All right, if that's the way you want it, you're under arrest for manslaughter, Stark. I've heard enough to justify that."

"Arrest!" Elaine exclaimed. "Sheriff, you can't be serious! We didn't do anything wrong—"

Stark motioned for her to be quiet, and Hammond said, "Be glad you're not under arrest, too, ma'am. But I reckon you were just doing what this crazy husband of yours forced you to do."

For a second Stark was afraid Elaine was going to come up off that running board and go after Hammond, and he was ready to get in her way and hold her back if she tried it. The last thing they needed right now was for her to wind up behind bars, too. He needed her on the outside to get in touch with Sam Gonzales as soon as possible and get started on a legal solution to this madness.

Luckily, the same thoughts must have gone through Elaine's head, because she stayed where she was. From the look in her eyes, though, she would have cheerfully carved Hammond a new one if given half a chance.

Stark was still a little stunned and disbelieving that Hammond would arrest him, but now that he thought about it, the move made sense. Those were Ramirez's men lying dead in the road and burned up in the SUV, and Hammond was being paid off by Ramirez. He would want to demonstrate to the Vulture that he was looking out for Ramirez's best interests.

Stark suddenly worried that if he was taken to the Val Verde County Jail, he might never come out of it alive. There were all kinds of ways a man could die while in police custody: an arranged fight in the lockup, a faked escape attempt, even a suicide that was really anything but. Hammond might think it would really be a feather in his cap where Ramirez was concerned if he could get rid of Stark without any suspicion falling on the Vulture himself.

On the other hand, if Ramirez wanted Stark dead, as seemed very likely, he would probably want everyone to know that he was responsible. Ruthlessly crushing his enemies and their families just added to Ramirez's mystique and power. But would Hammond realize that, or would he try to curry favor by getting rid of Stark right away?

There was no way of knowing, but Stark knew he would need to be on his toes from here on out. He couldn't afford to let his guard down even for a minute.

Those thoughts flashed through Stark's mind as Hammond continued, "Turn around and put your hands behind your back, Stark. You'll have to be cuffed."

Stark complied with the order. Hammond snapped the cuffs on him. It was a humiliating feeling, and Stark grated his teeth together in anger and frustration.

"Get hold of Sam and have him meet us at the jail," Stark said as he looked down at Elaine. She nodded in understanding. "And call the ranch and get somebody out there to see to Newt and Chaco."

"No need for that," Hammond said. "My men are already on the scene. The medical examiner will take custody of the bodies."

Stark looked around at the sheriff. "They'd better be treated right."

"Don't you worry about that," Hammond said. "You got bigger problems on your plate right now, Stark."

Stark was put into the backseat of Hammond's Blazer with a deputy to guard him. The sheriff drove back to Del Rio. When they got to the sprawling complex that made up the sheriff's office and jail, Stark saw that Elaine had done what he asked of her. Sam Gonzales was waiting on the steps outside the entrance.

Gonzales was a stocky man in his fifties with prominent ears and close-cut gray hair. He was in shirtsleeves, with his tie loosened against the heat. As Stark was taken out of the backseat of the Blazer, Gonzales hustled over and said, "I want to talk to my client, Sheriff. Has he been read his rights?"

"He sure has," Hammond replied. "Ask him yourself."

Stark nodded when Gonzales looked at him. "The deputy went over them while we were coming into town. Anybody who's watched TV in the last twenty years knows 'em anyway."

Hammond grunted. "Maybe so, but you ain't gettin' any grounds for appeal from this office, Stark." To the deputy he snapped, "Take him in and book him."

"I want to talk to him," Gonzales insisted.

"After he's been booked." With that, Hammond took hold of Stark's left arm while the deputy took the right. Between them, they marched him into the building.

The next little while was a disconcerting mixture of the familiar and the bizarre. Familiar because, as Stark had said, he had watched countless scenes on television and in the movies of a suspected criminal being fingerprinted, photographed, and booked into jail. Bizarre because he had never expected to find himself in such a situation. When it was finally over, though, he found himself in a small room furnished with only a table and a couple of chairs. He still wore his own clothes, minus his belt, hat, and all his other personal belongings, and Sam Gonzales sat across the table from him, a worried look on his round face.

"This is bad, John Howard," Gonzales said.

"Not too bad," Stark said with a shrug. "I halfway expected the ol' *ley de fuego* on the way into town."

Gonzales stared at him. "You really thought they'd shoot you and say you were trying to escape?"

"The possibility crossed my mind." He looked around. "Just like the possibility that this room is bugged."

"I don't care if it is," Gonzales said, a touch of defiance in his voice. "You're not going to tell me anything except the truth, and since I know you're innocent, the truth isn't going to hurt you."

Stark wished he could be that sure. He was certain he hadn't committed manslaughter; Ramirez's men had been trying to kill him and Elaine, and they had acted in self-defense. Only a total miscarriage of justice would arrive at any other conclusion. Unfortunately, given the situation, such a miscarriage was entirely possible. The truth might not be any protection at all.

"Just tell me what happened," Gonzales said. "From the beginning, and don't leave anything out."

For the next fifteen minutes, Stark did so, starting with the shots he had heard that morning and the worry he had felt about Newt and Chaco. As the story unfolded, Gonzales began to look more and more concerned.

When Stark was finished, the lawyer said, "I don't know, John Howard. Hammond can make a reasonable case for arresting you, and it's entirely possible that a judge would find cause to bind you over for trial."

"What about self-defense?" Stark asked.

"The problem is, you didn't *see* those men in the SUV shoot Newt and Chaco. For all you knew when you went after them, they didn't have anything to do with that."

"You know good and well they did!" Stark said in exasperation. "They were the only ones out there."

"You can't prove that."

"And they shot at us!"

Gonzales shook his head. "Maybe because they didn't know why you were chasing them and *they* were afraid of *you.*"

"That's crazy!"

"Of course it is, but you don't have any concrete evidence to support your side of the story. It's just your word."

"That's always been good," Stark said tautly.

"Yes, but not as good as physical evidence. You don't have any of that."

Stark wanted to get up and pace back and forth. He controlled the urge by placing his hands palms down on the table and pressing hard against it. "Both the men who survived the wreck tried to shoot me," he pointed out.

"Again, they could have been acting in fear of their own lives. After all, John Howard, you *had* just shot out their tires and caused their vehicle to crash, a wreck in which two of their companions perished."

"Good riddance," Stark growled.

"You need to be careful about that attitude." Gonzales sighed. "Understand, I believe you and think that you were right about those men. I'm just telling you how Hammond will make it look to the press."

Stark frowned. "The press?" he repeated. "What does the press have to do with this?"

"This day and age, everything. Hammond will put out a statement blaming you for everything and making you out to be a crazy killer. Oh, it'll be full of 'allegedlies,' but that's still what it will amount to."

"Can't you do anything about that?"

"I'll issue my own statement on your behalf, putting your side of the story out there," Gonzales promised. "You're well known around here and much more respected than Hammond is, and a lot of people will support you. But Hammond *is* the sheriff, and some folks will believe him, even though they'll think such behavior doesn't sound like something you'd do. I *think* public opinion will be on your side, but it's sort of a toss-up."

Stark looked around the little room. Suddenly it seemed much smaller, the walls much closer to him. Funny, he thought, he hadn't known he was the least bit claustrophobic until now.

"So how long will I have to stay locked up?"

"The district attorney will decide later today whether to continue with the case or not. I'll go see him as soon as I leave here and try to persuade him that he shouldn't pursue it. But if he does, and I think there's a good chance he will, you'll be arraigned late this afternoon or in the morning, and the judge will set bail then. You shouldn't have to spend more than one night in jail, and maybe not that much."

"Don't expect them to get in any hurry," Stark said. "Hammond will drag his feet and keep me behind bars as long as he can."

"There's only so much he can do once the process is started. Don't worry, John Howard. Even if this comes to trial, no jury is going to convict you."

"You never know," Stark said bitterly. "Remember that famous football player who's still walking around loose, and those liberal politicians who get away with everything from murder to lying to a grand jury."

"This isn't like that," Gonzales assured him. "There's just one more thing I want to know, John Howard: do you want me to handle this, or should I bring in a more experienced defense attorney from outside?"

Stark didn't waste any time thinking over the question. "You're my friend, and I trust you, Sam," he said. "Not only that, you were born and raised here, just like I was, and you know the folks around here better than any outsider ever could. You're in charge of the case. And the first thing I want you to do, even before you talk to the district attorney, is to call Devery Small and ask him to get the boys together to look after Elaine."

Gonzales extended his hand across the table. "Of course. I'll do that right away. Thanks, John Howard. I won't let you down."

They shook, and then Gonzales got up and knocked on the door. The deputy outside opened it. Gonzales looked back and said one more time, "Don't worry."

When the lawyer was gone, two deputies escorted Stark to a holding cell. The door slammed shut behind him with a clang. He sank down on the hard bunk and sat there.

There was nothing he could do now except wait. His fate was in the hands of other people. It was a bad feeling.

But not near as bad as knowing that Elaine was out there without him to protect her.

Seventeen

Norval Lee Hammond was in his office when his cell phone rang. He took it out of his pocket and thumbed the button to answer it. "Hammond."

"He wants to see you."

Hammond recognized the icy tones of the man called Ryan. That cold voice made a shiver go through the sheriff. The message that it conveyed was even worse. Hammond hadn't expected to be summoned across the border to the Vulture's sanctuary again so soon.

But he hadn't expected John Howard Stark to kill four of Ramirez's men, either.

"When?" he managed to ask.

"As soon as possible."

"Things are sort of busy here this afternoon. . . ."

"I'd advise you to find the time, Sheriff."

That didn't leave any room for argument. Hammond swallowed and said, "Sure. Sure, I'll be over as soon as I can."

Ryan broke the connection without saying anything else. Hammond set the phone down on the desk and looked at it, a feeling of revulsion going through him as if it were some sort of unclean serpent rather than an inanimate piece of twenty-first-century technology.

He had already spoken to the district attorney, a man named Albert Wilfredo. Wilfredo had been a little dubious about the case against Stark, but he had agreed to press charges and let a grand jury decide whether or not to indict him. The district attorney had been about to call the judge and see if he could set up an arraignment for that afternoon, when Hammond had asked him to hold off.

"I want Stark to stew a little first," Hammond had said. "It won't hurt for him to spend a night in jail."

Wilfredo had gone along with that, albeit a little reluctantly. Hammond didn't know what he was going to do, if anything, but he liked the idea of having Stark behind bars so that he could get at him if he wanted to.

Hammond had been acting mostly out of frustration and anger when he made the arrest, but since then he had come to realize that it was the right thing to do. Stark was powerless now. The real question was, what would Ramirez want done with him? Hammond had toyed with the idea of setting up some sort of fatal "accident" for Stark, but he didn't know if that would satisfy Ramirez. The Vulture might want his vengeance to be more personal than that. On the other hand, he might be happy just to get rid of the annoyance that Stark had become. Hammond just didn't know.

So he supposed it was a good thing he was going to see Ramirez. He could get a decision straight from the man himself.

He just wished it wasn't so damned scary dealing with him. And that bastard Ryan was always somewhere close by, giving Hammond the creeps.

He stood up and put on his hat, then went through the outer office and said to his secretary, "I'll be back in a while."

She just nodded and said, "Of course, Sheriff." She was a fine-looking Hispanic woman named Juanita, and she knew not to ask too many questions. That was one reason Hammond thought highly of her. That and the fact that she let him screw her every now and then and never got all weepy or started dropping hints that she might tell Willa Sue about their affair. Juanita was married, too, and had to be as discreet as he was. It all worked out very well.

Hammond drove across the International Bridge. It was the middle of the afternoon, and the late, hurried lunch he'd had wasn't hitting too well. He belched as he drove past the guards at the Mexican end of the bridge. They knew his vehicle and didn't bother stopping him. Things just worked a lot better on the Mexican side of the border, Hammond thought. Everybody knew their place, and money kept everything running smoothly. He had always admired the practicality of the Hispanic mind; they just took the money and went on about their business.

The guards at Ramirez's compound were a lot more diligent in their efforts. They searched Hammond even though he turned his revolver over to them. He knew the routine. Finally he was ushered into the cool, low-ceilinged den. Ramirez was waiting there, sitting on a low, heavy divan and sipping a drink. Ryan stood by the bar and seemed to be paying no attention to Hammond. The sheriff knew better.

"It has come to my attention that this man Stark is in your jail," Ramirez said without any greeting.

"That's right," Hammond said with a nod. "I arrested him on manslaughter charges earlier today."

"The men he slaughtered . . . they worked for me."

That didn't come as any news to Hammond, but at the same time, he wished Ramirez maybe hadn't been so blunt about it. "That's what Stark claimed, but he doesn't have any way to prove it. They were all Mexican nationals, and the SUV they were driving was registered over here to one of them. I've checked it out, and there's nothing leading back to you, Senor Ramirez."

"Of course not. Do you think I would arrange things any other way?" Ramirez finished his drink and set the empty glass aside on a stylishly rough-hewn table. "And yet, everyone knows those men worked for me. The whispers have already started. Stark killed four more of my men. *My* men."

Something Ramirez had just said jogged Hammond's brain. "Wait a minute. You said four *more* men?"

"That is correct. Last night he killed three. So that makes seven of *El Bruitre's* men who have been killed by this gringo." Ramirez's voice took on an angry edge. "Such news travels fast. No doubt they are already laughing in Bogota about how the Vulture is helpless to stop the slaughter of his men by this American."

"I'm sure that's not the case, senor—" Hammond began hurriedly.

"Shut up!" Ramirez roared as he sprang to his feet, his casual air abruptly discarded. "You know nothing! Nothing! Have you ever seen a pack of jackals, Hammond?"

The question took the sheriff by surprise. He blinked in confusion and stammered, "Uh, n-no, I don't reckon I have—"

"The men who inhabit my world are like a pack of jackals, always alert for any sign of weakness. If they sense even the slightest opening, they are always ready to attack, to rush in and grab the weak one and rip him to pieces! That is what they will try to do to me if they believe they can get away with it."

"I'm sure that will never happen, senor," Hammond said nervously. "Your reputation—"

Again Ramirez interrupted him. "My reputation suffers now with every breath this man Stark takes. I want him put down—immediately."

"You mean . . . killed?"

Ramirez gave him a withering stare of contempt. "Yes. I want him dead. As soon as possible."

Well, that was plain enough, Hammond thought. Ramirez didn't care how Stark died. But the more Hammond thought about it, the less sure he was that it would be a good idea to have it happen in jail.

"With all due respect, senor, Stark is in my custody. How's it gonna look if he dies in one of my cells?"

"And why, exactly, should I care how it *looks*?" Ramirez asked scornfully.

"Well, Stark's got a lot of friends in Del Rio. Probably more friends than I've got. And he's got a loudmouthed lawyer who's already talking to the press and hinting that Stark ain't safe in my jail. If something happens to him that's the least bit suspicious, it could blow the town wide open. That would have the feds on our asses in a heartbeat."

Ramirez waved off that protest. "You think I worry about your federal agents? That Border Patrolman, Purdee, has been trying to shut down my smuggling operation for years, and I run more drugs across the border now than I ever have. The United States government cannot touch me."

Hammond wasn't so sure about that, but he wasn't going to argue the point. Not with Ramirez in such a bad mood to start with.

"I'll do whatever you think is best," he said, "but I really think it might be better to wait a little while, until Stark is out of jail. Then you can take care of him without it coming back on me."

Ramirez frowned for a moment and then shrugged. "Perhaps you are right. Release Stark, and I will see that he is taken care of."

"You mean release him right now?"

"Why not, if it serves no purpose to keep him in jail?"

Man, the noose around his neck just kept getting tighter and tighter, Hammond thought. But maybe he could wiggle out of it yet.

"I can't just let Stark go," he said. "I've arrested him, the district attorney has agreed to go forward with the case, and he has to be arraigned; otherwise it's not gonna look right. But we can do that first thing in the morning, and once the judge sets bail, Stark will be back out where you can get to him."

Ramirez thought about it. The seconds ticked past, stretching out so that they seemed longer to Hammond. He felt sweat trickle down the back of his neck and between his shoulder blades. At last, Ramirez nodded. "So it shall be. Your precious reputation will not suffer, Sheriff. But there had better not be any slipups. The bail should not be so high that Stark cannot afford it."

"It won't be," Hammond said, thinking of old Judge Harvey Goodnight, who would have jurisdiction in the case. The judge claimed to be no relation to the famous old-time rancher Charley Goodnight from the Panhandle, but he was every bit as prickly and incorruptible as that pioneer cattleman had been. No one would even think of trying to bribe Harvey Goodnight. That wouldn't be necessary in this case. The judge would see that the case against Stark, while not insupportable, was weak, and he would set bail accordingly.

"One more thing before you go," Ramirez said.

"Of course, senor. Whatever you want."

Ramirez turned to Ryan. "Silencio, bring Alfonso in here."

Wordlessly, Ryan went to carry out the order. Ramirez strolled over to the bar and fixed himself another drink. He didn't offer one to Hammond. The sheriff stood there holding his Stetson in his hands, waiting, trying not to get too nervous as he wondered what Ramirez was up to now.

Ryan came back into the den accompanied by a heavyset Hispanic man. The newcomer looked a little anxious. Hammond understood the feeling. Nobody, with the possible exception of Silencio Ryan, liked to be summoned into the presence of the Vulture.

Ramirez greeted the man with a smile. "Alfonso, how are you?"

"Fine, Senor Ramirez," Alfonso replied.

"Really? I thought you might be feeling a bit, how do the Americans say, under the weather?"

Ruiz, that was the man's last name, Hammond recalled. He had seen him around before. Alfonso Ruiz was one of Ramirez's top gunners. Maybe *the* top man, other than Ryan.

Ruiz licked his lips and said, "No, senor, what would make you think that?"

Ramirez put his hands in the pockets of his perfectly pressed slacks. "I was told you were in the house of Flora Escobedo last night, and that you drank a great deal. So much, in fact, that you could not perform with the girl of Flora's that you picked out to be your companion. So naturally I thought you might be suffering from a hangover today."

Ruiz flushed and looked uncomfortable. "Those rumors are greatly exaggerated, senor. I not only performed, I left the girl begging for more. No amount of liquor could leave me unable to function as a man."

"Ah. I see."

Something about the way Ramirez said it made Hammond look at Ruiz and think, *You poor son of a bitch.*

Ramirez went on, his voice sharp and lashing like a whip now, "Then what is your excuse for failing me this morning?"

Ruiz blinked. "Failing you? I do not understand—"

"You were the leader of the men I sent to Stark's ranch this morning. You were to be with them, to see that they carried out their mission properly."

"Senor, I . . . I thought the men were capable . . . They were only supposed to kill the two old ones."

"So who did you put in charge?"

"Benito Sandoval—"

"The Drooler!" Ramirez screamed. "*El Salivotas!* And with him you sent Gordo, the Big Tamale, and the Dwarf! *Idiota!*"

Ruiz began to back away. "A thousand apologies, senor! I meant no harm. I truly believed those men could handle the job. And they did kill the two old men, just as they were supposed to."

"And were killed in turn by Stark," Ramirez said coldly, "making me look very bad in the process. I do not like to look bad, Alfonso."

Ruiz shook his head vehemently. "It will never happen again, senor—"

"No," Ramirez said. "It won't."

With that, his right hand came out of his pocket. A flick of his wrist opened the blade of the knife he held, and with blinding speed he stepped forward and plunged the knife into Ruiz's belly. Ruiz tried to jerk away, but Ryan had come up behind him, and now Ryan's hand clamped hard on the back of his neck, holding him in place as Ramirez leaned on the blade, driving it deeper. Ramirez ripped the knife from side to side, opening up Ruiz's belly so that the man's guts began to ooze out. Ruiz screamed in agony and shuddered, but he couldn't go anywhere with Ryan holding him.

Ramirez twisted the knife and bore down on it, slicing through Ruiz's abdomen. Blood flowed down Ruiz's legs, soaking his jeans and puddling at his feet, staining the woven throw rug on which he stood. Ramirez pulled the knife free and held it up in front of Ruiz's face so that Ruiz could see his lifeblood coating the blade.

"You disappoint me, Alfonso," Ramirez said between grated teeth. "I don't like to be disappointed."

He shoved the knife into Ruiz's throat and pulled it all the way across. More blood spurted. Ramirez stepped back quickly so the crimson flood wouldn't get on his fine linen shirt. When Ryan let go of Ruiz, the man folded up on the floor, twitching a couple of times as he died.

Ramirez turned toward a stunned Hammond, who had watched the whole gruesome incident in silence, not moving from where he stood. With a smile, Ramirez said, "My sister's youngest boy. She asked me to find a place for him in my organization. A nice boy, but sloppy. This is what happens to people who displease me."

Hammond managed to stammer, "I . . . I thought . . ."

"You thought I was no longer capable of getting my own hands bloody, Sheriff Hammond?" Slowly, Ramirez shook his head. "A good businessman knows how to delegate responsibility. But he also knows that from time to time he must handle his problems himself. Is this man Stark going to be a problem, Sheriff? Are *you* going to be a problem?"

"No, sir," Hammond choked out. "No, sir, I'll do whatever you say. You just give me the word, and I'll do it."

He knew he was groveling, and he hated himself for it. Once upon a time, Norval Lee Hammond had been a proud man and didn't take any shit from anybody. But those days were long past, and only an idiot wouldn't admit that. Hammond was a lot of things, but stupid wasn't one of them.

"All right," Ramirez said. "Go. And after Stark is released from jail tomorrow, you can wash your hands of the entire affair, Sheriff. It will be over as far as you are concerned."

"*Gracias, senor.*" Hammond backed toward the door. He fought the urge to bow and scrape like some damn house servant. "*Gracias,*" he said again.

Then he was outside and the door was shut and he could no longer see the bloody corpse of Alfonso Ruiz sprawled on the rug at Ramirez's feet. The air-conditioning inside the house had been cold, but Hammond's shirt was soaked with sweat.

Better sweat than blood, he told himself.

With an effort, he kept his hands from shaking as he reclaimed his service revolver from the guards and got into the Blazer. He drove away from the compound with a tight grip on the wheel. Ramirez was crazy, he thought. Utterly insane.

Yet he knew that wasn't true. There was nothing insane about the way Ramirez operated. Cruel, ruthless, completely devoid of anything other than evil, sure, but not insane. Ramirez just knew what worked. He knew how to make sure that nobody crossed him. Anyone who did would pay the ultimate price, as John Howard Stark was going to find out.

From one simple little incident—Tommy Carranza shoving around Ramirez's gringo lawyer in that parking lot—eleven men had died, with surely more to come. A war was brewing on the border, a war that might have serious consequences for Norval Lee Hammond. Regardless of the consequences, though, it was too late to stop it now. Things would have to play out. More blood would be spilled, and more men would die. The best Hammond could hope for was that he would be able to ride it out.

He took his hat off and sleeved sweat from his forehead as he drove across the bridge to Del Rio. His mouth had a bad taste in it. Ramirez had shown him today just how insignificant he really was. When he got back to the office, he would have to call Juanita in, get her on the desk, and fuck the shit out of her just to feel like any kind of man again.

And when he got home, he would fuck Willa Sue, too, even though she didn't like it much these days. That was just too damned bad for her.

Hammond took a deep breath, already feeling a little better as he thought about what he would do to the two women. One of these days, he thought. One of these days that little shit Ramirez would push him too far, and then he would see that Norval Lee Hammond wasn't a man to mess with. And if that peckerwood Ryan tried to interfere, Hammond would teach him a lesson, too.

After all, Norval Lee Hammond wasn't just the sheriff of Val Verde County. Once upon a time, he had been all-state.

After the body had been taken away and the bloody rug rolled up to be disposed of, Ramirez poured himself another drink and said to Ryan, "You know what to do, Silencio."

Ryan nodded.

"And after our friend Mr. Stark ceases to be a problem, perhaps it would be wise to turn our attention to the good sheriff Hammond."

Ryan nodded again. This time, he might even have smiled a little. It was hard to tell.

Eighteen

Elaine Stark snapped her purse closed, took a deep breath, and looked at herself in the mirror. After getting back to the ranch house, she had changed into a dark blue short-sleeved dress with a wide black belt. She left her legs bare—they were still good enough that she didn't need hose—and slipped her feet into a pair of sandals. A little makeup, a brush run through her short, graying blond hair, and she was ready to go.

She didn't know if the sheriff would let her see John Howard or not, but there was no way she could sit here and wait without even trying to get to her husband's side.

From the open door of the bedroom, Carmen Logales, whose husband was one of the hands and who worked on the Diamond S as a cook and housekeeper, said excitedly, "Several pickups are coming down the road, senora. Coming fast."

Elaine didn't know who the newcomers could be, but at this moment she didn't much care. If they were looking for trouble, she was in more than a mood to give it to them. She opened her purse again, reached inside, and took out the little .25 pistol she had put in there earlier.

"I'll deal with them, Carmen," she said as she left the bedroom and went to the front door.

When she stepped out onto the porch she saw the vehicles that had gotten Carmen so excited. Elaine relaxed as she recognized them. The one in the lead belonged to Devery Small. The others were driven by W.R. Smathers, Hubie Cornheiser, and Everett Hatcher. With dust billowing up from their tires, they came to a stop in front of the house.

Devery got out, a grim look on his face and a Winchester in his hands that he had picked up from the seat beside him. "Howdy, Elaine," he said. "The boys an' me heard about what happened. Are you all right?"

"Grieving over Newt and Chaco and mad as a wet hen at that so-called sheriff for arresting John Howard," Elaine replied, "but other than that I'm okay."

The other men had gotten out of their vehicles. They were all armed. "No more varmints lurkin' around?" Everett asked.

"Not that I know of." Elaine smiled. "But it's sweet of you boys to come and check on me."

"Sam Gonzales called me," Devery explained. "Said John Howard asked him to make sure you were bein' looked after." Devery glanced at the gun in Elaine's hand.

She said, "I can take care of myself, but I appreciate the sentiment. I was just on my way to town to see John Howard."

"The sheriff probably won't let you see him," Hubie said. "Hammond can be mighty contrary."

"And he sure won't let you in with that gun," W.R. pointed out.

Elaine looked down at the revolver. "I know." She turned and handed it to Carmen. "Put this back in my room, please."

Carmen handled the weapon gingerly. She nodded and said, "*Sí, senora.*"

Elaine was about to argue with the men some more about going to town, when the cell phone she had slipped into the pocket of her dress rang. She pulled it out and thumbed the button to answer the call. "Yes?"

"Elaine? Sam Gonzales here."

Elaine let out a sigh. "Hello, Sam. I hear that you've seen John Howard. Is he all right?"

"He seemed fine, other than being upset over Newt and Chaco and mad at Sheriff Hammond."

"Yes, that's John Howard," she said with a faint smile. "I was just on my way into town to see him."

"I wouldn't advise that."

Elaine frowned. "Why not?"

"From the story John Howard told me, Hammond could have arrested you, too, Elaine. If he sees you again it might remind him of that, and he could take you into custody right there in the jail. He's less likely to make a move against you if you're lying low out there at the ranch."

"You're sure about that?"

"Positive."

Her frown deepened. "I don't like it, Sam. My place is with my husband."

"Not behind bars, it's not. If you think John Howard is angry and upset now, think about what he'd be like if he knew you were arrested, too."

What the lawyer was saying made sense, Elaine supposed, whether she liked it or not. She tried one last gambit. "Did John Howard actually tell you to keep me away from him?"

"No, but that's my best legal advice to you."

She sighed. "All right. If you think it's best, I'll stay out here. I certainly don't want to make things any worse for him. Have you heard what's going to happen next?"

"I just left the district attorney's office. John Howard will be arraigned at nine o'clock tomorrow morning in Judge Goodnight's court."

"So he'll have to spend the night in jail?" Visions of a so-called accident that would prove fatal to her husband danced maddeningly in Elaine's head.

"That's right, but don't worry. He won't be placed in with the other prisoners. Since he's awaiting arraignment he should be kept in a holding cell overnight. I plan to drop in on him unannounced several times, just to make sure no funny business is going on."

"Thanks, Sam. You'll get in touch with me if anything changes?"

"Right away," Gonzales promised.

After she'd said good-bye to the lawyer, Elaine turned back to the other ranchers. "That was Sam Gonzales," she explained, unnecessarily since they had heard her end of the conversation. "He thinks it would be best for me to stay here and not go into town, especially not to the jail."

"That sounds like a good idea to me, too," Devery said. "I reckon you ought to call in all your hands, pass out some guns, and just hunker down until tomorrow. We'll stay here in the house, just to make sure nothin' happens."

Elaine nodded. "All right. I appreciate this, boys."

"Don't you worry 'bout it," Devery assured her. "We'd do most anything for ol' John Howard." He looked at the other men. "The way it turns out, looks like he's fightin' the battles that all of us should have been fightin' all along."

A deputy brought Stark's supper and slid the tray through the opening in the door. Stark was mighty hungry by that time, since during all the confusion he hadn't gotten any lunch. It had been a long time since breakfast that morning.

He lost some of his appetite, though, when he recalled that at the time he'd sat down to breakfast, Newt and Chaco had still been alive.

Still, he forced himself to eat, knowing that he needed to keep his strength up. He had just finished the meal when Sam Gonzales was brought down the corridor by a deputy. The man let Sam into the cell and then closed and locked the door behind him.

"How are they treating you so far, John Howard?" the lawyer asked.

"All right, I suppose," Stark replied. "Other than the fact that I never should have been locked up in the first place."

"We'll get our chance to argue that," Gonzales assured him. "In the meantime, I thought you'd like to know that your friends have gathered at the Diamond S, and they're not going to let anything happen to Elaine."

Stark heaved a sigh of relief and nodded. "I'm glad to hear it."

"I talked to her just a little while ago, in fact, and she sounded upset but otherwise fine. She was about to come into town and try to see you, but I convinced her that wouldn't be a good idea."

"Better just to wait," Stark agreed. "I don't want her to see me behind bars. Any word yet on when the arraignment will be?"

"Tomorrow morning, nine o'clock, with Judge Goodnight presiding."

Stark nodded. He could count on getting a fair shake from Harvey Goodnight. And that was all he asked.

"I've put in an official request that you be held overnight in this cell, alone."

Stark looked at Gonzales shrewdly. "You think it's possible Hammond might try to arrange a little accident for me?"

"Stranger things have happened." Gonzales rubbed his eyes for a moment. "From what I hear, you've made some powerful enemies, John Howard."

"If you reckon it'd be better for you and your family if you didn't handle my case, Sam, I understand."

Gonzales shook his head. "Absolutely not. You can put that idea out of your head. I'm on this case to stay, as long as you're satisfied with my efforts."

"More than satisfied so far," Stark said with a tired grin. He grew more solemn as he went on, "You'll handle all the arrangements for Newt and Chaco?"

"Of course. The coroner hasn't released their bodies yet and probably won't for a day or two, but I'll stay on top of the situation. You'll be out on bail in plenty of time for the funerals."

Stark nodded. It was funny, the twists and turns that life made. He had never considered the possibility that someday he would be out on bail. He was a law-abiding man who had fully expected to go through life without ever being arrested. It just went to show you that you never could tell what might happen.

For example, when he came home from Vietnam, he had thought he was through with war.

But now, a new war had come home to him, and it would be fought on the land where he had grown up, the land he loved. And above all, it was a war that he had to win.

The night passed quietly in the jail. Sam Gonzales dropped in again, but he didn't have any news and Stark figured the lawyer was just there to make sure he was still all right. Stark didn't sleep much. Every time he closed his eyes he was haunted by the memories of how he had found Newt and Chaco. Occasionally he thought as well about the burning SUV and the two men he had shot. Those images were equally vivid but not as disturbing. He was a little surprised that he could be responsible for the deaths of seven men in less than twenty-four hours and not be bothered too much by it.

The fact that those men had been vermin in human form probably had something to do with it, he decided.

The deputies woke him up at five the next morning. He had finally dozed off only a short time earlier, so a great weariness gripped him as he ate the dry toast and scrambled eggs they brought him for breakfast and drank the bitter coffee. His shoulders ached, and his eyes felt as if they had been taken out of his head, rolled around in some particularly gritty sand, and then popped back into their sockets.

Sam showed up again at eight o'clock and went over the procedures for the arraignment. "We'll plead not guilty, right?" Stark asked.

"You won't enter a plea at this time," Gonzales explained. "District Attorney Wilfredo will explain the basics of the case, and then I'll ask for a dismissal of the charges, but the chances we'll get it are small. The judge will bind you over, and the case will be sent to the grand jury."

"But I'll be released on bail, right?"

"That's right. If it's too high for you to make a cash bond, we'll go through a bail bondsman, but one way or the other you'll be released this morning."

"What then?"

Gonzales shrugged. "The case goes to the grand jury. That's probably where it ends. The grand jury will decline to indict you on the charges, and it's over."

"Can't be soon enough to suit me," Stark said. "One night in jail is more than enough."

"Well, at least there wasn't any trouble. I take it there wasn't?"

Stark shook his head. "Nobody came near me. It was a quiet night. Plenty of time for me to think."

He didn't add that what he had thought about was what would happen next. Not the arraignment or even the possibility of a trial, but what Ramirez would do next. A man like the Vulture wasn't going to let this pass, nor would he rely on the American justice system. He would want to take matters into his own hands.

"Have you talked to Elaine this morning?"

"Yes, and she's fine, just tired and worried," Gonzales said. "Everything was quiet on the ranch last night."

Stark nodded in relief. That was something good, anyway.

The deputies came along and shooed Gonzales out of the cell. Sam looked back over his shoulder and said, "I'll see you in court, John Howard. Don't worry. This is almost over."

Sam was a good man, Stark thought, but he was sure wrong about that. This wasn't anywhere near over.

A short time later he was put in the back of a jail van and taken over to the courthouse. He was handcuffed again for the transfer, and it was just as humiliating as it had been the day before, not to mention painful. Those damned handcuffs pinched. That was another thing he wouldn't have thought that he would ever experience firsthand.

Stark wasn't prepared for what was waiting at the courthouse. When the jail van came to a stop and the driver turned off the engine, Stark heard a low murmur that sounded almost like the rumble of distant thunder. A moment later, one of the deputies swung the rear doors open, and the thunder wasn't distant anymore. It was right there, surrounding the van, and it consisted of scores of voices yelling all at the same time. Bright flashes assailed Stark's eyes as he stepped out of the van with a deputy close on each side of him, but they weren't caused by lightning.

A double row of deputies formed a corridor through which he could walk. On both sides of that corridor were reporters and cameramen, taking his picture and shouting for comments from him. Stark ignored them as best he could, but he couldn't help glancing at them. Del Rio had a newspaper, a couple of television stations, and quite a few radio stations. There were probably some reporters from Cuidad Acuna here, too. But even so, there were more newspeople outside the courthouse than anyone could account for. Stations up in San Angelo and over in Austin and San Antonio must have sent reporters down here.

To cover one simple arraignment on manslaughter charges? That didn't make sense to Stark. He wasn't news.

But evidently he was, the way those folks were acting. Stark looked down at first; he had never been the sort to seek the limelight, even when he was a star athlete. But then he realized how that must look. He had seen news footage of other suspects doing the "perp walk." Maybe it wasn't fair, but any time he saw people like that looking down, or even worse, trying to cover their faces, he had assumed they were guilty. So after the first couple of steps his head came up and he looked around boldly at the crowd of journalists, meeting their curious gazes squarely, a man with nothing to hide and no wrongdoing on his conscience. It was just a gesture, and admittedly a small one, but it made him feel better anyway.

After running the gauntlet of the sensation-hungry media, Stark was led into the courthouse through a rear entrance and soon found himself in a small chamber adjacent to the courtroom where the arraignment would be held. Sam Gonzales waited for him there.

The lawyer summoned up a smile. "Are you ready for this, John Howard?"

"I wasn't ready for what I saw outside," Stark replied. "I wasn't expecting it, anyway. What the hell's going on, Sam?"

"The media statewide got hold of the story of what happened yesterday. There are news crews here from San Antonio, Austin, Houston, and Dallas. With that much coverage, the story may even go nationwide."

"How in the world did that happen?"

Gonzales shrugged. "I have a friend from college who works for the Associated Press."

"You leaked it, in other words."

"It's not a matter of leaking anything. That sounds sneaky. Your arrest and this morning's arraignment are matters of public record. I just pointed out what was going on and filled in some of the background."

"You mentioned Ramirez?"

"Not by name. I just talked about powerful Mexican interests involved in the drug trade."

Stark shook his head. "That's liable to just make Ramirez madder."

"Maybe, but the more attention that's focused on your case, the safer you ought to be, John Howard. Now that it's known what's going on, he won't dare make a move against you."

Sam had a much different opinion about what Ramirez would and wouldn't dare than he did, Stark thought. Ramirez might regard all this media attention as a further insult to his pride and be all the more determined to exact a violent, public vengeance.

On the other hand, Ramirez already wanted him dead. It couldn't get much worse than that.

Could it?

"Have you seen Elaine this morning?"

Gonzales nodded. "She's in the courtroom, along with a couple of your friends. They were the only ones who could get in. All the other spaces are filled with journalists."

Stark sighed and said, "Well, let's get this dog and pony show on the road."

"Unfortunately, the court operates on the judge's timetable, not ours," Gonzales said.

They didn't have to wait very long, though, before a bailiff came in and got them. They walked through a side door into the crowded courtroom that instantly got a lot noisier until Judge Harvey Goodnight, already seated at the bench, smacked his gavel a few times and loudly called for order in the court. Just like on TV, Stark thought. He was learning all kinds of things.

He saw Elaine sitting in the front row of spectator seats, flanked by Devery and W.R. She gave him a brave smile, which he returned. They said more with their eyes, though, as a man and woman who have been married for more than thirty years can do quite easily.

Sheriff Hammond was nowhere to be seen, Stark noticed. The bailiff read the case number, and Albert Wilfredo popped up from the table where he was sitting to go through the charges against Stark. They started with assault with a deadly weapon, proceeded through reckless endangerment and involuntary manslaughter, for the two men who had died in the wreck, to voluntary manslaughter, for the two men Stark had shot. Wilfredo concluded by asking that the suspect be held without bond, since he was a flight risk and an obvious danger to the community.

Then it was Sam Gonzales's turn, and he asked for an immediate dismissal of the charges, a request that Judge Goodnight denied, as expected. "This is a serious matter," the portly, bearded jurist said. "Serious enough that it ought to go to the grand jury so evidence can be heard. I'm binding over your client, counselor." Goodnight scratched his ear. "Now what about this bail?"

Gonzales pointed out that John Howard Stark was a life-long member of the community, had been born and raised here, had gone to school here, married, and raised a family of his own here. "John Howard Stark is anxious to prove his innocence and clear his name, Your Honor," Gonzales said. "He's not going anywhere. And as for him constituting a danger to the community . . ." Gonzales paused meaningfully. "There are some who would say that John Howard Stark's actions have provided a *service* to the community."

That comment caused quite a hubbub, of course, including an objection from Albert Wilfredo, and once again Judge Goodnight had to pound the gavel and call for order. When it was restored, he said, "Kindly refrain from editorializing, counselor."

"Of course, Your Honor. My apologies."

Goodnight looked at the district attorney. "Your objection is overruled, Mr. Wilfredo. Defense counsel's pointed comment is being disregarded by the bench. However, I fail to find that the defendant constitutes a flight risk or a danger to the community, so I'm ordering that bail be set—"

"The state requests bail be set in the amount of ten million dollars, Your Honor," Wilfredo broke in.

Goodnight glared at him, obviously not liking the fact that Wilfredo had interrupted him. He cleared his throat and went on, "As I was saying, bail will be set in the amount of five thousand dollars." He smacked the gavel down on the bench before anybody could say anything else. "Court's adjourned."

"Five thousand dollars in a case where four men died?" Wilfredo yelped anyway. Judge Goodnight ignored him, got up, and walked out of the courtroom as the bailiff bellowed for everybody to rise.

Gonzales turned to Stark. "Do you have five grand in cash, John Howard?" he asked. "If you don't, I can get it."

"There's that much in the bank," Stark said. "Elaine can withdraw it." He looked over at her, and she nodded. She was only a few feet away from him, with only a wooden railing separating them, but when she started to reach out toward him, a deputy moved to block her. Stark growled a little when he saw that.

"It's all right," Gonzales said quickly. "You'll be taken back to jail now, while the bond is posted and processed. It shouldn't take much more than an hour. Hang in there, John Howard."

Stark nodded curtly. "I'm fine. Just get it taken care of, Sam."

As Gonzales predicted, all the paperwork took about an hour. But then he arrived at the jail, and the cell door was unlocked and Stark stepped out again. He signed some papers and all his belongings were returned to him. Gonzales took his arm.

"We'll go out the side door. The reporters are watching the front and the back. I figured you wouldn't want to deal with them right now."

"You figured right," Stark said. "I just want to go home."

"That's where Elaine and your friends are waiting for you. They thought it would be best not to add to the commotion."

A few minutes later, they stepped out through a narrow, unmarked door into an alley. A disreputable-looking pickup was parked there. "My uncle Gil's truck," Gonzales explained with a smile. "I thought if my car was parked back here, some of the reporters might notice it. They didn't pay any attention to this old junker, though."

"Good thinking," Stark said. He paused just outside the door to draw in a deep breath.

"I know what you're thinking," Gonzales said. "Free air. Smells good, doesn't it?"

Stark nodded, but he was thinking that no matter how good it felt to be out of jail, he wasn't a free man again. Not really.

Not as long as the threat from the Vulture was hanging over his head.

But he couldn't do anything about that now. "Let's go," he said hoarsely as he opened the passenger door of the old pickup. "I'm ready to see my wife again."

Nineteen

There was a crowd waiting at the ranch house, and they broke into cheers and applause when Sam Gonzales drove up in the old pickup and Stark got out. Elaine was standing on the porch, but she didn't have the patience to stay there. She ran down the steps to meet Stark and throw herself into his arms.

He hugged her tightly and then kissed her, and that brought more cheers from the crowd. As he came up onto the porch with an arm still around Elaine, his friends gathered around him to slap him on the back and shake his hand. They were congratulating him as if he had just hit the game-winning home run in the bottom of the ninth, he thought. But this was no game, and there might not be a clear-cut victor.

"We knew they couldn't keep you in jail, John Howard," Devery said. "You didn't do nothin' wrong."

"That'll be up to the grand jury to decide," Stark pointed out.

W.R. snorted in derision. "Ain't no grand jury in Texas gonna indict you for what you did, John Howard. Folks are sick an' tired of those drug runners and other criminals gettin' away with everything they do. If it takes goin' after 'em our own selves, folks are fed up enough to do it. You're a damn hero, man!"

Stark just shook his head. He didn't feel like a hero at all. He felt like a tired, grieving man who just wanted things to get back to normal. It might be a long time before that happened, though, if ever.

Just like at the Fourth of July celebration a few days earlier, people had brought food galore to the Diamond S. Once Stark started in on the fried chicken and potato salad and green bean casserole and homemade rolls, he discovered that he was hungrier than he'd thought he would be. It was a good lunch, and by the time he finished, he was stuffed.

Some of the visitors began to drift away after the meal was over. By late afternoon, all that were left were Sam Gonzales and Stark's closest friends, Devery, W.R., Hubie, and Everett. "You can relax now until the grand jury hearing, John Howard," Gonzales said. "That won't be for several weeks yet."

Stark nodded.

"What about Ramirez?" Hubie asked. "Ain't he liable to try something else?"

Gonzales shook his head. "I don't think so. He doesn't want a lot of bad publicity."

Stark still thought the lawyer had his head in the sand where Ramirez was concerned, but he didn't say anything. After all, there was a chance Sam might be right.

But Stark intended to be prepared for the possibility that Gonzales was wrong.

Devery said, "We can take turns stayin' over here, to sort of help you keep an eye on the place, John Howard."

Without hesitation, Stark said, "That won't be necessary. All you boys have spreads of your own to look after. You need to go home, take care of your ranches, and spend time with your own families."

"But just in case—" Everett began.

"You heard what Sam said. Ramirez isn't going to try

anything else. He had Newt and Chaco killed. He's had his vengeance."

A man like the Vulture could never have enough vengeance, though, Stark thought. Not until every one of the people he considered his enemies were wiped off the face of the earth. Stark didn't want any of his friends putting themselves in danger to look after him. That just wasn't his way. He was a man who stomped his own snakes, as the old saying went. Or in this case, shot his own vultures.

"If you're sure that's what you want . . ." Devery said reluctantly.

"I am," Stark declared. "I appreciate everything you fellas have done, especially coming over here last night to make sure Elaine was safe. But it's over now, and things need to start getting back to normal."

"I think that's the wisest course," Gonzales said.

There was a little more talk, and then the men climbed into their pickups and drove off. Gonzales was the last one to go. "I'll get Uncle Gil's truck back to him," he said with a smile as he sat there for a moment with the driver's door open. "If there's anything you need, John Howard, don't hesitate to call. I'll be in touch regularly and let you know right away if there are any new developments in the case."

Stark nodded solemnly and shook hands with Gonzales. "I'm much obliged, Sam."

With a wave, Gonzales drove off, leaving Stark and Elaine standing side by side at the foot of the porch steps. She reached over and took his hand, lacing her fingers through his. She squeezed his hand hard, and when he looked over at her, she smiled and said, "That was just about the biggest load of bullshit I've ever heard, John Howard."

Her reaction didn't surprise him. She had always been able to see right through him. He said, "You don't know that. It could turn out that Sam's right about Ramirez not doing anything else."

"We both know better. Yes, he's killed two of yours, but you've killed seven of his. Worse than that, you've hurt his pride and maybe damaged his standing with the rest of the drug lords. He *has* to wipe out you and everybody close to you. You know that . . . and what do you do? You send away everybody who could help you."

"Not everybody," Stark said softly.

She looked up solemnly at him for a moment before she breathed, "Damn, I'm glad to hear you say that, John Howard. What do you want me to do?"

"Start loading the guns," Stark told her. "Every gun in the house."

By nightfall all the guns were loaded and Stark had worked out his plan. The few ranch hands who lived on the Diamond S had been sent away, all of them leaving reluctantly. Now came the biggest chore of all, he thought as he walked into the living room. He found Elaine there, closing the cylinder of a pistol she had just loaded.

"We're ready, John Howard," she said.

"Not quite. There's still one thing to do."

"What's that?"

"Talk you into going over to Devery's place where you can lie low for a while."

She stared at him in surprise, and then her frown turned into one of anger. "You've gotta be kidding," she said. "You don't really think I'm going anywhere, do you?"

"I can operate a lot better and a lot more efficiently if I don't have to worry about you all the time," he pointed out.

That just made her angrier. "I haven't asked you to worry about me, have I?" Without waiting for him to answer, she went on, "How about me worrying about you? You think this is easy for me? Tommy's dead, Uncle Newt and Chaco are dead . . . A part of me says we ought to just pack up and get out of here! Let Ramirez have the place if he wants it so bad!"

"You don't mean that," Stark said, almost aghast at the very idea of abandoning the Diamond S. "I won't be chased off land that's been in my family for four generations. Starks fought and bled and died for this spread. This is *Texas*, by God, and the Diamond S is my part of Texas. No bastard like Ramirez is going to take it away from me." He paused for a moment and then added, "Besides, before I start soundin' too noble here, Ramirez doesn't want the ranch. He just wants to run drugs across it and everybody else's spread along this part of the border."

"And he wants you dead," Elaine said.

Stark nodded grimly. "I reckon that's true. He's Colombian, remember? He'll want to kill my family, too. For the first time, I'm almost glad David and Pete are over there in the Middle East where he can't get to them. But there's still you to think of."

She was still holding the pistol she had just finished loading. She lifted it and said flatly, "This is my home, too. I've lived here for over thirty years. I won't run . . . I *can't* run— any more than you can, John Howard."

He looked at her, searching her eyes for any signs of wavering. He saw none, and he knew that he would never budge her from her position. The only way he could get her out of here would be to take her physically over to Devery's and ask his friend to keep her there. And now that he thought about it, he wasn't sure ol' Devery was up to that task.

"Can you do what I say?" he asked.

"Of course I can. You're the ex-marine, not me. You tell me the plan, and I'll follow it."

Stark nodded. "All right. I hope you can, because both of our lives will probably depend on it . . ."

The night was dark, not much of a moon hanging over the landscape of the border country. Starlight filtered down like glowing haze but did little to illuminate the darkness under the trees around the ranch house.

Five shadows moved through that darkness, slipping around the house with silent stealth. Although the hour was late, almost midnight, most of the lights in the house seemed to be on. As if that would protect the occupants from the deadly fate that was closing in on them.

El Bruitre had a large organization. Even with the losses he had suffered recently, he had plenty of good men to draw from. These five were hardened, experienced gunners, men who could and would kill without hesitation. They were dressed in dark clothing and carried automatic weapons. They would show no mercy tonight. The *Deguello* might as well have been playing, as it played while Santa Anna's army surrounded the Alamo and its valiant defenders.

This was no siege. It would be one brutal, smashing assault, designed to take out the enemies of the Vulture with as little delay as possible. Silencio Ryan had thought to draw Stark out by attacking those near and dear to him first. That hadn't really worked. Through luck or sheer determination or a combination of both, Stark had wiped out the crew sent to kill Newt and Chaco. No more fancy stuff, Ramirez had decreed. Just hit Stark and hit him hard, wipe him out. If Ryan was offended by being overruled when it came to strategy, he gave no sign of it. But then, Silencio Ryan seldom gave much sign of any emotion.

The lead gunner, a man known as *El Duende*—the Goblin—was connected by radio with Ryan. *El Duende* had a headset with both an earpiece and a microphone attached to it, with wires that ran down to the battery pack in the small of his back. Ryan had equipped him as well with a small, head-mounted video camera, also with its own battery pack and transmitter. Ryan sat in the back of a black van a mile away, receiving the sounds and images sent back to him by *El Duende*. If all went well, Ryan could show the tape to Ramirez when he got back to the compound on the outskirts of Acuna. He was sure Ramirez would get a large amount of enjoyment out of being able to watch Stark and his wife die, even though it would be a vicarious pleasure.

At the ranch house, *El Duende* motioned silently for his men to spread out around the place. When he was ready, he would fire the first shots, and that would be the signal for his fellow killers to open up as well. They would pour so much lead into the house that no one inside it could escape alive. Though the house was old and sturdily built, the high-powered bullets would have no trouble punching through the walls and doors and anything else in their deadly path.

The Goblin found himself crouching underneath a brightly lit window. He raised himself enough to peer through it. He looked into a large, well-equipped kitchen that also served as a dining room. The table, covered with a white linen cloth, was set for a late, intimate supper for two, complete with a bottle of wine, two glasses, and a couple of unlit candles. At the stove, steaks were frying on the grill and something was bubbling in a pot. The room was empty at the moment, but with the food cooking like that, it was obvious that Stark's wife had just stepped out of the kitchen for a moment. *El Duende* flexed his fingers on the automatic weapon he held as he heard footsteps coming closer, approaching the door into the kitchen from the rest of the house. The smell of the steaks cooking drifted out through the open window and tantalized the gunner's nostrils. A shame that the food would probably get shot up along with the inhabitants of the house.

He spoke in rapid Spanish to Ryan, whispering that Senora Stark was about to come back into the kitchen. As soon as she did, the Goblin declared, he would open fire.

In the van, alarms suddenly went off inside Ryan's head as he watched the video feed. He had studied the ranch house at long range through binoculars. He knew it had a central air-conditioning unit, and this was a hot July night.

Why, then, was the kitchen window wide open like that, as if to draw someone outside right to it, like a moth to flame?

The kitchen door moved, swinging inward. With his face twisted in a grimace of anticipation, *El Duende* straightened all the way from his crouch and brought the machine gun to his shoulder. Ryan yelled something in his ear just as he pressed the trigger, but the words were drowned out by the chattering racket of the gunfire.

Then suddenly, with no warning, everything went dark.

Stark had already drawn a bead on the would-be killer. It had been easy, the way the guy was silhouetted against the light in the kitchen window. He pressed the trigger of the Winchester as automatic weapons fire ripped out and the lights went off. The old rifle, which was in perfect condition, kicked hard against Stark's shoulder as it cracked wickedly, but he hardly felt the recoil. He was already working the lever, jacking another cartridge into the chamber.

He wouldn't need it for his first target. The man slumped against the house, and his gun fell silent as his finger came off the trigger. Stark saw him fall, a deeper patch of darkness against the shadows, and knew that the shot had been true. The .44-40 bullet had smashed through the back of the gunner's skull, bored through his brain, and then ruined his face as it burst out the front of his head, leaving him dead on his feet for a couple of seconds before death caught up with the rest of his body.

Just because one gun had fallen silent, however, didn't mean that all of them had. All around the house, the other gunmen were firing in response to the signal from the first man Stark had killed. They didn't know yet that their leader was dead, so they were continuing with their mission.

Stark slipped out of the clump of mesquite where he had hidden and waited for the ball to start. He wore black from head to foot, and his face had been darkened with charcoal. It was his first time to fight in camouflage since Vietnam, and if he'd had time to think about it, the situation might have brought back a lot of memories. As it was, he couldn't afford the luxury of remembering. What was past didn't mean a damned thing. The future—staying alive and seeing to it that Elaine did, too—was all that mattered.

"Stay down, Elaine!" he whispered into the microphone attached to the headset he wore. It was hooked up to the cell phone in his pocket, as was the earphone tucked into his right ear. They had kept in contact that way, Stark whispering to her while he watched from the mesquites as the gunners closed in on the house. He had told her to go give the kitchen door a push, then duck into the garage, which was right next to the kitchen. The main circuit breaker box was right there beside the door into the garage. It had taken her only a second to hit the switch and kill the power everywhere on the place. The plan called for her to do that as she dived in between the pickup and the SUV parked close together in the garage. The two heavy vehicles would serve as protection from flying bullets. Elaine was supposed to get low between them and stay there. Stark had drained the gas tanks so a stray slug couldn't ignite them, and Elaine had a couple of pistols and a rifle with her. Stark figured it was the safest place for her.

He was on the move, circling the house, searching for his next target. Ramirez's men had to have noticed by now that the lights had gone off, and while that might have puzzled them, they didn't let it distract them from their mission. With each man posted at a different window, they emptied the magazines of their automatic weapons into the house, reloaded, and started firing again. Stark hated to think about the damage they were doing to the place—so he didn't. He concentrated on the task at hand instead, and when he had a good shot again, he took it. Once more the Winchester cracked and bucked, and a slug tore through the body of one of the gunners, spinning him around and dropping him to the ground. Stark came close enough to hear the ragged, bubbling breaths the man was taking and knew that he was shot through the lungs. After a moment the grotesque sound stopped.

That made another one dead, three to go. Stark cat-footed through the darkness. He had learned a lot from the Vietcong during the time he'd been in Southeast Asia. The VC dressed in black, moved fast, and were never exactly where you expected them to be. They struck from odd directions, so you couldn't anticipate their attacks. Stark had hated the little bastards, but he admired their fighting ability and their mastery of offbeat tactics.

He was at the front of the house now, and as he peered along the porch he saw one of the gunners standing in front of the picture window, laughing crazily as he fired. The glass was all blown in, and the spraying bullets were wreaking havoc in the living room. Angry that his home was being desecrated this way, Stark aimed and fired.

Just as he squeezed the trigger, though, the gunner's weapon ran dry, and he leaned forward to drop the clip. Instead of taking him in the head, Stark's bullet grazed the back of his neck. The man cried out in pain and lunged forward, diving through the shot-out picture window.

The bastard was in the house!

"Elaine!" Stark said urgently into the microphone. "One of them is inside! He's in the living room! Elaine!"

There was no reply. With a feeling of chill horror, Stark realized he hadn't heard a word from her since the shooting started.

He wanted to dash around the house and get into the garage to make sure she was all right, but he knew he couldn't. For one thing, he still had three enemies to deal with, and for another, if he came busting in there unannounced and she was all right, she might just shoot him before she realized who he was. He had to stick to the plan and take care of the other three gunners before he could go check on Elaine.

The man in the living room pretty much had to stay there. If he ventured elsewhere in the house, he might fall prey to his own companions' bullets. Stark stepped up onto the porch and moved as quietly as possible along it toward the shot-out window. He couldn't go in that way; the moonlight, dim though it was, was still brighter than the stygian darkness inside the house. If he tried to go through the window he would be silhouetted against that glow and present a perfect target. If the gunner trapped in there had any sense, he would have his weapon trained on the window and would fire at the first sign of motion there.

Stark reached down to his belt and took out one of the little cylinders he had tucked there earlier. Silently, he laid the rifle down on the porch and straightened. He took the Colt Model 1911A .45 from behind his belt on the other hip and racked the slide. Then he snapped the highway flare in half and tossed it through the broken window into the living room. A second later the flare burst into flaming life with a hiss, and the gunner started firing wildly.

Stark rammed his shoulder against the front door and knocked it open. Diving into the hall just inside the door, he rolled over and pointed the .45 through the arched entrance to the living room. The bright red flare showed him the gunner twisting around and letting off shots blindly in every direction. A couple of them whined over Stark's head. He fired the Colt three times, watching in satisfaction as the bullets crashed into the gunner's body and smashed him against the wall. He bounced off and fell loosely to the floor. He lay there without moving, in the stillness of death.

Then and only then did Stark realize he had been hit by one of the wild slugs. It had plowed a bloody furrow across the outside of his upper left arm, and as blood trickled hotly down his arm, the wound began to hurt like blazes. He gritted his teeth and ignored the pain as he stood up. He went into the living room long enough to stomp out the small fire on the carpet caused by the flare, and then he stepped back out onto the porch.

Something was wrong, and he knew immediately what it was: other than some fading echoes, the night was quiet again. The shooting had stopped. That meant the remaining two gunners had overcome the killing frenzy that had gripped them. That made them much more dangerous adversaries, and so did the fact that by now they must have figured out that something had gone wrong. Their simple murder mission was fucked. Now they were in a fight for their own lives.

Stark put the pistol behind his belt and picked up the rifle again. He headed for the far end of the porch, but before he got there a shadowy figure lunged around the corner of the house and opened fire. The gun in the man's hand stuttered and belched flame. Stark threw himself forward, firing the Winchester as he fell, working the lever as he landed and rolled and bullets chewed up splinters from the boards beside him. He fired again and saw the gunman fly backward as if a giant finger had poked him in the chest. The man landed on his back, arms and legs outflung.

As he pushed himself up, Stark felt a stinging on his face and another trickle of blood. One of those flying splinters had sliced across his cheek, opening a gash that hurt like hell. His muscles, still a little sore from the fight in the Blue Burro, ached in several places, and he knew he would have plenty of fresh bruises in the morning . . . if he lived that long. He winced as he took a step. His right ankle was a little twisted, but not so badly that he couldn't use it.

He reached the corner of the house and started along the side. The other gunman ought to be somewhere over here, he thought.

That was when he heard the garage door go up.

"Elaine!" Stark cried, unable to hold back the exclamation. He broke into a run, heedless of his safety, all thoughts of stealth gone now. The garage door had been securely locked, but one of those bastards could have blasted the lock apart with automatic weapons fire.

Careening around the corner, Stark saw the open garage, as black inside as the maw of a hungry beast. He had taken just a couple of steps in that direction when muzzle flame bloomed in the darkness. Something pounded hard against his right shoulder, knocking him off his stride. He knew he was hit and he tried to keep his balance, but he couldn't do it. He fell, losing the Winchester when he hit the ground. As he rolled over, pain engulfing his entire right side, he groped with his left hand for the butt of the .45 at his belt.

But that arm was wounded, too, and he was slow and

awkward. The pain of his injury seemed to hamper him not only physically but mentally as well. His brain processes just weren't working like they should. He knew he ought to be sending out nerve impulses to his muscles, commanding them to move and move fast, damn it, but everything was haywire now. He blinked as he saw the dark figure step into the open doorway of the garage and train a weapon on him. Stark's fingers finally closed around the butt of the pistol at his waist, but he knew he was going to be too late.

The lights in the garage came on, throwing a blinding glare in Stark's face. Shots roared as he involuntarily squeezed his eyes shut. When he was able to open them in narrow slits a moment later, he saw the final member of Ramirez's crew of gunners. The man had dropped his weapon and leaned against the pickup, one hand on it for support. Blood welled from his mouth. He swayed there like that for a second and then pitched forward onto his face. Stark pushed himself up into a half-sitting position and saw the dark bloodstains on the man's back.

Elaine stood there behind him, her arm outstretched, a pistol rock-steady in her hand. A tiny thread of smoke curled from the barrel.

From where he lay just outside the garage, Stark asked, "What took you?"

Slowly, Elaine lowered the gun. Her face was pale, completely washed out of color, but still composed. She stepped forward, bent to check for a pulse in the neck of the man she had just shot, and looked up to give her husband a nod.

"He's dead."

"Good," Stark said. "I'm pretty sure all the others are, too."

"*Pretty* sure?" Elaine repeated.

"Best I could do at the time."

"Stay there. I'll check."

"I'm not going anywhere." Stark was too weak and numb to move. "Be careful."

She was back only a few minutes later, her face still

ashen and her features tightly under control. "Were there five of them?"

"That's right."

"They're all dead, then." She dropped to a knee beside him. "You look like shit, John Howard."

"Feel like it, too," he grated. "Are you all right? I got worried when your phone went dead."

"Bad choice of words," she said dryly. "I'm sorry. I dropped it when I went diving into the garage, and the battery popped out, and my foot kicked it and sent it flying, and I just couldn't find the damned thing in the dark. I knew you'd be worried, but I figured it was best just to wait for you to come for me."

"Instead, one of those killers came for you," Stark said, his voice bitter with self-recrimination.

"That wasn't your fault. Anyway, I got him. We're a team, John Howard, and a mighty good one at that."

"Yeah," Stark agreed softly. "A mighty good team."

"Let's get you into the truck. You need a doctor and a hospital."

"You'll have to put gas in it," Stark grunted as she helped him to his feet. "Cans are in the storage shed." His right side was covered with blood. "I want to take a look around first, see how much damage was done to the house."

"I can tell you that: it's shot to hell. But that doesn't matter. It's just a house. We're what's important, and we're fine. At least, we will be once we get you patched up."

Stark would have agreed with her. He opened his mouth to do so. But then the world went away and he was too busy passing out to worry about anything else.

Twenty

The smell of flowers was so strong when he woke up, he thought for a second that he must be at his own funeral. He expected to hear the organ start playing a dirge at any moment.

Instead, he heard an unfamiliar voice saying, "Ah, he's waking up now."

"It's about time." That voice belonged to Elaine, and Stark felt a vast wave of relief wash over him at the knowledge that she was all right.

He managed to pry his eyes open and was glad that the first thing he saw was her face as she leaned over him with an anxious frown. "John Howard?" she said. "Are you all right?"

Stark tried to answer her, but his mouth didn't want to work. Finally he was able to wrap it around some words. "I'm . . . fine . . . how about . . . you?"

"Don't worry about me," she told him. "You're the one who's been unconscious since last night."

"Last . . . night?"

"That's right, Mr. Stark." The owner of the other voice moved into Stark's line of sight. He was a young Asian man in a white lab coat over casual clothes. "You lost enough blood that you went into shock, and I can tell from looking at your other assorted bruises and scrapes that you've been mistreating your body lately. You're not a young man anymore, you know."

Stark closed his eyes for a moment to bring his temper under control. Even as weak as he was, he didn't like being talked to in such condescending tones. When he opened his eyes again, he said, "I reckon you must be a doctor."

The young man nodded. "That's right. Dr. Alvin Lu. I just moved here and started working at the hospital."

"Dr. Lu has taken good care of you, John Howard," Elaine put in.

"Where's . . . Doug?"

"He was by to check on you earlier, and he said he'd be back around lunchtime, but to call him if there was any change in your condition. I'll let his office know that you've woken up."

Stark nodded slowly. He trusted Doug Huddleston more than he did some snot-nosed kid. Seemed like they were making doctors younger and younger all the time. And then he realized that he was starting to sound like Uncle Newt. The thought made a pang of sorrow go through him.

He looked at Lu and asked, "What's . . . the extent . . . of the damage, Doctor?"

"Well, you have two bullet wounds," Lu replied without looking at Stark's chart, "one in your right shoulder, one in your upper left arm. The one in your shoulder is the more serious of the two. I cleaned and sutured the one in your left arm, and it should be fine. As for the other, the bullet went straight through, luckily missed the bone, and didn't deflect and do even more damage. In time you should regain the full use of that arm."

"How much . . . time?"

"A month, maybe six weeks. You also have a cut on your face that required a couple of stitches. I have some experience with cosmetic surgery, so I went ahead and did that myself, rather than calling in a specialist. There shouldn't be much of a scar."

"I reckon I'm past worrying too much . . . about how handsome I am," Stark said. "Anything else?"

"Just the loss of blood and general wear and tear on the body. My medical advice would be to take a vacation as soon as your shoulder is healed up enough for you to travel. Go to Acapulco or some place like that. Lie on the beach in the sun for a few weeks, and get a lot of rest. You need it."

"That sounds wonderful, Doctor," Elaine said. "You don't know this workaholic husband of mine, though. He'll say that he's got a ranch to run."

"It's the truth," Stark growled.

Lu said, "I'll let the two of you work that out. Right now I have other patients to check on. I'm glad that you're awake, Mr. Stark. I didn't think we were going to lose you, but you never know."

With that he left the room, which had flower arrangements sitting on every available space. Stark waited until the door was shut, then said, "Kid could use some work on his bedside manner."

"Yes, but he's a good doctor," Elaine said as she sat in a chair beside the bed. She reached out and took hold of Stark's left hand with both of hers. She squeezed it tightly. "You really had me worried, John Howard."

"Why? You know how tough I am. I got shot up before, in Vietnam."

"Yes, but then I didn't have to see you lying there covered with blood, with your face so pale you looked dead. By the time you got home from over there you were pretty much yourself again."

Stark nodded. "I knew I was coming home to you. That gave me plenty of incentive . . . to heal up."

She smiled and held his hand, and they sat there quietly for a while, just glad to be with each other. Stark felt his eyelids getting heavy. He tried to keep his eyes open, and when

Elaine noticed the struggle, she said, "It's all right, John Howard. You go right ahead and sleep. You need the rest."

"Don't want to . . . go away from you . . . again."

"You won't," she told him. "You'll be right here, and I'll be with you. We'll never be separated again."

The news that Stark was awake and recovering from his wounds got around fast. Devery, W.R., Hubie, and Everett were the first ones to come by to see him. After handshakes all around, Devery got down to business by saying, "We've all been thinkin', John Howard. You set us up."

Stark frowned. "How do you figure that?"

"You knew Sam Gonzales was wrong. You knew Ramirez was gonna come after you again. We could've stayed to help you, but instead you sent us all home."

"It wasn't your fight," Stark said.

"The hell it ain't," Hubie put in. "It's every decent citizen's fight. The courts have put the criminals' rights above ours for so long I reckon we just got used to goin' along with that, even though it don't make a lick of sense."

W.R. said, "We forgot how to fight back. But we're learnin' again."

"We're learnin' from you, John Howard," Everett added. "You've showed us the way."

Stark couldn't sit up, but he was able to lift his head from the pillow. "Now, hold on just a minute," he said. "I never set out to show anybody the way to anything. I just wanted to protect my ranch and my family."

"That's what we want, too," Devery insisted. "That's why we're gettin' together with all the other ranchers and farmers and even some folks from here in town, and we're puttin' together a patrol system. We're gonna do what the government can't—or won't—do: shut down the border and keep this little chunk of Texas safe from invaders."

"Because that's what they are, you know," Everett put in. "Invaders. Just like an army tryin' to come in here and take over and have ever'thing their own way. Well, it ain't gonna be like that no more. No, sir."

Stark looked around at the solemn faces of his friends and said, "Y'all are serious about this, aren't you?"

"You're not the only one who can fight back against evil, John Howard," Devery said. "It's our fight, too, and pretty soon those damn drug runners are gonna know it."

Stark looked over at Elaine. "I don't think I'm going to be able to talk any sense into their heads."

She smiled and said, "About as much chance of that as there is of anybody talking sense into *your* head, John Howard."

He gave a grim chuckle as he let his head back down on the pillow. "I know when I'm beat," he said. "But you boys better be careful. You don't know what you're letting yourself in for."

"It's the bad guys who don't know what they're in for," Hubie said with a grin. "But they're fixin' to find out."

Stark had been glad to see his friends. His next visitor wasn't so welcome.

The door of the hospital room swung open not long after Devery and the others had left, and Sheriff Norval Lee Hammond came in. He took his hat off, nodded politely to Elaine, and then said to Stark, "I hear you killed five more men last night. Gettin' to be a habit with you, ain't it?"

Before Stark could answer, Elaine said sharply, "My husband only killed four men last night, Sheriff. I killed the fifth one. Have you come to arrest us both this time?"

"I'm still conductin' an investigation," Hammond growled. "I'm not ready to make any arrests."

"That's because we didn't commit any crime," Stark said. "Those men were heavily armed, they were on my land, and they shot up my house. Not even you and Wilfredo can make this look like anything other than an open-and-shut case of self-defense."

Hammond's face flushed, and his jaw was tight as he

replied, "Like I said, I'm still conductin' my investigation. In the meantime, I've got a deputy stationed right outside your door."

"To make sure I don't escape?" Stark held up his bandaged left arm, which had an IV line attached to it. Several monitors were hooked up to sensors stuck to his body in various places. His right shoulder was heavily bandaged and immobilized. "I don't think I'm goin' anywhere in a hurry."

"The deputy is there to stand guard and make sure nobody bothers you," Hammond explained. "Don't waste your breath saying thanks."

"I won't."

Hammond started to turn angrily toward the door, but he stopped and said, "Look, Stark, I know you don't like me and don't think much of me. To tell you the truth, I don't give a damn what your opinion of me is. But no matter what you think, I'm tryin' to do my job the best way I can."

Stark just looked at him for a long moment and then said, "If you really believed that, Sheriff, I could almost feel sorry for you. But I don't think you do. I think you know better."

Hammond just glared at him for a second and then walked out.

After a moment, Elaine said, "Far be it from me to say anything good about the sheriff, but I'm glad he put a deputy on the door."

"Why?"

She stood up and went over to the window. The blinds were closed and the curtains had been pulled all day. Now she opened them and stepped back so that Stark could look outside.

"So that somebody will keep the locusts out," she said.

Stark stared in disbelief. The room was on the ground floor of the hospital, so he had a good view of the street outside. It was clogged with vans that had TV station call letters and logos plastered on them. Several of the vehicles had tall antennas raised so that they could beam satellite transmissions directly back to their home bases. The lawn in front of

the hospital was packed with people. At least three field reporters were doing stand-ups, talking solemnly into hand-
held microphones while cameramen with video cams on their
shoulders trained the equipment on them.

"Good Lord," Stark said. "They're gonna run out of hair
spray and mousse at Wal-Mart."

Elaine broke up laughing as she closed the blinds again.
"Tell me about it," she said. "You're news, John Howard, big
news. The story is all over Texas by now."

Stark winced. "I never wanted that."

"No, but it's the twenty-first century, so you've got it.
Nothing like a little information overload."

"They can yammer all they want to, as long as they leave
me alone."

"In other words you're glad I've turned down the dozens
of interview requests so far."

Stark couldn't fathom why that many journalists would
want to talk to him. He said, "Keep turnin' 'em down."

"I intend to."

For the next twenty-four hours, Stark drifted in and out of
sleep. The IV pumped fluids and antibiotics into him, and
his own natural strength, the iron constitution that a lifetime
of hard work had given him, began to assert itself. By the
next day he felt better. By the day after that he was starting
to get restless. All this lying around in bed got on his nerves.
He wanted to be up and doing something.

Elaine had kept her promise to stay by his side, sometimes carrying it to unreasonable levels. But even she had to
leave to eat and sleep and make sure the ranch was function-
ing. She never went back and forth from town to the Diamond
S alone, though. Stark had talked to Devery and arranged
things so that Elaine would always have an armed escort. If
she chafed under that restriction, she gave no sign of it. She
wanted Stark's mind to be as easy as possible while he was
recuperating.

She was gone during the afternoon of the third day while
Stark sat up in bed and read the newspapers that had been

brought in earlier. Although his battle with Ramirez's men was still front-page news, the aftermath of it was below the fold now. Liberal politicians squawking in Washington and anti-American sentiment and violence overseas had reclaimed their usual top-of-the-page spots.

Stark read that day's story about what had happened on the Diamond S and learned that the five dead men had been identified. All of them were Mexican nationals, in the U.S. illegally, and they all had criminal records on the other side of the border. That came as no surprise to Stark. The Mexican government had issued a statement deploring the American vigilantism that had cost the lives of five of the country's citizens. That stance wasn't unexpected, either, thought Stark. It went right along with the postmodern, politically correct thinking that said people should never take steps to protect themselves from violence and evil; that was the government's job, and if the government couldn't handle it, well, that was just too bad.

A sidebar to the main story was headlined: SHERIFF WARNS SO-CALLED CITIZENS' PATROL. The story said that Sheriff Norval Lee Hammond had called a press conference to announce that vigilante activities would not be tolerated in Val Verde County. "If you're thinking about taking the law into your own hands, you'd better think twice," Hammond was quoted as saying. Devery Small, the spokesman for what he described as a citizens' activist group, had replied that there would be no need for such organizations if only the sheriff's department would do its job the way it was supposed to.

Stark chuckled as he read that. Devery and Hammond both liked to talk, and he figured they could go back and forth at each other like that all day. He grew more solemn as he read that there were already unofficial reports of shots being exchanged between the citizen patrols along the border and smugglers who were trying to bring drugs across. No one had been killed, at least not as far as anybody knew, but the potential was there.

Stark lowered the newspaper as the door of the hospital

room opened. He expected to see Elaine, but instead a stranger stepped into the room and let the door swing shut softly behind him. Before it closed completely, Stark caught a glimpse of the deputy standing stiffly on guard in the hallway.

The man who had just come in was tall and slender, a little stoop-shouldered, in his forties. He had brown hair that was thinning and carefully combed over a bald spot. He wore a gray suit and a dark blue tie, and he might as well have had a neon sign on his head announcing that he worked for the government. "Mr. Stark?" he said.

"I reckon you know who I am," Stark said. "Who're you?"

The stranger reached inside his suit coat and took out a leather folder. "My name is John Kelso," he said as he opened the folder and held it out toward Stark. The folder contained a badge and an identification card, both of them quite official-looking. "Please take this and have a good look at it. I want you to be certain I am who I say I am."

Stark took the folder and studied the card. Kelso's photograph was on it, as well as the words DRUG ENFORCEMENT ADMINISTRATION. That explained how Kelso had gotten past the deputy. Stark closed the folder and tossed it on the foot of the bed, within easy reach of his visitor.

"What does the DEA want with me?"

Kelso picked up the folder and slipped it back inside his jacket. "We want you to stop what you're doing," he said bluntly.

Stark smiled and lifted his left arm so that he could gesture gingerly at the hospital bed. "Stop recovering from being shot, you mean?"

"You know what I mean, Mr. Stark," Kelso said. "We want you to put an end to this war you're fighting against alleged drug smugglers from across the border. You're putting a strain on relations between the United States and Mexico."

"You mean I'm embarrassing the government because all the news stories point out that you haven't been able to do a damn thing about the flood of drugs coming across the Rio Grande."

Kelso's face flushed angrily. "You don't know what the DEA can or can't do, Mr. Stark. You're not privy to the inner workings of the organization. But it's the job of the government to stem the tide of drugs. It's not up to private citizens like you and your friends."

Stark couldn't help but grin. He said, "There must be some truth to those rumors about Devery and the boys shooting it out with drug runners."

"I'm not here to confirm or deny rumors. I believe you were formerly a member of the Marine Corps, Mr. Stark?"

The sudden shift in the direction of the conversation took Stark by surprise. "That's right. I was a leatherneck. Served in 'Nam."

"Then you understand the concept of serving your country and doing what's best for America. Unless, in your zeal to cause trouble, you've forgotten."

Stark breathed heavily, struggling for a few moments to rein in his temper before he trusted himself to speak. "I haven't forgotten anything, mister. And no chickenshit little bureaucrat is going to come in here and tell me I *caused* this trouble. It came to me."

"Oh?" Kelso said coolly. "What about the altercation in a Mexican nightclub known as the Blue Burro, approximately a week ago? That's a long way from your ranch, Mr. Stark, and yet you killed three men there."

"You don't know that," Stark snapped.

"I may not be able to prove it, but I know it, and so do you. That's where all this trouble started, and *you* started it, Mr. Stark."

Stubbornly, Stark shook his head. "That's a damned lie. It started in Tommy Carranza's barn. He was the first one to die, and I didn't have anything to do with that. Tommy was my neighbor and one of my best friends."

"And now his family is in hiding. Somewhere in the Cheyenne, Wyoming, area, I believe."

How the hell did Kelso know that? Then Stark remembered that the man worked for the government. They had a way of finding out whatever they wanted to know, but only when it suited their own purposes.

"Leave Julie and the kids out of this," he said. "Let them grieve for Tommy and get on with their lives."

"We have no intention of involving Mrs. Carranza and her children in this matter," Kelso said. "But we're not going to tolerate a bunch of so-called vigilantes breaking state and federal laws."

"Nobody's breaking any laws except the drug smugglers. Why don't you crack down on them?"

Kelso ignored the question. "There could be charges of conspiracy, racketeering, incitement to violence, violations of international treaties . . ."

"You'd really put men in jail for trying to defend themselves?" Stark stared at the government man in disbelief.

"We have a legal system to deal with criminals—"

Stark snorted in disgust. "And it deals with them so well that killers and rapists go free every day of the week on technicalities, while innocent people put more bars on their windows and more locks on their doors. A few rich folks who can afford it live in gated, guarded communities, while everybody else who just wants to live a safe, law-abiding life has to take their chances with all the two-legged animals running loose."

"You're exaggerating, Mr. Stark. It's not that bad."

"It's gettin' there," Stark said heavily. "And you and the rest of the bureaucrats like you aren't doing a thing to stop it."

"Well, we can stop *you*," Kelso said, "and we can stop your friends. You'd better pass along that warning to them. You're rocking the boat—"

"Lord help us!" Stark exclaimed.

"You're rocking the boat," Kelso went on doggedly, "and we won't put up with it." He gave a curt nod. "Good day, Mr. Stark."

Stark's lips drew back from his teeth. "Get the hell outta

here, you weasel, before I get up outta this bed and beat you to death with an IV stand."

Kelso smiled thinly. "Threatening a government agent isn't going to help your case. Or have you forgotten that you're still facing manslaughter charges?"

"Get out," Stark said again. He started to swing his legs off the bed.

Kelso backed quickly toward the door. "Remember what I told you. You'd better use your influence to put a stop to this, or you'll be in deep trouble, Stark."

Stark's bare feet hit the tile floor. The hospital gown gaped open in the back, but he was too mad to care about his butt hanging out. He grabbed the IV stand with his left hand and stood up.

Kelso hustled out of the room. Stark was glad to see him go. The sight of the smarmy bastard made him sick. He was dizzy, too, since he hadn't been on his feet that much in the past few days.

He sat down slowly on the edge of the bed and took several deep breaths. Gradually, the spinning in his head settled down. He hoped Elaine wouldn't find out about this. She wouldn't like it that he had gotten out of bed without her there to make sure he didn't fall. She probably wouldn't be too happy about him threatening to wallop a government man with an IV stand, either.

Kelso had deserved it, though. The very idea of him coming in here and talking like that to a wounded man!

Still, Stark knew he was going to have to discuss this with Devery and the others. They all had homes and families. They couldn't afford to have the government after them. But the decision would be up to them; Stark couldn't make it for them.

What had happened to the world? he asked himself as he leaned back in the hospital bed. The government was supposed to uphold the law, protect the country's borders, and keep its citizens safe. Instead, in a mindless quest for "tolerance" and "diversity" that in reality was neither tolerant nor diverse, it was opening the borders, letting lawlessness run unchecked, and the only real protection a citizen had for himself and his family was what he could provide with his own two hands.

Despite all the good in the country—and Stark was still convinced that the United States was the greatest, most decent nation on the face of the earth—there were still dark alleys where evil lurked, and that evil was protected by incompetent, vainglorious government toadies like Kelso who were more concerned with their own image than anything else. It was a sorry state of affairs, and as long as the elitists on both coasts had an iron grip on the media and controlled as much of the political climate as they did, nothing was going to change unless it was for the worse. Stark struggled not to give in to the despair that he felt creeping into his soul.

There was always hope as long as good men fought the good fight, he told himself. They might be outnumbered, but they couldn't give up. He would tell Devery, W.R., and the others what Kelso had said, but he knew they wouldn't abandon what they had started. He knew because if he had been in their place, he wouldn't have quit. He *couldn't* quit.

Not as long as there was breath in his body.

Twenty-one

When Elaine came back in, Stark didn't say anything to her about Kelso's visit. He could tell she was upset about something, though, and finally she said, "A government man came out to the ranch today, John Howard."

Stark sat up in bed. "A tall, skinny bastard named Kelso?"

She nodded. "That's right. He said you were going to get in bad trouble if you didn't stop causing problems with Mexico. He wanted you to persuade Devery and the others to give up their patrols, too."

"That son of a bitch!" Stark burst out. "If I'd known he'd been out to the ranch bothering you, I really would have bent that IV stand over his head!"

"He came here, too?"

Stark nodded. "Yeah, and gave me the same line of crap. The DEA is embarrassed that we've been calling attention to all the drug smuggling going on along the border."

"You didn't promise him anything, did you?"

"Of course not. I still respect the government, I guess, whether it always deserves it or not, but not some flunky who's just trying to protect his ass and his budget."

Stark was angry, but he forced himself to calm down. He had already started thinking about getting out of the hospital, and he knew if he got too upset, he might cause himself a relapse and be stuck here that much longer. He told Elaine to ask Devery to come see him tomorrow.

"We'll hash it all out," Stark said. "The boys deserve to know what they're letting themselves in for. I don't expect any of them to give up, though."

"They won't," Elaine agreed. "They're too stubborn . . . just like another old rancher I know."

"If I didn't have all these wires and lines hooked up to me, I'd show you just how old I am, woman," Stark said with a mock growl.

"You get a little stronger, John Howard, and I might just hold you to that."

Stark watched the TV news that night before going to sleep and was glad to see that there was nothing about him on it. The media were gradually losing interest in him. The newspaper stories had moved to the inside pages. There was nothing about the citizens' patrols, either. Evidently, everything was quiet along the border right now. A fella could almost believe that Ramirez had decided it was all too much trouble and moved his operation elsewhere.

Stark knew better than to think that, however. Vultures were patient birds, able to circle for a long time before they finally swooped down on their prey. Ramirez was just waiting for the right time to strike again, but that time would come. Stark was sure of it.

The TV news trucks were gone. So were the newspaper and magazine reporters. The mob had moved on at last, Silencio Ryan thought as he surveyed the dark, quiet street in front of the hospital.

The mob had moved on—and it was time for him to move in.

He walked along the street, just a guy in a baseball cap. Nobody who saw him would remember much about him.

When he was a block past the hospital, he turned into a side street and strolled past an assisted living center. Nearly all the windows were dark at this late hour. Ryan kept an eye on them anyway as he walked by, watching for the telltale flick of a curtain. A lot of old people didn't sleep well at night, and they didn't have anything better to do than to look out their windows and remember a time when they were young and vital.

Ryan never gave it much thought, but he would have said that the odds were against him living to be an old man. On the other hand, he had survived for this long, and considering some of the dangers he had gone through in his life, the odds must have been against that, too.

John Howard Stark didn't know it yet, but the odds against *him* living to see another sunrise had gone up considerably tonight.

"I don't care how you do it, just get in there and kill him," Ramirez had said, his voice shaking with rage. The smooth facade that the leader of the drug cartel had constructed over the years was slipping. This damn gringo Stark had killed a dozen of his men now, and yet Stark still drew breath! It was insane!

What was even worse, Stark's activities had inspired some of the other foolish gringos to stand up to the drug runners, instead of hiding their heads in the sand as they had for so many years. Twice in the past few days, Ramirez's couriers had been attacked as they crossed the river into Texas. Both times the drug runners had been forced to retreat in the face of deadly accurate fire from hidden riflemen. Ramirez had seethed when he heard the news. Those Texans were not supposed to have the *cojones* to defy him this way. They never had before—until Stark came along.

So Stark had to die. Ramirez had allowed Ryan to set up the assault on Stark's ranch, the assault that had ended with five more good men dead. Tonight Ramirez had said, "Kill him yourself, with your own hands. Watch him die with your own eyes. Or if you cannot do that . . . I have some rocket-propelled grenades I bought from an arms dealer. Blow up the whole fucking hospital if you have to. But kill Stark."

Ryan knew which window marked the location of Stark's room. An RPG placed right through the glass would do the job, all right. He could kill Stark that way without leveling the whole hospital. Ramirez was too mad to be thinking straight. Blowing up a hospital was something even the sluggish, politically paralyzed American government could not ignore. Even one grenade might be too much. Better to slip in, accomplish the job, and slip back out with as little fuss as possible. A surgical strike, so to speak.

That was why Ryan was approaching the back of the hospital now. The idea of killing an already wounded man in his hospital bed didn't really appeal to Ryan's aesthetic sense, but orders were orders. And once Stark was dead, chances were this whole newly organized civilian resistance to the drug trade would fall apart. Stark, after all, was the figurehead for the movement.

Of course, they also ran the risk of making him a martyr, which might cause even more trouble. But Ryan would deal with that when and if the time came.

A delivery truck was backed up to the rear doors of the hospital, and a couple of guys were using dollies to wheel in cases of institutional-sized cans of food. A hospital security guard—not even packing a gun, for Christ's sake!—stood beside the doors. The guard glanced at Ryan, only slightly curious, and said, "Hey, pard, you're not supposed to be back here."

"Where's the emergency room?" Ryan asked as he came closer. He lifted his right hand, which had a bloody swath of cloth wrapped around it. "I cut myself pretty bad."

"Shit, I'd say so. Look, the entrance is around front, but I guess you can come through this way—"

By that time Ryan was close enough. The little pistol had a noise suppressor screwed onto its barrel, and the cloth wrapped around his hand would muffle the sound of the shot even more, but all that played hell with accuracy, so he had to be close before he fired. He raised his hand and shot the guard in the right eye at a distance of about a foot. The pistol made hardly any sound at all. The bullet popped right through the guard's eye and bored on into his brain. It was a small-caliber round and didn't have the power to blow a hole through the skull, so it bounced and rattled around in there, mushing even more of the unlucky guard's gray matter. Not that he felt it, since he was already dead and sliding down the wall behind him.

One of the delivery guys came out of the hospital, saw the guard going down, and said, "Hey, what's wrong with him?"

"I don't know," Ryan said. "I think he passed out."

The deliveryman pushed his empty dolly aside and rushed over. Ryan moved aside to get out of his way, and as the man bent over Ryan shot him through the ear. That was just as effective. The man went down, sprawling across the dead guard's body.

That left just the other deliveryman. He came out a moment later and walked right into a bullet.

Ryan piled all three bodies on the lift at the rear of the truck, thumbed the button, and rode up with them. He rolled them into the back of the truck, hopped out, and pulled down the door. As far as he could tell, no one had seen what had happened, and it would be a while before anybody realized there was something wrong back here. By that time, he would be long gone.

He walked into the hospital, cradling his right wrist in his left hand so that the bloody bandage was prominent. He had rearranged the swath of cloth a little so that the scorched bullet holes weren't as visible.

It was late, after visiting hours, but a few visitors were still there, as usual. The nurses hadn't gotten around to running off everyone just yet. Nobody paid much attention to Ryan, though. With that makeshift bandage on his hand, they just assumed he was supposed to be there. If anyone had asked him, he would have used the emergency room story again. Or told them he was looking for X-ray, as the mood struck him.

He paused at a corner and looked around into a hallway where patient rooms were located. The nurses' station was halfway along the corridor, at an intersection where another hall met this one. One nurse stood at the counter, writing on a chart. She didn't glance toward Ryan. He knew that Stark's room was three doors past the nurses' station, on the right. Ryan didn't have any doubt about that. He had always had a superb sense of location and always knew exactly where he was in relation to everything else around him. That innate talent was one of the things that had kept him alive this long.

A buzzer sounded, and the nurse at the counter put the chart aside and walked around into the corridor. She went to a room on the left, several doors past the room where Stark was. She would probably be in there a few minutes, Ryan thought. He moved on around the corner and walked quickly, purposefully, toward Stark's room. All his instincts told him he wouldn't get a better chance than this.

He had just reached the nurses' station when he realized something was wrong. There was no deputy outside Stark's door. Ryan had checked with contacts inside the sheriff's office. Hammond still had a deputy assigned to guard Stark. But the deputy wasn't there . . .

Which meant he had to be somewhere else.

"Hey! Can I help you, mister?"

Ryan paused and looked over at the area behind the counter at the nurses' station. The deputy was sitting back there in a swivel chair. He'd probably been flirting with the nurse who'd been writing on the chart. He wasn't supposed to leave his post at the door of Stark's room, but how much discipline could you expect from a force whose leader was firmly in the pocket of the biggest drug smuggler in Mexico?

Ryan stopped, gave the deputy a pained smile, and lifted the hand with its bloody bandage. "Is the emergency room down this way?"

"No, man, it's back the way you came in. You blind?" The

deputy stood up and came over to lean against the counter and point back along the corridor. "What'd you do to yourself, anyway?"

"I guess I'm just careless," Ryan said. He made as if to unwrap the bandage. "I think I cut it down to the bone. . . ."

The deputy leaned over to look, and Ryan shot him through his mouth, which was hanging open. The man went up on his toes and then fell facedown across the counter. Ryan shoved him away. He fell limply behind the counter where he couldn't be seen unless someone walked around there.

Ryan looked down at the spots of blood on the counter and shook his head. That was messy. When the nurse came back she would see them right away. He took a handkerchief from his pocket and wiped up the blood, careful not to leave any smudges. That might give him a few more seconds, and a few seconds could be important.

He already had a sense that time was slipping away. He couldn't afford to waste any more of it.

John Howard Stark had to die . . . *now.*

Stark hated sleeping on his back, but with his left arm and his right shoulder both wounded, he didn't have any choice. The left arm was much better, almost healed in fact, but it still twinged in pain if he rolled over on it during the night.

His head jerked up on the pillow, and his eyes opened. He blinked as he looked around the room. The overhead light was out, but the light in the bathroom had been left on, with the door pushed almost all the way shut. That gave enough illumination for him to see that the room was empty. He had finally talked Elaine into going home and getting a good night's sleep in her own bed while some of their friends stood guard. She had been sleeping in the chair in the hospital room every night, but nobody could get any decent rest doing that. As Stark looked around the room, he felt a touch of loneliness. He was used to having his wife around.

He was curious, too. Something had woken him from a sound sleep. It hadn't been a nightmare; at least he didn't think so. He couldn't remember even having any dreams, good or bad. But something had roused him from his slumber. Maybe one of the machines hooked up to him had beeped or something. They did that from time to time.

The door began to hiss open on its pneumatic closer.

Stark sat up in bed, figuring one of the nurses was coming in. She had probably made some noise out in the hall, and that was what woke him up. He hoped she wasn't bringing him some pill to make him sleep better. He had never understood why they would wake you up in a hospital to give you a sleeping pill.

But it wasn't a nurse. It was a man in a baseball cap, with a bandaged hand. He stopped short when he saw Stark sitting up in the bed. "Sorry, pard," he said. "I'm turned around." He came closer and started to hold out the bandaged hand. "I was lookin' for the emergency room . . ."

"I know you," Stark said suddenly. The hat and the clothes were different, but he recognized the voice.

It belonged to the man he had talked to in the Blue Burro, the cowboy who had told him where to find the three men who had killed Tommy Carranza.

Stark's comment made the man pause, and that gave Stark the chance to throw himself out of the bed to the right, toward the window. The IV needle ripped out of the back of his left hand, but he didn't notice the pain. He heard a couple of small coughing sounds, followed by the rattle of bullets hitting the metal bed frame after tearing through the mattress where he had been lying a heartbeat earlier.

One of those tall, rolling carts found in hospitals sat to the right of the bed. Stark grabbed it and lifted it as the gunman fired again. He heard the wind-rip of the bullet past his ear. That just added to the chemicals coursing through Stark's bloodstream. Despite his bad shoulder and wounded arm, he heaved the piece of hospital furniture up and tossed it across the bed at the would-be assassin.

The man had to duck back to avoid the thing. It crashed against the door with a loud racket. Stark was tangled in the wires and leads attached to all the monitoring equipment. He yanked on them and pulled over a couple of pieces of apparatus. They fell with a huge crash. Stark crouched as the gunman thrust his hand in the door again. The door wouldn't open all the way because of the cart Stark had thrown against it. A couple of shots spat out. Stark reached down, found a bedpan, and threw it at the door. It was plastic, of course, and wouldn't do any damage, but the killer flinched instinctively, anyway.

Then the guy disappeared, and Stark heard running footsteps out in the hall. The assassin was trying to get away. Stark's anger boiled up inside him and urged him to give chase, but he knew he couldn't. Adrenaline and survival instinct had saved his life, but the shape he was in, there was only so far he could push himself. He already felt a hot wetness at his right shoulder, as if the wound there had opened up again. Stark slumped against the bed and held himself up.

People yelled and screamed out in the corridor, and a few seconds later the door opened part of the way, stopping with a jarring impact against the cart. "Mr. Stark! Mr. Stark, are you all right?"

The voice belonged to one of the nurses. Stark recognized it. "I'm okay," he called back. "Be careful. There's a guy out there with a gun."

"He's g-gone." The nurse's voice caught, and she muffled a sob. "He . . . he killed Deputy Reynolds!"

Stark didn't know any of the deputies by name, and since they worked for Norval Lee Hammond he didn't have much respect for them, either. But he was sorry to hear that one of them had been killed.

"Have you called the police?" he asked.

"They're on their way. My God, wh-why would anybody *do* this?"

Because they were all in the middle of a war, Stark

thought. A war that some people blamed him for starting. He knew that wasn't really true. Ramirez had started this war.

And God help him, Stark didn't know how it was going to end. All he knew was that more people would probably die first.

BOOK THREE

He who follows in death's wake
risks all to gain little
only his soul.

   —Ling Yuan, second-century Chinese
    warrior/philosopher

Twenty-two

All the uproar that had gone before was only a prelude to what followed the attempt on Stark's life in the hospital. Sheriff Hammond would have preferred to keep things quiet, but there was no way even he could cover up four cold-blooded murders and an attack on a badly wounded patient.

Dr. Lu was on duty in the emergency room that night, and when he finished changing the dressing on Stark's wounded shoulder, he said that Stark was lucky not to have damaged himself even more. The wound had broken open again, but only slightly, and it hadn't bled much. "You've set back your recovery, but only by a couple of days," he had told Stark.

"Better than letting that son of a bitch shoot me," Stark had replied. "That probably would have taken a mite longer to recuperate from."

Lu could only shrug and nod.

The hospital was crawling with cops and the street outside was clogged once again with the news media by the time Elaine arrived the next morning. "I heard about what happened on the news this morning," she said as she hurried to Stark's bedside. "Are you all right, John Howard?"

"I'm fine," he assured her. "Made the morning news on the radio, did I?"

"The radio?" she repeated with a frown. "John Howard, you were on *The Today Show* and *Good Morning, America.* Probably on CBS and Fox and CNN, too, but I didn't check."

Stark grimaced. "The story's gone national, has it?"

"That's right. I guess the fact that you were almost murdered in your hospital bed caught the attention of the networks. And four innocent bystanders *were* killed."

"I know," Stark said with a sigh. "I can't help but feel sort of responsible for that."

"Don't you dare," Elaine said promptly. "Nobody's to blame but Ramirez and that hit man he sent after you."

Her mention of the killer made Stark think of something. "Can you let Hodge Purdee know that I'd like to see him?"

"The Border Patrol agent? Sure. I didn't think you had much use for government types these days, though."

"Purdee's different. He and I talk the same language."

"I'll give him a call. In the meantime, the reporters are clamoring again, wanting to interview you."

"This time I'll talk to them," Stark said. "I've been thinking about it, and maybe a little publicity is just what we need."

"It won't be a little. It'll be a lot."

"Whatever it takes," Stark said. "I want to talk to Purdee first, though."

Satisfied that he was all right, Elaine left to call Hodge Purdee. While she was gone, the door opened again and Sheriff Hammond and District Attorney Wilfredo came into the room.

Even though Stark wasn't glad to see them, he decided he might as well try to be polite. "Sorry about your deputy, Sheriff," he said.

Hammond gave a curt shake of his head. "Not your fault, Stark." The man looked haggard, and his eyes were haunted. He had to know that the man who'd killed the deputy, the security guard, and the two deliverymen worked for the Vulture . . . which in a way meant that they shared the same employer. If that fact gnawed at Hammond's insides . . . well, he had it coming as far as Stark was concerned.

"Mr. Stark," Wilfredo began, "I'm here to inform you that there will be no charges filed against you as a result of the incident last night—"

"Well, that's good to know," Stark broke in sarcastically, "especially since I was just trying to keep that bastard from killing me."

Wilfredo took a deep breath, controlled his temper, and went on, "And my office has determined that no charges will be filed against you in regards to the deaths of those men on your ranch. Your actions and those of your wife have been officially ruled self-defense . . . although the way you were waiting for them still gives me some concern."

"Just bein' prepared," Stark said. "What about the other charges?"

"That case has already been sent to the grand jury. It'll have to play out in due course." The district attorney made a face. "To be honest with you, though, I don't expect an indictment."

Something in Wilfredo's voice told Stark that the man had given up. He knew this particular hand was stacked against him, and he was practical enough not to beat his head against a stone wall, to mix that metaphor, Stark thought. Wilfredo was telling him that for all intents and purposes, the official prosecution of him was over.

The unofficial *persecution* might be a different matter.

Stark looked at Hammond. "Can I expect a better job of protecting me the rest of the time I'm here, Sheriff?"

"I'll increase the guards," Hammond said bitterly. "To tell you the truth, I'll be damned glad when you're out of here, Stark."

Stark nodded. "You and me both." He had more confidence in his own abilities to protect himself than he did in the sheriff's.

"That's all," Wilfredo said. "I'll be in touch with Sam

Gonzales and cover the same ground with him." He turned to leave but paused to say, "I hope you're proud of yourself, Mr. Stark. Because of you, the whole valley is in an uproar."

"That's what's wrong with the whole thing," Stark shot back. "The valley should have been in an uproar long before now over everything that criminals like Ramirez have gotten away with." He switched his gaze to Hammond. "For example, Sheriff, do you have any leads to the man who attacked me and killed those other men?"

"We're investigating," Hammond snapped.

"But when it turns out the guy works for Ramirez, you won't do anything about it, will you?"

"I told you before, Stark—I do my job." With a big hand, Hammond jerked the door open and stalked out before Stark could say anything else. Wilfredo followed, a worried look in his face.

Stark settled back against the pillows behind him. Wilfredo, in his opinion, was an honest man, but one trapped in a corrupt, ineffectual system. Hammond was just rotten, right to the core. Both of them were a danger to the honest people of the valley.

Of course, Stark thought, some would say the same thing about *him*.

Hodge Purdee came in around lunchtime. Elaine was back and was sitting in the chair leafing through a magazine.

"Hello, John Howard," Purdee said as he shook hands with Stark. "Sorry I haven't been by to see you before now. We've been mighty busy lately. I suppose you know that, though."

Elaine got to her feet. "Would you two like me to leave?"

"No, that's all right," Stark told her. "Anything I've got to say to Hodge I can say in front of you."

"And I certainly have no objection to your presence, Mrs. Stark," Purdee said. "With all due respect, you make even a hospital room look better, ma'am."

She smiled and sat down again.

Stark chuckled and said, "Stop flirting with my wife long enough to answer a question for me, Hodge."

"Sure, if I can. Answer the question, that is. I can stop flirtin' with Mrs. Stark, but it'll take an effort."

Stark grew more serious and asked, "Did you send me an e-mail a while back?"

Purdee frowned. "An e-mail? No, I don't recall ever sending you an e-mail, John Howard."

"Not even an anonymous one?"

"No. What's all this about?"

"I've got another question first. Do you know a man in his late forties, early fifties, still in very good shape, with red hair and kind of a rawboned face? He's not fair-skinned like most redheads, either, but dark enough that he could have some Hispanic blood in him."

Purdee thought about it for a moment and then shook his head. "I don't think I've ever run into somebody who looks like that. Who is he?"

"The fella who tried to kill me last night. I thought he might work for you."

"John Howard!" Elaine exclaimed.

Purdee's face purpled with anger, and his hands clenched into knobby fists. "Damn it, I thought we were friends!" he exploded. "By God, if you weren't shot up and in a hospital bed, I'd—"

Quickly, Stark held up his hands, palms outward. "Hold on, both of you. I didn't put that very well. Just listen for a minute, and I'll explain what I'm talking about."

"It better be good," Purdee snapped.

Stark talked for several minutes, starting with the mysterious e-mail he had gotten that put him on the trail of Tommy's killers, the trail that had led him to the Blue Burro. He went on to explain about the man he had talked to in the strip club and how he had taken him for one of Purdee's informants. He finished up by saying that the same man had been the one who'd attacked him the night before.

"I wasn't really accusing you of anything, Hodge," Stark concluded. "As soon as the guy showed up here and started shooting at me, I knew you hadn't sent him."

"No, and I didn't send you that e-mail, either. I'm a little disappointed that you believed I'd try to make an end run around the law that way, John Howard."

Stark shrugged. "I had just talked to you not long before, and I knew how frustrated you were by the whole situation along the border. I just figured you were trying to do something about it the only way you knew how."

"Well . . . I'm not saying I might not have done something like that . . . but in this case, I sure didn't."

Elaine asked, "But then who sent that e-mail? The man in the Blue Burro?"

"That's my best guess," Stark said with a nod.

"Who is he?"

"He must work for Ramirez. His top killer, maybe."

Purdee shook his head. "That doesn't make any sense. Why would he set up three of Ramirez's own men like that?"

"Maybe he wasn't setting them up," Stark said. "Maybe they were just the bait in the trap."

"To lure you in," Elaine said. "And you went, just like a mouse to cheese."

Stark smiled. "Yeah. And the redhead could have figured that if Ramirez's men weren't able to kill me, he'd have a better idea of just what he was up against."

"Like a test," Purdee said. He thought it over and nodded. "It makes sense, sort of, anyway. Who knows how a cold-blooded killer's mental processes work? He could have considered the lives of three men a small price to pay to see you in action, John Howard."

"Lambs to the slaughter," Elaine murmured.

"Not lambs," Stark said. "Those three tortured and killed Tommy. They had it comin'."

"I'm not arguing with you about that. But it's starting to look like this man may have been manipulating things all along."

"Yeah, and I don't like bein' anybody's puppet," Stark said. "But he's seen now what I can do. From here on out, it may be him against me, pure and simple."

"You're in no shape to have some crazed killer after you," Purdee said. "You'll need guards around the clock . . . better guards than Hammond can provide. I'll see what I can do, John Howard."

"I'm obliged," Stark said. "But only until I'm back on my feet."

"What happens then?" Purdee asked.

"Then I start taking the war to Ramirez," Stark said grimly.

Before Purdee left, Stark asked him about Kelso, the DEA man. Purdee knew him and didn't think much of him. "Officious prick," were his exact words, and Stark concurred with that judgment.

"Still, you don't want to get too far on the bad side of the DEA," Purdee had warned him. "They're bad boys to have as enemies."

"So am I," Stark had said.

Now he was nervous, as nervous as if he were about to go into battle, maybe even more so. From the door of the hospital room, Elaine said, "Are you ready?"

Stark took a deep breath. "As ready as I'll ever be. Let 'em in."

Elaine opened the door to admit the network news correspondent and the camera crew that followed her.

The reporter was an attractive brunette woman in her mid-thirties. She wore a stylish pair of glasses, as if that would make her seem more intelligent and serious, but her skirt was also short enough to show off a good pair of legs. She began the report the camera crew was taping by saying, "I'm here with Del Rio, Texas, rancher John Howard Stark, who finds himself in the hospital as the result of an attack on his home by gunmen working for the leader of an infamous

Colombian drug cartel." She turned to Stark. "Mr. Stark, as I understand it, you're not safe from these criminals even here in the hospital."

"That's right," Stark said, feeling a little uncomfortable as he looked into the camera. The red light on it was annoying. "Last night a man working for Ernesto Ramirez, better known as the Vulture, got into the hospital and tried to kill me. He murdered four men on his way in."

"And how do you know this assailant works for Senor Ramirez?"

"Because Ramirez has sent men to try to kill me before. Some of his men succeeded in murdering my uncle, Newton Stark, and one of my ranch hands, Chaco Hernandez. Before that, Ramirez had my neighbor and friend Tomas Carranza tortured and killed."

The reporter lifted the microphone back to her mouth. "These are serious charges. What are the local law enforcement agencies doing about them?"

"The sheriff's office is investigating . . . so Sheriff Hammond says."

"Do you think Sheriff Hammond isn't handling the matter properly?"

Stark shook his head. "I'd prefer not to comment on that."

Hammond would be furious when he saw this tape, Stark thought, but that was just too damned bad. Ramirez probably wouldn't be happy, either.

"You've had your own legal troubles . . ." the reporter said, letting the statement trail off so that it turned into a question.

"Yes, I have," Stark admitted, "but they all stem from the fact that I stood up to Ramirez. You see, Ramirez is used to getting his own way around here. He moved in across the border a while back, and he's been smuggling tons of drugs into the United States ever since. Hardly a night goes by that one of Ramirez's shipments doesn't come across the river somewhere. In fact, that's what started this whole mess. Ramirez wanted to pay Tommy Carranza to look the other way while Ramirez's drugs crossed Tommy's land. He wanted to turn the Carranza ranch into a narcotics superhighway, I reckon you could say. But Tommy said no, and he decked the lawyer that Ramirez sent to talk to him. That made Ramirez mad enough to have Tommy killed."

"You know all of this for a fact?" the reporter asked.

"I'm completely convinced it's the truth."

"Then why don't the authorities do something about it?"

"Some of the federal agencies are trying, but they're under-staffed and underfunded. I guess stopping the poisoning of America isn't as important as some pork barrel project some-where else or the latest round of social engineering experi-ments that the government wants to pawn off on us. Some of it's just a matter of too much red tape. As for the local law enforcement agencies . . ." Stark shrugged. "You'd have to ask them about that."

"We will," the reporter promised, and Stark imagined that Norval Lee Hammond would be starting to squirm even more. She went on, "What about this so-called citizens' pa-trol you've started?"

"Now hold on a minute," Stark said. "I didn't start that. I support it a hundred percent, but I can't take any credit for it. That's just an example of folks standing up for themselves and taking some responsibility back into their own hands in-stead of relying for everything on a government that's too big and uncaring to get the job done anymore."

"Some people say they're taking the law into their own hands, not responsibility."

"If the legal authorities did what they're supposed to, the people wouldn't have to take such extreme action to look after themselves. Look, I know the men who have organized these citizens' patrols. I've known them for years. They're good men, honest men, law-abiding men. But they're tired of their homes, their livelihoods, and their families being threatened by a bunch of no-account thugs whose every breath is a waste of perfectly good air." Stark knew he was getting wound up, but he couldn't help it. He hadn't rehearsed what he was going to say. He was just speaking from the heart. "None of them want to take up a gun and kill or even injure somebody else. These are peaceable men. But they're just tired of what's going on down here. This is Texas. This is America. We don't just let evil people come in and attack us without striking back. Sure, there's an element in the press and in the government that wants to blame us for everything, to say that if somebody comes after us, we must've done something to deserve it. That's bull! This is the best country on earth, and the one most likely to just let folks live and let live. This mess here in Val Verde County, it's just one example of what's going on all over the country. The will of the people is supposed to *mean* something, but it doesn't anymore. We sit back and let the criminals and the drug smugglers and the terrorists do as they damned well please and wring our hands and complain that somebody ought to do something about it." Stark paused and took a deep breath. "Well, down here on this stretch of the border, somebody *is* doing something about it. The people are standing up for what's right." He nodded grimly at the camera. "That's all. I'm talked out."

The reporter looked a little stunned. She had probably gotten more of a response than she was counting on. And as a member of the media, she had probably heard some things she didn't want to hear. Slowly, she raised the microphone to her lips again and said, "Ah, thank you, Mr. Stark. Very eloquently put."

Stark knew there wasn't a damned thing eloquent about what he'd just said. But eloquent or not, it was the truth.

And when that tape hit the airwaves, he thought . . . well, the old saying about the fan and the shit came to mind.

Twenty-three

"What do you mean the network won't run it?"

Elaine shook her head. "They say it's too inflammatory and one-sided."

"God *damn*!" Stark slammed a fist down on the bed rail. "They'll give airtime to every left-wing nutcase who wants to spew venom about everything he *thinks* is wrong with the country, and they won't show what I've got to say about somebody doing right for a change?"

"I'm sorry, John Howard," she said with a shrug. "There are plenty of other reporters you can talk to. One of those fellas who has a talk-radio show called and said he'd like to have you on."

Stark was aware of talk radio, of course, but had never listened to it much. He was too busy and just didn't have the time. "You think it's a good idea?" he asked.

"It can't hurt. You want me to call them back and say you'll do it?"

Stark considered for a moment and then nodded. "Sure. It's not that I think what I have to say is so all-fired important. But there's been a lot of publicity about this mess, and I'd like to get my side of the story out there."

Elaine nodded. "I'll get in touch with them."

That afternoon when she came back in, she seemed excited. "What's going on?" Stark asked her. "Did you talk to that radio fella?"

"Yes, but there's more happening than just that, John Howard," she replied. "Somebody at the TV network must have seen the interview with you and thought it wasn't right of them to refuse to air it. He snuck out a copy somehow and posted it on a Web site."

"I'm on the Internet?" Stark said with a frown.

"That's right, and other people have downloaded it and reposted it. You're all over the Web, John Howard. It's estimated that over a million people have downloaded the video in the past hour, and the number is just going up."

Elaine picked up the TV remote and turned the set on, changing the channel over to one of the cable news outfits. A well-groomed anchorman sat there talking about Stark and the Internet video. A photograph of Stark seemed to float over his left shoulder.

"Well, I'll swan," Stark said as he stared at the screen.

Elaine smiled. "They say it's going to be the most downloaded video since that rich girl's sex tape."

Stark reached up with his left hand and scratched his head. "I don't know if that's a distinction I want or not," he mused.

"Whether you want it or not, you've got it. Get ready for your fifteen minutes of fame, John Howard . . . although I've got a hunch it's going to last longer than that."

Elaine was right about that. During the next few days, as Stark recuperated from his wounds, he did interviews with numerous magazine and newspaper reporters. More TV camera crews showed up, too. Now that the original interview was freely available on the Internet, the networks considered themselves scooped, and they were scrambling to do damage control. The big-name talk-radio hosts were after Stark as well, and he talked to them as much as he could.

Another man might have let all the attention go to his head. Stark regarded it as a necessary evil. He was worried, though, that the whole thing was taking on a life of its own and mushrooming into a media sensation. Such things were often just nine-day wonders. The public grew obsessed with them overnight, and then forgot about them almost as quickly. Hell, he thought, even the 9/11 attacks had shut up the liberal carping for only a short time before they went back to trying to tear down everything good about the country. This border skirmish was tiny compared to that.

The story seemed to have legs, though. By the time a few days had passed, the term "Stark's War" had become part of the national vocabulary. And Stark himself was a national hero: an honest, hardworking Texas rancher smiting the evil drug lords who had killed his uncle and were polluting America with their poison.

Vengeance is mine, sayeth the Lord, according to Scripture, but for many people, that vengeance now seemed personified in John Howard Stark.

When he walked out of the hospital after being released, with a circle of his friends around him, the crowd of media was waiting, as was a large gathering of the citizens from Del Rio and the surrounding area. Cheers went up from them as Stark walked out with Elaine at his side. His left arm was healed except for a little stiffness. The right shoulder was in good shape, too, although he would have to be careful with it. His strength had returned, and despite the regulation about leaving the hospital in a wheelchair, he had walked out on his own two legs. He nodded to the reporters who crowded around and said, "No comment," to all their questions. He had talked enough, said what he had to say.

It was time now for action.

Silencio Ryan watched Stark from the back of the crowd. He wore a Stetson and sunglasses, and no one paid any attention to him. All eyes were on Stark at the moment. Ryan could have gotten him then, even though lining up the shot in this crowd might have been difficult, but he probably wouldn't have been able to escape and he wasn't ready to spend the rest of his life in jail. Unfortunately there wasn't a good spot to set up with a sniper rifle and take care of Stark from long range.

Anyway, Ramirez had changed the orders. Stark's death was no longer the top priority for the volatile Colombian. He had gone back to wanting to inflict as much pain as possible on Stark before finally killing him. Ramirez flip-flopped as much as a Democratic presidential candidate.

So for now, Ryan watched and waited and planned, and tried to ignore the fierce little flame of rage that burned in the back of his brain. Stark should have been dead by now, and the fact that he wasn't gnawed on Ryan's guts. He had always prided himself on his lack of emotion, but somehow Stark had gotten under his skin.

He would follow orders and let Stark live for now, let him live so that he could suffer even more, but Ramirez had better not wait too long, Ryan thought as he slipped away from the crowd. The killing urge could be denied for only so long.

"Damn, it's good to be home," Stark said.

Elaine squeezed his hand. "It's good to have you home."

Sam, Devery, Hubie, W.R., and Everett were all gathered in the living room of the Diamond S ranch house. Stark had changed to comfortable clothes, and now he leaned forward on the sofa where he sat, clasped his hands together between his knees, and said, "Fill me in on what's goin' on."

Devery grinned. "You mean you ain't heard of Stark's Army?"

Stark grimaced. "Good Lord. Who came up with that?"

"The media, of course," W.R. said. "Can't fight Stark's War without Stark's Army."

Stark shook his head. "This ain't right. I've been sittin' in the hospital for the past week. Anything that's gotten done, you boys have done it, not me."

"Nobody would've ever done *anything* without you startin' it, though, John Howard," Devery said. "And it's not just around here, either."

Hubie said, "Show him the video."

Elaine picked up the TV and VCR remote. "The boys taped these stories off the news, John Howard." She turned on the machines and started a tape playing.

Stark sat there and watched as the stories unfolded. All along the border, the word had gotten out that some decent Americans were taking a stand and making a difference, and between Del Rio and El Paso—and even beyond into New Mexico and Arizona—the good citizens were rising up to repel the invaders and criminals. They had formed a loose alliance, the organization referred to as "Stark's Army."

Elaine paused the tape, and Devery said, "That's what the news folks call it, but the people who are actually doin' the work don't bother with such things. They're just out to stop the bad things that've been goin' on."

Stark nodded in understanding, and Elaine started the tape again. Several news stories played out before Stark's astonished eyes:

In Eagle Pass, Texas, another border town farther down the Rio Grande, a band of heavily armed robbers from below the border attempted to rob a supermarket, only to be thwarted by the shoppers in the store at the time, including a good number of elderly citizens and housewives. A couple of the bandits were knocked out by a hail of canned goods and then disarmed, and the citizens had used those weapons to get the drop on the other would-be thieves. The gang had been herded into a large walk-in freezer and locked up before the police were called, and when authorities finally arrived, the key to the freezer was mysteriously missing for a good while before it turned up. The bandits were half-frozen and nearly suffo-cated before they were let out and taken into police custody.

Over in Arizona, in the small town of Palominas, three illegal aliens tried to carjack a woman taking her daughter to school. The Border Patrol and the local cops were nowhere to be found, but several bystanders took action, rushed to the screaming woman's aid, and had beaten the carjackers severely by the time the police finally arrived.

In Eunice, New Mexico, some of the locals flushed out— literally—a band of drug runners (which included a high-ranking official in the Mexican military) by pumping raw sewage through the drainage pipe the men were using to enter the country. Stark couldn't help but laugh at the sight of the bedraggled, stinking, sewage-covered drug runners being rounded up at rifle point by the citizens and then turned over to the authorities.

He wasn't laughing, though, when in each case some of the participants in the vigilante actions brought up his name and explained that they had been inspired to take action by "that fella down in Texas who's started fightin' the drug smugglers."

"Somebody's liable to get hurt," he said when Elaine had stopped the tape and turned off the TV. "Sure, it makes folks feel good when a bunch of old ladies throwing cans of baked beans knock the stuffing out of some robbers, but they could just as easily have gotten themselves killed. That could've turned into a bloodbath."

"Yeah, it could have," Devery said, "because one of those bandits admitted after they were captured that they planned to take everybody in the store, march them into that same freezer, and mow 'em down."

Stark stared at him in disbelief for a moment before saying, "You mean they would have killed everybody?"

"No witnesses," Devery said. "That was the plan. But it didn't come about, John Howard, because those folks have heard about you and they decided to stand up for themselves. If they hadn't, they'd likely all be dead now."

Elaine perched on the arm of the sofa next to Stark and put a hand on his shoulder. "You see, John Howard," she said, "you've already made a big difference. You've saved lives . . . just by being the big stubborn galoot that you are."

Stark laughed. "Thanks . . . I think."

There was a moment of silence, then Hubie said, "Well . . . what do we do now?"

Stark looked around at the circle of his friends. "You go on with what you've been doing," he said, "only I'm part of it now. I'll get my guns cleaned and loaded and be ready to go with you tonight." He glanced at Elaine. "You planning to argue with me about it?"

"No," she said. "I know better. I want you to be careful, John Howard . . . but you go get 'em."

Despite their self-deprecating natures, Devery and the others had done quite a job of organizing. Drawing on the ranchers up and down the river and from the townspeople as well, they had put together a force of at least sixty men who were willing to fight to protect this area of Texas from the onslaught of the drug runners and gang lords. Not everyone in the group went out on patrol, though. The homes of the men involved were always protected. The Diamond S, especially, was well guarded, since it was the home of the man who had started the opposition to Ramirez.

Stark was tireless as the days passed. July turned into August, that hottest month when the sun was always a brassy red ball in a washed-out sky the color of beaten silver. Temperatures topped one hundred degrees every day, often reaching as high as 110 or 112. One scorcher even got up to 117. But at night, the dry air cooled quickly, and even ninety-five degrees felt fairly pleasant in the low humidity.

The night was when Stark's Army operated, because that was when the enemy was active.

Stark still didn't care for the whole "Stark's Army" business. The way he saw it, his efforts weren't any more important than those of his friends and neighbors. The country didn't see it that way, though. The nine days' wonder had turned out to last considerably longer. There were still newspaper and TV stories nearly every day, and the coverage intensified every time there was a battle between the Texans and the drug runners. Several times each week, Stark and his friends found themselves battling it out with the Vulture's men, Winchesters and deer rifles and old army pistols against automatic weapons and Saturday night specials. The defenders were usually outgunned, but they were better shots and fought with the zeal of men protecting their homeland. As W.R. put it, "Hell, most o' them punks learned how to shoot by watchin' TV and movies. They're so busy holdin' their guns sideways and tryin' to look cool, they can't hit a damned thing! Meanwhile, us fellas who grew up plinkin' at jackrabbits and coyotes can do more damage with a handful o' bullets than they do with a whole blamed magazine!"

The patrols cruised up and down the river roads, on the lookout for couriers crossing the river. Using his military experience, Stark had set up a staggered schedule so that the smugglers could never tell when one of the patrols might come along. Usually, the smugglers turned back under heavy fire and escaped back across the river. On occasion, though, they abandoned their convoys, in which case Stark and the others burned the heroin and cocaine shipments.

Sheriff Norval Lee Hammond sat in his office and seethed. He sent men out to the scene of every shoot-out as soon as he heard about it, to recover the bodies of the smugglers who had been killed, if nothing else. He made no arrests, even though he knew good and well who was responsible for this carnage. Hell, the entire country knew! It was in the papers, on the TV, and on the radio. The lines of every conservative talk-radio show were jammed with people calling in to voice their support for Stark and his friends. The network news anchors reported the battles with stern faces and solemn voices that conveyed their disapproval, but Stark's War meant ratings, so they couldn't ignore it. In the halls of Congress, northeastern politicians bloated from decadent lifestyles and decades of holding office stood up and bellowed empty rhetoric about the dangers of vigilantism, while their conservative counterparts just shrugged and got on with the business of running the country. The leading contender for the Democratic nomination in next year's presidential election, a female senator from California, shrilly denounced John Howard Stark as un-American and a dangerous demagogue.

Stark just shook his head in wonder when he read that comment. He hadn't given any interviews or allowed any news stories to be taped about him since leaving the hospital. With all the yapping going on in the country, he was one of the quietest souls around. As for the un-American part, he didn't see anything the least bit un-American about defending his country. And that was all he was doing. It all seemed so simple to him.

When he said as much to Elaine, she just told him, "You're too dumb, John Howard. You're hopelessly behind the times. You still believe in right and wrong. To those people, there's no place in the world for that. There is no right and wrong to them; it's only a question of what you can get away with."

"I couldn't live like that," Stark said.

"Neither could I, and if you look around, you'll see there's a whole lot of people in this country who agree with you."

But not the *New York Times*. The very next day, that bastion of the liberal press ran a boxed editorial on the front page agreeing with Madame Senator from California and denouncing Stark as an unstable vigilante, no doubt traumatized by his service as a marine in that evil, immoral war in Vietnam. The editorial called for Stark's arrest, demanded that the Justice Department move in and restore order along the border, and suggested that there should be a congressional investigation of the whole matter.

"Yeah, a bunch of congressmen holding a hearing . . . *that'll* stop the drug smuggling," Stark said when he read the editorial in a copy of the paper Devery had brought out from Del Rio.

"They don't want to stop the smugglin'," Devery said. "They just don't want you stoppin' it."

Stark was inclined to agree with him. Smuggling in tons of drugs that would drain the economy and kill tens of thousands of citizens was less of a crime in the eyes of the federal government than a bunch of honest Americans standing up for their rights. Stark wadded the paper into a ball and tossed it into the cold fireplace. By the time winter came around and he wanted a nice fire, the paper would be dried out enough to make really good kindling. He didn't have a cat, or he would have put it in the bottom of the litter box.

That evening, Stark patrolled along the river with Everett Hatcher and Hubie Cornheiser. They were in Hubie's pickup, and he was behind the wheel. They were supposed to rendezvous in fifteen minutes with Devery, W.R., and another rancher named Hopkins.

Stark heard the sound of a loud engine approaching, but there was nothing ahead of them and no headlights behind. He had just started to say, "Do you boys hear that?" when a jeep roared up out of the night and raced past them.

Flame lanced from the muzzle of the machine gun mounted on the back of the jeep. Heavy slugs smashed into the front of the pickup, piercing the radiator and sending a cloud of steam hissing out from under the hood, which sprang its catches and popped up. Tires exploded under the lead onslaught, even as Hubie spun the wheel and sent the vehicle careening toward the edge of the road. With a spray of gravel and a cloud of dust, the disabled pickup came to a halt, its engine dying. The three men inside it were shaken, but none of them were hurt.

"What the hell!" Hubie exploded into the silence.

The jeep, still running without headlights, zoomed on up the road and disappeared into the darkness.

"We been ambushed!" Everett said unnecessarily. All three of them knew what had happened.

Then Stark heard the rumble of an engine and the grinding of gears. He twisted his head and looked out the back window. In the moonlight, he saw a large truck come around a bend in the road behind them. He recognized the type from his days in the military. It was a deuce-and-a-half with a canvas-covered back, the sort of truck that several dozen troops would climb into to be transported from one place to another.

"Boys," Stark said, "I think we're about to have company. A lot of company."

Twenty-four

As Stark barked orders, the three men piled out of the pickup, carrying their rifles. The Rio Grande was to their left, about a quarter of a mile away, with nothing but open ground between the river and the road. The other way, the landscape was more rugged and broken, covered by mesquite trees and scrub brush and cut by gullies.

"Come on," Stark snapped as he started in that direction. "We've got to get off the road."

Searchlights on the approaching truck blazed into life and washed over the three men as they ran into the brush. The truck's brakes squealed as the driver brought it to a skidding halt. Stark heard orders being shouted in Spanish as men tumbled out of the covered back, doubtless well armed and ready to hunt down the three gringos. Rifles cracked and bullets zipped through the air as the men began to fire at the Texans. Stark, Hubie, and Everett ducked lower and ran deeper into the brush. Branches clawed at them, tore their clothes and skin, but they bulled past the obstacles. Getting scratched up was a whole heap better than getting shot.

The ground suddenly went out from under Stark's feet and he tumbled down a slope, landing with a jarring thud at the bottom of a gully. The fall wasn't far, only about ten feet, but the impact was enough to knock the wind out of him and make his right shoulder ache where he had been shot. He heard noises close by, including some muffled curses, and realized that Hubie and Everett had taken the same tumble.

Stark crawled toward them and hissed their names. "John Howard?" Hubie said.

"You boys all right?" Stark whispered. The shooting continued, but none of the bullets whipped through the brush near them. The men from the truck must be firing blindly into the night.

"My knee's a mite wrenched," Everett replied, "but other than that I think I'm okay."

"Just shook-up a little," Hubie said. "What do we do, John Howard?"

The wheels of Stark's brain turned rapidly. His sense of direction was always reliable, and he could tell the gully ran north and south. To the south it probably ran through a culvert under the road and then continued all the way to the river. There was no telling how far north it went. North, though, would take them farther away from the men who were out to kill them, and that struck Stark as a good thing.

He had managed to hang on to his rifle as he fell, and so had Hubie and Everett. As soon as Stark had confirmed that fact, he said, "Follow me. Stay low and make as little noise as you can."

The gunmen were still firing their weapons, so Stark didn't think it was very likely they would be able to track the three men by ear. They were making too much racket for that. Still, it wouldn't hurt to be careful. Mustering as much stealth as he could, he came up in a crouch and started along the bottom of the gully. It was a mixture of sand and gravel, and he knew that during the occasional cloudbursts the area had, the gully would run full of floodwater making its way down to the Rio Grande. They didn't have to worry about flash floods tonight; the sky was clear and dotted thickly with stars overhead.

After a few minutes, the shooting stopped. Stark paused and whispered, "Whoever's in charge finally got them to settle down. They were all keyed up and trigger-happy."

"Who do you think they are, John Howard?" Everett asked.

"The jeep and the truck are both military issue. Could be Ramirez's men stole them from the Mexican army." After a moment he added, "Or those could be Mexican soldiers down there. From what I hear, a lot of their commanders have close ties with the drug cartels."

"Hot damn!" Hubie exclaimed. "You mean Mexico's invadin' us *again*?"

"Well, sort of. I reckon what they're really after is shutting down our patrols."

"How'd they know who we are?" Everett asked.

"With the contacts Ramirez has, he probably wouldn't have any trouble finding out the license numbers of all our vehicles. They could have been hidden somewhere off the road, waiting for us to drive by, checking all the plates through night-vision glasses."

"This really is turnin' into a war, ain't it?" Hubie said.

Stark nodded. "I'm afraid so. We'd better get movin' again. They're probably spreading out to look for us right now."

The three men began working their way north again. The gully twisted and turned, and several hundred yards farther on, it came to an abrupt end. Stark climbed part of the way up the slope so that he could take a look around. The gully came out in the middle of a large, open stretch of ground. There wasn't any cover for at least a hundred yards.

He grimaced and bit back a curse. He didn't know how close their pursuers were. When he listened, he could hear voices calling softly back and forth behind them. If he and Hubie and Everett emerged from the gully and tried to reach the shelter of the mesquite trees, they might make it unseen—or they might not. Stark wouldn't put it past the searchers to have men back there scanning the whole area with night-vision binoculars.

"Now what?" Hubie asked when Stark slid back down beside him and Everett.

"We're in a fix, and there's no getting around it," Stark said. Quickly, he laid out the situation and then said, "I wonder if we wouldn't be better off going back the way we came."

"Right back at 'em, you mean?" Everett asked, sounding confused.

"That's right," Stark declared. "They're spread out looking for us. If we can slip past them and get back to that truck . . ."

"I get it," Hubie said. "We can grab it for ourselves and use it to get out of here."

"That's the idea. How's it sound to you boys?"

"We're with you, John Howard," Hubie said without hesitation.

"Lead the way," Everett added.

Once again Stark cat-footed along the bottom of the gully, heading south this time toward the road and the river. He paused every few steps to listen, not wanting to run smack-dab into the killers who were looking for them. If the searchers had found the gully, they might send some men along the bottom of it.

That was exactly what had happened, he realized a few minutes later when he heard the crunch of footsteps on the gravel and the soft whisper of voices. He motioned Hubie and Everett against the side of the gully and pressed his back to it alongside them. All they could do now was wait for the men to come to them and try to strike without attracting the attention of the other pursuers.

Stark felt his nerves drawing tighter and tighter. He was barely breathing. The tramping of footsteps was almost on top of him and his companions before he saw the dark shapes moving through the shadows. He thought there were four of them, but he couldn't be sure.

If it came down to a fight, they would have to attack hard and fast in order to keep the men from yelling or loosing a burst of automatic weapons fire. Either of those things would bring more of the pursuers down on them in a hurry.

Stark, Hubie, and Everett remained utterly motionless as the four men moved past them, no more than six feet away, without seeing them. Stark began to hope that the men would go on up the gully without noticing them.

But some instinct must have warned one of the men, because he looked back over his shoulder, stopped abruptly, and exclaimed, *"Madre de Dios!"*

Stark lunged forward, planting the butt of his rifle right in the middle of the man's face. He felt the satisfying impact and heard the crunch of bones shattering. The man went down hard, either unconscious and out of the fight or already dead. In a continuation of the same move, Stark rammed the barrel of the rifle into the midsection of another man. That one grunted and bent over, putting his face in perfect position to meet Stark's sharply upthrust knee.

Hubie and Everett had jumped the other two and were grappling with them. Hubie was young and fairly athletic and was holding his own with his opponent, rolling with him across the floor of the gully. Everett, on the other hand, was older and not in as good a shape. The man he had tackled managed to throw him off. With a snarled curse, the man swung the barrel of his gun toward Everett. Stark saw what was about to happen but knew he couldn't get there in time to stop it.

He didn't have to. Everett kicked the man looming over him, the heel of his boot driving hard into the man's groin. The man yelled in agony and his finger jerked on the trigger, but the barrel of the gun had dipped so far that the burst of lead went into the man's own feet, chopping them to pieces. His screech filled the night.

Well, that tore it, Stark thought. Every enemy in earshot now knew that the men searching the gully had encountered the fugitives.

Hubie was on top of his man, using the butt of his rifle to

batter the guy's face into something that only barely resembled human. Stark ran by him and called urgently, "Come on!" He bent to grab Everett's arm and haul him up on his feet. Everett stumbled a little but soon righted himself. The three of them plunged down the gully, heading back toward the road.

Stark figured the pursuers would have left some men at the truck. He had hoped to jump them silently, knock them out, and capture the vehicle. Clearly, that wasn't going to be possible now.

The only slight advantage he and his companions still had was that the rest of the men wouldn't know which direction they had gone after the fight in the gully. They would have to split up, some going north while others backtracked to the south.

Shouts behind them told Stark that the others had found the four wounded and unconscious men. The gully grew shallower, but Stark, Hubie, and Everett could still stay below the level of it by crouching as they ran. Stark saw the road in front of them, a silver ribbon in the moonlight. As he had thought, the gully led to a cement culvert under the road. Actually, there were two of the big pipes, each about five feet in diameter.

He led the way into the pipe on the right. A little water still remained in the bottom of it from the last rain. The tiny splashes that their feet made echoed hollowly inside the pipe, as did their heavy breathing. After a moment, Hubie whispered, "We can't stay here, John Howard. They're sure to look in this pipe."

"I know," Stark said. "We'll catch our breath for a minute, then move out and make for the river—"

He stopped short as he heard something. The sound of an engine told him that a vehicle was approaching. Stark hoped it didn't belong to some innocent traveler who was about to wander into the middle of this firefight. He doubted if the invaders from across the border cared who else got killed, as long as they bagged their quarry.

As the vehicle came closer, something about the sound of it struck Stark as familiar. He stuck his head out of the pipe and ventured a look along the road to the northwest. After a second he realized that the engine sounded just like that of the jeep that had shot up Hubie's pickup. He saw the headlights coming closer and recognized them as those of a jeep.

"You two out the other side!" he barked at Hubie and Everett. "If I start shooting, you do, too."

They didn't argue, just scrambled to follow orders. Stark climbed the short embankment to the road, showing himself in the glare of the lights. He brought his rifle up.

The jeep slewed from side to side on the asphalt as the driver slammed on the brakes. Someone shouted in Spanish. Stark figured they were trying to turn that machine gun around. Flame lanced from the barrel, but the gunners were too eager and started shooting before it was all the way around. The burst of fire went well to Stark's right, clawing harmlessly through some brush.

By showing himself, Stark had confirmed that those men were his enemies. He began to fire, aiming above the lights where the jeep's windshield would be. On the other side of the road, Hubie and Everett opened up as well. With a tinkle of broken glass, first one of the headlights went out, then the other. The machine gun started to chatter again, then abruptly fell silent. Stark knew one of their bullets must have found the man who'd been pressing the trigger.

He ran toward the jeep. No shots came from it. His eyes were still a little dazzled from the lights that had shone in them, but his night vision was beginning to come back. He saw three men in the jeep, one behind the wheel and the other two sprawled limply around the machine gun mounted above the rear seat.

Hubie and Everett weren't far behind him, although Everett's wrenched knee made it hard for him to keep up. "We got 'em!" Hubie called excitedly. "We got 'em!"

That was true enough. All three of the men in the jeep

seemed to be dead. Stark pulled them out and left them lying in the road as he and his companions climbed into the vehicle. The jeep's engine was still running. Stark was glad none of their bullets had smashed anything vital in it.

"Take the wheel, Hubie," he said as he dropped his rifle in the floorboard between the front and back seats and climbed behind the machine gun. "Everett, you're ridin' shotgun."

"What're we doin', John Howard?" Everett asked as he settled into the passenger seat. "Why don't we just get out of here?"

"They wanted a war," Stark said grimly. "We're just givin' 'em what they wanted."

Hubie let out a whoop. "Let's go!" He threw the jeep into gear and jammed a foot down on the accelerator. With a smell of burning rubber, the jeep tore off through the night toward the spot where the deuce-and-a-half was parked.

Running without lights as they were, Stark was able to see well enough in the moonlight to make out a large group of men around the truck as they approached at high speed. More men were running back toward the road. Someone must have issued an order for the men to regroup at the truck. They had to hear the jeep coming, but they probably didn't know yet that it had been commandeered by the three Texans.

They found out a minute later as Stark called to his friends, "Keep your heads down!" and thumbed the trigger trips on the machine gun. He had already checked the ammo belt and found that it still had over half its load. Back in his leatherneck days, he'd had a little experience with machine guns like this. Not much, mind you, but enough to use this one effectively. He sent a storm of lead at the truck and the killers gathered around it.

The bullets chewed through several men and flung their tattered corpses around like rag dolls. Tires exploded under the onslaught of machine-gun fire. Some of the men turned to run but couldn't outrun the flaming death that sought them.

Others scrambled for cover, only to find that there wasn't any. A few threw themselves flat and escaped the scything lead, but only a handful. Others, farther out in the brush, wisely dropped and crawled off, unwilling to throw away their lives.

The jeep swept past the disabled truck, Stark swinging the machine gun around to fire a burst into the canvas-covered back. A couple of men who had been hiding there leaped into the open, firing pistols toward the jeep. With a flick of his wrists, Stark hosed them with lead and sent them flying backward into the ditch. Then the jeep was past, and Stark shouted, "Turn around and we'll hit them again!"

Hubie stomped the brakes and spun the wheel, and the rear end of the jeep slewed around. When the compact little vehicle was pointed back the way it had come, Hubie hit the gas again and it leaped forward. Stark fired, concentrating on the rear of the truck, and after a moment, with a loud crumping sound and a burst of flame, the gas tank ruptured and exploded. A fireball climbed into the dark sky, lighting up the landscape for a couple of hundred yards around. Stark spotted a few men running away and sent a burst after them, more to hurry them along than anything else.

The light also showed him that the bodies scattered around the road and the burning truck wore civilian clothing, but he couldn't shake the hunch that these men were members of the Mexican army. He felt a little bad about killing them, knowing that it probably hadn't been their idea to invade Texas. On the other hand, they were up here illegally, they had been doing their damnedest to kill Stark and his friends, and he wasn't going to lose much sleep, if any, over what had happened.

Stark tapped Hubie on the shoulder and said, "Let's get out of here. Head for the spot we were supposed to meet Devery and the others."

"Will do, John Howard. Hey, Ev, you all right?"

"I'm fine," Everett replied, "other than this knee hurtin' like blazes." He twisted his head around and looked at Stark.

"No offense, John Howard, but I'm gettin' a mite old for rowdy-dows like this."

Stark laughed as he patted the cooling machine gun. "You and me both, Everett," he agreed. "You and me both."

Twenty-five

The news that a shot-up, burned-out truck belonging to the Mexican army had been found on the highway about ten miles out of Del Rio was a curiosity. So was the fact that an abandoned Mexican army jeep turned up a few miles down the road. There were bloodstains on the highway, but no bodies. Stark wondered a little about that. The survivors of the battle must have called for help. The corpses had been recovered and taken back across the Rio Grande, so that no one could prove the Mexican military had been involved. A high-ranking officer issued a statement saying that the truck and the jeep had been stolen, dissociating the military from the foray across the border, and no one could prove otherwise. Stark still had his suspicions, though.

So did the news media, most of whom jumped to the conclusion—accurately, it so happened—that Stark had had something to do with this. But again, no one could prove anything, and since Stark himself stuck to a firm "No comment," the story seemed likely to die a natural death after a few days.

It got pushed off the front pages and out of the newscasts a lot quicker than that, by a much bigger story.

In Loving, New Mexico, three of the locals out on a citizens' patrol confronted a band of border jumpers. Most of the group had surrendered without a fight; they were illegals, just looking for a better life across the border in the United States. However, two of the men had pulled hidden guns and blazed away, obviously unwilling to be captured, and the locals had been forced to shoot them. When the authorities responded to the incident, they discovered that the two dead men were not Mexicans at all. They were Arabs, and they were carrying detailed plans of some sort of industrial complex. That was more than sufficient to get Homeland Security involved.

There were enough news leaks so that most of the story got out to the public over the next few days. The dead men, one from Saudi Arabia and the other a Libyan, were known operatives for al Qaeda. They had entered Bolivia with fake passports and then made their way up through Central America and Mexico for the express purpose of slipping unnoticed into the United States. The plans they carried were those of a giant oil refinery in Texas City, Texas, between Houston and Galveston. Along with al Qaeda sympathizers they were to meet in Houston, the two men would have attempted to blow up that refinery in a gigantic explosion that doubtless would have spread to the other refineries lining the Houston Ship Channel, and before it was all over there probably would have been a swath of death and destruction twenty miles long and several miles wide, with casualties in the thousands, if not higher, and property damage in the billions. While not as symbolic as the 9/11 attacks on the World Trade Center and the Pentagon, the actual toll, both human and financial, of this attack would have been even higher.

But it had been thwarted, not by the government, but by three common men: a rancher, a barber, and the owner of a hardware store in danger of being run out of business by the big box discount behemoth that had moved in on the edge of Loving. Their vigilance and courage had saved the day.

And to a man, each of them told the media that they never would have gotten involved in such an effort as the citizens' patrol if not for the inspiration of John Howard Stark.

Drug smuggling, as bad as it was, was one thing—terrorism was another. That hot-button issue blew the lid off the news coverage. The War on Terror, thought to have been largely won during the previous administration, was on everyone's lips in Washington again. Homeland Security, which had endured numerous budget cuts because of the drain on the economy caused by the graying of the baby boomers with its inevitable boosting of entitlement expenditures, was now seen as incompetent to deal with the threat of terrorists entering the country. The sitting president, a Republican, was perceived by many as being not as strong on defense as his predecessor, an image caused in large part by his recognition of the financial realities; Madame Senator from California, the presumptive Democrat challenger, was so far to the left that no one gave any serious thought to her doing anything to stem the tide of trouble. She would be too busy blaming the United States for anything and everything and trying to figure out some new, creative way to raise taxes and fritter away the increased revenue on misguided social engineering. For days politicians on both sides of the aisle shouted at each other, each blaming the other side for what had almost happened.

And somewhere deep in the bowels of Washington, somebody sat down and told himself that John Howard Stark was the pain in the ass who had brought on this whole mess.

Stark held the sheet of plywood in place while Elaine hammered in the nails. They were working in what had been their son Pete's room until he left to join the navy. Like the rest of the house, it had been shot up during the raid on the ranch by Ramirez's men. In the weeks since he'd been released from the hospital, Stark had been working to repair all the damage done by high-powered bullets tearing through the house. His friends would have pitched in to help if he had asked them, of course. Stark was so well known, in fact, that he probably could have gotten the building supplies warehouse store in town to donate all the materials, and the contractors who worked in Del Rio would have donated their labor to set everything right.

But that would have been cashing in on what he had set out to do, and that was the last thing Stark wanted. Besides, he enjoyed this kind of task, and so did Elaine. It gave them a chance to work side by side and then step back, look at the fruits of their labor, and feel proud.

The cordless phone in Stark's pocket rang. He looked at Elaine, who said, "You can let go, John Howard. There's enough nails in this sheet to hold it."

Stark nodded and stepped back from the wall. He pulled out the phone and answered it.

The call came from the gate down by the river road. These days, Stark kept it closed and locked, and guards were on duty there around the clock. The man on the phone was the ranch hand named George. He said, "There's an hombre from the government here to see you, Senor Stark."

Stark frowned. The only government official he could think of who might be coming to see him was Hodge Purdee. He asked George, "Is it Senor Purdee from the Border Patrol?"

"No, senor."

George was the laconic type, so getting information out of him was sometimes like pulling teeth. "The guy's name isn't Kelso, is it?" Stark asked. The visit from the DEA agent in the hospital still rankled in Stark's memory.

"No, senor. He says his name is Calhoun."

Stark didn't know anybody from the government named Calhoun. Suspicious of some sort of trick, he said, "Is he alone?"

"*Sí, senor.*"

"Did he show you any identification?"

"*Sí, senor*. It says he works for the National Security Council."

Stark frowned. The NSC advised the president on security matters. Calhoun might be just a flunky . . . or he might be someone pretty high up in the government.

Stark was curious enough to want to find out. "Send him up to the house," he told George.

"*Sí, senor.*"

Stark broke the connection and returned the phone to his pocket. Elaine looked at him and said, "We've got company coming?"

"Somebody from the National Security Council," Stark said.

"My goodness. I'll get a pot of coffee on." She ran her fingers through her hair and then brushed sawdust off the short-sleeved shirt and the blue jeans she wore. "I should probably clean up a little, too . . ."

"You look beautiful," Stark told her, taking her in his arms for a quick hug. "You don't need to get all gussied up for some bureaucrat."

"Well, I appreciate the sentiment, John Howard, but I want to run a comb through my hair, at least." She slipped out of his arms and hurried from the room.

Stark walked out of the bedroom and along the hall to the living room. Through the newly installed picture window he could see the lane leading from the highway to the house. A moment later a car came along it and stopped in front of the house. It was a gray, late-model sedan, no doubt a rental car. The man who got out was also rather grayish, from his thinning, close-cropped hair to his conservative suit. He also wore a white shirt and a dark blue tie that the Texas heat seemed to wilt as soon as he stepped out of the air-conditioned interior of the car. As he came toward the house he slipped off a pair of sunglasses, folded them, and put them in his shirt pocket.

Stark opened the front door and stepped out onto the porch. "Morning," he said pleasantly enough. "I'm John Howard Stark."

The man paused at the foot of the steps. "Good morning, Mr. Stark. Thank you for agreeing to see me. My name is Zachary E. Calhoun. I have my credentials right here . . ." He reached inside his coat.

Stark reached back inside the open door and picked up

the shotgun that was leaning against the wall beside the door. He didn't point the scattergun at Calhoun; he just held it casually under his arm, where he could get to it in a hurry if he needed it. The sight of the weapon was enough to make Calhoun pause in his motion. The government man's eyes widened.

"I assure you, sir," Calhoun said, "you don't need that weapon."

"Just bein' careful," Stark drawled. "Better than bein' surprised."

"Well, uh . . ." Calhoun finished taking out a leather folder from his jacket. "I'm sure once you've looked at my identification you'll see that you don't have any need of that shotgun."

"I'm sure," Stark said. He leaned forward to take the folder. He flipped it open and studied the identification cards under clear plastic on both sides. There were several of them, all sporting Calhoun's photograph and thumbprint. One card identified him as a member of the National Security Council. The others said that he was authorized to enter the White House, the Capitol Building, the State Department, and several other governmental offices in Washington.

Stark closed the folder and handed it back to Calhoun. "Looks like you're who you say you are," he commented.

Calhoun nodded in satisfaction and put the folder away.

"Now," Stark went on, "if you'll just step inside so we can check your retinal scan . . ."

"What?" Calhoun burst out, looking shocked again.

Stark grinned. "I'm just joshin' you. Come on in, Mr. Calhoun, and tell me what I can do for you."

Stark stepped back to let Calhoun go first. The government man entered the house. Elaine came into the living room from the other side and said, "Oh, hello." Stark saw that she had not only brushed her hair but had put on a little lipstick as well.

"Mr. Calhoun, my wife, Elaine. Darlin', this is Mr. Zachary E. Calhoun, of the National Security Council."

"It's my pleasure, Mrs. Stark," Calhoun said smoothly, seemingly on more familiar footing now. "I've been hearing a great deal about you and your husband in recent weeks."

"Well, we never set out to be famous," Elaine said. "We're just common folks."

"Hardly. You've set the entire country on its ear."

"We never meant to do that. Down here we're just John Howard and Elaine. Have a seat, Mr. Calhoun. Make yourself comfortable, and welcome to our home."

"You're very gracious," Calhoun said as he sank into an armchair.

Stark sat down on the sofa, laying the shotgun beside him. "What can we do for you, Mr. Calhoun?" he asked again.

Before Calhoun could answer, Elaine said, "Now, John Howard, don't be rude. Mr. Calhoun, would you like some coffee?"

Calhoun nodded and smiled. "If it's not too much trouble."

"No trouble at all. I'll be right back."

She left the room. Calhoun looked across at Stark and said, "Your wife is quite charming."

"I've thought so for over thirty years," Stark agreed. "But I still want to know what a government man wants with me."

"Right to the point, eh? I can respect that." Calhoun leaned forward slightly and clasped his hands together. In a lower voice, filled with gravity, he said, "The president sent me down here to see you, Mr. Stark."

"The president himself?"

"Yes, sir. He wanted me to make it clear to you that I'm speaking on his behalf."

Well, that might be true or it might not be, Stark thought. He couldn't exactly call up the White House and check out the veracity of Calhoun's claim. For the moment, though, he would proceed as if the man were telling the truth.

"That's mighty impressive. I've never heard directly from

the president before. Back in the sixties, I enlisted in the marines before I got one of those letters that start out 'Greetings.' "

Calhoun nodded. "Yes, we're aware of your military record. A lot of people in Washington have learned a great deal about you in the past month or so, Mr. Stark."

"Why are y'all so interested in a rancher from Texas?"

Calhoun's voice had a certain crispness to it as he replied, "Don't be disingenuous, sir. You know perfectly well why you're of interest to Washington."

Stark shrugged. "I reckon I do. I just think it shouldn't be so newsworthy whenever a man and his friends stand up for what's right."

"Perhaps not, but this day and age . . . At any rate, you're now a famous man, not just in Texas, not just in Washington, but across the country. Even internationally. They've certainly heard of you in Mexico."

Stark was about to say he didn't doubt that, but Elaine came in carrying a tray with three cups of coffee, a pitcher of half-and-half, and a sugar bowl. "I didn't know how you take your coffee, Mr. Calhoun. I have artificial sweetener, too, if you'd prefer."

"One sugar and some cream is fine," Calhoun said.

Elaine set the tray down on a table, put sugar and cream in the visitor's coffee, and handed the cup to him. He sipped it appreciatively, nodded, and said, "That's very good."

Elaine handed Stark his cup, took her own, and sat down in another armchair. "Go ahead with whatever you were talking about, gentlemen," she said. "Unless, of course, you'd rather have some privacy."

"It might be better—" Calhoun began.

"Anything you've got to say to me, you can say in front of my wife," Stark said.

Calhoun wasn't fazed. "Of course," he said. He smiled briefly at Elaine and went on, "I was just telling Mr. Stark how famous he is in Washington right now." He looked at Stark.

"It's because of your influence that I'm here. I've come to ask a favor of you, Mr. Stark."

"If there's anything I can do for the country, I'd be glad to."

"I'm happy to hear that." Calhoun took another sip of his coffee, then set the cup aside. "What we'd like for you to do, Mr. Stark, is to use your influence to bring this so-called vigilante movement to a close."

Stark frowned. "The only ones calling us vigilantes are the network anchormen who don't like what we're doing. And what makes you think I could stop it?"

"You started it," Calhoun said bluntly. "The whole movement gets its impetus from you."

Stark shook his head. "All I've done is tried to protect my family and look out for my neighbors. If folks make it out to be more than that, that's their lookout."

"You know it doesn't work that way," Calhoun insisted. "You're leading by example, Mr. Stark. People want to do what you're doing."

Elaine said, "That's a good thing, isn't it? If not for the men over in New Mexico who caught those terrorists, Lord knows how much terrible damage would have been done."

"That's certainly true in that one case," Calhoun agreed, "but there are certain procedures to be followed, certain ways of doing things—"

"Or not doing things," Stark put in.

Calhoun was beginning to look annoyed. "Despite the good that's been accomplished by the activities of certain people along the border, they're also causing some problems."

"Like what?" Stark said.

"There's a considerable amount of friction between us and the Mexican government at the moment. If it continues, we run the risk of developing quite a diplomatic rift."

"Then maybe the people in charge of the Mexican government ought to stop worrying so much about covering their own backsides and root out some of the crime and corruption on their side of the border," Stark suggested. "That's where the trouble starts. If scum like the Vulture couldn't operate over there without the law bothering them, they wouldn't be smuggling drugs over the river into Texas."

"That's a simplistic way of looking at things—"

"The simplest solution is usually the right solution," Stark snapped.

"In a perfect world, yes, but there are political and socio-economic factors at play here that are far beyond your understanding—"

"Wait a minute," Elaine said sharply. "Did you just call my husband stupid?"

Calhoun held up his hands, palms out. "Not at all, not at all. I was just saying that the situation is very complex, and there are things we know in Washington that aren't common knowledge down here in Texas."

"You know what's going on better than we do, when we're the ones who live here?" Stark said. "I don't think that's very likely."

Calhoun plowed ahead, obviously intent on carrying out the mission that had brought him here, even though he must have sensed it unraveling. "Nevertheless, the president has asked me to ask you directly, Mr. Stark, to join with us in an effort to restore peace and security to this region. The president is confident that you'll see your way clear to do the right thing in this matter. After all, you've served your country so well in the past, what with your service in the marines, and we know that you'd like to serve it now as well."

Stark's eyes narrowed. "So what you want is for me to go on TV and talk to the newspapers and tell everybody who's taken up arms to stop the invasion of this country by drug smugglers and terrorists . . . to just quit it. To go home and put their guns away."

"Exactly," Calhoun said.

"No," Stark said.

Calhoun blinked. "No? But, Mr. Stark, you seem to have such a good grasp of the issue—"

"The issue is that you want everybody to go back to just lettin' the government take care of them and tell them what to think and what to do, from the cradle to the grave. Well, I won't do that."

"You said you'd do whatever you could to help the government—"

"No, sir," Stark broke in. "I said I'd do whatever I could to help the country. That's not the same thing as the government."

"Of course it is!" Calhoun exclaimed, his frustration finally getting the best of him. "What else is the country if it's not the government?"

Stark stared at the bureaucrat for a long moment and then sighed. "If you don't know that, Mr. Calhoun," he said, "I don't reckon I could ever explain it to you."

Calhoun's face reddened, but with a visible effort he brought his anger under control. "We've gotten off on the wrong foot here, and I apologize," he said. He managed to summon up a smile. "Here I've abused your hospitality, and you've made me so welcome in your home." He looked at Elaine. "I'm truly sorry, Mrs. Stark."

"That's all right," she said, always the good hostess. Stark knew that it took a lot to make her upset with a guest. She was a lot more tolerant than he was in that respect. A part of him wanted to grab Calhoun by the collar and chunk him out of the house.

Calhoun drank some more of his coffee, smiled again, and said, "I don't think I've explained myself fully here. When I said that we want you to join us, Mr. Stark, I meant that literally. There's a job waiting for you in Washington."

That statement came as a genuine surprise to Stark. "A job?" he repeated. "For me?"

"That's right. We'd like to offer you a position as a consultant to the director of Homeland Security. You obviously have a fresh, effective way of looking at things, and we think you could be a great deal of help to us in solving the problems of protecting the country from those elements that wish to harm it."

"Consultant, eh?" Stark said. "What's a job like that pay?"

Calhoun smiled. "A great deal more, I assure you, than you've ever made from ranching." He named a figure that made Stark and Elaine exchange startled glances.

Stark looked back at Calhoun. "How would this job work?"

Calhoun warmed to this subject. "Well, you'd consult with various other advisers to the director, and you'd have a staff that would handle research and things like that, so that you could make an intensive study of the problems that confront us and prepare reports suggesting possible procedures that might have a beneficial effect. These reports would go directly to the desk of the director, of course, and then his staff would study their feasibility—"

"And not one damned thing would ever get done," Stark said.

Calhoun was taken aback. "What?"

"Any report I wrote would get tossed in a stack with a dozen other reports and ignored. But in the meantime, I'd be sitting in some office somewhere, out of sight and out of mind, until everybody forgot about me. Things down here along the border would go back to the way they were before, where the drug smugglers could get away with whatever they damned well pleased, killing whoever they wanted and bringing more and more of their poison into the country." Stark came to his feet, and his voice was harsh with anger as he went on, "But I'd be drawing my fancy government salary for being quiet, wouldn't I? That's why you really came here, to pay me off and shut me up."

"You don't understand—"

"There you go, callin' me stupid again. But I'm smart enough to know a skunk when I smell one."

Rattled by Stark's sudden vehemence just when he had thought things were starting to go well again, Calhoun turned in desperation to Elaine. "Mrs. Stark, please help me convince your husband to listen to reason."

Elaine smiled sweetly at him. "Mr. Calhoun, would you like some more coffee?"

Calhoun blinked, obviously surprised by the question. "Uh, no, thanks."

"Then get the hell out of my house, you government whoremaster." Still smiling, Elaine added, "Pardon my language, please."

Gaping, Calhoun looked back and forth between Stark and Elaine and finally settled his baleful gaze on Stark. "I warn you, there'll be some very serious repercussions accompanying your unfortunate decision not to cooperate."

"I don't cotton to being warned in my own house," Stark said. "I believe my wife asked you to leave."

Calhoun stood. "You'll—"

"I know," Stark broke in wearily. "I'll regret this. That's what fellas like you always say right about now. But you know what I really regret?"

Calhoun just stared angrily at him and didn't say anything.

"I regret not tossin' you out on your ass before now," Stark said. He reached down and picked up the shotgun from the sofa. "You're leaving."

Without a word, Calhoun turned and stalked out of the house. Stark and Elaine followed him to the porch and watched him get in his car, slamming the door hard behind him as he did so. Stark still carried the shotgun tucked under his arm. Calhoun drove away fast.

"The nerve of that son of a bitch!" Elaine said.

"He was right about one thing, though," Stark said slowly. "The government can come down mighty hard on us if they want to. They make for a bad enemy."

Elaine slipped an arm around Stark's waist and leaned her head against his shoulder. "I don't care. I'm almost ashamed to live in a country where the people running it care more about how things look than they do about standing up for what's right." She looked up at him. "It won't always be that way, will it?"

"I'd like to think it won't," Stark said.

But he didn't know anymore. Truly, he just didn't know.

Twenty-six

It had been such a long time since Ramirez was his former cool, calm self that Ryan had almost forgotten what that was like. For a couple of months now, ever since Ramirez had first heard the name John Howard Stark, the drug lord had been getting more and more erratic. If Ryan hadn't known better, he would have suspected that Ramirez was using some of his own product. Ramirez was on a natural high, though, brought on by rage and hatred. Time was, he had been gentle with the young girls he had brought to the compound; now they were always bruised and battered when they left the place. Ryan had even had to arrange for a discreet burial out in the desert after one of the girls had collapsed on her way out, bleeding from the nose and ears. She had died a short time later.

Ramirez had been really furious when he heard about the attack on Stark and his friends by the Mexican army. One of the commanders had been trying to curry favor with him, but the man had gone about it the wrong way, not knowing that Ramirez had already put Silencio Ryan in charge of tormenting Stark.

For Ryan's part, he was eager to confront Stark again. His failure to kill the Texan in the hospital still rankled. Ryan hadn't expected Stark to recognize him and react so quickly. They had talked only briefly in the dim, loud strip joint, and yet Stark had known who he was and realized that he was a threat. The man claimed to be just a simple rancher, but he had the skills and instincts of a seasoned warrior. It was all natural with Stark, too; Ryan had investigated him thoroughly and knew that Stark had lived a peaceful life for decades.

But that talent for violence had come back to him quickly, something that once learned was never forgotten.

Ryan came into Ramirez's office and found the drug lord slouched behind the desk, unshaven, his white suit rumpled and sweat-stained. Ramirez was really letting himself go.

"What are you doing about Stark?" Ramirez asked without preamble.

"Just what you ordered," Ryan replied coolly. "Making his life miserable before I finally kill him."

Angrily, Ramirez slapped a palm down on the desk. "You are doing nothing!" he shouted. "It has been weeks since you made a move against Stark!"

Ryan kept a tight rein on his emotions. "It takes time to arrange things," he said with a shrug. "You want this done right, I assume, not some crazy grandstand stunt like that army commander tried to pull."

Ramirez sneered at him. "I think you are afraid of Stark."

Ryan licked his lips and spent approximately three seconds thinking about how he could kill Ramirez and be miles away from the compound before anybody else knew that the Vulture was dead. It could be done easily . . .

But not yet, he decided. The pay was good, and Ryan had always felt a certain loyalty to his employers, even when they didn't deserve it. That was just the way he was. Ramirez had better not push him much further, though.

"I'm not afraid of Stark," he said. "I just want to do things properly, so that you'll have a suitable vengeance on him. I ask for patience, Don Ernesto."

Ramirez liked that "Don Ernesto" shit, Ryan knew. It made him sound like a noble, old-fashioned *hacendado* rather than the sleazy, drug-smuggling criminal that he really was. Somewhat mollified, Ramirez nodded and said, "All right. But I want action soon, Silencio. Understand?"

"As a matter of fact," Ryan said, "I'm ready to launch the first phase of the new operation right now. Today."

A wolfish smile tugged at Ramirez's mouth. "Really? That is good, very good. And will it cause pain for that gringo bastard?"

"Yes," Ryan said, not having to ask which gringo bastard Ramirez was talking about. "It will cause Stark much pain."

In the wee hours of the morning following the firefight with the Mexican army, Stark and his friends had gone back out to the river road with some spare tires and replaced the shot-out ones on Hubie's truck. Then they had towed the pickup back to Hubie's ranch so the law wouldn't be able to impound it as evidence. The vehicle was too shot up to ever be repaired, and since Hubie couldn't very well file an insurance claim on it, it was a total loss.

Like the other ranchers struggling to make ends meet with the current market conditions, Hubie wasn't exactly rolling in the dough. However, when Stark put out the word that donations were needed, enough money came in from the citizens of Val Verde County so that Hubie's friends were able to buy him another good, used pickup. Plenty of folks in Del Rio and the surrounding vicinity supported what Stark and the others were doing. They knew that in the long run, this stretch of the border would be safer than it had been before.

On this day, Hubie planned to patrol a section of his ranch, and he had asked Devery, W.R., and Everett to come along, as much to show off his new pickup as anything else. The four of them gathered at Hubie's ranch house, but before they set out to drive across the rugged landscape along the river, Devery begged off on that part of it.

"My missus has got a doctor's appointment today," he explained. "She likes for me to go with her."

"Nothin' serious, I hope," W.R. said.

Devery shook his head. "No, just, you know, female stuff."

The other three men said, "Oh," and nodded sagely, even W.R., who wasn't married. None of them wanted to discuss the subject any further.

"Y'all go on," Devery continued, "and I'll see you later, maybe tonight."

"Sure thing," Hubie said. "Tell Kate we, uh, hope everything, uh, goes all right."

"Sure." Devery nodded, knowing good and well that he wouldn't even tell her he'd mentioned the doctor's appointment to the fellas. In Devery's experience, ladies liked to be discreet about that sort of thing.

He got back in his own pickup and drove off, while behind him Hubie, W.R., and Everett piled into Hubie's truck.

They headed northwest on a dirt road about a mile from the river. They didn't expect to encounter any trouble in the middle of the afternoon like this, but that didn't mean they were being careless. Three rifles hung in the rack behind the seat, and each man was armed with a pistol as well. They were ready to deal with any problems they might run into.

"You boys hear about the visit John Howard got from a government man?" Hubie asked as he drove.

"You mean the fella who came to see him in the hospital?" Everett asked.

Hubie shook his head. "No, this was just yesterday. He told me about it on the phone last night. Seems somebody from the National Security Council came to see him."

"What'd he want?" W.R. asked.

"He offered John Howard a job in Washington."

The other two men stared at Hubie. "Lord have mercy!" W.R. exclaimed. "He ain't gonna take it, is he?"

Hubie snorted and replied, "Hell no. Come to find out, all the fella really wanted to do was to get John Howard to put a stop to our patrols. He wanted John Howard to speak out against what we've been doin'. The impression I got is that we've been embarrassin' the government because we've done so much more to slow down the drug traffic than they ever did."

"Bunch o' pencil-pushin' pissants," Everett said. "I hope John Howard told the bastard to go sit on a stump."

"Pretty much," Hubie said. "He won't be goin' off to take no job in Washington any time soon, let's put it that way."

He drove on, and it was only a few minutes later when Everett suddenly said, "Hey, look over yonder on that ridge! Who's that?"

Hubie and W.R. looked off to the right, where Everett was pointing, and saw a vehicle driving along the top of a ridge that paralleled the road, about three hundred yards away. Dust boiled up from its tires.

"That's one o' them damn Hummers, ain't it?" W.R. said.

Hubie slowed the pickup to a stop and leaned forward to peer through the windshield. "Looks like it to me," he agreed. "Son of a bitch! I'll bet Ramirez is tryin' to run some drugs across here in broad daylight, thinkin' that we won't be keepin' as close an eye on the place durin' the day."

"I'll bet you're right, Hubie," Everett said excitedly. "Are we goin' after 'em?"

"Damn straight," Hubie said as he pressed down on the gas and turned the wheel of his new pickup. The vehicle shot off the trail and started across open country toward the ridge. The terrain here was flat and the driving was almost as easy as on the road.

Whoever was driving the Humvee must have seen them coming. The boxy, heavy-duty vehicle swerved and disappeared on the far side of the ridge. "He's runnin'!" W.R. whooped. "Can you climb that ridge in this truck, Hubie?"

"I know a way through to the other side," Hubie said. "There's a gap comin' up."

Sure enough, the ridge shelved down into a saddle a short distance farther on. Hubie's pickup climbed the slope without any trouble and shot through the gap. The Humvee was still ahead of them, barreling along a flat that gradually dropped down while the sides rose to form a shallow canyon.

"Get the rifles down," Hubie directed W.R. and Everett. "They're liable to put up a fight."

"They might outnumber us," Everett said, "and them Hummers are built like a damn armored car. Maybe we oughtta call for some reinforcements, Hubie."

"No time for that," Hubie argued. "The way they're runnin', they'll be long gone before anybody but us could catch up to 'em. We better call and let somebody else know what's goin' on, though."

W.R. nodded in grim agreement with that suggestion and took his cell phone out of his shirt pocket. He opened it, looked at the display, and said, "Damn it, we're cuttin' in and out of the service area. I don't know if I can get through or not."

"Try Devery and John Howard anyway," Everett said.

W.R. thumbed in a number. "I'll try John Howard first. Devery's got his wife to tend to." After a moment he said disgustedly, "It ain't goin' through. Reckon I'll see if I can get hold of Devery."

While W.R. was making the call, Hubie continued following the fleeing Humvee. He knew from the way the other driver had taken off and was still driving recklessly that whoever was in the Hummer was up to no good. Folks just out joyriding wouldn't act so guilty, he thought, even if they were trespassing to do it.

"Devery!" W.R. said abruptly into the phone. "Devery, can you hear me? Damn it . . . I got a connection, but it's still cuttin' in and out . . . Devery, me an' Hubie an' Everett are chasin' some drug runners in a Hummer along . . . where the hell are we, Hubie?"

"The other side of Comanche Ridge!" Hubie said. "We're goin' down the valley toward Solomon Wash!"

"Past Comanche Ridge headin' toward Solomon Wash!" W.R. relayed into the phone. "Damn it, Devery, if you're talkin' to me, I can't hear you. I hope you can hear me. Devery? Devery!" Grimacing in disgust, W.R. looked at the others and said, "He's gone. The damn thing's dead as it can be."

"But he heard you, didn't he?" Everett said.

"I hope so, but I don't know. I never heard more than a word or two he said."

"Well, try again in a minute," Hubie suggested. "Maybe we'll come to a spot where the phone works better."

"Down in this canyon? I don't think so."

By now the trail had led them into a canyon about fifty yards wide, with a relatively level sandy floor and red sandstone walls that jutted straight up about twenty feet. The Humvee was still in front of them, only about a hundred yards ahead now. And it couldn't go anywhere except straight ahead; not even a Hummer could climb those sheer walls on either side.

But of course, neither could the pickup, Hubie suddenly realized.

Alarm bells went off in the back of his head. If the Humvee was trapped down here, so were they. He tapped the brakes, unsure what to do.

"What's wrong?" W.R. asked.

"I dunno. Boys, I got me a bad feelin' about this . . ."

Up ahead, the Humvee suddenly whipped into a turn and then came to a stop so that it was sideways in the path of the pursuing pickup. Men carrying automatic weapons leaped out of the vehicle and took cover behind it.

"Oh, shit!" Hubie exclaimed. "It's a trap!"

And he had waltzed right into it, he thought bitterly, taking the bait and swallowing it without the least hesitation. John Howard never would have allowed himself to get into a fix like this.

There wasn't time for that, he told himself. They were in for a fight, so they had to concentrate on that.

He hit the brakes and brought the pickup to a skidding, sliding, dust-billowing stop. Even over the sound of the engine, he heard the popping and ripping sounds of gunfire. "Give us some cover while I try to get us out of here!" he said to W.R. and Everett as he spun the wheel and hit the gas again.

He felt the pickup shivering under the onslaught of lead as he tried to turn it around. So far none of the tires had gone, but that might not last. W.R. and Everett fired their rifles out the rear and side windows. When the nose of the pickup was pointed back up the canyon, Hubie stomped on the accelerator again.

They had barely gotten started when he saw the twin pillars of dust coming toward them. At the base of each of those pillars was another Humvee. Hubie felt his heart sinking as he realized they were well and truly trapped.

"Comin' up in front of us!" he called.

"Shit!" Everett said. "Look up on the sides o' the canyon! They're all around us!"

Indeed, two more Humvees had appeared on each wall of the canyon. Men scrambled out of them and began firing down at the bouncing, careening pickup. Just like the Comanches and Apaches who had hunted in this land more than a hundred years earlier, they had their quarry boxed in.

Hubie suddenly braked and spun the wheel again. W.R. and Everett were thrown to the side by the violence of the turn. "What're you doin'?" W.R. yelled.

"There's just one Hummer ahead of us the way we were goin' to start with," Hubie explained. "He can't block the whole canyon. If we can get past him and get to Solomon Wash, we got a chance."

"Give it a try," Everett said.

Hubie sent the pickup roaring back toward the Humvee they had pursued into the canyon. It was still stopped where it had been. Hubie angled to the right, hoping to get around the vehicle on that side. Even in the bright sunlight, the flickers of gunfire from the muzzles of automatic weapons could be seen around the Humvee. Bullets hammered into the pickup. It kept going, though, its engine straining valiantly.

The left front tire blew as one of the flying slugs finally found it. As the rim dug into the sand and gravel, the steering wheel seemed to come alive and jump out of Hubie's hands. He yelled as the pickup tipped to the side and started to go over. "Hang on!"

That was all they could do as the pickup rolled twice and finally came to a stop upside down. The cab hadn't crumpled too much, and although Hubie was shaken and disoriented, he didn't think he was hurt too bad, if at all. He was lying on the roof of the cab in a tangle with W.R. and Everett.

"Hey!" he said urgently. "Hey, are y'all all right? W.R.! Everett!"

One of the other men groaned. Hubie fumbled for the door handle and after a moment was able to shove the driver's door open. It swung back with a screech of twisted, tortured hinges. He crawled out.

He saw blood dripping on the ground and realized it was coming from him. He reached up and found a gash on his forehead. No time to worry about that now. For the moment, the shooting had stopped, but it wouldn't stay that way once the ambushers realized there were survivors in the wrecked pickup.

Hubie twisted around and peered into the cab. He could see the faces of both of his friends. Everett was conscious, but his features were twisted in pain. W.R. looked to be out cold.

"Everett! Everett, you hear me?"

Everett blinked and focused on Hubie. "Lord, Hubie!" he gasped. "I think my leg's broke!"

"Can you crawl out of there?"

"I . . . I can try. Gimme a hand."

Hubie reached in and grasped Everett's hand. He hauled back on it as Everett crawled toward him. Dragging his injured leg behind him, Everett emerged from the wreck.

"What about W.R.?"

"I don't know," Hubie said worriedly. He reached in and searched for a pulse in W.R.'s thick, corded neck.

As if on cue, W.R. regained consciousness with a sputtering curse. "Wha . . . what the hell happened?"

Hubie saw a rifle barrel and reached into the cab to grab it. "Can you move, W.R.? Are you hurt bad?"

"I dunno . . . I think I'm okay . . ."

Hubie pulled out the rifle and reached into the truck for another one he had spotted. "We've gotta get under the truck bed. It's the only cover we got."

He knew the shooting could start again at any second. He was a little surprised that it hadn't already. Then the sound of derisive laughter drifted to him through the scorching air, and he knew why the gunners weren't shooting. They were having too much fun laughing at the gringos they had trapped.

A good shot at one or two of 'em, Hubie thought. Right now, that was all he asked.

W.R. crawled out of the pickup. He was scratched and bleeding like Hubie but seemed to be all right otherwise. He took one of Everett's arms and Hubie took the other, and they started trying to drag their friend under the protection of the overturned truck bed.

Guns cracked and bullets kicked up dust only a few feet away from them. The firing increased. Hubie cried out as he felt a bullet burn his calf. But he didn't let go of Everett, and a second later all three of the men were able to roll under the pickup bed. That shielded them from the men on the canyon walls, at least. They lay on their bellies, breathing heavily.

"Now what do we do?" Everett asked between teeth gritted against the pain of his broken leg.

"We try to hold out until help gets here," Hubie said. "I'll bet Devery and John Howard are on their way right now, maybe even some of the other boys."

W.R. fumbled in his pocket. "Maybe I can try callin' 'em again . . . Shit! My phone's busted all to pieces."

"So's mine," Everett said when he checked. And Hubie's phone was up there in the cab somewhere, out of reach. Hubie looked through the open rear window of the cab, but he didn't see the phone anywhere. Lord knew where it had gotten tossed to when the truck rolled over.

"I just thought o' somethin'," W.R. said. "With the truck upside down like this, can't they shoot right at the fuel tank?"

Hubie went cold all the way through. What W.R. said was true. Sooner or later, one of those gunmen was bound to realize what a tempting target the gas tank was. Maybe they had already figured that out, and the only reason they hadn't blown up the truck so far was that they were getting a kick out of keeping the Texans pinned down. He could just imagine the sons of bitches up there grinning and chuckling.

Taking one of the rifles with him, he slid over closer to the edge of the protected area under the truck bed and risked a look out. He could see in both directions. The Humvee they had chased in here was still parked where it had been. The two Hummers that had boxed them in were stopped now, too. Hubie sighted on one of them with the rifle and pulled the trigger. He saw one of the headlights shatter.

That just increased the rate of fire from the ambushers. Hubie pulled back, blinking rapidly from the grit that one of the bullets threw in his eyes when it hit the ground near him.

"Now look what you did," W.R. said. "You went an' made 'em mad."

Hubie didn't know whether to laugh or cry. "Aw, shut up, you old walrus," he said with a strained grin.

"Fellas," Everett said, "we ain't gettin' out o' this, are we?"

"Sure we are," Hubie said. "Devery and John Howard—"

"Ain't gonna get here in time, and you know it. Those damn drug runners have got us this time."

W.R. wiped the back of his hand across his mouth. "Yeah, it sure looks like it."

Everett went on, "I just want y'all to know I've never known a better bunch o' fellas than you. It's been an honor to be your neighbor and your friend, and I'm sure glad I got to know you."

"Same here, old son," W.R. said.

Hubie grimaced. "I hope they rush us."

"Why?" Everett asked.

"Because if they do, we got a chance to take some of 'em with us. If they just sit off yonder and take potshots at us, there ain't nothin' we can do about it."

"Yeah," W.R. said with a slow nod. "I'd sure like to know I did for a couple of 'em."

It seemed that they weren't going to get that chance, though. The shooting stopped, and a voice shouted, "Hey, gringos, look what we got for you!"

"What in blazes?" W.R. muttered. Unwise though it might be, he and Hubie crawled to the edge of the protected area and looked out.

Hubie's eyes widened in horror as he saw a couple of men at one of the Humvees fooling with a long, thick tube. "That's a goddamn rocket launcher!" Hubie cried.

He brought up the rifle he still held and began firing as fast as he could. Beside him, W.R. did the same. Behind them, Everett whooped, "Give 'em hell, boys!"

Suddenly, an explosion rocked the ground underneath them, and smoke and dust and rocks billowed up next to the Humvee. Hubie yelled, "We got the son of a bitch! We set off the rocket before they could shoot it at us!"

Indeed, the Humvee had been blown over on its side and was burning. The blast must have wiped out several of the killers from below the border at the same time.

"Look at it," Hubie said as Everett painfully pulled himself up alongside him and W.R. "Ain't that a pretty sight?"

"Not as pretty as a Texas sunset," W.R. said, "but I reckon it'll do."

The three men lay there grinning at the burning Hummer, so they never saw the rocket that came from the other side of the canyon, struck the pickup, and blew it apart in an earth-shaking explosion.

Twenty-seven

Stark and Elaine were just sitting down to lunch when the cell phone in Stark's pocket rang. Stark answered it and heard Devery Small's excited voice on the other end.

"John Howard, Hubie and W.R. and Everett are chasin' some drug smugglers over on Hubie's ranch! I just got a call from W.R.! You reckon we oughtta go help 'em?"

"What? Slow down, Devery," Stark said.

Devery took an audible breath. "W.R. called me on his cell phone. The connection was bad, so I could only hear part of what he was sayin'. And I don't think he heard a word I said, even though I was yellin' my head off into the damn phone."

"Where were they?"

"The other side of Comanche Ridge, I think. I ain't sure. And I thought I heard W.R. say somethin' about Solomon Wash."

Stark knew where those places were on Hubie's ranch. He said, "I'll head over there right now. Ought to take me about thirty minutes to get there."

"I'm in Del Rio and got Kate with me, so it'll take me a mite longer. But I'm on my way!"

Elaine was already on her feet. "You want me to go with you, John Howard?"

He shook his head. "Not this time. I'd feel better if you stayed here where it's safe."

"You know I can take care of myself," she protested.

He kissed her quickly on the forehead as he went past. "I know. But not this time."

He knew she wanted to argue with him, but she just sighed and nodded. He got his hat and one of the rifles and went out the door. He had taken to wearing the Colt .45 Model 1911A all the time now, so it was on his hip.

A feeling of annoyance gnawed at him. He had just gotten back to the ranch house after spending the morning out checking his own fences, and he had been looking forward to a good lunch and then some time spent with Elaine. Instead he had to go see what sort of trouble Hubie and W.R. and Everett had gotten into.

Stark frowned guiltily as he got into the pickup. He didn't have any right to feel that way, he told himself. Hubie and the others were just doing the job they had all set out to do, and they might be in real trouble.

Stark's worry grew stronger as he drove toward Hubie's ranch. It was unusual for the drug runners to try anything during the day; their business was more of a nocturnal one. Maybe they had some special operation going on. Special, and dangerous.

When he reached the ranch, he was stopped at the gate by a couple of Hubie's hands armed with shotguns. "How you doin', Mr. Stark?" one of the men asked.

"All right," Stark said curtly. "You boys heard any shooting from over toward Comanche Ridge?"

The cowboys frowned. "No," said the one who had greeted Stark. "But that's a good ways over northwest. Thought we heard a couple o' peals of thunder from off in that direction a while ago, but you can see for yourself there ain't a cloud in the sky."

"We figured we just imagined it," the other hand put in.

Stark's concern grew. He didn't like the sound of what he had just heard. "I think there might be some trouble up there involving your boss. Can you call the ranch house and send some men that way?"

"Sure thing, Mr. Stark." The men looked at each other worriedly. "You reckon Hubie's in trouble?"

"Could be," Stark said. "I'm on my way to find out now. When Devery Small comes up, tell him where I've gone and for him to come right on."

He drove past the guards and took a small dirt road that was little more than a pair of ruts. He knew it was the quickest way to Comanche Ridge and Solomon Wash beyond. By going this way he would bypass the ranch headquarters.

It seemed to take forever to reach Comanche Ridge. Before he got there, he spotted a column of black smoke rising on the far side of the ridge. When he saw it, his hands tightened on the steering wheel and he muttered, "Damn it, boys, what did you run into?"

Doggedly, Stark pressed on. He reached the gap in the ridge, drove through it, and turned to the left, toward Solomon Wash. He saw the smoke rising directly in front of him now. That wasn't a good sign.

A few minutes later, he was close enough to see that the smoke came from a burning vehicle that was lying on its top, upside down. Stark's heart thudded heavily in his chest. He couldn't be sure, but he thought it was Hubie's new pickup. What the hell had happened? Had the pickup wrecked somehow, rolling over and catching fire? The damage seemed to be too much for that. It looked more like the pickup had been blown to pieces in an explosion. Of course, the gas tank could have gone up . . .

And where were Hubie, W.R., and Everett?

Stark had the horrible feeling that he already knew the answer to that question.

He drove almost all the way to the burning wreck before

he stopped some twenty yards away. The worst of the fire was over. The pickup was nothing more than a blackened, broken hulk by now. Carrying his rifle, Stark got out of his pickup and approached the wreck carefully. The flames had died down, but a lot of heat still came from it.

Stark bent over and tried to peer underneath what was left of the truck, but he couldn't see anything. Everything was twisted and melted and burned. It was going to take some professionals to get in there and find out exactly what had happened. Stark straightened and shouted, "Hubie! W.R.! Everett! Anybody around?"

No answer came back to him except the echoes of his own voice from the sandstone walls of the canyon.

Stark had been hoping against hope that his friends had gotten out of the wreck somehow and walked off, looking for help. If that were the case, they ought to still be in earshot. Maybe they weren't, though. He pointed the rifle at the sky and fired three times, working the lever between each shot. That was a universal distress signal, and the sound of the shots would carry for a couple of miles. Surely Hubie and the others hadn't gone any farther than that.

Hoping that he would hear some answering shots, Stark listened intently for several minutes. Again, echoes were his only answer.

He bit back a curse, tried not to give in to despair just yet, and started looking around. Some distance off, maybe an eighth of a mile, he saw a black smudge on the ground that looked like a burned spot. He walked over there and saw that some of the brush had indeed been on fire recently. There was also a little crater in the ground, as if an explosive had been detonated here. But that was all. He didn't find any other evidence of anything odd and violent having gone on.

With his face locked in grim lines, Stark turned and went back to the destroyed pickup. The heat coming from it had diminished. Stark was able to get close enough to hunker on his heels and poke the barrel of his rifle through an opening underneath the wreckage. He raked it back and forth until the front sight caught on something. Stark pulled it toward him.

He let out a startled yell and jerked back, sitting down hard on the sandy ground as horror coursed through him. The sight at the end of the rifle barrel had caught inside the empty eye socket of a blackened skull. Stark dropped the rifle and scuttled backward, staring at the skull.

And the worst part of it was, the skull seemed to be staring back at him.

Stark knew he was looking at part of what remained of one of his friends.

With an effort, Stark fought off the horrified reaction. He wasn't ashamed of it, but this wasn't the time or place for it. He got to his feet, drew his pistol, and looked around. Whoever was responsible for this slaughter might still be around.

That seemed unlikely, though. Everything was quiet again, now that the echoes of Stark's yell had died away. The killers had probably done their grim work and then left. Stark wondered if all three of his friends were under that wrecked pickup. He was afraid that would turn out to be the case.

The sound of an engine made him turn his head. He saw several vehicles coming through the gap in Comanche Ridge. He was expecting Devery and some of the hands from the ranch, but instead he saw that the vehicles coming toward him had flashing lights on their roofs.

Someone had called the authorities.

Stark holstered his pistol and went back to his pickup to wait. There were three vehicles approaching him, two sheriff's office cars and the black Blazer that Norval Lee Hammond himself drove. Hammond was leading the way.

Anger bubbled up inside Stark as he looked at the Blazer. Hammond's boss Ramirez was responsible for what had happened here today. Stark was sure of it. The destroyed pickup must have been hit by a rocket or something like that. A drug lord like Ramirez would have access to weapons like that. He probably had plenty of contacts among the shadowy underworld of illicit arms dealers.

The Blazer rocked to a stop. The door swung open and Hammond climbed out. The sheriff had always been a little ponderous, as athletes gone to seed usually are, but now he moved like an old man. His face was haggard and his eyes were sunk deeper than usual in his head. He looked like a man who hadn't been sleeping much lately. Stark didn't feel sorry for him, though. Hammond's worries were his own doing. And nobody would sleep very well after deliberately crawling into bed with a vulture.

"Lord have mercy," Hammond said as he looked at the burned-out pickup. "What happened here?"

"You tell me," Stark replied tautly.

"How would I know? I just got here."

Stark started to say something about how maybe Ramirez had told Hammond what was going to happen today, but he managed to hold the comment back. Maybe Hammond was telling the truth for a change. He didn't deserve the benefit of the doubt, but Stark would give it to him anyway . . . for a while.

"I'm pretty sure that pickup belongs to Hubie Cornheiser," Stark said. "He and W.R. Smathers and Everett Hatcher were out here today having a look around—"

"Looking for drug smugglers, you mean?" There was a contemptuous edge to Hammond's voice.

"Having a look around," Stark repeated stubbornly. "They saw something suspicious and were going to check it out. That's all I know. I just got here not long ago myself."

"How did you find out what they were doing?"

"They called Devery Small and tried to tell him about it. The connection was bad, and all he got for sure was that they were out by Comanche Ridge." Stark inclined his head toward the ridge, just in case Hammond wasn't familiar with the geography of the Cornheiser Ranch. "Devery called me, and we decided we'd both come out here, just in case the boys were in trouble."

"Where's Small now?" Hammond asked sharply.

"He hasn't gotten here yet. He was in Del Rio when he talked to me, so he had farther to come."

Hammond nodded. "Well, he won't be able to get in when he gets here, because I left a unit at the gate to keep anybody from going in or out until I found out what the trouble was."

"How did you hear about it?" Stark asked.

He thought for a second that Hammond was going to tell him it was none of his business, but then the sheriff said, "I got an anonymous tip that some men had been killed out here. I figured it would be more of your vigilante work, Stark."

Stark kept his temper on a tight rein. "You'd better call in the Texas Rangers, Sheriff. I think this might be more than your office can handle. This pickup was hit by a rocket, or something like that."

"A rocket, eh?" Hammond walked closer to the wreck, then suddenly stopped short. "Shit!" he exclaimed. "Is that a *skull*?"

Stark swallowed the sickness that threatened to well up in his throat. "I was poking around under there with my rifle, and that got caught on the barrel."

"Shit!" Hammond said again. He looked a little green around the gills as he turned away from the wreckage. "Call back to headquarters," he said to one of the deputies. "We're gonna need Crime Scene and the coroner."

Stark opened the door of his truck and stepped up into the cab. As he sat behind the wheel, Hammond turned sharply toward him and snapped, "Hold on, Stark. You're not going anywhere."

"Wasn't intending to," Stark replied. "I just thought I'd get out of the sun while you do your work."

"Oh. Well, stay right there. I'm sure I'll want to talk to you some more."

Stark sat in the pickup, sweating in the heat, as Hammond and one of the deputies walked around the burned-out truck. Hammond was talking and the deputy appeared to be taking notes, but Stark couldn't hear what was being said. Then Hammond went back to the Blazer and shut himself up in it for a good while. The vehicle had tinted windows, so Stark couldn't really see what Hammond was doing. He thought the sheriff was talking on the radio, though.

More official vehicles arrived a while later, including a van that belonged to the sheriff's Crime Scene team. Photographs were taken, measurements were made, diagrams were drawn. A couple of ambulances drove up, followed by the coroner's car. The deputies and the EMTs started the grim work of recovering the remains from the pickup. Stark had to look away until they were finished with that.

Hammond was in and out of his SUV, evidently burning up the airwaves. After a while he came over to Stark's pickup and said, "We found the remains of three people under that pickup, Stark. It'll take a while to identify them, of course, but we're pretty sure they were male. Likely your three friends."

Stark nodded. "Likely," he agreed, his voice thick with emotion. He pointed and said, "There's a spot over there where it looks like there was another explosion."

"We'll have a look, don't worry."

"You still need me?" Stark wanted to get home so he could tell Elaine what had happened. She was going to have her work cut out for her, making sure that Hubie's and Everett's wives were taken care of.

"Stick around awhile longer," Hammond said curtly.

Stark shrugged. He could sit here all day if he had to. It wouldn't be comfortable, but he could do it.

True to his word, Hammond had the other blast site photographed and examined, too. It was late in the afternoon by now. Stark was hungry, having missed lunch. There was nothing in the pickup to eat, and anyway, every time he glanced toward the wreckage, he lost his appetite for a while.

Finally, Hammond talked on the radio some more, then trudged over to him and said, "Why don't you get out of the pickup for a minute, Stark?"

"What is it?" Stark asked as he dropped to the ground and rested a hand on the windowsill of the opened door. "You decide to let me go at last?"

"Not exactly." Several deputies had drifted over with Hammond, and now they moved up closer to him and Stark. "John Howard Stark, you're under arrest. Turn around so that you can be placed in handcuffs."

For a second, Stark's brain couldn't comprehend what he was hearing. "Under arrest?" he repeated. "What the hell for?"

"Murder," Hammond said.

All Stark could do was stare at him for a long moment. Then he exploded. "Murder! What in blazes are you talkin' about, Hammond?"

The sheriff jerked a thumb toward the ruined pickup. "You're being arrested for the murders of three victims, positive identities unknown, presumably Hubert Cornheiser, Everett Hatcher, and William R. Smathers."

"You're out of your damn mind! Those boys were my friends. I didn't have anything to do with this!"

"I thought you were on the scene a little too conveniently, Stark," Hammond went on, as if he hadn't heard Stark's response to that wild accusation. "You were trying to throw suspicion off yourself by being found on the scene."

Stark shook his head. "That's the craziest damn thing I've ever heard."

Again Hammond ignored him. "I had some of my deputies go out to your ranch and have a look around. They found a couple of used RPG tubes hidden in your barn, Stark. What did you do, miss with the first grenade before you zeroed in with the second one?"

This was insane, almost beyond Stark's comprehension. "Why would I blow up three of my best friends?" he yelled, waving an arm toward the wreckage.

The deputies closed in more, as if they thought Stark was about to attack the sheriff.

Hammond smiled faintly. "I've heard rumors about a falling-out between you and the rest of your so-called vigilantes, Stark. Seems they thought you've gotten a little power-mad since you've become such a celebrity. The rest of them had had enough, but you wouldn't let them quit. You'd lose your place in the spotlight if the rest of your gang deserted you."

Stark shook his head. Madness, sheer madness. But Hammond wasn't through.

"My informants tell me that you've been trying to buy arms on the black market. Rifles and pistols aren't enough for you anymore. You want to have your own private little army, so you need things like rocket-propelled grenades. And I guess you tested out a couple of them today and got rid of the men who must have threatened to expose your crazy scheme."

"This is crazy, all right," Stark muttered, "but I'm not the one who's a lunatic."

Hammond was back to ignoring him. "Now turn around so you can be cuffed, or my men will take you into custody by force." Hammond rested his hand on the butt of the pistol at his waist. "After seeing what you did to Cornheiser, Hatcher, and Smathers, I almost hope you *do* resist arrest, Stark."

Hammond might kill him, Stark thought. He probably had orders from Ramirez not to, but he could always claim that Stark had attacked him and given him no choice. Stark stood there tensely for a couple of heartbeats longer, then slowly turned around and placed his hands behind his back.

The pieces of this puzzle were clicking into place in his brain. It had all the earmarks of an elaborate revenge plot. Just coming after him and attempting to kill him wasn't enough to satisfy Ramirez anymore. The lull over the past few days had been just the calm before the storm. Three of Stark's friends were dead, and Stark himself was being arrested for the crime. No doubt the "evidence" that Hammond's deputies had found in Stark's barn had been planted there. Ramirez would probably get one hell of a kick out of this when he heard about it.

The cuffs clicked into place around Stark's wrists. They chafed just as much as they had the other time he'd been arrested. This was getting to be a damned unpleasant habit.

Hammond grabbed Stark's arm and shoved him roughly toward the cruisers. "Take him back to town and lock him up," he ordered a couple of the deputies. "Be sure and read him his rights. Everything by the book, boys. We don't want any judge throwing this one out."

"If a judge throws it out, it'll be because he knows you're insane as well as corrupt, Hammond," Stark said.

Hammond's hands clenched into fists, but he didn't throw a punch. He was being too careful for that. This was the culmination of a plan designed to humiliate and humble John Howard Stark.

"Take him," Hammond hissed.

But it was only the first step in the Vulture's revenge, Stark thought.

As bad as this was, he sensed that worse was coming.

Twenty-eight

When the car with Stark in the backseat drove out through the gate to Hubie's ranch, Stark saw Devery's pickup parked on the shoulder of the river road. Devery was leaning against the fender, but he straightened and lunged forward as he spotted Stark in the cruiser.

"John Howard!" he yelled. "John Howard, what happened?"

Stark leaned forward and hunched his shoulders up, lifting his hands so that Devery could see they were cuffed behind him. "Call Sam!" Stark shouted as the deputy at the wheel stomped the gas and sent the car spurting away. He didn't know if Devery had heard him or not. If not, he hoped that his friend had been able to read his lips.

Stark settled back against the rear seat and twisted his neck to look behind the car. He saw Devery's pickup pulling out onto the road to follow the cruiser. Stark couldn't be sure, but he thought that Devery was talking on the phone as he drove. He hoped Sam Gonzales was in his office today.

The ride into Del Rio seemed longer than it really was. Stark felt as if he'd been hit between the eyes by a two-by-four. Not only were three of his best friends suddenly, gruesomely dead, but he was being blamed by the law for it.

Of course, he didn't believe for a second that Sheriff Hammond really thought he was responsible for what had happened to Hubie, W.R., and Everett. Hammond knew good and well that Stark hadn't killed them. The very elaborateness of the plot against him—rocket-propelled grenades hidden in his barn, for God's sake!—indicated that Hammond was probably in on it. At the very least, Hammond had received "anonymous" tips telling him what to do, and he must have known those tips came from Ramirez.

But it was unlikely either he or his attorney would be able to prove any of that, Stark thought. He wasn't by nature a despairing man, but it seemed to him now that the jaws of the trap had closed securely on him.

By the time they reached Del Rio things didn't appear any more promising to Stark. He looked for Sam Gonzales but didn't see the lawyer. The deputies took him into the jail, went through the whole rigmarole of photographing, fingerprinting, and booking him again. When he asked to be allowed to make a phone call, one of the deputies said, "As soon as the sheriff gets back, he'll tend to that."

Stark was put into a holding cell. His gun, belt, boots, hat, and everything in his pockets had been taken away from him. He sat down on the bunk as the door of the cell clanged shut. The sound put his teeth on edge.

He had been there about half an hour, staring at the floor without really seeing it, when the door down the corridor opened and footsteps approached the cell. They stopped just outside, and a deputy peered in through the reinforced glass window set in the door at eye level. A key rattled in the lock.

"Your lawyer's here," the deputy said as the door swung open. "Come on out." He stepped back, a hand on the butt of his pistol. Two more deputies stood nearby, Stark saw as he stepped into the hall. Both of them were ready to draw and fire, too, if need be.

"You boys must think I'm Clyde Barrow come back to life," Stark said.

"Who?" asked one of the deputies. He was maybe twenty-two years old.

Stark just shook his head and said, "Never mind. Just take me to my lawyer."

When one of the deputies opened the door to an interview room furnished with a table and two chairs, though, it wasn't Sam Gonzales whom Stark saw sitting at the table. It was Devery Small. He had put on a tie, but other than that he still wore jeans and a khaki work shirt. His Stetson sat on the table.

"Thank y'all," he said to the deputies. "That'll be all for now. I got to talk to my client in, uh, private. Confidential-like. You know."

Stark walked into the room. The deputies didn't try to stop him. As he sat down across the table from Devery, the door closed.

Stark leaned forward and hissed, "What the hell are you doin'?" He threw a glance at the mirror on the wall, knowing it was probably one of those two-way jobs. Hammond might have the room bugged, too, even though such things were supposed to be illegal.

"Take it easy, John Howard," Devery replied. "Are you all right? Anybody try to hurt you?"

"I'm fine, just flabbergasted to find myself under arrest again. Where's Sam?"

"He said he couldn't get here for a while and for me to come to the jail and say I was your lawyer and demand to see you. I got the feelin' he was afraid Hammond an' his boys might try somethin' funny, and he wanted a witness on hand so's they'd behave themselves."

Stark snorted. "Hammond's not going to do anything to me. If I'm right about what's going on here, he's got his marchin' orders, and they don't include killing me."

"John Howard, what *is* goin' on?" Tears shone in Devery's eyes. "Is it true what I'm hearin', that Hubie and W.R. and Everett are all dead?"

Stark nodded grimly. "I'm afraid so. Barring some sort of miracle, they're all gone . . . and after the past couple of months, I don't reckon I believe in miracles anymore."

Devery put his head down and stared at the table for a long moment, breathing hard as he struggled to control the emotions coursing through him. Finally, when he was able to look up again, he said, "Ramirez?"

"There's no one else who could have been behind it," Stark said.

"But . . . he hates you worse'n anybody else. You're the one he's tried to have killed in the past. Why go after Hubie and the other fellas?"

Stark spread his hands. "Look around, Devery. Three of my best friends are dead, and I'm in jail charged with killing them."

"Yeah," Devery said, nodding slowly. "Yeah, I reckon I can see it. He wants you to suffer, John Howard. It's just pure meanness, plain and simple."

Stark couldn't argue with that. Pure meanness was about as good a description as he had ever heard of Ernesto Ramirez.

"What do we do now?" Devery asked. "We got to get you outta here. This ain't right."

"That'll be Sam's job. There's nothing you can do, Devery, except see to it that Elaine stays safe."

Devery nodded again. "You got it. Your place'll be guarded round the clock."

For a while they commiserated with each other over the deaths of their friends, sharing memories of Hubie, W.R., and Everett. Then, suddenly, the door of the interview room was jerked open and Hammond strode in, an angry expression on his flushed face.

"This ain't your lawyer," he snarled as he pointed a finger at Devery. "You're under arrest for . . . for impersonating an attorney, you little pissant!"

"No, he's not," Sam Gonzales said from behind Hammond.

"Devery works for me part-time as a legal assistant, and as such he was entitled to see our client."

Devery wiped the back of his hand across his mouth. "Uh, yeah, that's right. I'm one o' them, whatcha call 'em, pair of eagles."

Hammond grimaced, his lips drawing back from his teeth. He jerked a thumb over his shoulder. "Get out," he snapped. "And I ain't gonna forget about this!"

Devery grabbed his hat, got to his feet, and hurried out of the room, giving Stark one last reassuring glance as he departed.

Coolly, Sam Gonzales stepped past Hammond and set his briefcase on the table. "I'll need to talk to my client now, Sheriff," he said. "I'll thank you to leave us alone."

Hammond moved closer to Sam and put his face only inches away from the lawyer's. "You think you're so goddamned smart," the sheriff said between clenched teeth. "But you're really just a dumb pepper belly."

Gonzales paled, but he kept his temper under control. "You should leave now, Sheriff," he said quietly. "You really should . . . unless you want to violate Mr. Stark's rights even more than they've already been violated."

Hammond shook his head and pointed at Stark. "Nobody's violated his rights. Nobody! Everything's been done strictly by the book, and I dare you to prove otherwise . . . greaser."

Sam reached for his briefcase, and Stark saw the lawyer's fingers trembling slightly as he undid the catches. "I'll talk to you later, Sheriff," he managed to say.

Hammond finally swung around and went to the door. He cast a baleful glance at both Stark and Gonzales before he went out and slammed the door behind him.

"Thanks, Sam," Stark said.

"For what? I haven't done anything yet."

"You didn't haul off and hit Hammond in the mouth. That's gotta be helpful."

Sam smiled thinly. "You're probably right. But it sure

would have felt good." He took a deep breath, opened the briefcase, took out a legal pad and a pen, and said, "All right. What the hell's going on here, John Howard?"

Stark spent the next half hour telling Gonzales about the worried phone call from Devery, his hurried drive over to Hubie's ranch and out to Comanche Ridge, and the grisly discovery he'd made in the canyon leading to Solomon Wash. Sam's normally pleasant, round face became grim and drawn as he listened.

"I'd heard the rumors," he muttered when Stark was finished, "but that's not like hearing it firsthand. I'm sorry, John Howard. That must have been an awful experience for you."

"Yeah, but not as bad as it was for Hubie, W.R., and Everett."

"I'll do everything I can for their families. Right now, though, it's more important to do what I can for you. Is there anything else you can tell me?"

Stark thought about it for a minute and then shook his head. "You know as much about it as I do."

"What do you think Ramirez's ultimate goal is?"

"To make life as miserable as possible for me before he finally kills me?" Stark guessed.

"You think he still wants to have you assassinated?"

"It seems likely. Unless he gets such a kick out of the idea of me going to prison that he decides to let that play out."

"I wouldn't be surprised," Sam said. "A man like Ramirez probably has plenty of contacts inside the penitentiary. If you're convicted and sent to prison, he could have you killed there any time he wanted." Sam hesitated. "But he might have even worse things in mind."

A humorless smile stretched Stark's mouth under the dark mustache. "You're not tellin' me anything that I haven't already thought about, Sam."

Gonzales put away his legal pad and pen and closed the briefcase. Briskly, he said, "Other than the circumstantial evidence of you being on the scene, which really doesn't amount to anything, the main thing supporting Hammond's case against you is the fact that those grenade launchers were found in your barn. Our first course of action is to attack that search as unlawful, and therefore get the evidence thrown out."

"Anyway," Stark said, "isn't it obvious that if I'd used those damn grenades, I wouldn't have kept the launchers in my own barn?"

Gonzales shrugged. "Killers do odd things, John Howard. They hang on to evidence for no good reason, and it ultimately winds up convicting them. Not that I'm saying you're a killer. I don't believe that for a second." He hesitated, then asked, "But I'll have to know . . . where were you this morning?"

Stark's mouth quirked. "I was out checking fence . . . alone."

"Nobody saw you? Nobody can swear that you were on your ranch all morning?"

"Nope," Stark said with a shake of his head. "Not that I know of. I don't have an alibi that'll hold up."

"Well, you shouldn't need one," Gonzales said confidently. "We'll get this whole mess tossed out at the arraignment, if they don't decide to drop it before then. I can't imagine Wilfredo letting Hammond bully him into looking like a fool, again."

Stark nodded. He hoped Gonzales was right.

But after today's shocking incidents, he no longer felt that confident about anything.

Except for the fact that the world was going to hell, and he was going right along for the ride.

Elaine came to see him that evening. Devery was with her, and he said, "I tried to tell her you wanted her to lie low out at the ranch, John Howard, but that wife o' yours is mighty stubborn."

Stark pulled Elaine into his arms and hugged her. "That's the truth," he told Devery as he grinned over Elaine's shoulder.

She punched him lightly in the stomach. "Is that any way to talk about somebody who came to see you and make you feel better?"

Stark leaned down and kissed her, not caring that Devery and one of the deputies were standing right there a few feet away. "You make me feel better, all right. The whole world makes more sense when you're around."

The deputy told Devery, "You'll have to wait outside. Only one visitor at a time back here."

"Sure thing," Devery agreed. "Take it easy, John Howard."

"Only way to take it," Stark said.

The deputy ushered Devery away and shut the door. Stark and Elaine sat down side by side on the bunk. "Tell me all about it," she said.

Stark shook his head. "You don't want to know all about it. There are parts of it I don't even want to think about again."

"Well then, tell me as much as you can. As much as you want to."

Stark talked for a while, glossing over the most grisly parts of the story. When he'd been brought back to the holding cell after his talk with Sam Gonzales, he had gone over the place as best he could and hadn't found any bugs, so he was reasonably confident that no one was listening in as he explained his theory about Ramirez being behind this frame-up.

When he was done, he had some questions of his own. "When Hammond's men came to the ranch and searched the barn, did they have a warrant?"

Elaine nodded and said, "Yes, the deputy who was in charge made sure that I looked it over good and then he gave me a copy of it before they ever started searching. I told him he was wasting his time. And then they came out of the barn carrying those . . . those things."

"They had to be planted there after I left."

"Couldn't the deputies themselves have planted them?"

"It's possible," Stark said, "but I think it's more likely some of Ramirez's men, maybe even the killers themselves, slipped onto the ranch and put them in the barn." A chill went through him as he thought about the Vulture's men being that close to Elaine without anyone knowing about it. "I think most of the deputies are reasonably honest and do their jobs the best they can, despite Hammond being crooked." He paused and then asked, "Did they find anything else? Did they search inside the house?"

"They searched *everywhere*," Elaine said. "They said the warrant gave them the authority to search the entire premises."

"I'm surprised they got Judge Goodnight to agree to sign that warrant," Stark muttered.

"Judge Goodnight didn't sign it. It was signed by Judge Bates."

Stark frowned. Louise Bates was a local justice of the peace, a lawyer from somewhere in the Northeast who had moved to Del Rio a few years earlier with her husband when he retired from his job with a big chemical company. He was still relatively young, but his health was bad and his doctor had advised him to seek out a warm, dry climate, something Del Rio had in abundance. Stark had never heard anything bad about Louise Bates, but he supposed not being a Texan and having been in the area only a few years, she wasn't fully aware of what was going on in the Rio Grande valley these days. Her liberal background, too, would make her quick to leap to conclusions whenever anybody starting throwing around words like "vigilante."

"I reckon it's legal," Stark said, "or Hammond wouldn't be trying to get away with it. He knew Harvey Goodnight wouldn't sign a warrant for a fishing expedition like that."

"So if Sam can't get the search thrown out, the evidence will go in and you'll be charged again, this time with murder." Elaine's hands knotted together.

Stark took them, separated them, and held them in his

own hands. "It'll be all right," he told her. "Everybody knows it's crazy to accuse me of killing those fellas. Hammond can frame up all the evidence he wants, but no one will ever believe him."

"You don't know that, John Howard. All he's got to do is convince a jury. Twelve people. There are probably a lot more people than that in Val Verde County who don't like you. Not everybody thinks you've been doing the right thing by fighting Ramirez, you know."

Stark nodded grimly. "I know. That's why we have to fight these charges tooth and nail. I trust Sam, and I don't plan to give up."

"Neither do I. I've never given up on you, John Howard, you know that. Even when you were over there in Vietnam, with all that fighting and dying going on all around you, I always had faith that you'd come home safely to me." She rested her head against his shoulder. "I have faith in you now."

That made Stark feel better than he would have thought possible under the circumstances. He put an arm around her and sat there holding her for a long time as they drew strength from each other. Two halves of one whole. That was the way it had always been with them, and nothing could ever change it.

Twenty-nine

Stark spent a restless night, his sleep haunted by nightmares of what he had found in that desolate canyon the day before. He was sure that by morning he must look as bad as he felt.

After breakfast Sam Gonzales stopped by with the news that the arraignment would be at two o'clock that afternoon. "Normally it would have been this morning," Sam said. "They're dragging their feet for some reason, probably because Wilfredo doesn't really want to go forward with the case and Hammond is pressuring him to do so."

"Elaine told me the search warrant was signed by Louise Bates."

Gonzales nodded. "I found that out and talked to her. She said Sheriff Hammond called her and told her it was an emergency, that if he didn't act fast your ranch hands might dispose of the evidence against you." The lawyer shrugged. "I hate to say it, John Howard, but I don't think the lady likes you very much."

"I don't even know the woman," Stark said in exasperation. "I think I was introduced to her once, at some civic function."

"Yes, but she's from Massachusetts. She doesn't believe

in anyone taking the law into their own hands. She says there's never any justification for that."

Stark frowned for a moment, but then he began to laugh. He put his head back and just about roared with amusement.

Gonzales stared at him, and when Stark's laughter began to die away, he asked, "What's so funny?"

"Somebody from Massachusetts thinking that there's never any justification for taking the law into your own hands. I'm sure glad Sam Adams and Paul Revere and the rest of those old boys up there didn't feel that way. You'd look damned silly with a powdered wig on, Sam."

Gonzales grunted, and then that mental image made him laugh, too. "When you're right, you're right, John Howard. In the meantime, I'll go get ready for the arraignment. It doesn't look like we'll be able to dodge it."

Sam departed, leaving Stark alone again. He had extracted a firm promise from Elaine the night before that she would stay out at the ranch today, no matter what happened. Devery and some of the other men were guarding her around the clock, and Stark figured she was safer there than in town. He had worried all along that Ramirez might try to strike back at him by hurting the people he cared about. That was what had happened with Hubie, W.R., and Everett. He didn't want Elaine falling victim to the same fate.

Late in the morning—or at least what felt like that time; without a watch Stark couldn't be sure—footsteps once again approached the cell, and the door was unlocked. A deputy said, "Come with me, Mr. Stark. You've got another visitor."

Stark followed the man down the corridor, thinking that Sam was probably back, but when he was taken into the interview room, he saw that a stranger was sitting at the table. The man was black and middle-aged, with gray hair and glasses that gave him a slightly professorial look. The dark, sober suit he wore, though, practically shouted that he was a government man.

"Mr. Stark," the man said without offering to shake hands,

"my name is Raymond Whitby. I'm with the Internal Revenue Service."

Stark resisted the temptation to make some crack about the IRS being after him now, too. There was too much of a chance that was exactly the case. Instead he nodded in acknowledgment and said, "What can I do for you, Mr. Whitby?"

"Nothing. I'm just here to inform you that the Service has filed charges of tax evasion and nonpayment of taxes against you, and we're hereby seizing your property, both real and personal, to satisfy the debt that you owe the government."

Stark was still standing. He had to lower himself slowly into the chair across from Whitby as all of that soaked in on his stunned brain. "That's not possible," he finally said.

"Oh, it's very possible, I assure you," Whitby said. He picked up a briefcase from the floor at his feet, opened it, and took out a thick sheaf of papers. "Here are copies of all the documents relating to the case, including your tax returns. You'll see that for the past five years, you've underpaid your taxes to the tune of . . . let's see here . . ." Whitby looked down at one of the papers, but Stark had the feeling the government man knew exactly what the numbers on it were. "Yes, two hundred thousand dollars. Approximately. It's actually a bit more than that."

Stark shook his head. "I've barely made that much taxable income in the past five years. There's no way I could owe that much in taxes. Just look at my tax returns."

Whitby turned the documents around and pushed them across the table. "Look at them yourself, Mr. Stark."

Stark picked up the top paper, which was one of his tax returns. He and Elaine had always done their taxes themselves, rather than hiring an accountant, so Stark was very familiar with the forms. He stared for a moment at what was written on this one, and then his eyes snapped up to Whitby.

"This isn't my return!"

"I believe it is," Whitby said calmly. "Turn it over. You'll see your signature, along with that of your wife."

Stark flipped the document over and saw the familiar handwriting, but he still shook his head. "It's not possible. This has been forged, or changed somehow."

Whitby snapped his briefcase closed and said smugly, "That's what nearly all the tax cheats say when we finally catch up to them."

Stark resisted the temptation to throw the stack of papers in the IRS agent's face. "I still say you can't just seize my property. You have to go to court."

"Certainly we do have seizure powers. To put it bluntly, if we say you owe us money, we can take everything you own, and *you* have to go to court to get it back if you think we're wrong." Whitby smiled. "Of course, under your current circumstances, I think you're already going to be busy in court without dealing with this matter."

"You son of a bitch," Stark breathed.

Whitby smiled again. "I work for the IRS, Mr. Stark. I've been called much worse than that."

"You know a man named Ramirez?" Stark asked suddenly.

"Who?" For a second, Whitby's confusion seemed genuine. Then he said, "Oh, you mean that alleged drug smuggler you're feuding with. I've read about the man in the newspaper; that's all."

Stark actually believed him. Not even Ramirez had the power to bring the IRS into this game on his side. But Stark wasn't through.

"What about Calhoun? Zachary E. Calhoun? Or John Kelso?"

Whitby shook his head. "Never heard of either of them."

Stark, though, had seen the flicker of recognition in Whitby's eyes when he mentioned Calhoun's name. The man from the National Security Council was behind this, Stark thought. Calhoun worked for the president. He could bring enough pressure to bear to get the IRS to go along with the campaign to break Stark. It was hard to believe that the United States government would go to so much trouble to ruin one of its own citizens just because they regarded him as an embarrassment.

It wasn't really the government, Stark reminded himself. It was just the petty little bureaucrats who liked to think they were in charge. They had forgotten that their real bosses were the people . . .

But the people had allowed them to forget about that. The people had taken the power that rightfully belonged to them and placed it in the hands of men and women like Whitby and Calhoun and Kelso. Because it was easier that way. Because they felt safer, whether they really were or not. Because the press and the politicians constantly told them that was what they were supposed to do. *Don't think for yourselves. Trust us. We'll take care of you.*

We're from the government, and we're here to help you.

Stark gave a hollow chuckle.

"Something funny?" Whitby snapped.

"No. Not a damned thing. Are you going to leave me anything at all?"

Whitby shrugged. "Photographs, personal effects, things like that. We'll be seizing your property, including the house and all the other buildings, your cattle, your farming equipment, everything of tangible value."

"What about my wife?" Stark said tautly. "That's her home."

"She signed the returns, too. She's equally liable. But we're not completely heartless, despite popular belief. Some of our agents have gone out there today to inform her of the situation, and she'll be given a reasonable amount of time to vacate the premises."

Stark felt his tension ease slightly. Sam Gonzales didn't need anything else on his plate right now, especially something like a fight with the IRS, but it was going to be up to him to buy Stark and Elaine some more time.

"Twenty-four hours," Whitby added.

Stark stared at him for a second, then exploded, "What?"

"Mrs. Stark will be given twenty-four hours to vacate.

Approximately. We'll be generous and call it noon tomorrow."

Stark sat there, stunned. He wanted to dive across the table and smash his fist into Raymond Whitby's face. But he knew that wouldn't accomplish a damned thing except to get him deeper in the hole that was threatening to swallow him.

He was starting to understand how the fella Job, back there in the Old Testament, must have felt.

Elaine tried cleaning and puttering around to keep her mind off what was happening, but that effort was a dismal failure. She couldn't stop thinking about John Howard being locked up in that little cell, waiting to find out whether he was going to be put on trial for the murders of three of his best friends. It was all crazy, of course, but their whole life was that way these days.

Having Devery Small and a couple of other heavily armed men underfoot all the time didn't help matters. Elaine was grateful for their presence, though. There was no telling what a madman like Ramirez might do.

She was in the kitchen when Devery came in and said, "There's a car comin' up the road, Elaine. I don't know who it is."

She sighed. "More trouble, I'd bet."

"Well, you stay inside here while me an' the boys see about it."

She nodded, but as Devery went out to greet the newcomers, she drifted into the living room and stole a look through the curtains over the picture window. She saw that a man and a woman had gotten out of the car, which was a dark, late-model sedan. Evidently the woman had been driving. She was in her thirties, blond and attractive, wearing gold-framed glasses. The severe suit she wore and the way her long hair was pulled back told Elaine that she was either in business or from the government. Probably the latter, Elaine decided.

The man was tall, a little paunchy, with brown hair. Devery talked to both of them for a moment, then turned and gestured toward the house. They all started that way.

Elaine met them at the door. Devery gave her a worried look and said, "Elaine, these folks are from the Internal Revenue Service. I checked their bona fides."

"Thank you, Devery." To the strangers, she said, "Come in, please. Can I get you something, some coffee or iced tea?"

The woman shook her head without waiting for the man to respond. Clearly, she was in charge here. "No, thank you, Mrs. Stark. You *are* Mrs. Elaine Stark?"

"That's right."

The woman introduced herself. "Charlotte Grayson. This is Mel Littlefield, my associate."

"I'm glad to meet you," Elaine lied. "If this is something to do with our taxes, I'll do what I can to help you. My husband's not here right now—"

"We know where your husband is," Grayson said. "One of our agents is paying him a visit in jail." She turned to Littlefield, who put his hand inside his coat and took out a folded document. He handed it to Grayson, who handed it in turn to Elaine. She took it without really thinking. Grayson went on, "That's an official notice of seizure. The IRS is taking control of this property in lieu of payment of back taxes. Mel?"

Littlefield took out another paper and stepped forward to give it to Elaine. "This is an eviction notice," he said. He sounded a little regretful, but that might have been just a pose. "You'll have until noon tomorrow to vacate the premises, Mrs. Stark."

Devery couldn't stand it anymore. He burst out, "Wait just a doggoned minute! You're takin' the ranch and kickin' Elaine off of it?"

Grayson turned her cold stare on him. "That's right. And you are . . . ?"

Devery swallowed, evidently realizing that he was getting

into deeper waters than he wanted to. "Uh, my name's Devery Small," he said. "I'm one of John Howard and Elaine's neighbors and old friends."

"This matter doesn't concern you, Mr. Small," Grayson said. "It's between Mr. and Mrs. Stark and the government."

"It's crazy, that's what it is!" Elaine stared down at the papers in her hands. "None of it makes any sense. We don't owe any back taxes! We've always paid what we owe, and paid it on time."

"Not according to our records. Our agent should be going over all this with Mr. Stark right now. I suggest that if you have any questions, you talk to him."

"No, I'm going to talk to your boss," Elaine snapped. "You can't just waltz in here and tell me to get the hell out of my own house!"

Again sounding almost apologetic, Littlefield said, "Actually, we can, Mrs. Stark. It's all perfectly legal. But if you want to speak to our supervisor, that would be just fine." He took a business card out of his pocket and held it out toward her. "Here's the number you should call—"

Elaine snatched the card from his hand, crumpled it, and threw it on the floor. "Don't think you can come in here and pull this good cop, bad cop routine on me. As far as I'm concerned, one of you is just as bad as the other."

"We're both equally dedicated to our jobs," Grayson said. "And I believe we're through here." She nodded. "Good morning, Mrs. Stark. Remember, you're to be out by noon tomorrow."

Elaine didn't trust herself to speak. She was too mad for that. She was afraid she might start spitting curses at the two visitors. She was even more afraid she might light into that Grayson woman and knock that smug expression off her face. The IRS agent was twenty years younger and probably worked out, but Elaine had spent thirty years working on a ranch. With an effort, she controlled herself and stood there silently, not moving, as Grayson and Littlefield left the house.

Elaine heard the car doors shut, and then the vehicle drove off.

"Well, I never heard so dang much craziness in all my life," Devery said. "Hell, John Howard's so law-abidin' he'd even pay a parkin' ticket if he got one, or an overdue fine at the library. He sure never cheated Uncle Sam on his taxes."

"No," Elaine agreed quietly. "No, he didn't."

Devery scratched his head. "What are you gonna do about it? I'll take you into town if you want, so you can talk it over with John Howard."

"He's got enough to worry about right now, especially if the IRS paid him a visit, too." She summoned up a smile. "Devery, I may have to come and spend a few days with your family."

"You're welcome as long as you want to stay," Devery said immediately. "And don't you worry about this. We'll get it all straightened out. I'll bet John Howard's already talked to Sam Gonzales and got him workin' on it. Sam'll get an injunction against the government. You just wait and see. You won't have to go anywhere."

Elaine appreciated Devery's optimism, even though she didn't think he believed those sentiments for a moment. Fighting the government was nearly always a losing battle.

"Calhoun," she said softly.

"Who?"

"The government man who came to see us before. The one who wanted to give John Howard a cushy job and shut him up. He's behind this."

"Yeah." Devery nodded. "Yeah, I bet you're right." He shook his head. "Lordy, it ain't enough that we got to fight a bunch o' bloodthirsty drug smugglers. Now we got our own government comin' down on us. It ain't right. It just ain't right."

"No," Elaine agreed, "it's not."

But for the life of her, she didn't know what they could do about it.

* * *

That afternoon she sat in the book-lined study, behind the desk where John Howard worked on the taxes and all the other bookkeeping that was required to keep the ranch running properly. She had taken out the files and pored over the copies of everything she could find relating to this problem, and as far as she could tell, everything was exactly the way it was supposed to be. The problem was, the IRS had different documents.

It was a frame-up, pure and simple, she thought. But even so, it might take years of work by high-powered attorneys to overcome the false charges. They didn't have that much time, and they certainly didn't have the money that a protracted court battle would take. The government would win in the long run, just through its sheer size. The Stark family would be ruined, no matter what the outcome.

It wasn't fair, she thought as tears rolled down her cheeks. They were good citizens, always had been. Good Americans. John Howard had served his country in Vietnam. Their sons were in the Middle East at this very moment, working to defeat terrorism and make the world a safer place for everybody. But evidently such sacrifices no longer counted for anything.

Elaine's gaze dropped to a framed photograph on the desk. It had been there for thirty years and showed a much younger John Howard Stark standing in front of a ramshackle tent with five other men. All of them wore military fatigues, carried rifles and machine guns, and had belts of ammunition draped around their bodies. Heavily armed like that, they should have looked like fierce warriors, but they were all grinning and somehow they looked like overgrown kids. The camaraderie was palpable between them, even in this old photograph.

Elaine blinked a couple of times and then wiped away her tears. An idea had begun to form in her mind. She opened a desk drawer and took out a black leather notebook. When she opened it, the pages were full of names, addresses, and phone numbers. She looked at the notebook, flipping through some of the pages, and then looked at the photograph again.

"John Howard," she said aloud, "I know if you were here you wouldn't want me to do this, but every instinct I've got tells me this is the right thing to do."

She pushed the welter of papers aside, pulled the phone closer, put her finger under one of the numbers written in the notebook, and began to dial.

Thirty

Jack Finnegan was lining up a putt when the phone rang. He knew how the nap of the carpet in his office broke; he had rolled thousands of golf balls across it over the years and ought to know by now. He ought to feel a little guilty about wasting his time on such things when he should be working, he thought, but he figured as long as he was using that shot glass for a target and not filling it with booze, that was a good thing.

His AA sponsor had told him he shouldn't even have a shot glass in his office. He should have gotten rid of it when he got rid of the wet bar. But some habits were even harder to break than drinking, and for Jack Finnegan one of them was stroking a golf ball across that thick carpet into a shot glass a few hundred times a day.

At the moment, though, his concentration was broken, so he sighed and turned to the desk without putting the ball. He picked up the phone and said, "Yeah, Darcy?"

The voice of his executive assistant said, "There's a woman on the line for you named Elaine Stark, Jack."

For a second the name didn't register with Finnegan. Then, as Darcy went on, "She said to tell you she's married to John

Howard Stark," Finnegan remembered her on his own. Sure, Elaine. Trim little blond number, married to his old marine buddy from 'Nam. Finnegan had met her at one of the unit's reunions, and he hadn't even hit on her. That had been back in the days when he was still sober most of the time. Good thing, too, because John Howard Stark was a big, tough son of a bitch, Texan through and through, and he probably would've handed Finnegan his head if Finnegan had started messing with his wife.

The banker took a deep breath. A call from the wife of an old friend wasn't good news these days. It probably meant that ol' John Howard had dropped dead of a heart attack or a stroke or something. And Finnegan was a year older than Stark, he reminded himself, and in a high-stress business to boot. He had smoked for years, drunk *waaaay* too much, and chased too much strange tail. Sure, he had given up the cigarettes and he'd been sober for four years, seven months, and nineteen days, but he still figured that he was about due for his own drop-dead moment. He didn't need to be reminded of that by having another old friend die.

"Jack? Do you want to talk to Mrs. Stark, or should I tell her you're already gone for the day?"

Finnegan glanced at the readout of the digital clock on his desk. Not quite two o'clock. That would be carrying banker's hours to an extreme.

"I'll talk to her," he said as he placed the putter on his desk. The top of the desk was empty except for the clock, the phone, and a small notepad.

A couple of clicks sounded in his ear, and then a woman's voice said, "Hello?"

"Elaine," Finnegan said warmly. "This is Jack. How are you?"

"Not doing too good these days, I'm afraid. I guess you've heard . . . about John Howard."

"No, I'm afraid not. No one's called me." Finnegan didn't have to force caring and concern into his voice. He found that he really felt those emotions. John Howard Stark had been a good friend. A damned good friend. Not to mention one hell of a soldier. Finnegan was convinced there was a good chance he never would have gotten out of that jungle hellhole alive if not for John Howard.

Elaine sounded a little confused as she said, "No, I, uh, mean you probably saw him on the news, or read about him in the papers."

"Oh." Stark was famous? He'd made the papers? This was the first Finnegan had heard of it. "No, I'm afraid I don't read much except the financial news these days, and I don't watch much TV."

That was because he couldn't stand the sound of it. It seemed to echo too much in the big, empty house since his wife had left. The kids, of course, had gone off to college some years earlier and never come back. His only contact with them was an occasional phone call.

"Jack, John Howard's in trouble," Elaine said. "He's in jail, and he needs help. I thought maybe some of his old friends—"

"In jail?" Finnegan exclaimed. A straight arrow like John Howard Stark? That seemed impossible. "What did he do? Do you need money? A good lawyer?"

"Right now, I . . . I don't know what we need."

Finnegan sat down in the big, padded executive chair. "Tell me about it," he said, more businesslike and focused now. "Start at the beginning."

She did, and by the time she was finished, Jack Finnegan was sitting up straight in his chair. The puffy, dissipated lines in his face seemed to have vanished. His voice was brisk as he said, "Don't worry, Elaine. I'll be down there as soon as I can, and we'll straighten all this out. Do you want me to call anyone else for you?"

"No, I . . . I've got a list of names and numbers here, all the men who were closest to John Howard in those days. I thought it would be better for me to call them myself."

"All right. I'll see you probably tomorrow. And again, don't worry."

She laughed quietly. "It's hard not to."

"I know," Finnegan said. "I know."

When he had said good-bye, he got his assistant back on the line and said, "Darcy, get hold of Arthur Baldwin. And book me on the first flight tomorrow morning to Texas."

"Texas?" Darcy repeated. "Jack, you've got an important meeting tomorrow."

"It'll have to wait," Jack Finnegan said, and as he hung up the phone he marveled at how good it felt to actually give a damn about something again.

It was deadline day, and Will Sheffield knew it would be a long, busy evening as he and the staff of the paper got it ready to e-mail to the printer. The whole process was easier now, of course, than it had been in the days before everything was done on the computer, but it was still a challenge to get everything into the paper that needed to be there and get it in the right place. Sheffield had spent the morning writing his editorial for this week's edition, a call for the city council of the small Tennessee town to find a way around a zoning controversy that threatened to put an old black man out of the home where he had lived for more than sixty years, just because he raised a few pigs in his backyard. Hell, the old man and the pigs had been there for years before some land developer had carved up the acreage next door and built fancy brick houses on it and sold them to a bunch of snobbish rich folks who decided they didn't want to live next to a pig farm. It wasn't a racial issue; some of the new home owners were black, and they didn't want the pigs there, either. As Sheffield had put it in his editorial, the whole thing stank, and not just because of the pigs. The line was a little too cute, maybe, but he hadn't been able to resist the temptation to use it.

When the phone on his desk rang, he took his attention away from the computer where he had been laying out the paper. "*Banner*, this is Will. Can I help you?" This was his private line, so it probably wasn't somebody calling to put a want ad in this week's paper. Although you never knew. No phone number was completely private in a small town.

"Will, this is Elaine Stark from Texas. John Howard's wife? We met a few years ago at a reunion?"

"Of course." Sheffield had no trouble remembering her. She'd been smart and pretty—he wouldn't have expected John Howard Stark to marry anyone who wasn't—and she had hit it off very well with his wife, Janet. "How are you? How's old John Howard?"

A sudden thought struck him. He wouldn't have been that surprised if John Howard had called him, although several years usually went by between times when they talked. The fact that Elaine was on the phone instead meant that there might be trouble. Sheffield hoped his old friend and comrade-in-arms wasn't sick . . . or worse.

"John Howard's in some trouble, Will. He needs help."

Sheffield frowned, leaned forward, and turned off the monitor. "Tell me about it," he said without hesitation. "What can I do?" But before she could say anything, he remembered the wire service stories he'd read in the past few weeks, and he said, "Oh my God. This is about that drug smuggler, isn't it?"

"That's part of it."

Sheffield ran his fingers through his thick brown hair. He had been distracted at first, but it was coming back to him now. He had seen reports on the network news about Stark's crusade to stop the drug smuggling and how its influence was spreading along the country's southern border. There had even been a tie-in with some sort of terrorist plot to blow up an oil refinery in Houston or somewhere. Being in the news business, he was ashamed that he hadn't kept up with the story more closely, especially since it involved an old friend.

But he lived in a small town and edited and published a

small-town paper. News to him meant a bad wreck out on the highway, vandals breaking into one of the elementary schools, a record catfish being pulled out of the lake by a twelve-year-old boy, Little League games, and how the high school football team was going to look this fall. National news seldom if ever crept into the pages of the *Banner*.

Elaine told him what had been going on. The whole story was crazy, fantastic, like something out of one of the thrillers that Sheffield had written after it became obvious to him that no publisher was going to buy his novel about a sensitive young man growing up in the hills of Tennessee during the sixties, deciding to be a writer, and then going off to war. Of course, nobody had bought the thrillers, either, and he had given up on them after writing three during his spare time. By then he had been working on the paper for a while and had gotten a bank loan in order to buy out the former publisher, who was retiring. Writing local news stories wasn't the same as penning the Great American Novel, of course, but Sheffield had grown to like it, and the *Banner* had supported him and his wife and their growing family reasonably comfortably, especially after Janet had gotten her real estate license and started selling houses.

None of which would have been possible if John Howard Stark hadn't saved his ass on numerous occasions in-country.

When Elaine finished telling him about it, he said simply, "I'm on my way."

She said, "Will, I hate to impose on you like this—"

"I'm on my way," he said again as he stood up. "And don't worry about a thing. You've got the power of the press on your side now."

The only problem was, he thought, with all the enemies lined up against John Howard Stark, that might not be enough. It might not be anywhere near enough.

"Now, don't take these on an empty stomach," Henry Macon said as he handed the bottle of pills to the elderly woman on the other side of the counter. "Be sure to eat a little something first. That'll keep your stomach from getting upset."

"Thank you, Henry. You're a good boy, you know that?"

Macon smiled. "Yes, ma'am." Aunt Luella Carson could call him a boy because she was eighty-five years old and had known him all his life, just like she knew most of the folks in this Cedar Rapids neighborhood. And it *was* a neighborhood, not a damn "hood," like some of the kids had called it back in the nineties. The way slang changed, he supposed they called it something else by now, but Macon didn't know the current terminology. He had long since stopped listening to most of the things that came from the mouths of morons who didn't know which way a baseball cap was supposed to be worn. The backward caps and the baggy pants always reminded him of Leo Gorcey and Huntz Hall and the rest of the Bowery Boys he had watched in old movies on a round-tubed Philco when he was a kid. He sometimes wondered how many of the local gangstas realized that their chosen fashion style had originated with a bunch of white, Jewish juvenile actors who had plied their trade more than sixty years earlier. Very few, he guessed. Actually, none.

Philistines, he thought. Barbarians.

Except for Alicia Keys. That girl could *sing*. He'd heard 78s of Billie Holiday when he was young, and Alicia was right there with her. The current generation wasn't completely worthless. Just damned near.

Macon watched to see that Aunt Luella got out of the pharmacy all right. She was spry for her age and went everywhere on her own, and nobody bothered her. Everybody on the street knew better. This was a good street, with thriving businesses and some nice homes farther down. The closest crack house that Macon knew of was six blocks over, and the people who haunted that area seldom drifted over here. But sometimes they did, so Macon worried that someday a couple of them might carry their turf wars over here and start shooting at each other. If that ever happened, innocents like Aunt Luella might be in the cross fire.

He couldn't protect everybody. He knew that, even though it had taken him some time to come to terms with it. He had come back from the marines with a whole new sense of self-worth and a determination to transform the world in which he had grown up. He had transformed himself first, working his way through college and getting a pharmacist's degree. Then in the seventies, when the so-called urban renewal began, he had managed to lease an abandoned storefront and start his own business. The pharmacy had been successful, enough so that eventually he'd been able to buy the building in which it was located. He and his wife, Edith, had moved into the apartment upstairs. During the gentrification boom of the eighties, he could have sold the building for a considerable profit, but he had hung on to it. Now the neighborhood was racially mixed but still predominantly black. The yuppies had moved in, stayed awhile, and moved on, most of them. The ones who had stayed had grown out of that frantic, wealth-obsessed lifestyle and were now solid citizens, part of the community. It was a fine place to live most of the time, and Macon was proud to have been a part of it for so long.

That pride was one reason he was so angry when he spotted a kid he had never seen before shoplifting some perfume from the cosmetics area.

For a moment Macon considered letting him go. The kid was about fifteen, and he was probably stealing the perfume to give to his girlfriend. Macon remembered being fifteen and in love.

But then he checked the kid's feet and saw the hundred-dollar sneakers that had probably been bought with drug money, and he thought that if the kid did have a girlfriend, she was probably knocked up by now, and he came out from behind the counter and covered the ground between himself and the thief with the long strides of a man who was six five.

He reached out and his hand came down on the kid's shoulder. "Wait a minute," he said. "I think you forgot to pay for something."

The kid twisted around and said, "Pay f' *this*, mo'fucker." His left hand had stuck the perfume down one of the large pockets of the drooping jeans. His right came out of the pocket on the other side holding a gun.

Macon's eyes widened. He had been robbed several times at gunpoint during the years he had owned the pharmacy. Before that he had gone through the hell that was Vietnam. So he was no stranger to violence.

But now, as time was shaved into tiny fragments of seconds, he saw how fast the kid was moving and knew that he wouldn't have time to get out of the way of the shot. He was going to die right here in the store he had worked so hard to make a success, shot with a cheap, nickel-plated Saturday night special by a punk kid. The gun was probably stolen, and the ID numbers would have been filed off of it. The kid would run out the door while Macon fell bleeding to the floor and his life leaked out all over the place, and oh God, Edith was upstairs and would probably hear the shot and come rushing down to see her husband lying there, dying, and if they were both very fortunate there would be just enough time for her to cradle his head in her lap and say good-bye to him . . .

Or screw it, he could just take the gun away from the punk kid and shove it up his ass. His hand went down as the gun came up, and the long thick fingers closed around the cylinder as the hammer snapped on the web of skin between Macon's thumb and fingers. He wrenched the gun out of the kid's grip and backhanded him with it, sending him flying backward into a greeting card rack. The kid went down, tangled with the rack.

Macon said to Lois, the girl who worked the register at the cosmetics counter, "Call nine-one-one."

Her head jerked in a frightened nod. "Are you all right, Mr. Macon?"

He looked down at his hand. It was bleeding and it hurt, but he felt fine. He smiled and said, "I'm all right."

The kid had a broken jaw. He was also wanted for questioning in a couple of drive-by shootings. After getting Macon's statement, the police hauled the kid off to the hospital to get his jaw wired up before they took him to jail. Macon worried a little that the kid's friends might try to retaliate against him for what he'd done. It wasn't like he'd had a lot of choice in the matter, though. Once he had decided not to let the kid get away with shoplifting, events had taken their own course.

He was thinking about that when the phone rang and he scooped it up and said, "Macon Drugs."

"Henry?" A woman's voice.

"Yes, ma'am. Can I help you?"

"Henry, it's Elaine Stark. I hope you remember me."

Macon remembered her, all right, and when he hung up the phone thirty minutes later, he hoped Edith would understand when he told her that he had to go to Texas.

The shrimp boats left early in the morning, before dawn, worked the beds out beyond St. Charles Island, and were back in the small town of Fulton by midafternoon, tying up in the boat basin across the road from the tourist cabins. This part of the Texas coast had two main industries, fishing and tourism, and those two merged along the several-mile-long stretch of Fulton Beach Road, with its dozens of small motels and restaurants along with the boat basin and several wholesale seafood companies. Rockport, the somewhat larger town right next to Fulton, was even more touristy with its long beach and maritime museum and annual art festival during the summer. By and large, though, the area was one of the most unspoiled anywhere along the Gulf coast. As soon as Nat Van Linh had seen it, back in the middle seventies, he knew this was where he wanted to settle and raise his family.

Of course, at the time he'd been barely out of his teens and had neither wife nor children—or a job or any prospect of one, for that matter—but he had known that everything good would come to him in time. He had the boundless optimism of an immigrant from hell—or in his case, Vietnam, which in many ways was the same thing.

He stepped out onto the back porch of his restaurant, the Blue Gull, to watch the shrimpers come in. The porch overhung the water and was a popular place for lunch and dinner, but it was deserted now since the restaurant closed between two and four in the afternoon. Behind him the dining room was being cleaned up, and in the kitchen the cooks were getting ready for dinner. Most of the people who worked in the Blue Gull were family in one way or another.

Nat leaned on the railing around the porch and looked out over the bay, his eyes picking out the familiar shapes of several of the boats chugging slowly toward the basin. He owned six fishing boats, a nice-sized little fleet. Two of them were captained by his sons, the others by cousins. Nat's three daughters ran the restaurant, and his wife kept the books. These days, he was mostly just a figurehead, he supposed. He greeted the people who dined there and knew by name just about everyone in the area who came in, even occasionally. He knew many of the tourists who returned year after year, the people who always made a point of stopping in at the Blue Gull at least once during their stay.

"What're y'all doin', Uncle Nat?"

Nat looked around and saw his nephew Jimmy sweeping up around the tables, cleaning the porch after the lunch rush. Jimmy had been born and raised here in Fulton, spoke very little Vietnamese, and had a Texas twang in his voice that was the equal of any cowboy's. He was even on the high school rodeo team.

"Just watching the boats come in," Nat explained. Jimmy had worked here for only a short time, so he didn't know yet that Nat made a habit of this.

Jimmy paused in his work and leaned on the broom. "I worked on one of your boats last summer, did you know that?"

Nat shook his head. "No, I didn't." His captains took care of hiring their own crews.

"Man, it was hard. Gettin' up that early and workin' out in the hot sun all day . . . I like it here at the Blue Gull a lot better."

Where you can stand around and shoot the breeze with your uncle instead of doing your job? Nat thought. But he didn't say it. He knew you couldn't expect this younger generation to have the same work ethic that he and those like him had brought with them to their adopted country from Vietnam. Jimmy and his friends had no idea what it had been like living there: the grinding poverty, the constant fear, the never-ending struggle against the Communists . . . Nat's father had been an educated man, a professor of mathematics, who had died in a bombing in Saigon when Nat was ten years old. His mother had died not long after, and Nat had always wondered if grief had caused her passing. His older brother, who was seventeen at the time, had tried to keep the family together. His older sisters, who were fourteen and twelve, had sold their bodies to buy food. Nat and his younger brothers and sisters had become adept thieves.

By the time Nat was fifteen, he was out in the jungle, working as a scout and interpreter for the Americans. His older brother was in the South Vietnamese army. His older sisters had vanished somewhere in the quagmire of sex and drugs that was Saigon's red-light district. Nat never knew what happened to the three of them after the fall of Saigon. The chaos had swallowed them whole. But he had managed to get himself and his four younger siblings out of the country before the Communists caught them. Like thousands of others, they had set out into the South China Sea in a little boat barely worthy of the name. They had almost drowned more than once before finally reaching safety in the Philippines.

From there it had been a long hard struggle for them to immigrate to the United States, but determination and luck had been on their side. They had reached Texas at last, penniless, with little education, and except for Nat none of them spoke much English. The local fishing industry needed willing workers, though, and Nat and his family brought a willingness to work that paid off. In the short run it had kept them together and kept them eating; in the long run it had made them well-to-do, even rich by some people's standards.

So he couldn't get mad at Jimmy for loafing. Jimmy had never been hardened in the crucible that was Vietnam. But neither was Nat going to let him get away with being lazy, at least not for very long.

He was about to tell the boy to get back to work when one of the waitresses, his niece Kathy, came out onto the porch and said, "Phone call for you, Uncle Nat."

Kathy was in high school, too, a beautiful girl who was a cheerleader and also was on the math and science team. Nat smiled at her and asked, "Who is it?"

"A woman named Mrs. Stark."

Nat took a sharply indrawn breath. "Elaine Stark?"

"She didn't say," Kathy said with a shake of her head.

It had to be Elaine, Nat thought. She was the only Mrs. Stark he knew. He had thought about calling John Howard a few times during the past few weeks, when he'd read in the newspaper about what was going on down in the Rio Grande valley, but he hadn't. He realized now that he should have, because Elaine wouldn't be calling if something wasn't wrong.

As he walked into the restaurant and headed for the office to take the call, his mind flashed back to Vietnam, whether he wanted it to go there or not. Those had been dark, desperate, and dangerous times. Though Nat had worked for the Americans, he never really trusted any of them until he met John Howard Stark. John Howard had been different, a big, honest, tough man who didn't take any crap from anybody, as the Americans put it. By the time Stark left Vietnam, Nat had come to believe that everything good about America and Americans was embodied in him. If the foolish politicians and the so-called peace protesters who had actually lengthened the war had put someone like Stark in charge, Saigon wouldn't be known now as Ho Chi Minh City and thousands of people would not have been murdered in the Communist takeover.

But that was decades in the past, though often the hurt of it still seemed fresh, and Nat had learned to think more about the future. He picked up the phone in the office and said, "Elaine? This is Nat. What's wrong?"

"How did you know—" she began.

"The same way I always knew what John Howard was thinking during a firefight, and he knew what I was thinking. Just tell me what I can do to help."

She told him, and although it was an amazing, unbelievable story, he believed it. He had long since learned that in America, nothing was too outlandish or far-fetched to be true.

"I'm on my way," he said without hesitation when she was finished.

"Thank you, Nat."

"John Howard never let me down when there was trouble. I won't let him down." Nat paused. "Have you called any of the others from the old bunch?"

"Jack Finnegan, Will Sheffield, and Henry Macon. They're all coming, too."

Nat nodded. Good men, all of them, though from what he'd heard, Jack had had his troubles. "What about Rich?"

"I tried the last number John Howard had for him. It had been disconnected."

"Rich never stayed in one place for too long," Nat mused. "I might be able to find him, though. If I can, I'll bring him with me."

"All right. Thank you again, Nat."

"Don't worry, Elaine. We'll get this straightened out."

He hung up the phone and stood there for a long moment, his mind back in Vietnam again. What was it Rich Threadgill had always shouted when a firefight started? Oh yes . . . "The fuckin' marines have landed, asshole!"

The fuckin' marines were about to land on Del Rio, Texas.

Thirty-one

The arraignment was once again before Judge Harvey Goodnight. Sam Gonzales immediately objected to the search warrant signed by Justice of the Peace Louise Bates. District Attorney Albert Wilfredo immediately defended its legitimacy. Judge Goodnight studied the warrant in question for several minutes and then said, "I wouldn't have signed this thing, but the justice of the peace was within her rights to do so. I'll allow the evidence. Whether or not the trial judge will do the same will be up to him."

Sam looked over at Stark like something good had happened, but for the life of him, Stark couldn't see what it was.

The rest of the proceedings went quickly, and once again, although it was obvious Judge Goodnight thought the state's case was flimsy and probably shouldn't have been brought in the first place, it was enough to cause him to bind Stark over and send the case to the grand jury. The defense's motion for bail turned out differently, though. "Due to the seriousness of the charges and the high-profile nature of this case, I'm setting bail in the amount of two million dollars," Goodnight announced.

"I can't get anywhere near that," Stark muttered to Gonzales.

"We can arrange for it through a bonding company, but it may take a day or two." Sam tried to smile reassuringly. "Don't worry, John Howard. We'll have you out of jail before you know it."

After court was adjourned but before Stark was taken back to his cell, he got a chance to ask, "What was that you looked pleased about when the judge ruled the search warrant was legal?"

"He mentioned the trial judge," Gonzales explained. "If a trial was held here in Del Rio, it would be in Judge Goodnight's court. He was telling me that if I ask for a change of venue, he'll grant it."

"Is that what you plan to do?"

"If it ever gets to that point, yes. The farther we can get away from the valley, the better chance you'll get a fair trial."

"People won't know me somewhere else," Stark pointed out.

"Yes, but in Lubbock or Fort Worth or some place like that, Ramirez won't find it nearly as easy to intimidate witnesses or jurors. Strangers will be able to see right through the obvious attempt to frame you."

Stark still had his doubts, but he nodded. Sam was just trying to put as good a face on things as he could. Stark didn't blame him for that.

"I'll get to work on the bail," Gonzales promised as the deputies came up to lead Stark away.

Stark just nodded again. The whole thing was so surreal, like a bad dream, that at times he had to remind himself it was actually happening.

The clang of the cell door closing served as a reminder of its own. Stark sat on the bunk, leaned his head back against the wall, and closed his eyes. It was happening, all right. It was all as real as it could be.

He wondered if his life would ever be normal again.

* * *

Devery Small sat on the front porch of the Diamond S ranch house with a rifle across his knees and looked out at the night. There was an armed guard standing watch on each side of the house, but Devery was nervous anyway. So much had happened, so much that he never would have believed was even possible. Hubie and W.R. and Everett were dead, and John Howard was in jail, charged with their murder. That was crazy, of course. Devery didn't have to be told that John Howard hadn't had anything to do with those killings. He knew it with his gut. There were good guys and bad guys in the world, and John Howard Stark was one of the good guys. That was the way Devery saw it, anyway.

Sam Gonzales had been out here earlier, filling Elaine in on what had happened in court today. It had come as no surprise that John Howard was still in jail. Ramirez had pulled out the big guns on this. He was going to make sure that his enemy, John Howard Stark, suffered the torments of the damned.

Elaine had wanted to go into town and see her husband, but Sam had talked her out of it. John Howard would rest easier, he'd said, if he knew she was out here at the ranch, safe and sound. Grudgingly, Elaine had agreed.

She had told Devery that she'd called some of John Howard's old friends from the marines, and all of them had agreed to come down and do what they could to help. One of them, a banker from Chicago, had promised assistance in the form of a high-powered law firm from his hometown. One of the other guys was a newspaper editor, and when you were in trouble it never hurt to have a member of the press on your side. Devery didn't know about the others, but he figured John Howard could use all the friends he could get right about now.

Devery heard a faint noise from the other end of the porch and turned his head in that direction. He didn't see anything. He'd had the chair leaned back against the wall with only its back legs on the porch, balancing himself with a foot against the porch railing like Henry Fonda playing Wyatt Earp in *My Darling Clementine*. Now he sat up straight, letting the chair's front legs come down on the porch with a thump. He called, "Anybody there?"

No answer. Devery told himself he was just being jumpy. He was nervous, of course, and didn't mind admitting it. What fella in his right mind wouldn't be nervous in a situation like this? He stood up and pointed the rifle at the far end of the porch.

"If anybody's there, you better speak up, or I'm liable to go to shootin'," he warned.

The shifting darkness came from behind him. Some instinct must have alerted him, because he jerked his head around in time to see the black-clad shape lunge at him. He had just enough time to think, *It's a goddamn ninja!* before the cold steel pierced his body from behind. The knife thrust felt just like a hard punch, but the icy pain that penetrated far into his body told him he hadn't been hit with a fist. He arched his back in an involuntary effort to get away from the agony, but he couldn't escape it. The knife twisted inside him. He dropped the rifle. It fell to the porch with a clatter. An arm locked across his throat, holding him in place as the knife was withdrawn and then thrust into him again and again. Devery jerked hard a couple of times and went limp. He was no longer aware of anything except the pain that filled his consciousness. It blossomed like a flower, or like ripples in a pond spreading ever outward and outward. It grew until there was nothing else.

And then there really was nothing else. For Devery, everything was gone.

Silencio Ryan slid the knife out of the man's back and lowered him to the floor of the porch. He wiped the blood from the blade on the man's shirt and then straightened. This one had made a little more noise in dying than the others had, especially when he dropped the rifle. But it didn't really matter. All the guards had been disposed of, and that left his way clear to his real target.

Elaine Stark.

He had parachuted in, leaping out of a plane flying high overhead, above the Stark ranch. Landing about half a mile from the ranch house, he had buried the black chute and then jogged easily toward his objective. As always, it felt good to be operating alone, with no one to depend on but himself, and more importantly, no one else along to make a mistake and jeopardize the mission.

The first thing he had done was to move around the ranch's outbuildings, unseen and unheard, leaving the deadly little packages he took from the backpack he wore. Then he closed in on the house itself and its pitiful guards who thought they could stop anyone from getting to the woman. Ryan had killed them all without even breaking a sweat. He was ready now to do the job that had brought him here.

He turned away from the body of the last man he'd killed, toward the front door. It was locked, but he needed only a moment to get past that. As he eased into the house, he heard the soft murmur of voices. A television, he decided after a couple of seconds. No one was with Mrs. Stark. She sought distraction from her problems through the medium of television, like so many other people.

The voices came from upstairs. She was in her bedroom, watching TV. Ryan came to the staircase. Smiling under the soft black hood he wore, he started up.

"Freeze, you son of a bitch," she said from behind him. "Don't move, or I'll blow you in half."

Elaine had come downstairs to raid the refrigerator, leaving the TV on in the bedroom upstairs where she had been watching it. She was a little surprised that she was hungry. With all the trouble that was going on, she would have thought that worry would rob her of her appetite. But that wasn't the case, and so she had padded barefoot into the kitchen, wearing the oversize T-shirt that she slept in over her panties. She hadn't bothered turning on the light. After thirty years, she knew where everything was. She opened the refrigerator door—

And heard something out on the front porch.

It wasn't a very loud noise, but something about it made her stiffen with one hand still on the refrigerator door. She eased it closed, killing the light and plunging the kitchen into darkness again. She moved over to the door that led into the old-fashioned pantry. A loaded shotgun was just inside that door. She picked it up and then walked quietly toward the hall that led from the front door toward the rear of the house. The stairs to the second floor were about halfway along that hall.

Elaine stood just inside the open kitchen door, barely breathing, listening intently. A part of her wanted to call out to Devery and make sure he was all right, but instinct warned her against it. She heard a rattling from the front door. Somebody trying to get past the lock?

That proved to be the case. The front door opened, its hinges squealing a little, the sound so soft she never would have heard it if she had been upstairs. Elaine held her breath now, not trusting herself to be absolutely quiet if she didn't.

A dark shape moved past her, a deeper patch of shadow drifting toward the stairs. Up there on the second floor, the bedroom door was open, and enough light spilled out into the hall so that Elaine was able to make out the man's silhouette as he started up the stairs. She had no idea who he was, but he was clad all in black and had a hood of some sort over his head, either as a disguise or to make him blend in more with the darkness or both. The one thing she could be sure of was that he was up to no good. She stepped into the corridor, her bare feet making no sound on the hardwood floor, and moved to the base of the stairs. As she lined the barrel of the shotgun on the intruder's back, she said, "Freeze, you son of a bitch. Don't move, or I'll blow you in half."

The man froze. He stood stock-still, there on the stairs, his head slightly tilted at an odd angle. He looked almost like he was sniffing the air.

That seemed to be indeed what he was doing, because a moment later he said, "Gun oil, some sort of fragrance—probably from soap or shampoo—and a touch of hair spray. That would make you Mrs. Stark, and I don't doubt that you're armed."

"Damn right I am. I've got a twelve-gauge pointed right at your back. Who the hell are you, mister?"

He didn't turn around to answer her. His voice was slightly muffled by the hood over his head. "My name is Silencio Ryan. I've had the pleasure of making your husband's acquaintance a couple of times."

The man from the strip joint, Elaine thought with a sharply indrawn breath. The one who had shown up later at the hospital and tried to kill John Howard. The one who undoubtedly worked for Ramirez the Vulture.

For a second, Elaine thought about simply squeezing the trigger, going ahead and killing him. She didn't doubt that he deserved it. But that would make her a murderer, and while she had no trouble with the idea of killing to protect herself or someone she loved—she had already done that, after all—she couldn't bring herself to gun this man down in cold blood, no matter who he was or what he had done. Instead, she said, "Back down off those stairs, slow and easy."

Ryan did as he was told, one step at a time, and as he did, Elaine backed away toward the front door. "Devery!" she called. "Devery, are you out there? I need some help!"

"You won't get it from him or any of the other guards," Ryan said. He didn't have to explain what he meant by that.

"*Devery!*" Elaine cried, an edge of near-hysteria creeping into her voice. Was she alone out here with this black-clad killer? "Chuck! Rusty! Steve!"

The other guards didn't answer either. Elaine stopped as her hip bumped the small table in the hallway where one of the telephones sat. She could still call for help—if he hadn't cut the wires into the house. Her cell phone was upstairs, where it wouldn't do her a bit of good now.

The phone was to her right, so she had to hold the shotgun in her right hand and reach across her body with her left hand to grope for it in the darkness. The move was awkward, and the shotgun weighed enough so that it was difficult for her to hold it steady with one hand. And all the time, she had to keep her eyes on Ryan. She realized now she should have told him to stay on the stairs. The light wasn't as good down here, so she couldn't see him quite as well. It might have been a good idea to keep more distance between them, too. But she wasn't a former marine. She didn't have the sort of tactical experience that John Howard did.

She found the phone and picked it up. She heard the dial tone even without bringing it to her ear and heaved a sigh of relief that the line hadn't been cut. Ryan had slipped up there, she thought. Holding the phone in her left hand, she used that same hand to fumble around for the numbers on the base. Working by feel, she found the 9 and pushed it. Now the 1 . . .

The barrel of the shotgun had drifted off-target without her being aware of it. Ryan must have noticed it, though, because he spun and dove to his left. Elaine cried out and jerked the trigger instinctively as she tried to point the weapon at him one-handed. The roar of the shotgun going off in the hallway was deafening. She had no idea if she had hit Ryan or not. She wasn't even aware that she had dropped the phone.

Grabbing the shotgun with her left hand, too, she pumped another shell into the chamber and looked for Ryan. God, she couldn't see him anymore! Where was he? Had he run off?

He came up beside her, seemingly materializing from the floor like some kind of dark demon rising from the netherworld. His hand closed over the barrel of the shotgun and wrenched it to the side, even as Elaine jerked the trigger again. The charge of buckshot went into the wall, blowing a hole the size of two fists in it. Ryan twisted the gun. Elaine's finger caught in the trigger guard and broke with a sharp snap. She screamed in pain.

His other hand closed around her neck and jerked her closer to him. She couldn't get any air past his iron grip. Even though she tried to fight, her muscles didn't seem to want to work right. She managed to punch him a few times, but the blows were weak and ineffective.

With his other hand, Ryan reached up and pulled the hood off his head. With his face only a couple of inches from hers, he said, "There's someone across the border who would like to meet you."

Bright red skyrockets were going off behind Elaine's eyes. She was so desperate for air that although she heard Ryan's words, she barely comprehended their meaning. Blackness was closing in her brain.

She felt his other hand exploring her body through the T-shirt. He lifted it, reached around her, slid his hand down inside her panties to squeeze her flesh. "I wish there were more time," he said, "but unfortunately, there's not. Good night, Mrs. Stark."

The rockets were all gone now. No longer did they arch across the black velvet curtain inside her head. That curtain had closed all the way, shutting out all awareness from Elaine Stark.

Ryan checked for a pulse in her neck. It was there, beating strongly and steady. His touch had been sure and precise, squeezing hard enough to cut off her air and make her pass out, but not enough to crush her larynx or do any other real damage. In a short time, she would wake up and be fine except for a certain amount of soreness and bruising on her throat.

She was actually hurt less than he was, he thought. He hadn't been able to avoid all the buckshot from the first blast. A couple of the pellets had torn into his right side. One of them had just cut a painful but shallow furrow in the skin, but the other had lodged there. When he pulled his shirt up and checked the wounds, he could feel it, a leaden lump under the skin. But he was in no danger from it, and it could be extracted later when he got back to Ramirez's compound with the woman. The pain was nothing; he could ignore that.

Bending slightly, he draped the woman's limp body over his left shoulder and picked her up. Shouts came faintly to his ears from outside. He walked quickly to the front door, which was still open, and stepped out onto the porch. When he looked toward the bunkhouse, he saw that lights had come on in there. The ranch hands had heard the shotgun blasts and knew something was wrong. As Ryan reached into a pocket with his right hand and pulled out the little transmitter, he saw the door of the bunkhouse jerked open. A man started out.

Ryan thumbed up the cover and pressed the button on the transmitter.

The bunkhouse came apart in a huge, fiery explosion that sent a ball of flame soaring high into the night sky. The cowboy who had just emerged from the building was caught in the holocaust and thrown forward a good twenty feet, shrieking in agony as fire wrapped around him. His screaming didn't stop when he hit the ground. He writhed for several seconds before he finally grew still and silent. His clothes and hair continued to burn.

The explosion that had destroyed the bunkhouse and everyone inside it had been so large that it had drowned out the other blasts. But the rest of the ranch's outbuildings, including several cottages where the married ranch hands lived with their families, were shattered and burning as well. The slaughter was complete. Every building at the ranch headquarters had been devastated except the main house, and no one was left alive but Ryan and Mrs. Stark.

Ramirez would be very happy when he heard about this. But that would be just the start of his joy, because he would still have Elaine Stark to deal with. Ryan had heard Ramirez ranting about what he was going to do to the woman. It would be a kindness to her if he broke her neck right now and went back to tell Ramirez that her death had been an unavoidable accident.

Ryan was not, however, in the business of being kind. He carried Elaine's unconscious form well away from the house and laid her on the ground. As he straightened he heard the throbbing beat of wings over the crackling of flames. The helicopter's pilot had been waiting for the explosions. They were the signal to him to come on in. As the sound of the chopper grew louder, Ryan walked back over to the house, took another bundle from his backpack, and tossed it through the open front door and down the hallway. He went back to stand beside Elaine as he triggered the explosives. The blast tore a fiery, blazing hole in the center of the house, and the flames began to spread rapidly.

The downdraft from the helicopter's blades beat at Ryan as the aircraft lowered to the ground nearby. There was plenty of light for the pilot to see by. Ryan picked up Elaine and carried her toward the chopper. She murmured and stirred slightly, but she didn't regain consciousness. There was another man besides the pilot inside the helicopter. He leaned down to help Ryan lift Elaine into the craft. Ryan climbed in after her, and a moment later the chopper lifted off, banking and soaring into the night, leaving the Diamond S below and behind it. The ranch looked as though it had been hit by an artillery barrage or a bombing raid. The fires burned brightly, flames clawing at the darkness, smoke climbing high into the sky.

Ryan never looked back.

On the porch of the big house, Devery Small coughed and stirred slightly. He coughed again, and the pain that went through him dragged him out of the dark abyss that had claimed him and back into consciousness. He hurt like blazes, and for a second that was all he could think about.

Then he became aware that a heat even worse than that of a summer day in Texas was pounding down on him from behind. He struggled to lift his head and look around. When he finally managed to do so, he saw through bleary eyes that the wall of the house was on fire. The flames had climbed all the way up the wall and were starting to eat away at the roof over the porch. Even in his stunned, pain-wracked state, Devery realized that if he didn't move, the burning porch roof would soon fall right on top of him.

He started to crawl. It wasn't easy. His fingers scrabbled at the planks of the porch while his booted toes pushed feebly at them. He moved a little, a couple of inches, no more. Redoubling his efforts, he pulled himself along, getting a little closer to the edge of the porch. Again and again, he inched toward safety. The heat grew worse, until he felt as if he were inside an oven, roasting like a turkey.

His fingers closed over the edge of the porch. He grasped it and pulled as hard as he could.

With a cracking sound, the roof gave way and began to come down.

Devery felt himself falling. Fiery debris pelted him, burning him, making him cry out in pain. He landed on the ground and more agony shot through him. He rolled, trying desperately now to get away from the heat. Somehow he wound up on his hands and knees and crawled for a short distance before he found the strength to surge up onto his feet and launch into a stumbling run. As badly as he was hurt, he knew he didn't have much strength left. He staggered on, putting the blaze as far behind him as he could.

When he tripped and pitched forward onto his face, he hardly knew it. But he felt the fresh burst of agony when he landed, that was for sure. He lay there, the taste of sandy grit in his mouth, and fought to hang on to awareness, but it was a losing battle.

Once again a black tide washed over him, engulfing him so that he knew nothing more.

Thirty-two

Stark was eating his breakfast when the door of his cell opened. He'd spent a restless night, not surprising under the circumstances, and he wasn't really hungry, but he was forcing down the scrambled eggs, sausage, and toast anyway. The coffee was a little better.

He looked up, expecting to see one of the deputies, but Sheriff Norval Lee Hammond stood there instead, one hand grasping the edge of the door. Hammond's face was ashen, and his voice was hoarse and strained as he said, "Come on out of there, Stark."

Stark set the plate aside as a chill went through him. Hammond looked like he had just gotten some terrible news. Maybe the charges against him had somehow been thrown out after all, Stark thought, and he was about to get out of here. He got to his feet and asked, "What is it?"

"Your lawyer's here." Hammond inclined his head. "Come on."

Stark stepped out into the corridor. Two deputies had accompanied the sheriff, and they looked as pale and shaken as Hammond did. Stark frowned. He was starting to get the feeling that more was wrong than he had bargained for.

"What's going on here, Hammond?" he asked sharply.

"Just go talk to Gonzales." Hammond's voice was dull now, as if beaten down by shock.

Stark started walking toward the interview room where he always spoke with Gonzales. The deputies stood aside to let him by. Neither of them would look at him, Stark noticed.

By the time he reached the open door of the interview room, he was almost running. He saw Sam Gonzales sitting at the table inside the room, staring down at his feet.

"Sam?" Stark said. "Sam, what's wrong? What's happened?"

Gonzales lifted his head, and Stark saw that the lawyer's eyes were red. There were wet streaks on his face where tears had rolled down his cheeks. He tried to speak, but the words seemed to lodge in his throat.

Elaine.

The thought seared through Stark's brain. Something had happened to Elaine. His guts went watery with a fear stronger than any he had ever known in his life, stronger even than the terror of a nighttime attack by the Vietcong.

"John Howard," Gonzales finally managed to say. "I . . . I'm so sorry. . . ."

Stark lunged into the room, wild with fear now, and grabbed the lapels of Gonzales's suit coat. He jerked Gonzales to his feet and yelled, "What happened? Goddamn it, tell me what happened!"

"The r-ranch," Gonzales stammered out. "G-gone. The house . . . the bunkhouse . . . all the buildings . . . gone . . . burned down . . . there were explosions, some sort of explosions . . . Elaine's gone, John Howard."

Stark just stared at him for a long moment, dizzyingly sick as if the entire universe had been twisted inside out, and finally he was able to croak, "Dead?"

"Gone," Gonzales repeated with a shake of his head. "Gone! We don't know where she is, or what . . . what happened to her."

Stark's brain frantically clung to the shred of hope that Gonzales had just tossed him. If Elaine had disappeared, then there was a chance she might still be alive. A slim chance, to be sure, but it was still there. Slowly, the maddening whirligig of emotion that had seized Stark began to ease its pace. A deep breath rasped in his throat as he drew it into his body. He said, "What about Devery and the others who were out there?"

"Devery's alive," Gonzales said, "but just barely. The others . . . everybody else . . . oh God, John Howard, none of them made it. They're all dead."

That was another hammer blow that almost floored Stark. His friends, all the ranch hands who had worked for him, even the wives and children of some of the men . . . gone, all gone. There had probably been eighteen or twenty people all told on the ranch. How could they all be dead, just like that?

"What happened?"

Hammond answered from the doorway. "We're still investigating. Best we can guess right now, somebody planted explosives all around the buildings and then set them off. Everything burned to the ground."

Stark was still holding Gonzales's lapels. He let go of them and swung toward the sheriff. "Your boss did this," he said hollowly.

"I work for the people of Val Verde County."

"You work for Ramirez, and we all know it. This is his way of getting back at me. He murdered my friends and framed me for it, got me thrown in jail. Now he's kidnapped my wife and wiped out everybody on my ranch." Stark started toward the door. "Get out of my way, Hammond."

Hammond thrust out a hand. "Hold on there, Stark! You're still in custody until bail's arranged. I know you're upset, but you're not goin' anywhere!"

"Get . . . out . . . of . . . my . . . *way!*" Stark roared. He threw himself at Hammond, swinging a wild punch. All he knew, all he could think about, was that he had to get out of here and get to Ramirez's place somehow. He could still save Elaine, even if it cost him his own life!

Hammond ducked the punch and grabbed him, tackling him around the waist. The deputies rushed in and threw themselves on Stark as well. Sam Gonzales got hold of him from behind, shouting, "No, John Howard, no! This won't help anything!"

Stark bellowed and fought like an enraged grizzly. One of the deputies went flying backward to crash against a wall and then fall limply to the floor of the corridor, out cold. Stark began dragging the other three men, but their weight was too much and when Hammond managed to trip him, he went down, landing heavily with the three men on top of him. Something hit him on the back of the head, sending blinding pain through his brain. He found out later that it was Hammond's baton that had struck him, but right then it didn't matter. The blow stunned him long enough for the deputy to get some cuffs on him. Stark writhed impotently on the floor.

"Get him up and get him back in his cell!" he heard Hammond shout. "Damn it, Gonzales, the only reason I'm not gonna throw the book at Stark over this is that I know how upset he is."

"Because of something the man you work for did," Gonzales said.

Stark heard the meaty sound of a fist striking flesh. "Be careful, counselor," Hammond grated. "You'll trip and hurt yourself again."

"You won't get away with that, Sheriff," Gonzales said thickly. In the small part of his brain that was still coherent, Stark knew that Hammond had just punched the lawyer. Sam was wrong, though. Hammond *would* get away with it, because Hammond was one of the bad guys, one of the evil ones who got away with everything they did. That was the way the world worked now. Evil went unpunished—hell, it was even rewarded most of the time—while a decent man who tried to do the right thing had everything he loved ripped away from him.

Stark was on his feet again. Hands gripped him, forced him to walk, marched him down the hall to his cell, and practically threw him into it. He slammed into the wall, bounced off, fell onto the bunk, and rolled off to lie huddled on the floor. The door crashed shut.

"Elaine," Stark whispered as tears filled his eyes. "Elaine . . ."

By the middle of the day, when they let Sam Gonzales speak to him through the slot in the door where his food tray was passed in and out, Stark had run the gamut of emotions. He had known paralyzing fear and numbing grief, seething white-hot rage and cold, calculating hatred. Now he was back to mostly numb.

"I've seen Devery at the hospital, John Howard," Gonzales reported. "He's in bad shape, but the doctors think he's got a fighting chance. He has three stab wounds in his back, and one of his lungs was collapsed. The killer was going for the heart, and he probably believed that he got it. What he didn't know is that Devery's heart isn't in the right place."

"What?" Gonzales's statement was puzzling enough to cut through the fog in Stark's brain.

"Devery's heart isn't located where most people's are. It's more in the center of his chest instead of on the left side. Doug Huddleston said that if anything, Devery's heart is a little on the right side. It's considered a congenital defect, but it saved Devery's life."

"I didn't know that," Stark muttered.

"No reason for you to. Devery didn't go around telling people that his heart's in an odd place."

"I'm glad he's got a chance to make it." Something occurred to Stark. "Was he able to talk? Did he say anything about what happened?"

"All he saw was one man, the man who stabbed him. There must have been more, though." Gonzales passed a shaking hand over his face. "I went out there, John Howard. The destruction was . . . awful. One man couldn't have done it by himself."

"That depends on the man," Stark said, thinking of the

son of a bitch from the Blue Burro, the one who had killed four men at the hospital and come damned close to killing Stark himself.

How many people had died since this whole thing started? Stark couldn't answer that, but he knew the toll had to number in the dozens. Many of them had been innocent men, women, and children who happened to be in the wrong place at the wrong time.

And what was behind all the tragedy? It wasn't even money, Stark realized bleakly. Sure, he and his friends had put a dent in Ramirez's drug smuggling operation with their patrols, but he doubted if they had actually cost the Vulture more than a few thousand dollars. A drop in the bucket compared to what Ramirez made in a year's time from his poison. No, it was pride, nothing but vainglorious pride on the part of Ramirez, who couldn't stand for anyone to defy him. Anyone who had dared to do so had to be punished, and to such an extreme that everyone from the Rio Grande to Ramirez's home in Colombia would know that the Vulture was a bad man to cross.

Pride. Stark could barely conceive of it causing so much bloodshed, and yet it had.

"What about the bail?" he asked. "When am I getting out of here?"

Gonzales sighed. "Not any time soon, I'm afraid. The bail has been raised to twenty million dollars."

"Twenty million! What the hell's wrong with Judge Goodnight—"

"The judge didn't do this," Gonzales said. "He's been taken off the case. It's been reassigned to a federal court. The judge there raised the bail."

"Why?"

"Those rocket-propelled grenades were stolen from an army supply depot six months ago. You're getting the blame for that now, and since they were used in the commission of three murders, the feds have declared that they have a right to step in and take over. The Justice Department is talking about bringing charges of civil rights violations against you, too. And since you tried to escape, they say you're a flight risk. It could have been worse. The federal prosecutor originally asked for fifty million dollars."

Stark closed his eyes and leaned his forehead against the cool metal of the cell door. Almost all he could think of was Elaine, but this latest round of maneuvering against him by the federal government was so ridiculous that he couldn't ignore it. Ridiculous, but effective, he thought. If the bureaucrats had their way, he would never be a free man again. He would spend the rest of his life behind bars, simply because he had embarrassed them.

It wasn't just *Ramirez's* pride that had gotten him in this mess, he realized.

Of course, his life behind bars might not be that long. Once he was in prison, Ramirez would be able to have him killed at any time. The bureaucrats could probably arrange a fatal "accident," too, if they wanted to. And there wouldn't be much Stark could do about it.

"I'll keep working on it, John Howard," Gonzales said. "I'll do what I can to set things right. For one thing, I've been in touch with the Texas Rangers."

"Can they help?" Stark asked dully.

"Well, it would have been better if I had gotten them down here before the feds came in, but they'll do what they can. And I've been in touch with the Mexican authorities about trying to find Elaine. If they can search Ramirez's house—"

Stark snorted contemptuously. "If they search Ramirez's house, you can bet they won't find anything. They'll look the other way if they do. Half the police force is in his pocket, and so are the army commanders over there."

"Don't give up," Gonzales insisted. "I haven't."

But it's not your wife in the hands of that monster, Stark thought. He bit back a groan of despair as he wondered if he would ever see Elaine alive again.

*   *   *

Late in the afternoon, Sam Gonzales paid another brief visit to the jail. He didn't have much to report, only that he had been in touch with David and Peter, and both of Stark's sons had been granted emergency leave to return to the United States. They were on the other side of the world, though, and it was going to take a couple of days for them to get home. Stark nodded. He wasn't looking forward to having to explain to the boys everything that had happened. He knew he didn't come off lily-white in this affair. His own pride and stubbornness had played a part in it. That didn't matter at the moment, though. There was plenty of blame to pass around, with most of it going to Ernesto Diego Espinoza Ramirez.

When Stark heard footsteps approaching the cell a short time later, he figured one of the deputies was bringing his supper, even though it was a little early for that. He was going to send the food away; he didn't think he would ever have an appetite again.

But instead a key rattled in the lock and one of the deputies swung the door open and announced, "You've got another visitor, Mr. Stark." The young man's tone was respectful.

"Who is it?" Stark asked. He sure as hell didn't want to talk to the press, which he imagined was having a field day with this story. The vigilante's life collapses around him . . . the perfect cautionary tale for the liberal media.

"He said his name is Jack Finnegan."

Stark's head jerked up. Jack? Jack Finnegan? Stark hadn't seen him or even talked to him for several years. What was Jack Finnegan doing in Del Rio, Texas? Wasn't he supposed to be in Chicago, running that bank he had inherited, making money hand over fist, getting drunk, and screwing every woman at the country club except his own wife?

"Are you willing to see him?" the deputy asked. "I can't force you to."

"Sure," Stark said. "Sure, I'll talk to him. Good old Jack."

He got to his feet and stepped out into the corridor. There were three more deputies waiting there, all of them with their batons drawn. They were ready to jump him and batter him into unconsciousness if he tried anything. Stark smiled thinly.

"Take it easy," he said. "I'm a peaceable man."

Yeah, just like Wild Bill Elliott used to say . . . just before he beat the hell out of Roy Barcroft.

The deputies escorted Stark down the hall to the interview room where Jack Finnegan was waiting. Finnegan greeted Stark warmly, shaking his hand and using his other hand to clap Stark on the shoulder. "I won't ask how you are, John Howard," Finnegan said. "I know it's a world of shit right now."

"You got that right," Stark grunted. He waited until the deputies had gone out and closed the door; then he asked, "What are you doin' here, Jack?"

Finnegan looked down at the table for a second, then raised his eyes to Stark again. "Elaine called me," he said bluntly. "She said you were in trouble and needed help. If I had to guess, I'd say you didn't know anything about her getting in touch with me."

"No," Stark said slowly. "I didn't. But I'm not surprised. Did she call anybody else from the old unit?"

"Will Sheffield and Henry Macon are here in town, too. We all ran into each other at the airport. That's also where we found out about . . . what happened at your ranch. Is there any new word?"

"About Elaine, you mean?" Stark sighed. "If there is, they haven't told me. As far as I know, she's still missing."

"Which means she could still be alive."

Stark nodded. "I keep hangin' on to that hope . . . but it's hard, Jack. It's really hard."

"You know who took her?"

Stark met his friend's gaze squarely. "Of course I do."

"So you know where she is now."

"Probably."

Finnegan took a deep breath. "Then it seems to me somebody needs to go in there and get her. Sounds like a job for a marine recon unit."

"No, Jack," Stark said, shaking his head. "That's crazy. There's only three of you—"

"Four if we get you out of this hoosegow."

"You got a spare twenty million bucks for the bail?"

"As a matter of fact . . . no. I could raise part of that. Give me enough time and I could probably get all of it. But we don't have that much time."

Stark frowned. "It sounds like you've already been talking to Sheffield and Macon about this."

"We rode over here together, after we pored over all the newspaper accounts we could find and talked to that lawyer of yours. He seems like a good man, but my attorney is flying in tomorrow to lend him a hand. What we're worried about is that tomorrow might be too late."

"Jack . . . you're fifty-five years old. Sheffield and Macon are fifty-four, like me."

Finnegan smiled. "True. We've all been getting junk mail from the AARP for quite a while now. But we haven't forgotten what it was like over there in 'Nam. We can still kick a little ass, John Howard."

Stark could see that Finnegan wasn't going to listen to reason. "And you're a drunk," he said, hoping the cruel words would shock some sense into his friend.

But Finnegan just smiled again and held out his hand. It was rock steady. "All too true," he said, "but a drunk who hasn't tasted booze in over four years."

Stark met Finnegan's eyes squarely for a long moment, and in that moment hope was reborn in him. In an assault on Ramirez's compound, four men would be vastly outnumbered.

But the *right* four men might have a chance.

Stark reached out and took that rock-steady hand Finnegan was showing him. "What are you going to do?" he asked as he gripped Finnegan's hand firmly.

"I don't exactly know yet," Finnegan replied, "but you need to be ready when we do it, John Howard."

"I'll be ready," Stark promised. "And it had better be soon."

Thirty-three

The three men had gotten just one rental car since their destination was the same. Will Sheffield was behind the wheel as they headed out to the Diamond S. They would need a place from which to operate, a command post, so to speak, and Finnegan thought that Stark's ranch might be the best spot.

"Won't there still be cops all over it?" Macon asked.

"That's what we're going to find out," Finnegan said. He was sitting in the backseat, sprawled out a little. Macon was riding shotgun. "They've had part of last night and all day today to go over the place for evidence, so they're probably through with it by now. Let's face it, how extensive of a crime scene investigation are you gonna get in Del Rio, Texas?"

"Some of these small towns have good police departments," Sheffield put in.

"Yes, but the sheriff's department here is as corrupt as they come, remember?"

Macon said, "Yeah, well, you said John Howard told you the feds are part of this now."

"Let's just take a look around and see," Finnegan suggested. "No need to worry about it until the time comes."

Macon looked back at him and frowned. "I like to worry. I'm an adult. It's what I do."

Finnegan just grinned.

He felt sorry for John Howard, of course. The poor bastard had had shit dumped on him from every direction at once. And he had to be out of his mind with worry about his wife. Finnegan was worried about Elaine, too.

But in a way, he was having the time of his life. For too many years, making a lot of money was the only thing that had been important to him. And he had made a lot of money, no doubt about that. Sheffield and Macon were doing all right for themselves, but Finnegan could have bought and sold both of them many times over. All that money, though, hadn't done a damned thing to make him happy. Neither had booze, drugs, or sex.

Now he had a chance to help an old friend and to put some serious hurt on a bad guy who really deserved it. *That* excited Finnegan. He leaned forward a little and asked, "Anybody know where we can get some guns? A *bunch* of guns?"

Stark ate his supper after all, even though he had thought earlier that he wouldn't. Now that there was a chance he might be able to do something to help Elaine, he knew he had to keep his strength up.

Lights out was at nine o'clock. Even though Stark didn't expect anything to happen until after that, the time dragging by so slowly still gnawed at his nerves. Questions haunted him. Where was Elaine now? What was happening to her?

Was she even still alive?

The bare bulb in the cell's ceiling finally went out. Some light still came in through the window in the door. Stark sat on the bunk, knowing there was no point in lying down. He wasn't going to sleep.

Some time later, he heard sirens, a lot of them. They had

to be pretty loud for the noise to penetrate into the window-less cell. The fire department was close by, and there were also emergency sirens mounted on poles throughout the town. From the sound of it, all of them were going off at the same time. Stark frowned, wondering what could be going on. The emergency sirens were activated in the event of threatening weather. Was a tornado bearing down on Del Rio? Such storms were rare in this area, but not unheard of. Stark stood up and began to pace tensely as the sirens continued to howl.

Jack Finnegan had implied that he and Sheffield and Macon were going to try to break him out of here so they could go after Elaine. Could this commotion have something to do with that? Stark asked himself. He couldn't think of anything that his old friends could have done to cause such an uproar.

Footsteps approached the door. Stark swung toward it, his muscles taut, waiting to see what, if anything, was going to happen.

A key rattled in the lock. Stark clenched his hands into fists. If one of the deputies was there, Stark was going to jump him and take his chances. He had to get out of here, and he couldn't wait any longer.

The door opened, letting light from the corridor into the cell. Stark squinted at the man dressed all in black who stood there.

"Come on out, John Howard," Jack Finnegan said. "We just paid your bail."

"What?" Stark said, glad to see Finnegan but confused by what his friend had just said.

"Well, metaphorically speaking, anyway," Finnegan continued. "We didn't come up with twenty million bucks, but we did figure out a way to make sure nobody cares what's going on here at the jail."

Stark stepped out of the cell. "What did you do?" he asked warily.

Finnegan grinned. "A tanker truck full of toxic waste just overturned on the highway at the edge of town. The stuff's spilling all over the place."

Stark's eyebrows went up in surprise. "What! This is my hometown, Jack. You can't just—"

"Relax, John Howard," Finnegan said as he led Stark toward the front of the building. "It's not really toxic waste. In fact, it's mostly pancake syrup. But the fire department and every cop in town don't know that. They scrambled out there to try to contain the spill and keep a panic from breaking out. There were only two guys left here."

They had reached the front of the jail. Stark saw a couple of deputies slumped over the desks there. He said worriedly, "You didn't—"

"Of course not, they're fine. Henry and I just knocked them out. They'll have headaches when they wake up, but that's the extent of the damage."

Stark nodded. He didn't want the blood of innocent men on his hands.

Henry Macon waited at the door, also dressed all in black like Finnegan. He had a shotgun in his hands. He nodded curtly to Stark and Finnegan and said, "Will's waiting in the car. Let's go."

The three men hustled outside. The rental car was at the curb. They piled in and Sheffield hit the gas.

Stark and Finnegan were in the backseat. As the car pulled away from the jail, Stark said, "How in hell did you get hold of a tanker truck filled with syrup and make it look like it was hauling toxic waste?"

Finnegan grinned and rubbed his fingers together. "Money talks, John Howard. If you're willing to put out enough dough, you can get almost anything done, and it doesn't take much time, either. Plus I have an attorney who has a lot of connections all across the country, some of them a little on the shady side of the law."

"How much have you spent so far?"

Macon looked back at them from the front seat. "You might not want to ask that, John Howard," he advised.

"A little over a million and a half," Finnegan said proudly. "Had to pay a premium, you know, for speed."

"A million and a half?" Stark repeated.

"Money well spent," Finnegan assured him. The grin disappeared from the banker's face. "If it helps us get Elaine back safe and sound, it'll be worth every penny, John Howard. Don't you worry about that."

Stark sat back and rode in silence for a few minutes. When he spoke again, he said, "Y'all are liable to get in a lot of trouble over this. You know that, don't you?"

"We know," Sheffield said.

"Now ask us if we care," Macon said.

"You've got families, jobs, good lives that you've made for yourselves. You're risking all that just to help a friend?"

"Hell of a thing, ain't it?" Finnegan said.

Stark nodded slowly. "Yeah," he said. "A hell of a thing. No matter how this turns out, I owe you, all of you. Any time I can ever help you, just let me know."

Finnegan chuckled and said, "You're assuming we won't all spend the rest of our lives in jail."

Stark didn't know what to say to that. They were in this too deep to back out now. They had to go ahead, play out the hand, and see what happened.

He realized they were on their way to the ranch. He said, "The Diamond S is the first place the authorities will look for me."

"They're going to be too busy with that toxic spill to look for you for a while, remember?" Finnegan said. "Anyway, that's not where we're going. We scouted out a place not far from there that looks like it's been deserted for twenty years."

Stark nodded. "The old McCarthy place. It looks like that because it *has* been deserted for twenty years. The old man who owned it died without any heirs. He also hadn't paid his property taxes for several years, so the county took it over. They've been trying to sell it all this time, but it's such a hardscrabble spread that nobody wants it."

The McCarthy Ranch was actually a pretty good hiding place, Stark thought. It was reasonably close to his ranch, it had an old house on it and a tumbledown barn where they could hide the car, and most people had forgotten it even existed. They could hide out there until they were ready to move against Ramirez and have a reasonable expectation of not being found.

It would have to be pretty soon, though, because they couldn't count on more than a few days' grace. Then Hammond or someone else was bound to remember the old ranch and come out there to have a look around.

The turnoff to the Diamond S was approaching. Stark leaned forward and said to Sheffield, "I want to have a look at my ranch."

"That's not a good idea, John Howard," Finnegan said. "When we checked the place this afternoon, there were still a couple of deputies out there."

"They've probably been called in to help deal with that overturned truck," Stark pointed out. "Wasn't that the idea, to get all the law enforcement in the county concentrated there?"

"Yeah, but we can't be sure there's nobody at the Diamond S."

"We won't stay long," Stark said grimly. "But I have to see what Ramirez did to my home."

Finnegan sighed. "It's a dumb move, but I suppose I know how you feel. Take the ranch road, Will."

Sheffield nodded and wheeled the car into the turn.

Finnegan was right, Stark thought. He was risking his freedom, and theirs, just to see the destruction with his own eyes. He felt compelled to do so, however.

The moon was bright enough so that Sheffield was able to cut off the headlights and drive without them as he approached the ranch headquarters. There was no point in announcing their presence any more than they had to. As they came within sight of the blackened ruins that marked the locations of the main house, the bunkhouse, the barns, and the other out-buildings, Sheffield put the car in neutral, turned the engine off, and let it coast to a silent stop so he didn't have to use the brakes. He had already taken the bulb out of the dome light, so the car remained dark as the four men opened the doors and stepped out.

Stark stood there beside the vehicle and looked around, and as the extent of the terrible destruction soaked in on him, he felt his heart hardening even more with anger and hatred. Ramirez was responsible for this. Ramirez had de-stroyed everything Stark had worked for decades to build. And when he took Elaine, he had ripped out what remained of Stark's heart and soul. Getting her back was his only chance to regain his humanity, Stark thought.

"Don't move," a voice snapped from behind them. "You're covered."

Stark tensed, ready to throw himself to the ground in case any shooting started. On the other side of the car, Macon started to turn, the shotgun in his hands. Stark expected to hear the blast of gunfire shattering the nocturnal peace.

Instead, another voice called sharply, "Rich! No! Put the gun down!"

Stark had thought there was something familiar about the first voice, though he hadn't heard it in years. The second one he definitely recognized. "Nat!" he exclaimed. "Nat, is that you?"

A short, slender shape came out of the darkness. "John Howard!" Nat Van Linh said. He reached out to grasp Stark's hand and pump it. "Lord, it's good to see you!" Nat turned his head and added, "Rich, put the gun down and come over here."

"You sure about that, Nat?" rumbled the hoarse voice that had first challenged them from the darkness.

Quietly, Nat said, "These are our friends, Rich, like I told you. They're John Howard, Will, and Jack."

A figure stepped out from the shade of a cottonwood tree. In the moonlight, Stark saw that he wore ragged blue jeans and a dark T-shirt. His hair was long and a little tangled, and he had a close-cropped beard. He carried a long-barreled pistol in his right hand. The silvery moonlight reflected off the glasses he wore.

Stark hadn't seen him for twenty years or more. He suspected that in daylight, there might be a lot of gray in that sandy hair. But other than that, Rich Threadgill didn't appear to have changed much.

"Rich," he said. "It's good to see you again."

Threadgill came closer. "John Howard? Is that really you?"

Stark held out a hand and said, "It's really me."

Threadgill ignored the hand and threw his arms around Stark in a bear hug. Stark gasped a little, both from the strength of the embrace and the fact that Threadgill evidently hadn't bathed or changed clothes in a while. That came as no surprise; cleanliness wasn't a big concern for someone who lived on the streets. The surprise was that Threadgill was still alive after all these years. Stark had assumed that his old friend's lifestyle would have claimed him a long time ago. Drugs, alcohol, violence . . . all were part and parcel of a life lived on the streets.

It hadn't had to be that way. Threadgill had relatives who would have taken him in and given him a place to live. Stark had talked to some of them in the past. They had tried to help Threadgill when he came back from Vietnam, but any time he moved in with one of them, he never stayed very long. He was too restless. Nor had he been able to hold a job for more than a few weeks before he got in a fight, mouthed off to a supervisor, or simply stopped showing up for work. He drank some, but booze wasn't his problem. He could control that. What he couldn't control were the inner demons that never gave him any peace.

It would have been easy, of course, to blame Vietnam for what had happened to Rich Threadgill, but Stark knew that wasn't really the case. Threadgill had been . . . eccentric . . . before he ever joined the marines and was sent to Southeast Asia. His parents had died while he was in high school and he had learned to take care of himself then. He had managed to graduate, but he knew that further education wasn't for him. He didn't want to be tied down anywhere. So he'd enlisted and found himself in that steaming, dangerous jungle along with Stark, Finnegan, Sheffield, and Macon. That was where he'd really come into his own. Going back stateside to a life of peace . . . well, that just hadn't worked out.

Stark slapped Threadgill on the back several times as the man hugged him. He heard sobs and realized that Threadgill was crying. "It's all right, Rich," he said. "I'm glad to see you, too." Looking over Threadgill's shoulder at Nat Van Linh, he asked, "Where did you find him?"

"In Dallas," Nat replied. "I'd gotten a postcard from him about a year ago, mailed from a halfway house up there. He wasn't staying there anymore, but the people running the place had an idea where I might find him. He was there, living under an overpass. That's why it took me longer to get down here. We came to the ranch expecting to find Elaine."

"She called you, too?"

"That's right." Nat looked around at the devastation. "What happened here? Where is she, John Howard?"

Finnegan took Nat's arm. "Come on, buddy, we'll fill you in. You may not know it yet, but you just stepped into a world of trouble."

Stark finally disengaged himself from the sobbing Threadgill and gently but firmly got the homeless man to sit down on the trunk of the rental car. Threadgill dragged the back of his hand across his eyes and said, "Nat told me you were in trouble, John Howard. I want to help you."

"That's right, Rich. I've had a lot of trouble the past couple of months. And now a drug lord across the border has kidnapped my wife."

"Elaine? I remember you showin' us her picture when we were over there in 'Nam. She was really pretty." Threadgill obviously didn't remember it, but he had met Elaine a couple of times since they'd all come back from the war.

"She still is," Stark said, and he hoped fervently that that statement was true.

The other four men gathered around the car. Finnegan had explained the situation to Nat Van Linh by now, and Nat asked, "What do we do now, John Howard?"

"Head on over to the McCarthy place, I guess," Stark said. "Then we can start trying to figure out how to arm ourselves and how we'll attack Ramirez's compound."

"I'll leave the strategy to you, John Howard," Finnegan said. "You were always better at that than any of us. But as for the weapons, I've got that taken care of. They ought to be here tomorrow."

Stark frowned at him. "What are you talking about, Jack?"

"I told you, my lawyer's got all sorts of contacts, including people who know how to put their hands on guns that can't be traced. They'll be delivered to that other ranch tomorrow."

Stark grunted. "More of that million and a half you've spent?"

"Well, actually most of the cost will be over and above that."

"I can't ever pay you back. You know that."

"You got me out of that damned jungle alive," Finnegan said. The other men all nodded. "Chances are none of us would have survived without your help, John Howard. *We're* the ones who can't ever pay *you* back."

Stark looked at each of them in turn, saw the trust and affection on their faces, and finally nodded. He said, "Let's get out of here."

But before they could move, the distinctive throbbing sound of a helicopter's engine came beating through the night.

Thirty-four

The helicopter didn't necessarily have to have anything to do with them, Stark thought, but it didn't pay to take any chances. "Get under the trees," he barked, instinctively falling back into the habit of giving orders when he and his companions were in a potentially dangerous situation.

"What about the car?" Macon asked as the six men hurried over into the thick shadows underneath the cottonwoods.

"Nothing we can do about it now," Stark replied. He wished they were better armed. They had the shotgun, which Finnegan had bought in a Del Rio sporting goods store that afternoon, and Threadgill's long-barreled old pistol. He'd had the gun for decades, and Stark didn't know if it would even fire.

The sound of the chopper's engine grew louder. Looking up through the branches of the trees, Stark caught sight of its running lights. He had hoped that the helicopter just happened to be flying over the ranch on its way elsewhere, but judging from the way the lights were moving, it looked like the Diamond S might actually be the chopper's destination.

"Who could that be?" Sheffield asked quietly.

"The black helicopters, man," Threadgill said. "Haven't you heard of the black helicopters? They're comin' for us!"

He started out from under the trees, brandishing the pistol as if he intended to shoot down the chopper with it. Stark grabbed his arm and stopped him before he could go more than a couple of steps. "Wait a minute, Rich," he said. "Maybe that chopper doesn't have anything to do with us."

Threadgill gave a shake of his head, as if something annoying was buzzing in his ear. "Medivac," he said. "Gotta be medivac, comin' to get the guys who were hit and take 'em back to base."

"No, Rich, we're not in-country," Stark told him, speaking quietly but insistently in an effort to get through his friend's muddled memories. "Just take it easy."

Threadgill still seemed confused, but he lowered the pistol and said, "I'm okay, John Howard. Really, I'm okay."

Stark doubted that, but maybe Threadgill would be able to keep it together until after the helicopter was gone. Maybe it hadn't been a good idea for Nat to bring Threadgill with him, he thought. If Threadgill was able to reach back into the past and regain the combat prowess that had made him one of the best fighting men in the unit, he would be an asset in the raid on Ramirez's compound. But if he went nuts in the middle of a firefight and could no longer distinguish friend from foe . . .

Burn that bridge when you come to it, Stark told himself. Right now, he wanted to know what the hell that helicopter was up to.

The chopper had slowed and was hovering over the ruins of the ranch house. As Stark looked up at it, something came out of the helicopter. Stark couldn't see that well in the darkness, but he would have sworn that some sort of bundle had just been tossed out. A second later, as it landed with a heavy thud between the burned-out ranch house and the devastated bunkhouse, Stark knew he'd been right. Something *had* been thrown from the chopper.

In that heartbeat when whatever it was had been plummeting toward the ground, Stark had wondered if it could be a bomb. Had Ramirez sent his men back to finish the job of destroying the Diamond S? When it hit would the whole ranch be transformed into a gigantic crater? Stark wouldn't put it past Ramirez to have himself a pocket nuke.

That was a crazy thought, of course, and the thing hadn't exploded when it hit the ground. Now, as the chopper swung around and started back south, Finnegan said, "What the hell was that?"

"We'd better find out," Stark said.

He started forward, followed by the other men. Macon came up beside him, carrying the shotgun. "Better let me go first, John Howard," he said. "Just in case whatever's up there needs a load of buckshot."

Stark nodded. "All right. But the rest of you be ready for trouble."

Macon moved out in front, taking the point. He kept the shotgun trained on the long, shapeless bundle that lay motionless on the ground. Circling it, he called to the other men, "It looks like something wrapped in canvas. You think we can risk a light?"

Sheffield slipped a small flashlight out of the pocket of his black jeans, also purchased at the sporting goods store that afternoon. "John Howard?" he asked.

"Go ahead," Stark told him.

Sheffield thumbed the switch, and a narrow beam of illumination sprang out from the flashlight. He played it over the object, which was indeed something wrapped in canvas, just as Macon had said. Rope had been tied around the thing in several places.

Stark's guts knotted as he saw the dark stains on the canvas. Something had soaked through it, and every instinct in his body told him it was something bad.

"Open it up," he said in a voice as hollow as if it had come from inside a grave.

Finnegan took hold of Stark's arm. "John Howard, maybe we'd better go back to the car for a minute—"

"Open it up," Stark commanded again. "Nat, I never knew you not to have a knife on you. Cut those ropes and unwrap that canvas."

Nat looked around at the others. Nobody moved.

"Do it!" Stark roared.

Finnegan shrugged and nodded to Nat. "Go ahead."

With a sigh, Nat took a folding knife from his pocket and moved toward the canvas-shrouded bundle. He knelt beside it, opened the knife, and began sawing on the ropes.

Stark stood there, sick and numb, feeling almost as if he had been displaced from his own body and was just observing this developing horror from somewhere else. But in the back of his mind a panic-stricken voice had begun to gibber, and each beat of his heart sent a desperate "No!" of denial through his brain. His chest was tight and painful, as if a giant belt had been drawn around it, and he wondered fleetingly if he was having a heart attack.

The ropes parted under the keen edge of Nat's knife. When all of them were cut, he folded back the canvas. . . .

The lifeless face of Elaine Stark, her features bloody and twisted in agony, was sharply limned by the beam from Will Sheffield's flashlight. Sheffield cried out in horror and jerked the light away.

But it was too late. What John Howard Stark had just seen had been burned indelibly into his brain, a nightmare image that would be with him for the rest of his life.

He threw back his head and howled in agony like a wild animal.

Finnegan grabbed at him but missed as Stark lunged forward. "Stop him!" Finnegan yelled. "John Howard, no!"

Macon tried to get in Stark's way, but he was bowled over as if he weren't there, despite being taller and heavier than Stark. Shouldering Nat aside effortlessly, Stark dropped to his knees beside his wife's body and cried out again in incoherent pain as he took her face in his shaking hands. "Elaine!" he choked out as he leaned over her, tears falling from his eyes to land on her face and wash away a little of the blood.

"Elaine . . . no, God, no, please, God, no . . . Elaine . . . I'm
so sorry . . . so sorry . . ."

His whole world had been ripped from under him, turned
inside out, transformed into a wrenching nightmare of grief
and loss. He shook and shuddered as the tears flowed.
Leaning over, he pressed his cheek to hers, shaking even
more as he felt the coldness of her flesh. She had been dead
for quite a while. All during the afternoon and evening, while
he had dared to hope again, it had already been too late to
save her.

Ramirez . . . *the Vulture* . . . what else had he done to her?

The others were standing back, allowing him to be alone
with her, so they weren't close enough to stop him as he
began pulling away the rest of the canvas, uncovering her
body. Stark cried out again as he saw the blood, dark in the
moonlight, the mutilation, the indignities that had been heaped
upon her. He hoped wildly that she had been dead before those
terrible things were done to her, but in his heart he knew that
probably wasn't the case.

Finnegan came up and took hold of his arm. "John Howard,
come on," he said softly. "There's nothing you can do—"

Stark backhanded him, sending him flying. Finnegan
landed with an "Ooof!" and rolled over a couple of times.

Sheffield, Macon, and Nat looked at each other, not knowing what to do. Stark was no longer even aware of them. At
this moment, he was mindless, totally consumed by his grief.

So he never saw Rich Threadgill step up behind him,
wasn't aware of Threadgill's arm rising and falling or the
butt of the heavy old pistol thudding against his head. Stark
pitched forward into the darkness that had already engulfed
his soul and now claimed his physical being as well.

He wasn't out long, only a couple of minutes. Threadgill
might not have any idea how to cope with normal, everyday
life, but he could hit a man with a gun butt just hard enough
to stun him without doing any real damage. In that couple of

minutes, Stark's friends had used their belts to tie him hand and foot. He came out of his stupor roaring with rage. He looked around wildly, tossing his head back and forth, and saw that they had carried him underneath the trees.

Threadgill came over and knelt beside him, putting a hand on Stark's shoulder. "Take it easy, John Howard," he said, and the strength in his arm pressed Stark to the ground with ease.

"Elaine!" Stark gasped.

"The others are takin' care of her. Don't you worry. We'll see to it that she's laid to rest proper."

Stark closed his eyes and groaned. The feeling of loss was still sharp and agonizing inside him, and yet a certain numbness had crept into his consciousness, dulling the pain, if only infinitesimally. The human organism could only endure so much agony—physical, mental, or spiritual—before it began taking steps to protect itself. Stark's grief had already reached that threshold.

"Remember that night at the camp near Duc Pho?" Threadgill asked quietly. "I tried to teach you how to play the harmonica, and all you could do was make it squawk like a cat with its tail bein' stepped on. And then Will told us all about the book he was gonna write, and Jack said when he got back home he was gonna take over the bank from his daddy and make a lot of money, and I reckon he did, sure enough, and ol' Henry didn't say much, but then ol' Henry never said much, did he? and neither did Nat."

Threadgill kept talking, reminiscing quietly, his brain seeming clearer now. He knew the memories he brought up were in the past and wasn't confusing them with the present. The words calmed Stark, and gradually his breathing and his pulse slowed, approaching normal levels again. The pain was still there, like a persistent toothache, only a million times worse, but a part of him realized that he was going to have to learn to live with it. The only alternative was to surrender, to give himself over to madness, and that way lay only death.

That was unacceptable. He had to cling to sanity so that he could cling to life. No matter how much he might wish it were otherwise, he had to continue living.

He had things to do.

Finally, he broke into Threadgill's monologue by asking, "What are they doing, Rich?"

Threadgill hesitated. "Well, they're, uh, gettin' Elaine ready . . . cleanin' her up . . . I mean . . . Henry found a shovel that wasn't burned up too bad in the barn, and he said he could dig . . . aw, hell, John Howard . . ."

"It's all right," Stark told his old friend. "I know what you're trying to say, Rich. You think you could untie my hands and feet?"

"Jack said to keep you—"

"That's when I was out of my head," Stark broke in. "I'm all right now."

That was a lie, of course. He would never be all right again. No matter what happened, he would always be incomplete. But he was functional again. The old instincts had come back to him. His brain was working, and he knew what had to be done.

"Well, all right," Threadgill said. "But if Jack bitches at me, it ain't my fault."

He unlashed the belts from Stark's hands and feet. Stark hadn't been tied up so long that his extremities had gone numb. He was able to climb to his feet without much trouble. He saw the others about twenty yards away, under the cottonwoods, gathered around something.

He knew what it was, what it had to be. When he and Threadgill walked up and the other four men drew back, Stark saw that they had taken Elaine's body from the blood-stained canvas and wrapped it carefully in a thick blanket.

"I found that blanket in the house, John Howard," Nat said. "It was partially burned, but there was enough left . . ."

Stark nodded. Enough left for a burial shroud, that was what Nat meant.

"We could call the authorities, give them an anonymous tip," Finnegan said. "That way it could all be done legally and, well, properly. . . ."

Stark shook his head. "There wouldn't be anything proper about turning her over to Hammond," he said harshly. "This was her home. She'll be laid to rest here, by people who loved her, and nobody will ever know the place except us. And my boys, if I live to show them."

The other men nodded in agreement. Macon, who stood there holding a shovel with a charred handle, said, "You just tell us where, John Howard."

Stark turned to gaze toward a small hill that overlooked the ranch headquarters. "Up there," he said.

Then he turned back to Elaine and knelt beside her, pulling back the blanket to reveal her face. As Threadgill had said, the men had cleaned her up, washing the blood from her face and combing her hair. Stark looked at her for a long moment. He didn't lean down to kiss her lips. To his way of thinking, that would have been a hollow gesture. Elaine— her soul, her essence, her spirit, whatever you wanted to call it—was already gone. Stark touched her hair, her cheek, rested a fingertip on her lips for a moment. The lines of pain had been smoothed out somehow. Stark didn't know how his friends had accomplished that, but he was grateful to them for it.

Stark leaned his head back and looked up at the heavens, seeing the stars through gaps in the cottonwood branches. If what he believed was right—and he *believed*, so it must be— she was already up there somewhere, gazing down at him. If he knew her, and after more than thirty years he damned well ought to, she was hurting for him, not for herself. She would wish she could reach down somehow and take his pain away from him, ease the burden of grief that still threatened to consume him. And she would want something else . . .

Vengeance.

A vagrant night breeze rustled through the cottonwoods. Stark heard the words being carried on that breeze . . . *I love you, John Howard. I will always love you. And when the time comes, I'll see you again. But until then . . .*

The breeze became a wind and whipped harder through the leaves.

Go get 'em, John Howard. Get the bastards.

Vengeance is mine; I will repay, sayeth the Lord. Stark knew the Scripture and believed in that part of it, too.

But he figured that the good Lord could spare some vengeance for Elaine Stark, and he was just the one to deliver it.

Thirty-five

She was laid to rest atop the hill, with a lonely mesquite tree for a marker. The ranch was spread out before her, and in the distance, across the river in Mexico, rugged mountains loomed darkly. The wind still blew. It nearly always blew on top of this hill, Stark knew. Clouds drifted across the moon as he and his friends stood there by the grave. They had worked a long time on it, trading off with the shovel. The grave was deep. Once it was partially filled in, they had placed a layer of rocks inside it, wedging them in securely so that nothing could get to the body. Then the rest of the dirt was shoveled in, and gravel was spread over it to hide it. The law would probably be out here the next morning, if not earlier, searching for any sign of Stark, and he didn't want them finding the grave. He didn't want them disturbing her.

When they were finished, Will Sheffield said a prayer. Henry Macon said one as well. The others were silent, including Stark. Anything he had to say would be said in private. Later, maybe, when this was all over, he would come back out here and make his peace with what had happened. But that was too far in the future to even think about.

"We'd better get out of here," Stark said. "We're lucky Hammond hasn't come lookin' for us already."

Nat had a rental car hidden on the other side of a stand of trees a few hundred yards from the remains of the house. He had driven it up there earlier when he and Threadgill heard the other car coming, since they didn't know whom the vehicle belonged to. Threadgill had been left to get the drop on the newcomers. Now Nat fetched the other car and fell in behind the one Sheffield was driving. They had found the deserted McCarthy Ranch while it was still light, and Sheffield wasn't sure they would be able to now that it was dark. Stark was able to tell him where to drive, though, and within half an hour, they pulled up in front of the abandoned ranch house. The others got out, and Sheffield and Nat drove the cars into the old barn with its leaning walls and sagging roof. With luck, the barn wouldn't fall down while the cars were parked in it.

The six of them gathered in the house. Sheffield shined the light around to make sure no rattlers had crawled into the place. The furniture was all gone, but they sat down on the floor to wait for morning.

"Tell me about the guns," Stark said.

"They should be delivered out here by sometime tomorrow afternoon," Finnegan said. "Heckler and Koch MP Five machine guns, L Eighty-five assault rifles, and the latest fashions from Glock, Smith and Wesson, and Colt. Prime stuff, John Howard. But we're not just talking guns here. We've got body armor and forty-millimeter grenade launchers coming, too."

Stark grunted. "Sounds like enough to fight a war."

"A small war, maybe," Finnegan said, pride in his voice. "We're going to be outnumbered, right?"

"Probably ten to one."

"Well, all that gear will help knock down the odds."

"And you were able to get all this because you know a lawyer?" Stark sounded dubious.

"A lawyer who sometimes handles high-profile cases, like that of a certain alleged arms dealer." Finnegan nodded. "Oh yeah, I had to call in plenty of favors for this one. But it's gonna be worth it." He laughed. "Free trade . . . ain't it grand? Just call it one of the blessings of democracy."

They had stopped at a grocery store, too, as well as the sporting goods store, and the trunk of the rental car was full of bottled water and prepackaged food. It wouldn't make for a very nutritious diet, but they wouldn't have to live on it for long. Macon passed around bottles of water and a box of granola bars. Nat opened a container of beef jerky and handed out the strips of tough, dried beef. Just like earlier, when his supper had been brought to him in the jail, Stark had no appetite but ate anyway.

"What time is it?" Threadgill asked.

Finnegan pressed a button on his watch, lighting up the digital display for a second. "Twelve forty-seven," he said.

"Is that all?" Stark asked. A little after midnight? It seemed as if a lot more time had passed since his friends had snatched him out of the Val Verde County Jail. It seemed like a shift in geologic eras, in fact, when he compared life before he had seen what was wrapped up in that canvas, and after. . . .

"How did they know we were there?" he asked aloud.

No one seemed to want to answer. Finally, Sheffield said, "You mean, back there at your ranch . . . ?"

"They didn't know," Finnegan said. "That's the only thing that makes sense."

Nat said, "But then why would they . . . I mean . . ."

"Why did they bring Elaine back?" Stark said heavily. "Jack's right. They didn't know we were there. It was just coincidence that we were. Ramirez probably didn't even know you boys broke me out of jail tonight. He had Elaine's body brought back and left somewhere it was bound to be found. In fact, he probably intends to tip off Hammond about it. That way Hammond could tell me all about it."

"He's doing all this to punish you," Macon said.

Stark nodded. "That's right. He wants to hurt me as bad as he possibly can." Stark took a long drink of water from one of the bottles and then wiped the back of his hand across his mouth. "What he doesn't realize is that he's accomplished his goal. He's hurt me as bad as he possibly can . . . but I'm still here. And now I'm loose, where *I* can go after *him*."

"Sounds to me like this fella Ramirez is a damn fool," Threadgill said. "If he had a grudge against you, John Howard, he should'a just gone ahead and killed you first thing."

"Yes," Stark said. "He should have. But he didn't."

"Like I said, damn fool. Got any more of that jerky, Nat?"

Ryan said, "The chopper's back. It's done."

Ramirez lolled back in the bathtub and nodded in satisfaction. "Good. Make sure Hammond is notified."

The bathroom was so opulent it should have been in a despot's palace somewhere, all gold and ivory and thick carpet. Ramirez had the jets in the big spa tub running full blast, swirling hot water around his body. He had been in there for hours. He was going to look like a prune when he finally got out.

Ramirez was just trying to feel clean again, Ryan supposed, after the things he had done to Elaine Stark.

Raping her, and letting a dozen of his men rape her, hadn't been enough for Ramirez. He had tortured her, too, personally using cold steel and hot flame to inflict so much agony on the woman that by the time it was over she had been nothing more than a mutilated husk of a human being, whimpering and pleading for death. Even then, Ramirez had withheld that release from her, choosing to make her suffer even more. With her blood coating his hands and spattered all over his face and clothes, he had stood there and waited for her to take her own sweet time about dying. Only the time hadn't been sweet at all.

Ryan had seen and done a lot of bad things in his life. He had killed innocent men in cold blood, more than he could ever remember. He had carried out torture himself, when it was necessary. But he had never taken any pleasure in the work other than a certain amount of pride in a job well done, certainly not the sort of giggling glee that Ramirez had taken in what he'd done to Elaine Stark.

It wasn't right.

Stubbornly, Ryan shoved that thought out of his head. He tried not to think about how easy it would be to kneel beside that sunken tub, force Ramirez's head under the water, and hold it there until he drowned like the mad dog that he was. Even considering it, however briefly, was unprofessional. Right and wrong never entered into Ryan's decisions. Only life or death, and, to a lesser extent, profit or loss.

Still, he knew the time was coming for him to move on. There were no legal, binding contracts in the world in which he lived; he was a free agent and could leave Ramirez's employ any time he wanted to. Ramirez might not like it, but that was just too bad. If he tried to stop Ryan from going, he would quickly find out that when Ryan's loyalty ended, he made for a dangerous enemy.

In the big tub, in the swirling water, Ramirez sighed and went on, "I just wish there was some way Stark could be there when they find her. He should see what his foolishness has caused."

"Maybe he already did," Ryan said. The faintest trace of a smile pulled at his lips.

Ramirez sat up sharply, splashing in the water. "What? What do you mean by that, Silencio? Stark is in jail!"

Ah, now this was the good part, getting to lay some news on Ramirez that would shake him up a little. Ryan said, "Not anymore. Someone got into there earlier tonight and broke him out."

Ramirez slapped both hands against the water and started cursing. Ryan let the profane outburst run its course, and then he continued, "The chopper pilot says there was a car parked out at Stark's ranch when he dropped the body. He couldn't see the license plate or really tell much about it, but it was there. Seems to me that Stark might have gone there, since he was on the run by that time."

"*Madre de Dios!* Who did this? How?"

"I'm not sure. I'd say that some of Stark's rancher friends might be behind it, but to be honest, they don't seem competent enough to me to have pulled off something like this. Whoever's responsible for it staged a distraction. They wrecked a truck on the outskirts of Del Rio and made it look like it was leaking toxic waste. Turns out it wasn't, of course, but it drew all of Hammond's men away from the jail except for a couple of deputies, who got knocked out when Stark was set free."

"He must be found! Do you hear me, Silencio? I had taken everything away from Stark, including his freedom! He must be found and taken back to jail, so that he will spend the rest of his life in prison, a toy of men who will do my bidding. Failing that, he must be killed. But first, he must be found!"

"Of course, Don Ernesto."

Ramirez was too upset to hear the mocking tone in Ryan's voice. The Vulture could rant and rave all he wanted to, but in the end, his words were meaningless. Ryan's instincts told him they would not have to go looking for John Howard Stark.

Before it was over, Stark would come to them.

They took turns sleeping during the night. Two men were always on guard, even though Stark knew it was very unlikely anyone would find them here on the old McCarthy place before several days had passed. When it was his turn to sleep, Stark's rest was troubled and fitful. His dreams were haunted. In his mind's eye he saw Elaine as she had been when she was a young woman, fresh and beautiful, and then as a wife and mother and his partner on the ranch, older, more mature, but every bit as beautiful, if not more so, and then finally as she had looked when he pulled back that bloodstained canvas, and the horror of it all was just too much for him. After he had snapped awake a couple of times with his heart hammering and tears in his eyes, he made sure he didn't go back to sleep. Instead he got up and wandered through the deserted house, trying to be quiet so the others could sleep. He thought about the old man who had lived here so long ago. Stark had never known him well, but McCarthy had had his own life, full of the same small triumphs and bitter defeats, the moments of bliss and the long dark hours of despair, the loved ones who make life worth living but who are all too often gone too soon. Glory and tragedy, laughter and tears, and it was all multiplied millions and millions of times over, no, billions, all over the world, as men and women ceaselessly struggled to capture the fleeting wonder of life before succumbing to the ultimate triumph of death.

Stark was damned glad when it got to be morning.

They breakfasted on water, hot canned soda, and junk food. Judging by the haggard looks on the faces of the other men, they hadn't slept well, either. They hadn't been married to Elaine, of course, so they didn't feel the same level of grief that Stark did, but they were human, after all, and what they had seen would have disturbed anyone except the most sociopathic monster.

"If the weapons come today, we can move tonight," Stark said, preferring to think about tactics rather than . . . other things. "We'd better try to figure out our plan of attack. It's too bad we don't have more intel about Ramirez's place."

"Where can we get some?" Finnegan asked.

Stark shook his head. "Damned if I know. There was a newspaper article a while back, an exposé I guess you'd call it, about Ramirez, and if I remember right, it had a couple of aerial photos of his place."

Finnegan reached for his briefcase, which had been brought in the night before along with the food. "Hang on. Let me work the Net for a while."

"How are you gonna hook up to the Internet?" Stark asked with a frown. "Even if you've got a laptop in that briefcase, there's no phone line out here. Hasn't been for years."

Finnegan grinned and took out a computer no bigger than a hardback book. "Another of the miracles of digital technology. This brick is part of a wi-fi network. Wireless Internet, you know."

Stark just shook his head. "If you can do that, more power to you, Jack. You've left me behind, though."

Finnegan opened the little computer, booted it up, established a connection, and was soon searching through the archives of the Del Rio newspaper. It didn't take him long to locate the story about Ramirez that had gotten its author killed, dismembered, and scattered up and down the Rio Grande. Stark told the others about that.

"A damned shame," Finnegan said, "but the guy's death won't be in vain. He's going to help us bring Ramirez down." Sitting cross-legged on the floor with the computer in front of him, he pulled his briefcase over and took out more apparatus, including a cable. In minutes he had a small, battery-powered printer hooked up and spitting out prints of the two aerial photographs that accompanied the news story.

Stark and the others huddled over those photos all morning, studying them and figuring out the best way to approach the Vulture's compound and get inside. "Once we're in we don't know what we'll find," Sheffield pointed out.

"No," Stark agreed, "we don't. We'll have to improvise. The important thing is to get to Ramirez."

"You want him for yourself, John Howard?" Macon asked quietly.

Stark had to think about that question, but not for very long. "I want the son of a bitch dead," he said. "I don't care who does it. If you have a shot, take it." He looked around at the others, and they all nodded in understanding.

"What sort of men does he have working for him?" Nat Van Linh asked.

"A few Colombians, but mostly just typical Mexican

gunners and drug runners. They're plenty tough and dangerous, I suppose, don't get me wrong about that, but to Ramirez
they're just cannon fodder. There's another man, though. . . ."
Stark thought back to the times he had seen the one he was
talking about. "He's probably Ramirez's personal bodyguard
and top lieutenant. About fifty, I'd say, and he looks Mexican . . . dark skin, high cheekbones, hawk nose . . . except he
has red hair. And he's damned dangerous when he wants to
be."

That last statement came from Stark's musing about everything that had happened. He was convinced there had been
times when the red-haired man could have killed him. The
only real try he'd made had been when Stark was in the hospital, though, and his luck had been bad there. He hadn't
been part of the gun crew that had invaded the ranch, nor the
bunch that had killed Newt and Chaco. Stark wouldn't have
been surprised if the man had been around somewhere during those operations, though, monitoring things and seeing
just how well Ramirez's gunners carried out their missions.
He had to wonder, as well, if the man had been responsible
for kidnapping Elaine and laying waste to the Diamond S. It
seemed like something he would be capable of.

Like a gun, though, the redheaded killer couldn't fire
himself. Somebody else—in this case, Ramirez—had to
point him and pull the trigger.

"Watch out for him," Stark concluded. "With luck we can
get through all the other men between us and Ramirez. I
don't know about that hombre."

"He's one man," Finnegan said. "We'll get him. Don't
worry, John Howard."

Stark was going to worry, though. He had seen too much
not to.

Nat leaned over one of the photos and said, "Shouldn't we
be thinking about our exit strategy, too?"

Threadgill laughed. "You don't really think we're gettin'
out of there, do you, Nat?"

"Damn it," Stark snapped. "I didn't ask you fellas to go

on a suicide mission." He looked away. "Maybe we'd better just call it off. It was different when . . . when we thought Elaine might still be alive. I was willing to risk everything to save her. Now I don't know. I can't ask the five of you to give up all you have . . ."

His voice trailed off into a long moment of silence that none of the others seemed willing to break. Finally Will Sheffield said, "You're not asking us, John Howard. This is strictly a volunteer job." He looked around at the others. "Right?"

"That's right," Macon said. "And that's why I think Nat's got a point. Let's figure out how we're going to get out of there alive. You can't stop me from going with you, John Howard, but I *do* want to get back home."

After a moment, Stark nodded. "Fair enough. Let's get to work figuring this out."

They had been strategizing for another hour or so, snacking and swigging from the water bottles as they did so, when Finnegan's cell phone rang. He answered it and after a moment handed it to Stark. "Tell this fella exactly how to get here, John Howard."

Stark took the phone and said, "Hello? Who's this?"

"You don't need to know that, friend," a man's voice said. Finnegan shook his head at the same time and moved his hands back and forth, warning Stark not to pursue that line of questioning.

"You're right, I don't," Stark said. "You need directions out here?"

"Yeah. Any time you're ready. Starting from Del Rio."

It took Stark only a couple of minutes to give the man detailed directions for how to find the old McCarthy ranch house. When Stark was finished, the man said, "See you in an hour," and broke the connection.

Stark handed the phone back to Finnegan. "Can that fella be trusted?"

"All the trust that money can buy," Finnegan replied with a smile. "He wouldn't have survived in the illegal arms business as long as he has if he was in the habit of double-crossing his clients."

Stark just shook his head. "You've got some friends who are handy to have, Jack."

"Oh, they're not friends," Finnegan said. "Just . . . business acquaintances." He looked around. "My friends are all here."

Stark knew what he meant. He just hoped that friendship wasn't going to get all his friends killed.

Thirty-six

The truck arrived in the early afternoon. Stark and the others heard the rumble of its engine before the vehicle itself came in sight. They waited in the house, Macon holding the shotgun and Threadgill cradling his pistol, until they were sure who the visitors were. Stark kept a close eye on Threadgill. It wouldn't take much to set him off and start him shooting.

The truck was a big old panel job with MASSEY PLUMBING painted on the sides. Two men were in the cab. The driver killed the engine, opened the door, and hopped out. He was a short, skinny man wearing an untucked cowboy shirt with the sleeves cut off and a straw Stetson with a tightly curled brim and a battered crown. His hair was pale, his skin sunburned. When the passenger climbed out, he proved to be much bigger, with broad shoulders and a prominent gut. He wore his brown hair in a buzz cut.

"Hey, Jack!" the little man called. Stark recognized his voice from the brief phone conversation earlier. "Anybody home?"

The men stepped out onto the sagging porch. "I'm Jack," the banker said.

The little man grinned and slapped the truck fender. "Got your merchandise here."

"Let's have a look."

Everyone gathered around the rear of the truck. The big man ran the sliding door up its grooves. The interior of the truck appeared to be full of plumbing equipment: stacks of plastic and copper pipe, bins full of faucets and washers and plastic elbows and joints, pipe wrenches hung on racks, a couple of plungers and a drain auger, even an old toilet.

Stark frowned. They couldn't fight Ramirez and his small army with this junk.

But then the little sunburned man climbed into the back of the truck and worked hidden catches and swung up trapdoors in the floor and pulled out the racks of tools and equipment to reveal a small-scale armory. As Finnegan had promised, there were assault rifles and submachine guns and grenade launchers and more than a dozen pistols. Helmets, Kevlar vests, and strap-on body armor hung from hooks. It was like the inside of a SWAT van; only a few moments' work would cleverly conceal all of the lethal cargo.

"There ya go," the little man said. "If you're satisfied, Jack, make the call."

Finnegan looked at Stark. "What do you think?"

"There's plenty of ammo for all of this?" Stark asked.

"You bet, hoss," the little man replied.

"And the truck goes with it?"

"Yep."

Stark nodded. That would make the approach to Ramirez's place easier, all right. He looked at Finnegan and nodded again. Finnegan took out his cell phone, thumbed in a number, and in a moment said simply, "Do it." He broke the connection and looked at the little man. "The money is on its way to the Caymans right now."

"Done and done," the little man said happily. He took a cell phone of his own from his shirt pocket and made a call. "Come on in."

A few minutes later an SUV drove into sight. "There's our ride outta here," the little man explained. "Pleasure doin' business with you boys."

Sheffield spoke up. "When you sell weapons to people, don't you ever wonder what they're going to do with them?"

The little man grinned and shook his head. "None o' my business, hoss." He motioned to the big man. "Come on, Billy."

They climbed into the SUV. The vehicle's windows were so darkly tinted that it was impossible to see into it. The driver wheeled it around and drove away.

"That was just creepy," Macon said.

"There's a whole lot that goes on in the world that normal guys like us never see," Finnegan said.

"That's all right with me," Nat said. "I've seen enough trouble to last several lifetimes." He glanced at Stark and added, "So, I guess a little more won't hurt, will it?"

"This'll be the last of it as far as I'm concerned," Stark said. "One way or another, this ends tonight."

The bridge over Amistad Dam spanned the Rio Grande at the southern end of Amistad Reservoir, north of Del Rio. There were customs offices at both ends of the bridge, but the checks the agents ran on vehicles passing back and forth over the dam were cursory. Late that afternoon, Sheffield and Threadgill drove the plumbing truck across, explaining to the Border Patrol agents that they were on their way to a job at a hacienda on the Mexican side of the border. Tradesmen such as plumbers and electricians crossed the border all the time, coming and going. An hour later, Stark and the others crossed in one of the rental cars. The back was full of fishing equipment now, bought at one of the marinas on the U.S. side of the reservoir, along with Mexican fishing licenses. Finnegan, who was at the wheel, grinned up at the agents and commented, "I hear the catfish are really biting up around the Arroyo de Caballo."

"You plan to rent a boat at the marina on the other side?"

"Yes, sir."

"Watch out for the buoys in the middle of the reservoir, especially if you're out there after dark."

"Will do," Finnegan promised. He gave the agents a little wave as they motioned him on across the dam.

He turned right toward the marina when he reached the other side. The marina was some six miles up the shoreline of the reservoir, but Finnegan turned again before he reached there, this time onto a dirt road that led to the southwest and curved back toward Cuidad Acuna. Earlier he had called up topographical maps of the area on his computer and they had planned out their rendezvous and the route they would follow to Ramirez's compound on the southeastern edge of the Mexican border city.

The plumbing truck was parked at a lonely crossroads in the middle of some semiarid farmland where a few Mexican families managed to scratch out a living. Sheffield and Threadgill got out when they saw the rental car approaching. Dusk would be upon them soon.

With the group together again, Stark took the wheel of the car and led the way to an isolated draw. He parked there. If they made it back to recover the car later, all well and good. If not, some Mexican who chanced upon it would find himself the recipient of some good fortune.

Safe from prying eyes in the back of the truck, the men uncovered the armament and combat gear and began getting ready for the assault on the Vulture's nest. They shrugged into the Kevlar vests, strapped on helmets and body armor, buckled on web belts and hung flares, flash-bangs, and H-E grenades on them. They holstered Heckler & Koch 9mm pistols and loaded the assault rifles and shotguns. Threadgill tucked his old hog leg behind his web belt. "These newfangled guns are pretty nice," he said, "but I want this ol' man stopper o' mine with me, too."

"I'm just thankful you don't refer to it as Old Betsy," Finnegan said with a grin.

When they were ready, Stark said, "I'll drive the rest of the way. Rich, you're with me. The rest of you, in the back."

"Good luck, John Howard," Macon said.

"Yeah," Sheffield echoed. "Good luck."

"To us all," Nat added.

"Let's go get them motherfuckers," Threadgill said.

Jack Finnegan just looked at Stark and nodded. The banker's wry attitude had vanished after his quip about Threadgill's old revolver.

The four who were riding in back climbed into the truck. Stark pulled the door down and dogged its catches in place. He and Threadgill went to the front of the truck. Stark paused before stepping up into the cab. He looked off to the west, where the sun had dropped behind the low mountains that sprawled across the landscape. The afterglow remained, painting the sky with stripes of brilliant orange and red and streaks of pale blue that faded almost to white on the edges. It was a beautiful sunset. Stark knew that one reason the sunsets were so spectacular these days was the increased amount of pollution in the air from heavy industry in northern Mexico. That knowledge wasn't enough to detract from the sky's beauty at this moment.

Any sunset would seem beautiful, Stark thought, when there was a good chance it was the last one a fella was ever going to see.

He would have given anything if Elaine could have shared this one with him.

That was when he seemed to sense her presence beside him and feel her breath warm against his ear. *I'm with you, John Howard*, she seemed to whisper. *I'll always be with you.*

"John Howard?" Threadgill said.

Stark took a deep breath. "Let's go," he said as he pulled himself up into the cab and settled behind the wheel.

A moment later, the truck bounced away over the rough desert road as the brilliant colors began to fade from the arching sky behind it.

"What have you found?" Ramirez demanded. "Who is responsible for this debacle?"

As always when he visited Ramirez, Sheriff Norval Lee Hammond wished he could stop sweating so much. It was a hot night, of course, but that wasn't the cause of his discomfort. Not the sole cause, anyway. Ramirez looked mad enough to chew nails. He could certainly chew the head off a corrupt civil servant who had failed in his duties and let down everyone who had ever believed in him.

Willa Sue and the kids had been gone when he stopped by the house on his way over to Cuidad Acuna. No note, just some sort of legal paperwork saying that she was filing for divorce from him. Who the hell would'a thunk it? He never would have believed that the bitch had the balls to do such a thing.

The angry thoughts were hollow, though. Deep inside, he was hurting. This was just one more case where life hadn't worked out the way it was supposed to for Norval Lee Hammond.

"We still don't know who broke Stark out of jail," he said. "My deputies never saw whoever knocked them out. The guys who tricked up that tanker truck and wrecked it were hired to pull the stunt for a movie, they said. They were paid in cash, and well paid, at that. We're looking for the guy who hired them, but I doubt if we'll ever find him."

Ramirez pointed a finger at Hammond. "You had better find Stark, that's all I can say. You'll be damned sorry if you don't, Hammond."

Hammond was already sorry that he'd ever had anything to do with the Vulture. He wished he could change it, take it all back. But people wished that all the time, about all sorts of things, and nobody had ever succeeded in doing it yet.

"We've got another problem," Hammond said.

Ramirez frowned. Silencio Ryan, who lounged against the wall of Ramirez's den, never changed expression. Problems apparently meant nothing to him.

"There are some feds in town who worry me," Hammond went on.

"There were already federal agents involved, according to

what I've been told. And it was a federal judge who raised Stark's bail and moved the case out of local jurisdiction." Like most criminals, Ramirez was fairly conversant with the ins and outs of the law.

"I'm talking about *different* feds," Hammond said. "To tell you the truth, I'm not sure they even work for the government at all. I don't know who they are. But they seem to pop up all over the place, and they do what they want to like they're even more used to getting their way than the usual run-of-the-mill bureaucrat. I think they're spooks."

"Ghosts?" Ramirez said, confused by the terminology. He spoke English fluently, but it wasn't his native tongue.

Hammond shook his head. "No, some sort of . . . secret agents, I guess you'd say. Anyway, we've already got the Texas Rangers and Justice Department investigators and God knows who else poking around Del Rio. We don't need anybody else."

"You worry too much," Ramirez said with a chopping motion of his hand. "Just find Stark. That's your only job right now."

Hammond nodded. "I'll do my best, Senor Ramirez. Can I go now?"

"Go," Ramirez said with a contemptuous flip of his wrist. He turned toward Ryan. Clearly, he had already forgotten Hammond. "Silencio, I am so tense with anger I think I may have a stroke. Bring me a girl."

"I'm not a pimp, Don Ernesto," Ryan said.

Ramirez looked surprised. Hammond felt that way. He had never heard anyone deny Ramirez anything he wanted, not even Ryan. Hammond lingered, curious to see what was going to happen.

"Silencio, I am hurt," Ramirez said, but it was anger that smoldered in his eyes, not hurt feelings. "You have brought girls to me before."

"No, if you'll think back, I haven't. You've ordered your servants to do so in my presence plenty of times . . . but I'm not one of your servants."

Ramirez looked like he wanted to argue with that statement, but he controlled himself and said, "If you feel that such a task is beneath you, I understand, *mi amigo*. I'll summon Pablo and have him bring me what I need."

Ryan nodded curtly. "You do that."

Well, well, Hammond thought. The lapdog that Ramirez had been so eager to sic on everybody else had shown some teeth to his master. Ramirez's grip on everything had been slipping for weeks now, slowly but surely. This show of defiance on the part of Ryan was just another sign of that.

Ramirez glared at Hammond. "You are still here?" he snapped.

"I'm just goin', right now," Hammond said. He turned toward the door and put on his hat.

But before he could leave, the ground suddenly rocked under his feet. For a split second he thought it might be an earthquake. Such things occurred occasionally in this part of the world.

Then the roar of a huge explosion rolled over the compound, and Hammond knew it wasn't an earthquake that had caused the ground to shake. It was something even worse, something he had been halfway afraid of in the back of his mind.

"Stark," he whispered.

Stark had driven to within a quarter mile of the compound before parking the plumbing truck on a side road next to an auto junkyard. Ramirez's estate was on the other side of the junkyard, across a small creek, and up a bluff on the far side. It wouldn't have much of a view, but Stark doubted that Ramirez cared about that. Judging by the aerial photos, the junkyard was the best avenue of approach. It was surrounded by a barbed wire fence, but there were no alarms of any sort. A pair of wire cutters made short work of the fence.

Of course, the junkyard's real protection was of the four-legged variety. The men hadn't penetrated more than a hundred yards into the auto graveyard before three snarling, slavering, half-starved dogs came loping around a pile of smashed cars and charged toward them.

Stark bounced a tear-gas grenade at the dogs. It went off with a muffled bang, hopefully not loud enough to alert the guards at the compound on top of the bluff. The dogs got one whiff of the stuff and took off whimpering, their tails between their legs. Stark and his companions waited a moment for the gas to dissipate in the night breeze, then moved forward again. Enough of the stuff was still in the air so that their eyes stung a little, but that cleared up in a hurry.

They reached the far side of the junkyard, cut the fence there, and splashed across the shallow creek. The bluff wasn't so steep that it couldn't be climbed, though the task was more difficult in body armor, carrying the load they were carrying. The night was hot enough so that they were wet with sweat by the time they reached the top.

At the top of the bluff was another barbed wire fence. Stark was sure this one was rigged with alarms, so they couldn't just cut it and waltz through. The six men separated, spreading out around the perimeter.

Stark crouched beside the fence, peering through the strands of barbed wire at the main building about a hundred yards away. It was a low, sprawling adobe house in the Spanish style, with foot-thick walls, a red tile roof, and wrought-iron gates that opened into an interior courtyard. Several other smaller but similar buildings were scattered around. One of them would be the quarters for Ramirez's gunners; another was where the various vehicles were garaged. There was a tennis court, dark at the moment.

And a building that housed a generator, because Mexican electric power was notoriously undependable. They had studied the photos and seen the heavy wires leading from that building to the main house, and Stark had recognized them as the sort of power line that was hooked up to a generator. Most ranch houses were rigged the same way.

A generator required gasoline. One big enough to power

Ramirez's entire compound would need a lot of fuel. Stark didn't think Ramirez would be satisfied with less than the best. It made sense that the gasoline supply would be stored in the same building as the generator, so it would be handy for refueling.

Macon had a backpack full of grenades, all of them wired together to make a powerful bomb. His job was to get into that generator building and blow up the gasoline. The only way to do that was to cut the wire and set off the alarms, but it wouldn't really matter.

Once that gasoline went up, everybody would know they were here anyway.

Stark was counting off the seconds in his head and knew that the other men would be, too. They had figured on three minutes for everyone to get in position. Then Macon would make his move.

Time was up.

Stark suddenly heard the shrill sound of alarms going off and knew that Macon had cut the wire. He readied his own cutters. If the wire had been electrified, it no longer was, because the circuit was broken. Macon had taken the pair of heavily insulated cutters, just in case. As he came to his feet, Stark listened for shots. It was always possible that Macon would encounter a guard on his way into the generator building. But no shots came, and Stark hoped that meant luck was with them. They had figured it would take at least a minute for Macon to get inside, set the jury-rigged bomb, and get out of there, paying out the wire that he would use to pull the pin on one of the grenades and set off all the others, that blast exploding the gasoline tanks in turn. Stark was counting in his head again . . .

Fifty-nine . . . sixty . . . sixty-one . . . sixty-two . . . sixty-three . . .

Had something gone wrong?

The world rocked and the generator building came apart as huge gouts of flame burst through the walls and the roof.

Stark said, "Yes!" and leaped to the fence. The wire spanged and coiled on itself as he swiftly snipped the strands.

Then he was through, assault rifle cradled in his hands as he charged toward the hacienda.

Jack Finnegan was glad he was wearing gloves. His hands were so sweaty that without them he might have dropped the wire cutters. His sense of humor seemed to have deserted him. Before she left him, that was one of the things his wife had hated about him. She'd always said that he would rather crack some wiseass joke than concentrate on their problems and really listen to what she was saying. "Hell yeah" had been his response. Who wouldn't?

Well, try as he might, he couldn't come up with any jokes as he waited for Macon to blow up the gasoline supply. In just a minute or so, he was going to be cutting that wire and then charging into a compound full of heavily armed men who wouldn't hesitate to gun him down. He was heavily armed, too, of course, and he was counting on the element of surprise to counteract the advantage in numbers that the defenders would have. But still, the odds weren't good.

That had never stopped him before, he thought. He had gambled plenty of times in his life. He'd lost more than he had won, too. But he was still here, wasn't he? Sure, he was a drunk fighting to hang on to hard-won sobriety, and he was pretty much alone in the world now, with no one to care about and no one to care about him, but he was still alive and kicking.

And it wasn't really true that he was alone. He had friends, good friends. They were out there in the darkness, waiting like him for the explosion that would signal the beginning of the battle. A smile tugged at Finnegan's mouth. He had taken what should have been a good life and turned it into shit. But now he had a chance to do something worthwhile again. Maybe, if he came through this night alive, this would be the beginning of a whole new life for him—

Then there was no time to think anymore, because the earth was shaking and fire lit the night and the smile was still on Finnegan's face as he went into battle.

There was a book in this, Will Sheffield told himself as he crouched beside the fence. Definitely. Even a writer without much talent, like a guy who published a small-town newspaper, ought to be able to get a compelling story out of six friends, six comrades-in-arms, banding together again after thirty years to take down an evil drug lord and avenge the murder of an innocent woman, not to mention all the other deaths Ramirez had ordered. This was the stuff of high drama. Not even he could mess it up.

Of course, he had to live through it first, before he could write about it.

He was crazy to be risking his life like this. He knew it. He had a wife, kids, a career that was important to a lot of people, even if it wasn't exactly what he'd set out to do. Somebody had to get the pictures of the senior class in the special graduation supplement every year. Somebody had to take the picture of twelve-year-old Bobby Ray Simmons holding up his record catfish that was almost as big as he was. Somebody had to write the obituaries and the birth and wedding announcements and attend the school board and city council meetings. Ask people what was most important to them about the town where they lived, and hardly any of them would mention the local newspaper. But there would be a big hole in their lives without it, and Sheffield knew that even if they didn't.

No, it wasn't the Great American Novel. That was just a myth, anyway, something dreamed up by college professors.

Still, if he lived to write it . . . in highly fictionalized form, of course . . . this would make one helluva yarn.

Sheffield was trying to come up with a good opening line

when the generator building blew up. Creativity would have to wait.

Now he had to go destroy stuff.

Nat Van Linh had always had the ability to mentally transport himself to another place, a better place. Not really, of course. He wasn't a teleporter like in some science fiction movie. But he could close his eyes for a moment and conjure up an image so real, so vivid, so lifelike that it was almost as if he were really in that other place. It was a skill that had come in handy when he was growing up in Vietnam.

He took advantage of it now as he waited in the darkness next to the fence.

In his mind he was back down on the Gulf coast, with a warm, salty sea breeze in his face, sand under his bare feet, seagulls gliding overhead as the waves lapped and bubbled on the shore. Though he had spent his youth first in the crowded confines of Saigon and then in the steaming, deadly jungles, he had known the first time he had walked out on the beach in Texas that he had truly come home. This was where he was meant to be.

Everything that had happened in the years since then, the love of family and friends, the success in business, all confirmed that initial impression. His life had achieved a harmony, a tranquility that resonated all the way to the core of his being. Now, as he waited for that tranquility to be shattered, he took a deep breath and drew strength from the peace that spread throughout his body and soul.

The earth trembled underneath him and the brightness of the flame was such that he saw it even through his closed eyelids. Nat blew out the breath and stood, moving quickly but not hurrying, and within him his heart was still at ease as he cut through the wire and moved into the compound. He was still smiling peacefully as a shadow lunged at him, cursing in Spanish, and Nat used the assault rifle in his hands to blow the son of a bitch in half.

Where was he? Oh yeah, Mexico. Gonna bust into this place and get the guy who killed John Howard's wife. That was it. Hold on to that moment of clarity. Remember why he was here.

But it was hard, so fuckin' hard. Was he back in 'Nam? No, this was Mexico. Were we at war with Mexico now? Must be, or else why would the marines be here? He'd have to ask John Howard about that. John Howard had never lied to him, never let him down.

Something was gonna blow up real good. Rich knew that much. And when it did, he was gonna cut through that fence and run toward that big house, and if anybody tried to stop him he was supposed to shoot them. Was Charlie in there? Must be, yeah, the VC must've taken over the place, that was it. Little bastards in their black pajamas. Who would've ever dreamed that they could fight so good?

What was he waiting on? The explosion. Don't move until then. Big explosion. He couldn't miss it. *Ka-blooie!* Yeah, man, he'd know it when it happened. But he almost missed it anyway, and it was a couple of seconds after the big blast before he remembered what he was supposed to do next. He shook his head, cut the wire, and stepped through the gap.

"Rock 'n' roll, man," he said aloud. "Rock and fuckin' *roll!*"

Macon checked the wire first. Electrified, of course. But the gloves he wore and the heavy insulation on the handles of the wire cutters would protect him from that. The night was quiet, but it soon wouldn't be. He put pressure on the handles. The first strand of wire parted.

Somewhere in the compound, an alarm went off.

There were eight strands of wire. Macon cut them in less than fifteen seconds. Then he was through, running toward the generator building. Enough light came from the house so that when he reached the door, he saw that it was locked. But the door wasn't meant to keep out a man who was six five and weighed two hundred and forty pounds. Barely slowing down, he lifted his booted right foot and crashed it against the door, close to the jamb. Wood splintered and cracked, and the door flew open.

He lunged inside, feeling for a light switch. Something brushed his face. He reached up and felt a pull chain. When he jerked on it, light from a bare bulb flooded the room. Squinting against the sudden glare, he saw the heavy generator, bulking on the concrete floor like some sort of misshapen metal toad. Beside it were at least a dozen fifty-gallon drums. Macon grinned as he shrugged off his backpack. The seconds ticked off in his brain. A little more than half a minute had passed since he'd cut the first wire.

He pulled out the roll of wire and dropped the backpack next to the drums of gasoline. He turned and started toward the door, and suddenly the guard was there, lunging at him and driving the blade of a long, heavy knife into Macon's body. Macon cried out in pain and dropped the wire and his rifle. The guard, a thick-bodied Mexican a foot shorter than him, tackled him and knocked him to the floor.

They rolled over, and that made the knife twist and tear inside him. Flailing, Macon got his right hand around the guard's neck. He squeezed hard, until it looked like the man's eyeballs were going to pop out. The guard slammed punches into Macon's face, but Macon ignored them. He held on for dear life. His superior strength forced the guard back, but Macon could feel himself weakening. Now or never, he thought.

He drove the guard's head against the concrete floor as hard as he could. The man's skull made a sound a little like a watermelon bursting open. He went limp as blood and gray matter began to pool under his head.

Macon pushed himself up onto hands and knees. He knew he was hurt bad. His insides were cut to pieces. And in the back of his head the countdown was still going on. Now it had been almost a minute. Too long, too long. The others were waiting on him, and they had to get inside quickly before the guards knew what was going on. They needed that distraction he was supposed to provide.

Blood dripped in a steady stream from the huge wound in his belly as he crawled across the floor toward the backpack. When he reached it, he picked it up and collapsed with his back propped against one of the drums of gasoline. He could smell the gas, but even stronger was the sheared copper smell of freshly spilled blood, a lot of it. He ignored that as he pawed inside the backpack.

Six seconds later, three guards carrying machine guns burst into the generator room and saw Macon sitting there, a backpack in his lap, the bottom half of his body awash in crimson. He was smiling, though, as he held up something and showed it to them.

In the two seconds that remained, they didn't have time to recognize it as the pin from a grenade. Then the flames of hell reached out and claimed them.

Henry Macon died thinking of his wife.

Thirty-seven

Ramirez leaped to his feet as the explosion rocked the compound. Even the normally impassive Ryan looked startled. But Hammond was more than startled. Panic bloomed inside him. He turned to run. He didn't know where he was fleeing, but he didn't care. He just had to get away.

"Silencio!" Ramirez cried. "Stop him!"

A shot cracked behind Hammond and something sliced across his upper right thigh, leaving behind a line of fiery agony. That leg folded up beneath him, dumping him heavily on the tile floor.

"I didn't say to shoot him!" Ramirez yelped.

"You said stop him," Ryan responded. "He's stopped."

Hammond rolled and writhed on the floor, clutching his wounded leg. Ryan came over to him. Somewhere outside the main house, gunfire chattered. Ryan brought his foot down on Hammond's bullet-torn leg, making the sheriff scream. Pointing the pistol in his hand at Hammond's face, Ryan asked, "Do you know anything about this?"

"Stark!" Hammond shouted, fighting through the pain in his leg. "It's got to be Stark!"

"That's what I figure, too." Ryan's eyes narrowed. "You didn't double-cross us, did you, Hammond? Maybe *let* Stark escape so he could come down here and get us off your back for you?"

Hammond jerked his head from side to side. "God no! I . . . I'd never do that!" He looked over at Ramirez, who stood there with his face carefully controlled but his eyes leaping around in fear and confusion. "I swear it! I would never betray you!"

"He is telling the truth," Ramirez said. "He is too cowardly a dog to try such a thing." The drug lord nervously wiped the back of a hand across his mouth. "Silencio, what are we going to do? It sounds like Stark has an army out there!"

"He couldn't come up with an army," Ryan said scornfully. "All hands were against him. A few friends, maybe. They'll never get in here, Don Ernesto."

"You're sure?"

Ryan nodded. "And if by some chance they do, I'll deal with them." He paused, then added, "But maybe you'd better get to the chopper, just in case."

Ramirez's head bobbed up and down in a spastic nod. "*Sí*. The chopper. And you come, too. We will leave Stark to my men."

Ryan was wrong, Hammond thought, although his mind was blurry with pain. Hammond had dealt with Stark enough lately to know that once the man made up his mind to do something, he wouldn't let anything stop him, not even death. If it took his last breath, Stark would make it in here.

Ryan left Hammond's side and moved toward Ramirez. Hammond rolled over and groaned.

"What about the sheriff?" Ryan asked.

"Leave him," Ramirez answered without hesitation. "Let Stark have him."

And Stark would kill him, no doubt about it, Hammond thought. But maybe not, if, when he burst in here, he found Hammond standing over the bodies of Ramirez and Ryan. Maybe Stark would be grateful enough to let him go.

Reaching up to grasp the edge of a table, Hammond hauled himself up and stumbled to his feet. All he had to do was jump Ryan and get his hands on the man's gun. He could do that. Hell, he'd been all-state, hadn't he?

With an incoherent yell, Hammond lunged after them. Ryan turned smoothly, not hurrying, brought up the pistol in his hand, and fired twice. Twin black holes appeared an inch apart in Hammond's forehead. The sheriff's momentum carried him forward another step before his nerves and muscles realized that he was dead and dumped him facedown on the floor. Ramirez glanced at the body, shrugged, and said, "He was of no more use to us anyway. Let's get out of here, Silencio."

Several men ran out of the gunners' quarters and headed for the blazing generator building before Stark could stop them. If they ran into Macon over there, he would have to deal with them. But there were probably still quite a few inside the long, low, red-roofed building. Stark pulled a flash-bang grenade off his web belt and heaved it through the open door. He turned his head, closed his eyes, and covered his ears.

The grenade went off with its blinding flash and high-pitched burst of sound that was more like a giant scream than a bang. The glare lasted only a second. Stark wheeled into the doorway and saw men scrambling around, most of them obviously disoriented. A few of them had managed to avoid the effects of the flash-bang enough so that they could see what they were doing as they tried to reach the door. One of those men spotted Stark and yelled a curse as he swung up a pistol.

Stark opened fire with the assault rifle.

The L85 bucked and roared in his grip as he sprayed the room with short, lethal bursts. The bullets flung men around like rag dolls. They danced and jittered as blood spurted from dozens of holes in their bodies. One by one they fell to the floor, which was awash with blood in a matter of seconds.

Stark threw an incendiary grenade into the pile of corpses and moved on. With a thump, the grenade burst behind him and spread an all-consuming fire from one side of the room to the other.

Gun flame bloomed in the darkness as Stark ran toward the main house. He heard the wind-rip of a pistol round passing close beside his head. Without breaking stride, he pulled a 9mm pistol from its holster with his left hand and triggered it twice, bracketing the place where he'd seen the muzzle flash. The second bullet found its target. A man screamed and the gun cracked again as he involuntarily jerked the trigger, but the bullet went harmlessly into the night sky.

A shadow moved behind the wrought-iron gate as Stark approached it. He dived forward as an automatic weapon opened up. A slug hit the top of his left shoulder but glanced off the Kevlar. Still, the impact was enough to numb that arm for a second. He gritted his teeth and fired the assault rifle one-handed. Sparks flew as lead spanged off the gate. But enough of them got through to stitch a line across the chest of the machine gunner. With a groan, he collapsed and died.

Stark scrambled up, shaking his left arm to try to get some feeling back into it. The gate was locked, but several rounds from the L85 blasted it open.

With the squeal of hinges, Stark kicked the door open and ran into a tunnel-like path that led to the courtyard in the center of the hacienda. Somewhere, in one of the rooms off that courtyard, he would likely find Ramirez, cowering like the rat that he was. The Vulture was ill-named; even a carrion bird could soar high in the sky, but Ramirez was a small, verminlike creature, more suited to a dark hole than the open heavens.

Stark advanced slowly toward the courtyard, ready for anything.

Will Sheffield, Nat Van Linh, and Rich Threadgill stalked toward the main house from different angles. Sheffield and Nat had noted that the barrackslike building where the gunners were housed was already on fire. John Howard's work, more than likely. But there were still plenty of guards spread out around the estate who hadn't been mown down and then trapped in that inferno. Some of them took potshots at the former marines as they moved through the darkness. More than once, they found themselves in fierce firefights as they closed in on the house. Nat took cover in some trees as bullets searched through the darkness for him and whistled close by his head.

Breathing hard, he crouched there. He had thought that he was in very good shape for his age, but now he knew he was wrong about that. He owned a restaurant and some fishing boats, for God's sake! He wasn't a warrior anymore. He wasn't even close to the fierce young man he had been thirty years earlier.

But he could still see pretty well in the darkness, he discovered. He spotted the guard moving through the trees toward him, searching for him, and all at once it was as if he were back in the jungle, waiting patiently for his enemy to come to him. Silently, Nat laid his rifle aside and slipped his combat knife from its sheath. Like an animal with its prey finally in reach, he came up from the ground, grabbed the man's hair with his left hand and jerked his head back, then used his right to slide the keen edge of the blade across the man's taut throat. Blood gushed hotly as the guard twitched and died. Nat let him go and stepped back . . .

Right into a bullet that plowed into his upper right arm through a gap in the body armor, breaking the bone and sending him spinning off his feet.

Pain blotted out everything else, filling his senses for a second. Awareness came back to him just in time for him to see the man charging at him, eager to finish him off. Nat's right arm was useless, but he felt around on the ground with his left hand, found the knife he had dropped, and lunged up with it, taking the guard by surprise. The blade sank into the man's groin. He screamed as Nat ripped the knife through his guts, but he managed to squeeze the trigger of the machine pistol in his hand as he fell forward, dying. At this range the bullets penetrated the armor and chewed into Nat's leg. He cried out as the guard fell on him, pinning him to the ground. Feeling himself weakening from shock and loss of blood, Nat tried to roll the dead weight off him. He couldn't do it.

He passed out while he was still struggling to free himself.

A hundred yards away, Sheffield had his own hands full. He was pinned down behind a small shed of the sort that was used to store lawn equipment. He hunkered low to the ground as automatic weapons fire tore into the shed from two directions at once. Unlike the main house and most of the other buildings in the compound with their thick adobe walls, the shed was a frame structure, and the wooden walls didn't do much to slow down the high-powered rounds. Another few minutes, in fact, and the gunners would have shot the thing to pieces, and then Sheffield wouldn't be able to hide behind it anymore. Knowing he couldn't stay where he was, he threw a flash-bang around one corner of the shed and then followed it, firing bursts from the assault rifle as he ran. A shot came from his left. He went down, rolled, and fired in that direction, then swept the L85 back to the right.

When he surged up onto his feet, nobody fired at him. Knowing that he'd been lucky, he put that behind him and moved on toward the house. He thought he caught a glimpse of someone—Rich Threadgill, maybe—ducking through an open door.

Threadgill had reached the house, all right. He had shot

some guys along the way. He didn't know who they were, but they had been trying to shoot him, so that was all he needed to know. Except for John Howard and the other four, everybody in here was an enemy, and it was okay to shoot them. John Howard had made that perfectly clear. So Threadgill was confident that he wasn't going to get in trouble.

He ran down a hallway with a tile floor. A couple of big Mexican guys in flowery shirts jumped out through an arched doorway and blasted away at him with pistols. Threadgill pulled his old long-barreled Colt. It boomed loudly in the narrow hall as he emptied it into the two Mexicans. The heavy-caliber bullets punched right through their torsos, knocking them back against the wall. Bloodstains bloomed on their shirts, but Threadgill couldn't see them very well against the background of colorful flowers. The men slid down the wall, leaving crimson smears on the adobe behind them. Threadgill moved past them into the arched doorway, holstering the Colt and lifting his assault rifle as he did so. There might be more enemies inside.

Instead there were a lot of women, a dozen or so, girls, really, except for one fat *mamacita* who spread her arms and tried to get between Threadgill and the young women who had been brought here for the Vulture's perverted pleasures.

The scene flickered and shifted in front of Threadgill's eyes. Instead of young, pretty Mexican girls, he saw young, pretty Vietnamese girls. He remembered you couldn't trust them no matter how pretty they were because sometimes they worked with the VC and more than one poor GI had wound up dead just 'cause he wanted some o' that *poontang* and got his throat cut instead. Sometimes they planted bombs, too, and blew soldiers to bloody little bits, and you just couldn't trust 'em because they were the enemy, Goddamn it, and John Howard had said it was okay to shoot the enemy. So Threadgill didn't pay any attention to the screaming that filled the room as he lifted the assault rifle and tightened his finger on the trigger.

Sheffield got to him just in time to knock the barrel of the rifle up so that the bullets tore into the ceiling instead. "No, Rich!" he shouted. "No!" He shouldered Threadgill aside.

That put him in just the right position to take the bullet that the fat *mamacita* fired from the pistol she had dug out of a pocket in her voluminous skirt. The slug hit Sheffield in the chest. It didn't penetrate the Kevlar, but it still felt like a punch from a giant fist that knocked him backward.

Threadgill caught his balance and brought the rifle to his shoulder. He fired one shot, blowing half the woman's head off. His mind had snapped back to normal, and as the woman collapsed, he looked past her body at the shrieking, terrified Mexican girls. He spoke enough Spanish to tell them to get the hell out of there, to run away home and never come back to this place of evil. There would be no place to come back to, anyway. By morning it would all be gone.

Scorched earth, baby, scorched earth.

Threadgill reached down, grabbed the stunned Sheffield's arm, and dragged him out of the way as the women stampeded past them. Hauling Sheffield to his feet, Threadgill asked, "You all right, Will?"

"Y-yeah. Just got the breath knocked out of me by that shot."

"I reckon we better go find John Howard."

Sheffield nodded. "Yeah." By now, he figured, wherever they found Stark, they would find Ramirez as well.

Bare lightbulbs lit the tunnel at fifty-yard intervals. The floor, the walls, the arched ceiling were all made of square-cut stones that oozed moisture. The tunnel had been here for a long time, hundreds of years, perhaps. It predated the compound that was above it now. Ryan figured that it had been built as an escape route by some of the early Spanish settlers who might need such a bolt-hole to save their lives in case of an Indian attack. The original hacienda was long gone, but the tunnel remained, and Ramirez had put it to good use once he realized it was there. It led from the main house to the big, barnlike hangar where the helicopter was kept.

Even down here, they could hear the gunfire and the explosions as the small-scale war aboveground continued. As they hurried along, Ramirez said, "Stark should be dead by now! How can they still be fighting?"

They were still fighting because Ramirez's hired guns were no match for Stark and his friends, Ryan thought. A hundred and eighty defenders inside the Alamo shouldn't have been able to hold off Santa Anna's army of thousands for thirteen days, either. A man fighting for a cause was always more dangerous than a man fighting for money.

Well, almost always, Ryan amended. He was the exception, of course.

"You can fly the chopper, eh, Silencio?"

"Sure."

"We will head for Mexico City and let this disaster die down before we return, eh?"

"Can't fly all the way to Mexico City on the fuel tank in that chopper," Ryan said. "We'll have to stop for gas a few times along the way."

"Yes, yes, whatever it takes." Ramirez was already thinking ahead. "When this is all over I will return here and rebuild my operation until it is bigger and better than before. Soon, from one end of Mexico to the other, no one will ever again dare to defy the will of the Vulture."

Never believe in your own hype, Ryan thought. Obviously, Ramirez had never learned that lesson. That was why he had pushed and pushed Stark, playing with him at times the way a cat might play with a mouse, until finally Ramirez had backed Stark into a corner from which there was no escape.

At least, so it had seemed. Stark had proven, was proving, otherwise, at this very moment.

If they made it to Mexico City, Ramirez could do what he wanted to. Ryan knew he himself would never come back to this place. He had never been a great believer in luck . . .

But he knew he had pushed his as far as he could push it.

* * *

Stark burst into the large, opulent room and knew at first glance that this was Ramirez's sanctum. He swept the assault rifle from side to side, ready to fire at any motion.

Nothing. The room was empty.

No, not quite empty, Stark saw. A man lay facedown on the floor, unmoving, a red puddle under his head. From the size of him and the uniform he wore, Stark recognized him as Sheriff Norval Lee Hammond. He got a toe under Hammond's shoulder and rolled him onto his back. The sheriff had been shot twice in the forehead at fairly close range. Stark wasn't surprised by that, because he had seen the gory mess the slugs had made of the back of Hammond's head when they exited. Stark felt no pity, not even a twinge, as he looked down at Hammond's corpse. The man had made his own choices, followed his own path, and this was where it had led him.

Of course, that was true of everybody. Stark had his own destination, and this wasn't it.

Where the hell was Ramirez?

He searched quickly, and in a small room down a narrow hallway, he found an open trapdoor. Steps led down into a stone-walled passage lit by an occasional bulb. Stark didn't hesitate. He descended into the underground passageway. It stretched out, seemingly endlessly, in front of him.

And as he paused there at the foot of the steps for a second, Stark heard the faint echo of shots from somewhere far ahead of him.

He didn't hesitate any longer. His feet slapping against the slick stones of the floor, he ran down the tunnel, every instinct telling him that he was on the right path.

The trapdoor at the other end was locked, of course, but Ramirez had the key. He fumbled with it, dropped it, and Ryan had to pick it up and unfasten the heavy padlock. He swung the trapdoor up and back.

They climbed out into the darkened hangar. "Start the engine," Ramirez snapped. "I'll open the doors."

That would be the most physical work the man had done in a long time, Ryan mused as he headed for the chopper. Well, other than raping and torturing Elaine Stark, of course. Ryan climbed into the cockpit, turned the switch on, and checked the gauges as the dashboard lights came on. Gas tank was full, battery was charged, everything looked good. The ceiling was high enough and the doors were big enough so that the helicopter could lift off and hover above the ground, then fly out of the hangar, rather than having to be wheeled out before it could take off. It took a skilled hand at the controls to accomplish that maneuver, but Ryan was capable of it.

The doors had hydraulic motors attached to them. Ramirez had to unfasten them, but then all he had to do was press a button and the doors would roll back on their own. With a rumble, they started to do so. The chopper's blades began to revolve lazily as Ryan started the engine.

Ramirez ran to the helicopter and climbed in next to Ryan. "Let's get the hell out of here," he said breathlessly.

"In a minute," Ryan said. The engine was still warming up, and the doors weren't all the way open yet. A reddish glare filled the gap, and from the looks of it, Ryan thought the whole compound must be on fire by now. Except for this hangar, which was off to the side, well away from the other buildings. Stark and his friends had ignored it so far. They would pay for that mistake.

Ryan reached for the controls and increased the engine's idle a little more, when the shape of a man appeared in the opening between the hangar doors. He strode forward confidently as the doors continued to slide open. Ryan's eyes widened in surprise as he saw that the man had an assault rifle cocked jauntily over his right shoulder.

Ryan shoved Ramirez out the right side of the cockpit and went diving to the left as the assault rifle came down and began to spit lead and flame at the helicopter.

* * *

"Going somewhere, boys?" Jack Finnegan shouted as he opened fire. He knew they couldn't hear him over the drone of the chopper's engine, but he didn't care. In the glare of the dashboard lights, through the Plexiglas bubble that enclosed the cockpit, he had recognized Ramirez from the newspaper photos. The other man, the pilot, had to be the one John Howard had warned them about. Both of them jumped for their lives as Finnegan sprayed the chopper with burst after burst from the assault rifle. The bubble shattered and bullets bounced around until the control panel was nothing but a torn-up mess. That helicopter wasn't going anywhere, despite the fact that its blades continued to turn.

Caught up in the destruction, Finnegan remembered the bodyguard too late. He swung the L85 in the man's direction, but the man had already rolled over and had a gun in his hand. It cracked wickedly as flame geysered from the barrel. The guy was good; he knew where to aim. Two slugs punched into Finnegan's abdomen, just below where the Kevlar vest ended and above the armor strapped to his thighs. In this light, under the circumstances, that was damned good shooting.

Finnegan was in no mood to appreciate it. He doubled over in agony and toppled forward, but as he fell he squeezed off one last burst from the rifle. He didn't know if he hit anything or not . . .

But by God, it felt good to go down fighting!

The luck that Ryan had never really believed in had just bitten him on the ass. There was no other explanation for it. Otherwise how could a blindly aimed shot fired by a dying man hit the gun in his hand and send it flying? Not only that, but the round also took off the index and middle fingers on Ryan's right hand. Blood spurted from the stumps as he rolled farther into the shadows near the wall of the hangar. He grabbed them with his left hand and squeezed hard, trying to stop the flow of blood. The pain was bad but nothing he couldn't deal with. It was unlikely, too, that he would bleed out just from losing a couple of fingers. But it could happen if he didn't get the situation under control.

One thing was certain: he was out of this fight. Ramirez was on his own, wherever he was. Ryan had lost track of him. No, wait, there he was, tentatively approaching the now motionless body of the man Ryan had shot.

Ryan lifted his head as he heard something. Footsteps, thudding on the stairs leading up from the tunnel.

Of course there was only one person it could be. Of course.

Ryan laughed softly as John Howard Stark climbed out of the tunnel and into the hangar.

The place was lit like an anteroom of hell, with the nightmarish red glare of flames spilling through the open doors but fading into shadows before it reached the far walls of the cavernous building. Stark saw the shattered helicopter with its blades still spinning and knew that Ramirez must have been trying to escape. That long tunnel had been a bolt-hole. A heartbeat later Stark saw the man near the doors, bending over a grim shape sprawled on the ground. Stark saw the helmet and the body armor and knew that the man on the ground was one of his friends. He couldn't tell which one, but he felt a pang of grief anyway. Another good man gone down, a victim of the Vulture's insane hatred.

And that was Ramirez himself, Stark realized as the man looked up at him. In this garish light, Ramirez looked like Satan himself, gloating over a tortured soul. Ramirez hesitated, made a tentative move toward the fallen man's rifle as if he intended to pick it up and fight back, but then he straightened and regarded Stark coolly.

"I know you," Ramirez called. "You're him. Stark."

Walking forward slowly, keeping his rifle trained on Ramirez, Stark nodded. "That's right. And you're Ramirez."

"You're a fool, you know. You've accomplished nothing except to get yourself and your friends killed. Still, I am glad to finally meet you, Senor Stark." An ugly grin stretched across Ramirez's face. "After all, I already had the pleasure of meeting your lovely wife."

Stark almost pressed the trigger then and wiped that grin off Ramirez's face. He waited, because he didn't know where the redhead was. The man had to be here somewhere. It would be a great pleasure to kill Ramirez, but the other man had debts to pay, too. Stark wanted to draw him out.

"Maybe I won't kill you after all," Stark said quietly. "Maybe I'll take you back across the border and turn you over to the law. We're going to have some real law in Val Verde County now, you know, with Hammond gone. I saw his body back in the house."

Ramirez shook his head. "It does not matter. No matter who is in charge, I will simply buy him, as I bought Hammond. You cannot fight me, Stark. It is a losing battle. And I am tired of this now." He raised his voice. "Kill him, Silencio! Kill him *now!*"

Nothing happened.

Ramirez's eyes widened. "Silencio!" he screamed.

Well, maybe he'd been wrong about the redhead, Stark thought. Maybe he was either dead or gone.

"Looks like you're on your own, Ramirez."

Terror, hatred, madness all raced through Ramirez's eyes. He took a step back.

At that moment, the man on the ground groaned.

Stark knew it was a mistake the instant he took his eyes off Ramirez, but it was too late to do anything about it. With blinding speed, Ramirez plucked a small-caliber pistol from behind his belt at the small of his back and fired. The bullet hit Stark in the throat and knocked him half around. He staggered and went to a knee, firing the assault rifle one-handed as he did so. His shot ripped through Ramirez's body and knocked the Vulture back even more. Ramirez managed to stay on his feet, though, and tried to bring the gun up for one last shot.

Inside the helicopter, a fire started by sparks from the shot-up control panel finally reached the gas tank. It erupted with a roar, blowing the chopper into pieces and sending the still-spinning blades loose into the air. The blast knocked Stark forward. What felt like a mighty wind passed directly over him.

He looked up in time to see Ramirez still standing there, eyes wide with horror and disbelief.

Then Ramirez's top half fell one way and his bottom half fell the other, sheared cleanly in two by the helicopter blades on their way out of the hangar.

"J-John Howard . . . ?"

Stark had fallen beside his wounded friend. He looked over into Jack Finnegan's face. Finnegan's features were smooth, seemingly without pain. But he had trouble speaking as he gasped out, "Did you . . . get him?"

Stark thought about that madly spinning blade and knew it had been guided by a higher power than anything he and his friends had been able to muster. But Ramirez wouldn't have been standing right there if not for what they had done.

"We got him, Jack," he said hoarsely. "We all got him."

"G-good." Finnegan swallowed. "I can't feel much, John Howard. Lucky, huh?"

"Hang on, Jack. We'll get out of here."

"No, I don't think so. Not me . . . anyway. But it's . . . okay. Probably . . . for the best . . . You know me . . . always find a way to . . . screw up . . ."

"Not this time," Stark told him. "Ramirez would have gotten away if not for you, Jack. You're the one who stopped him."

Finnegan smiled. "I ever tell you . . . I wanted to be . . . a pro golfer?"

Stark put his head closer to Finnegan's. "No," he whispered. "No, I don't think you did."

"Could'a been . . . good at it . . . You should see the way I . . . putt into a shot glass . . ." Finnegan's eyes opened wider. "Oh Lord," he said clearly. "John Howard, I . . ."

He sighed and his head relaxed against the ground. Stark closed his eyes and whispered, "Damn, damn," but it sounded more like a prayer than a curse.

Eventually he remembered that he'd been shot in the throat. He got a hand up there to check the wound and found that the bullet had plowed through the side of his neck, leaving a painful, messy wound, but not one that was life-threatening. He could tell from the amount of blood that it hadn't nicked a vein or an artery. He pushed himself up into a sitting position beside Finnegan's body and looked around. The fire had spread to the walls of the hangar. He ought to start giving some thought to getting out of here, Stark thought.

That was when Will Sheffield and Rich Threadgill ran in from outside and saw him sitting there. "John Howard!" Sheffield yelled.

Stark waved them over. He climbed to his feet with Sheffield's help. "Rich, get Jack," he said. "Let's get out of here."

Threadgill didn't move. He looked down at Finnegan and said, "Jack? Better get up, Jack."

"I'll take him," Sheffield said quietly. "Here, Rich, you help John Howard."

"Oh. Okay." Threadgill put an arm around Stark's waist and supported him as he hobbled toward the doors.

Once they were outside, well away from the burning hangar, Stark asked, "What about Henry and Nat?"

"We haven't seen them," Sheffield said with a shake of his head.

Stark nodded grimly. "By now they'll be on their way back to the truck, if they're able to. Get down the hill, go back through the junkyard, and get the hell out while you still can."

"What about you?"

Stark shook his head and looked down at Finnegan. "I'm staying here."

"John Howard, you're a wanted man."

"I know, and I don't intend to spend the rest of my life as a fugitive. With all these explosions and fires, the police and the fire department will be showing up here any time. With Ramirez dead, the Mexican authorities won't know what to do with me. They'll give me back to the Americans, just to get me out of their hair. I'll take my chances on our side of the border."

Sheffield hesitated. "You're sure about that?"

"Go back to your life, Will," Stark told him quietly. "Just one thing . . . look after Rich."

Sheffield nodded. "Well, all right . . . I guess. But I don't like it."

"Nothing about it to like. It's just what's got to be done."

Sheffield and Threadgill moved off into the darkness, Threadgill complaining about leaving Stark behind, Sheffield trying to reassure him that was what John Howard wanted. Stark sighed as a weariness greater than any he had ever known settled over him. Using his rifle to steady himself, he sat down on the ground next to Finnegan to wait. He opened his mouth, intending to say something to Elaine about how it was over now and how he had settled the score for her, but he stopped because he knew it wasn't true. Justice had been done, but justice didn't heal the wound and stop the hurting. It was just . . . better than nothing.

Stark looked at what appeared to be a mile-long procession of flashing red and blue lights approaching the compound and wondered if the huge empty feeling inside him would ever go away.

Ryan had gotten his belt off, knotted it around his wrist to form a tourniquet, and tied his handkerchief around the stubs of the first two fingers on his right hand. The bleeding had stopped. He felt a little light-headed, but he knew now that he was going to make it. There was a doctor downriver in Piedras Negras, across the border from Eagle Pass, who could be trusted. Ryan could walk into downtown Cuidad Acuna, steal a car, and be there before morning. Being short two fingers was going to be damned annoying in his line of work, but he supposed he would just have to figure out ways of dealing with it. Maybe he would go to work for the U.S. government, he thought with a smile as he trudged through the night. After all, they hired a lot of handicapped people. And he was now an American with a disability. . . .

He stopped for a moment and looked back at the hilltop compound. Flames and smoke climbed high into the sky above it. "Well, you raised hell, Stark," he said. "Hope you got what you wanted out of it. And I hope that one of these days, you and I cross paths again."

That thought brought a smile of anticipation to Ryan's hawklike face. He might have been able to kill Stark tonight, but both of them were wounded and it just hadn't felt right. Ryan had always followed his instincts, and tonight they had told him to walk away.

But one of these days . . . yes, one of these days . . .

Silencio Ryan moved on, and soon was swallowed up by the night.

Epilogue

Stark had spent more time in hospitals lately than he ever had in his life, and he didn't much like it. The only good thing was that he had friends here, too, and since he was ambulatory, he'd been able to walk down the hall and see Devery Small and Nat Van Linh. Devery was out of intensive care, but he'd be laid up for a long time. Nat, who had been found unconscious under the body of one of the guards at Ramirez's compound, would need even longer to recuperate, not to mention several surgeries to implant steel rods in his leg to replace the bullet-shattered bones. But the doctors thought there was a good chance he would walk fairly normally again, eventually.

There would certainly be enough money to pay for the best doctors in the world. The trust fund that Jack Finnegan had left to Stark would take care of that. Finnegan's lawyer had shown up the next morning after the battle at the Vulture's nest and gone right to work browbeating all the local authorities.

He hadn't been able to do anything about the feds, though. There were heavily armed guards within ten feet of Stark at all times, even when he was taking a leak. Federal marshals had taken charge of him when the Mexican police turned him over at the International Bridge, and he was still officially in their custody even though he'd been held in the hospital a couple of nights for observation.

The bandage around his neck was uncomfortable, but Doug Huddleston had warned him to leave it alone. "That's a pretty nasty scratch you've got there, John Howard. You don't want to get it infected."

After all he'd been through, Stark wasn't too worried about such things, but Doug was a friend, so he humored him.

Most of the past forty-eight hours had been spent talking to various law enforcement agents. Stark didn't think he had slept much in that time. Whenever he asked what was going to happen, the feds just shook their heads solemnly.

He was going to spend the rest of his life in prison, Stark thought. Well, so be it. A man's gotta do what a man's gotta do. It was an old, corny line, but there was a lot of truth in it, by God.

When he was alone for too long, he was haunted by thoughts of everything he had lost. Elaine, of course . . . that was the worst. But he couldn't escape the grief he felt over Jack Finnegan and Henry Macon, either. Macon had never made it out of that generator room. The Mexican authorities had let the U.S. agents examine the scene, and as best they could piece it together, the bomb Macon had been carrying had gone off while he was still in the room. Probably an accident . . .

Or not, Stark thought.

He was sitting on the hospital bed, with the TV on even though he wasn't seeing or hearing what was on it, when a man he had never seen before walked into the room. The guards outside had allowed him in, so he had to be a fed of some sort. He was about sixty, with graying dark hair and deep-set blue eyes. When he said, "Mr. Stark?" his voice had a Texas twang to it, although it was faint enough so that most people who didn't live down here wouldn't have heard it.

"Who else would be in here?" Stark asked.

The stranger pursed his lips. "Don't get all uppity with me, son," he said, sounding more Texas than ever. "You don't know it yet, but I'm here to give you a hand."

"You're from the government, and you're here to help? I've heard that song and dance before."

The man shook his head. "No song and dance this time, just some plain ol' truths. You have given Uncle Sam one helluva black eye."

Stark looked away, not wanting to have this argument again.

"You don't care about that, do you?" the stranger went on. "Somebody killed your friend, and you had to do something about it. Then it just grew from there until you had a damn war on your hands, you and your buddies. Oh, we know about the other two, don't think we don't."

Stark felt a pang of alarm and sat up straighter in the bed.

"Don't worry, we're not interested in goin' after them. They've gone back to their lives. Threadgill's stayin' with Sheffield in Tennessee. We got no real reason to bother 'em."

"Or Nat Van Linh, either," Stark said.

The man nodded. "As soon as Mr. Van Linh is able to travel, he can go back to Rockport. His part in this is over." The stranger looked squarely at Stark. "So is yours."

Stark grunted. "Other than the hundred and fifty years or so that I'll have to serve in a federal penitentiary."

"Nope," the man said with a shake of his head. "There are no charges against you, Stark, local, state, or federal. All the cases have been dropped."

Stark stared at him in disbelief. "What the hell are you talking about?"

"You ever hear of cuttin' your losses, Stark? You're a *hero*, son. You're Davy Crockett and James Bond and Spider-Man all rolled up into one. Oh, hell, the press and the liberal fringe in Washington may call you a crazed vigilante, but even they know better. They're just puttin' on a show because it's expected of 'em. They know that to most of the folks in this country, you're the man who went up against the drug lords and won. That's what really matters, that somebody did the right thing for once."

"Won," Stark repeated hollowly. "I don't feel much like a winner right now."

The stranger shook his head. "Doesn't matter. You're bigger than life. What you feel or don't feel doesn't matter a hoot in hell anymore."

Stark frowned narrow-eyed at the man. "What about that fella Kelso from the DEA?"

"Reassigned."

"Calhoun?"

"Retired from the National Security Council. He's going back to teaching political science at Georgetown . . . God help those poor kids who wind up in his class."

"The IRS seized my ranch," Stark said.

The stranger chuckled. "Now, here's how you can tell that you really got friends in high places, son, or at least people who want you to go away and be quiet: the Internal Revenue Service has admitted that it made a mistake. You never owed those back taxes. The Diamond S is yours again, free and clear."

Stark rubbed his eyes with the balls of his hands. He looked up and said, "So you're saying it's all over, like none of it ever happened?"

The stranger nodded gravely. "Like none of it ever happened. Except, of course, for the tragic losses of your wife, your uncle, and your friends. And for those you have the government's deepest sympathy."

Stark took a deep breath. "I don't know whether to believe you or not. I don't even know who you are."

The stranger smiled. "I'm the fella who cleans up the messes that other folks should've had more sense than to make. I reckon that's all you need to know."

"Yeah. I guess so."

"One more thing. You got some visitors waitin' outside. Actually, they've come to take you home. The doctors say they don't need to keep you here anymore."

The man went to the door and opened it, and Stark saw his sons standing there, tall and proud in their uniforms, and as they came in he felt the tears springing to life in his eyes. As they rushed in and hugged him and the back-slapping and carrying-on started, the stranger paused at the door and added one more thing before he slipped out of the room.

"Go home and live your life, John Howard Stark. No need to look back."

At sunset, he stood alone beside the grave on the hillside, hands in the hip pockets of his jeans, Stetson cocked back on his head. David and Pete had come up here with him earlier, and they had cried and prayed, prayed and cried, together. Now the boys were back down at the mobile home that had been moved onto the property until the ranch house could be rebuilt, along with everything else that was needed to make the Diamond S a working ranch again.

Everything but Elaine.

He took a deep breath and said, "I'm sorry. I got you and Newt and all the others into this, and you died because of it. I never meant for it to happen, but it did and I can't change it. I've . . . felt you with me since then. I know you're not mad at me. But I have to ask myself . . . was the price too high? Did it cost too much to do the right thing?"

Stark took off his hat. He told himself that he wasn't hoping for an answer, a sign of some kind to tell him that everything was all right, but he knew deep down that was exactly what he was waiting for.

Only it didn't come. The hot breeze blew and the sun began to sink behind the mountains across the river and a mockingbird sang somewhere in the cottonwoods, but none of those things was a sign. They were just . . . life going on.

Maybe that was the closest thing to it he was going to get, Stark thought.

"I tell you one thing," he said. "I'm the same man I've always been, but I'm changed, too. I followed along right behind death for too long. I risked everything, and I lost most of it. But I learned, too, and now I know that the world's a dangerous place. I think I'd forgotten that. I know it's got a lot of evil in it, and somebody has to stand up to it, stand up for what's right. I can do that. I can fight the battles that most folks can't. In the end, though, I'll really just be fighting for one thing, and I don't think I'll ever get it back."

He didn't have to say it. She would know. His real battle now was for one thing, one small and lonely thing . . .

His own soul.

John Howard Stark put on his hat and went down the hill toward home, and behind him the leaves of the cottonwoods stirred in the breeze and a voice seemed to whisper, *Oh, John Howard, you never really lost it. It's still there inside you. You just don't know it yet.*

But Stark didn't hear . . .

This time.